MW00329433

NOTHING BUT MURDER

By the Same Author

ENJOYMENT OF MURDER
MURDER AND MORE MURDER
THE ART OF MURDER
NOTHING BUT MURDER

NOTHING BUT

MURDER

By WILLIAM ROUGHEAD

With a Foreword by the Author

M. EVANS
Lanham • New York • Boulder • Toronto • Plymouth, UK

M. Evans
An imprint of The Rowman & Littlefield Publishing Group, Inc.
4501 Forbes Boulevard, Suite 200, Lanham, Maryland 20706
http://www.rlpgtrade.com

10 Thornbury Road, Plymouth PL6 7PP, United Kingdom

Distributed by National Book Network

Copyright © 1946 by Sheridan House, Inc.
First Rowman & Littlefield paperback edition 2014

All rights reserved. No part of this book may be reproduced in any form or by any electronic or mechanical means, including information storage and retrieval systems, without written permission from the publisher, except by a reviewer who may quote passages in a review.

Library of Congress Cataloging-in-Publication Data Available

ISBN 13: 978-1-59077-462-5 (pbk: alk. paper)

♾™ The paper used in this publication meets the minimum requirements of American National Standard for Information Sciences—Permanence of Paper for Printed Library Materials, ANSI/NISO Z39.48-1992.

Printed in the United States of America

FOREWORD

IT IS, FOR ME, both a privilege and pleasure once again to address an American audience and this, because I have ever received from the people and Press of the Great Republic so large a measure of kindness and encouragement.

Further, the course of my literary labours has been agreeably lightened and refreshed by divers valued friendships, resulting from generous appreciations of my work. Chief among these I reckon my association with Henry James, from whose all genial approval of my efforts to make murder palatable to the general, I received such stimulating sustainment. My relations with Edmund Pearson, also, afforded me the utmost satisfaction, and it is my proud boast that I was the means of setting his hitherto blameless feet upon the murderous course which he was so long and brilliantly to follow. Professor William Lyon Phelps, of Yale, was another man of letters who helped me on my criminous way. "I have been an admirer of your books for years," he wrote to me when in London in 1935 and hoped to come to Edinburgh to meet me. But the Fates forbade; and in his last letter before leaving England, he wrote: "Your books had won my mind and your letter has won my heart."

Rarely have I, as a modest writer, had, in the old Scots phrase, "so good a conceit of myself," as when I read in Alexander Woollcott's "Foreword" to the selections from my essays made by him in 1941 for The Readers Club, Inc., these heartening words: "In America, Roughead's fame is out of all proportion to the multitudes who would read his every page with relish and enrichment. In the White House at Washington, in a special section of the bookcases just outside the President's study, there is a carefully winnowed selection of detective literature deposited there by the Library of Congress and labelled The President's Shelf. On that shelf the rarest brews, in my opinion, are the work of Mr. Roughead."

Apropos of this, I should like to rebut the charge sometimes brought against me, of undue levity in dealing with so grave a matter as murder; and I think I can best do so by quoting a sentence from a letter written to me by my friend the Lord Bishop of Jarrow, in acknowledging a copy of Woollcott's book, which I had sent to him, and which he said he had read with "the keenest enjoyment." Thus his Lordship: "So many people think that wit consists in 'making jokes'; your way of exposing the objective humour of actual life is the real wit. The humour of truth is always the most humourous thing to be had; it does not need to be manufactured, but to be isolated by the discerning mind, and this you do exceptionally well." This episcopal approval absolves me from the animadversions of lay journalism.

For the present selection from my earlier essays I am not responsible, but I am glad to recognise some old friends in the admirable format which distinguishes American books. After British books, "produced in complete conformity with the authorized economy standards" this is to me a most welcome and refreshing change.

I am particularly pleased that the publishers have included "An Academic Discussion," which I specially wrote for Edmund Pearson in return for his introducing me to his so attaching heroine Lizzie Borden. He was so much delighted with it, he told me, that he carried about with him a proof of my article which I had sent him and insisted on reading it aloud to all his friends! I can only hope they shared his enthusiasm. "Locusta in Scotland" I am glad to see revived, as it was a great favourite of my friend Sir Hugh Walpole. Also, "Jessie King," of whom I cherish grateful remembrance as the protagonist of my first murder trial. The rest, being of age, may be safely left to speak for themselves.

William Roughead

12 BELGRAVE CRESCENT,
EDINBURGH.

CONTENTS

NOTHING BUT MURDER

AN ACADEMIC DISCUSSION:

A Macabre Conceit

A SPECIAL MEETING of the Society of Scottish Criminals—an Association not to be confounded with the respectable legal body bearing the same initials—was held within the Calton Jail, Edinburgh, on 31st September, 1924, Deacon Brodie, President of the Society, in the chair. There was a full attendance of members. The Secretary (Major Weir, G.O.M.) having read the minutes of the last meeting, censuring as crude and inartistic the technique of certain crimes lately perpetrated in England,—

THE PRESIDENT expressed his pleasure at seeing so good a house on an occasion which they must all feel to be one of national importance. *Nemo me impune lacessit* was the motto of their indomitable race; Scots folk were proverbially touchy, and when the supremacy of members in matters criminal was threatened, he knew he could rely on their whole-hearted support in order to uphold their criminous prestige. The Scots lawyer was justly jealous for the pre-eminence of his system of jurisprudence, the Scots surgeon was equally so in respect to his school of surgery, the Scots minister, be his denomination what it might, was persuaded that his particular path was the narrow and the only way. And if they found among the followers of these learned professions so strong an expression of what he might call clan feeling, were they, members of that numerous and gifted class whose young filled our reformatories, whose seniors occupied our prisons, whose illustrious forebears, according to the practice of the age which they respectively adorned, were "wirreit" at the stake and "brint in assis," succumbed to the embraces of the boots, the caspieclaws, and the pilniewinks, lost their heads beneath the irresistible pressure of the Maiden, were cast off the ladder in the Grassmarket, or made a more genteel retiral on the new movable platform or drop of which it was his proud boast to be at once the inventor, the architect, and the victim—(Applause)—were they, he would repeat, suc-

3

cessors to such glorious traditions and enjoying, albeit undeserv-
edly, so splendid an heritage—were they, he would again remark,
tamely to submit to the domination of transatlantic miscreants,
however distinguished in the exercise of their nefarious cult?
Perish the thought! The Society had received a copy of a work
which, he believed, had met with much acceptance beyond what
was colloquially termed the Herring Pond. It was an American
book, by an American writer, treating exclusively of American
crime—need he say that he referred to *Studies in Murder*, by
Mr. Edmund Lester Pearson?—and as such had been presented
to them for their edification and example. Now, certainly the
cases with which it dealt were very singular and striking, but he
had yet to learn that they surpassed or even equalled in merit
any of our Scottish *causes célèbres*. He himself was merely a
housebreaker—it might be one not unfamous in that lower walk
—and it was to him a matter of regret that he could lay no
claim to reflect that sanguinary beam which cast its ruddy glow
upon the reputations of so many of the gifted company whom
he had then the happiness to address. But speaking as a master-
burglar, admittedly at the head of his calling——

Mr. James Mackcoull *alias* Captain Moffat, said he yielded
to no man in loyalty to their respected President, who might be
a competent chairman and was reputed a capable cabinet-maker,
but whose pretensions to be considered an eminent housebreaker
were simply preposterous. He was rather to be deemed a bungler
than a burglar—they all knew what a hash he had made of the
Excise Office job; and his absurd enthusiasm for one Captain
Macheath—an Englishman, despite his name, and as he (Mr.
Mackcoull) was credibly informed, not even a real robber but a
person in a play—was unpatriotic and unbecoming a member of
their Society. If they wanted the genuine article let them remember the affair of the Paisley Union Bank and the Begbie
business, matters to which modesty forbade that he should do
more than allude.

Mr. David Haggart said that as their youngest member he
was naturally diffident in voicing his views, but he desired to
associate himself with the observations which had fallen from

the hon. and gallant member. Like Captain Moffat he had had the honour to combine housebreaking with homicide, and he thought that their amiable President was inclined to attach undue importance to his own purely burglarious performances—whether efficiently executed or not was beside the question. Still, it must always be borne in mind that Mr. Brodie had other and greater claims to the consideration and esteem of the Society: he had been for many years a member of Edinburgh Town Council. (Loud applause.)

THE PRESIDENT, after repeatedly bowing his acknowledgments, remarked that Mr. Mackcoull's title to be regarded as the originator of the Begbie Mystery was by no means generally admitted. De Quincey, in his celebrated essay, *On Murder, considered as one of the Fine Arts*, states that the murderer is to this hour undiscovered——

MR. MACKCOULL protested against the citation of an alien authority. He had not read the essay referred to, but he understood that the author unblushingly owned that he never committed a murder in his life, and it further appeared that the whole paper, while professing to be a panegyric on murder, was in fact poking fun at murderers and holding up their craft to ridicule and contempt. Such a production should be burnt by the public hangman, and ought not to be mentioned in polite society like the present.

MRS. JESSIE M'LACHLAN rose to a point of order. Their business, as she conceived, was to discuss whether certain American crimes were superior to the natural and kindly products of their native land. Her position was somewhat peculiar. She was only an honorary member, for though she had been convicted of murder, the credit of the deed actually belonged to their venerable friend Mr. James Fleming, the oldest member of the Society. ("Hear, hear.") Mr. Fleming, by reason of his advanced years and retiring disposition, was unable to be with them that night, but she was empowered to intimate his entire concurrence in the views she was about to express. She had been called, quite erroneously, "the Heroine of the Cleaver," and the fact that Mr. Pearson's most intriguing crimes were effected with a hatchet, or other heavy instrument having a cutting edge, had for her a sentimental interest. It might be natural or it might not—(Cries of "Yes" and "No")—but there it was, and she acknowledged a preference for those cases in which an axe or some similar implement was employed. Mr. Pearson's leading instance—that of Miss Lizzie A. Borden, indicted for a double parricide—was in its circumstances so remarkable as to establish a record. "It concerns," proceeded Mrs. M'Lachlan, "a middle-class New England home in 1892, consisting of a wealthy old gentleman named Andrew J. Borden; his second wife; Miss Lizzie, his daughter by the first marriage; and an Irish servant. The old man goes out on his affairs one morning about nine o'clock; his wife, after dusting the dining-room, goes up to the spare room to make the bed; Lizzie is about the house as usual; the servant is washing the downstairs windows, and later goes up to her room on the third floor for a rest. About eleven o'clock the father returns and is admitted by the maid, *who hears, as she opens the door to him, Miss Lizzie, on the upper landing, laugh.* He asks for his wife, and his daughter replies that she has gone out in response to a sick call. The old man then lies down for a nap on the sitting-room sofa; twenty minutes later the daughter calls to the servant that her father is dead. He lies on the sofa with his head horribly hacked by an axe. Doctors and neighbours arrive, full of pity for the bereaved daughter's plight. Where is the stepmother? She is found upstairs in the spare room, stretched upon the floor beside the bed, her head cruelly cut to pieces by an axe. Where had Miss Lizzie been while this dreadful massacre was in progress in that quiet house that sunny August morning? She was ironing handkerchiefs in the dining-room, and afterwards out in the barn, looking for lead to make sinkers for a fishing-line. Now, I entreat the attention of members to the amazing fact that it was proved by the doctors, from the condition of the bodies, that *the stepmother had been slain an hour and a half before the father,* so that the murderer, if he came from outside, must have had a discomfortable wait between the acts, besides exposing himself to the notice of Miss Lizzie and the maid. It is plain that the assassin, unless some sort of screen were used, must have been more or less splashed with blood. Miss Lizzie, who to the indignation of the great American public fell under suspicion of the local authorities, was free from bloodstains; but she was proved to have burnt a dress which she said was stained with paint. There was a choice of axes in the cellar, none of which was bloodstained, though the handle of one of them was freshly broken and the head, which fitted the wounds, covered with ashes. The family life had been unhappy; the daughter barely spoke to Mrs. Borden, whom she refused to address as mother; she took her meals apart from her parents, and constantly quarrelled with them about money matters. The old folk were ill that week with symptoms of irritant poisoning, and Miss Lizzie was shown to have tried to buy prussic acid the very day before the crime. But this evidence, by the mysterious operation of American law, was held to be inadmissible. Miss Lizzie duly 'tholed her assize' and was acquitted, to the gratification of the godly of Fall River, Massachusetts. She had been a notable church worker, enjoyed a high repute for piety, and was escorted throughout the proceedings of which she was the subject by a brace of pastors as a ghostly bodyguard. She succeeded to the family fortune. No suspicion attached to anyone else, and the murders remain a mystery. The genius of Miss Lizzie Borden inspired a contemporary poet to enshrine in delicately wrought verse the brilliant gem of her creation—a poem so charming and so brief that I am unable to forgo the pleasure of reciting it in full:

> Lizzie Borden took an axe
> And gave her Mother forty whacks;
> When she saw what she had done,—
> She gave her Father forty-one!"

(Applause.) Such, continued Mrs. M'Lachlan, was a bald outline of this beautiful and attaching case. There were in Mr. Pearson's volume other crimes also deserving the attention of the Society, as the Nathan murder, and the tragedy of the *Herbert Fuller*—a breezy tale of butchery on the high seas, but an examination of these, though alluring, would take her too far.

She would therefore confine her remarks to certain features of the Borden case which, in her judgment, rendered it as a work of art not inferior to any product of our home industries, with the possible exception of the Sandyford Mystery, upon which for obvious reasons it would be improper in her to dwell. For anything comparable to this great work they must go back to Elizabethan drama. That wonderful laugh, heard by the maid as she opened the door to the new victim—a touch worthy of Webster, with whose masterpiece in murder, *The Duchess of Malfy*, they as students of such literature were well acquainted —was only to be equalled in terrific effect by the kindred line in that great tragedy:

The Lord Ferdinand laughs—

MR. WILLIAM HARE of Messrs. Burke and Hare, West Port, purveyors by special appointment to Surgeons' Hall, said he was loth to interrupt a lady, but this was no laughing matter. In the absence of his senior partner, unavoidably detained in the Anatomical Museum, it fell to him to vindicate the fair fame of the capital of Scotland. What was this Yankee spinster and her paltry tale of victims compared with the sixteen items standing at the credit of the firm of which he had the honour to be a humble member? Mary Paterson and Daft Jamie could give old Mr. and Mrs. Borden a stroke a hole; in the words of the poet they were "familiar in our mouths as household words," and who in that room had ever heard before of Lizzie Borden and her parents? Had not his lamented friend and partner, Mr. Burke, in addition to his other services to humanity, enriched the language with a new verb, no less picturesque and handy than expressive of the accepted greatness of his genius?

MRS. CHRISTINA GILMOUR and MR. OSCAR SLATER, rising simultaneously, claimed the ear of the meeting. They had both had urgent occasion to leave Scotland for America—there was no suggestion of the slightest impropriety, for they travelled by separate routes and in different centuries—and they submitted that their joint experience of that deep-breathing, free-living country, which from the immunity it extended to perpetrators of the foulest and most atrocious crimes might be named a rogues' Paradise or malefactors' Mecca, affording a much needed model to less enlightened lands—(Interruption, and a voice, "Chew coke!")

THE PRESIDENT said he would not sit there to lie down under such gross and unfounded aspersions upon their common country. The hon. members must be extruded.

(This was forthwith effected, Mrs. Gilmour shedding tears, and Mr. Slater using language which, owing to his imperfect English, was fortunately unintelligible to the reporters. Order being restored,)—

MISS MADELEINE HAMILTON SMITH, who was received with loud and prolonged cheering which she gracefully acknowledged, said that she was deeply touched by so flattering a reception. Her position was even more irregular than that of Mrs. M'Lachlan. They had each, she believed, in their several ways conferred some little distinction upon their native city; but whereas Mrs. M'Lachlan was at least convicted, she herself, alas, had suffered that ambiguous finding "Not Proven," and consequently, by the rules of the Society, was ineligible for membership. Still, as heading their supernumerary list, she felt herself entitled to address the meeting. She might say at once that she did not share that lady's admiration for their American colleague, with whom Mrs. M'Lachlan's sympathies were, in the circumstances naturally enough, engaged. Both were exponents of what might be termed the slaughterhouse or poleaxe school. For herself, she had always preferred the rapier to the bludgeon. Not that she was to be taken as an advocate of cold steel, for indeed she was wholly averse from the employment of any lethal weapon whatsoever. She had no use for hatchets, daggers, knives, pistols, and such clumsy things, which were uncertain in their action, caused unnecessary inconvenience, and made a disagreeable mess. These were methods of barbarism, unworthy of a civilized and cultured community. (Cries of "Withdraw" and uproar.) Well, well, it was purely a matter of taste and personal feeling; she would withdraw the phrase to which hon. members excepted. (Applause.) But take her own case. Assume that she had in fact designed the elimination of the late M. L'Angelier; what would have been her situation that day had she lured him into the parental parlour, and disposed of him with the family poker upon the domestic hearth? Her brown silk gown would have been ruined, her papa's carpet stained, her mamma's antimacassars spoilt, and she herself would have had considerable difficulty in satisfying a jury that it was a case of suicide. No; there was but one method by which objectionable persons could be safely, surely, and swiftly removed, and that was by poison. It was easy to acquire, cleanly to employ, simple to administer— a child might use it—and it operated outwith the presence of the exhibitor, always an advantage to susceptible and nervous artists. True, it had one drawback: it was open to detection on chemical analysis; but that was a trifle in comparison with the risks which recourse to physical violence inevitably involved. The only point in the Borden case which at all appealed to her was Miss Lizzie's unsuccessful attempt to procure prussic acid, which, she was free to confess, did touch a sympathetic chord, and went some way to redeem an otherwise vulgar and second-rate performance. (Cheers, hisses, and a voice, "Keep your tail up.")

Dr. Pritchard, M.A., M.B., M.C., M.D., etcetera, etcetera, said he was sure they were all most grateful to Miss Smith for her highly instructive remarks, with which so far as her toxicological views were concerned he for one was in complete accord. He had considerable experience in various branches of their great profession, including such trifling affairs as forgery and fire-raising, and he was prepared to maintain that poison, wisely chosen and administered with tact, preferably by an affectionate relative or trusted physician—it had been his good fortune to act in both capacities—was the least exceptionable mode of effacing superfluous persons. It was in fact the only gentlemanlike, and he would add ladylike, resource. (Here the Doctor bowed to Miss Smith, who smilingly deprecated the compliment.) The hour was late, and he would not detain them longer; but he could assure Miss Smith that she need be under no apprehension as to her status in that assembly. It was no fault of hers that she failed to secure that conviction—and here he was sure he spoke for all his fellow-members—which in the considered judgment of the Society she had so richly deserved. (Repeated and prolonged applause.)

THE REV. JOHN KELLO, minister of Spott, said that as an apostle of peace he was officially opposed to deeds of violence. His own homely recipe—the strangling of his wife with a towel while engaged in prayer, and thereafter preaching to his flock an eloquent sermon—had been commended as humane, ingenious, and original. It was not, however, adapted for general use: his case was rare. In his younger days the gentle art of poisoning was yet in its infancy. It was chiefly practised by incompetent and obscure hags, to whom the ignorance of the time ascribed diabolic powers. He regretted that, sharing as he then did the popular delusion, he had burnt more witches than any man in Scotland, always excepting his late Majesty King James the Sixth, of pious memory. These youthful indiscretions, which in the light of later scientific knowledge he could not sufficiently deplore, received some countenance from the experiences of his American confrère, the pastor of Salem, New England, who in the year 1690——

At this stage it was discovered that the Secretary (Major Weir, G.O.M.), whose necromantic instincts were excited by the reverend gentleman's remarks, was about to raise the Devil; whereupon the reporters hurriedly left the hall, and we have no means of knowing what, if any, decision was arrived at touching the question in debate.

THE BOYS ON THE ICE;

Or, *the* Arran *Stowaways*

There remain in the deeds of Watt and Kerr the bones of as
strange and sad a story as has ever been told, of a record of
cruelty and suffering on an almost heroic scale.
GEORGE BLAKE: *Down to the Sea.*

EVER ON THE OUTLOOK as I am for fresh grist for my criminous
mill, I have frequently had occasion to deplore the increasing
scarcity of suitable provision for my requirements. All the old
famous trials have already been consumed, and not a few out-
of-the-way cases have furnished curious and, I trust, profitable
material. But, criminally speaking, the current supply is disap-
pointing.

The modern murderer may execute a capable and satisfactory
job, yet, when it comes to the trial, he invariably pleads insanity, and thus, so far as concerns his neck, gets away with it.
Divers eminent alienists enter the witness-box, and testify—on
such grounds as that in infancy he bit his nurse, in childhood
pinched his little playmates' toys, in youth specialized in sundry
sorts of devilry, in short, was what is popularly known as a bad
hat—that, scientifically considered, he is irresponsible for his acts.
So, instead of being well and truly hanged as in the good old
days, he is sent into retreat for a period vaguely described as "His
Majesty's Pleasure," while it becomes the public's privilege to
defray the expense of his maintenance for an indefinite number
of years—John Watson Laurie, the Arran murderer, lived at his
country's cost for forty.

I confess that as a layman (and a taxpayer) I never can see
why, if a murderer be conscious of the nature and quality of his
act, and knows that what he does is wrong and punishable, he
should not be held responsible for its consequences and suffer
accordingly. But the subtile science of psychiatry has disposed

13

of these antiquated forthright methods, and the murderer is now accounted the victim of his peculiar complex, and so ought to be pitied rather than punished. Two such cases, occurring in recent years, I have in mind. I attended both trials, and was struck by the strange similarities presented by the circumstances of the respective crimes, the unexpected and unusual course of the judicial proceedings, and their inconclusive and (as I venture to think) unsatisfactory results. These were, in order of date, the King's Park tragedy of 1934 and the Murrayfield murder of 1938. Each related to the slaying of an unfortunate girl by a young married man, who had been subject, from time to time, to alleged fits, and, while admittedly sane, was by the medical experts for the Crown held to enjoy the benefit of what they termed "diminished responsibility," and so escaped the last dread penalty of his hideous crime.

Later I am going to give an account of these remarkable cases, but that with which we are now concerned is happily free from such recondite complications, being a plain tale of brutality, practised upon hapless boys by two ship's-officers, whose only complex was a lust of cruelty. Had these nefarious mariners flourished in our own more enlightened days, doubtless their sadistic savagery would have been attributed to "emotional instability" or "altered consciousness," and they would have put to sea again with flying colours.

I

On 7th April, 1868, the wooden sailing-ship Arran, a vessel of 1063 tons register, sailed from the port of Greenock, on the Clyde, for Quebec. Her master was Robert Watt, 28 years of age, a native of Saltcoats in Ayrshire. The mate was James Kerr, 31 years of age, who hailed from Loch Ranza in the Isle of Arran. He was, incidentally, the captain's brother-in-law. The ship's company numbered 24, including the officers. The cargo consisted of coal and oakum, in view of the subsequent happenings an appropriate lading. Captain Watt is described as a weak but not naturally ill-disposed commander, whose milder disposition was dominated by the coarse, unfeeling character of his ferocious mate and kinsman. It is not without significance that each of these marine monsters was fully bearded.

When the *Arran* was well out at sea, and just as the carpenter was about to batten down the hatches for the voyage, there emerged from divers hiding-places in the ship's bowels seven young stowaways, surely a record for unauthorized passengers of tender years. The boys belonged to Greenock, came of poor but respectable parents, and were in varying states of destitution and distress. Their names and ages were as follows: Hugh M'Ewan, 11; John Paul, 11; Hugh M'Ginnes, 11; Peter Currie, 12; James Bryson, 16; David Brand, 16; and Bernard Reilly, 22. What induced these unfortunate children to secrete themselves in the *Arran's* hold does not appear. Reilly proposed to emigrate in search of work. Little Paul and M'Ewan were chums ashore, and probably acted in concert; the others seem to have adventured each on his own. "Please, sir," explained one of the infants, when interrogated by the captain, "we want to be sailors!" It was the second day of the voyage, the ship was leaving the Irish Channel, and it was too late to put back. But as the *Arran* was amply provisioned for four months, the anticipated length of the voyage out and home, including detentions, she could afford to feed the fugitives, and the bigger boys could work for their keep. The rations authorized by the captain were, in the circumstances, adequate: 5 lb. of beef per day, and 14 oz. of coffee, 7 oz. of tea and 5 lb. of sugar per week.

The ship running into heavy weather, the young stowaways suffered grievously from sea-sickness, and the mate, observing that some of them vomited pieces of meat, ordered the steward to stop all beef supplies, adding that "he was going to give them the ground of their stomachs before they got any more"! Presently the rations were by his command reduced to biscuits, which were doled out in such quantities as the good pleasure of the mate permitted: some days they got one biscuit each, sometimes one biscuit among four boys. But for the humanity of the cook, who furnished them with surreptitious scraps, they hardly had escaped death by famine. Further, some of them had scarcely any clothes and were barefooted; M'Ewan was a delicate child and spat blood; so that as the weather worsened their plight became truly pitiable. But pity was an item not included in the *Arran's* manifest.

It chanced that the boy Bryson was dirty in his person and habits, averse from work, and given to petty pilferings of biscuits, meal, and currants to satisfy his craving for food. A letter, written from Quebec on 10th June, 1868, by a member of the crew to his people in Greenock, gives a graphic account of the hellish conditions to which these poor lads were subjected:

> The boys were thinly clad, and were not able to stand the severe cold. The men could hardly stand it, let alone them. Two of the little ones had their bare feet, and as we were going so far to the northward amongst hail, frost, snow, and raining continually, none of them would keep on deck to work. As soon as the mate missed them, he went with a rope's end in hand and ordered them out, and as they came out gave them a walloping, and pretty often very severely. The captain never interfered with the mate and them till one good day the hatches were all opened, and the crew, on going to shift some oakum and coils of rope where the stowaways slept, found them all besmeared with filth. Then he gave them a thrashing, and made all hands clean it up. It would take too long to tell you how they were used, so I will give you the end of them. . . .

What that end was we shall see in the sequel. Meanwhile the full fury of the mate's ferocity was directed upon young Bryson, who afterwards was to give the Court the horrid particulars of his ill-treatment. I think it better to let the witnesses tell their own story, rather than to summarize it in narrative form. One gets from the actual words of the victims so much more vivid an impression of their incredible sufferings. But to enable you to appreciate their evidence I must indicate the course of that disastrous voyage, and the happenings that led to the subsequent trial of the captain and the mate before the High Court of Justiciary, when they were placed at the bar to answer for their crimes.

The flogging and the starving continued until, on 10th May, the Arran, which for some days had encountered packs of floating ice, became firmly embedded in an icefield in St. George's Bay, on the coast of Newfoundland, and her voyage was for the time suspended. Then, after further outrages upon the famished boys, for foraging for food in the temporary absence of their persecutors—who had gone for a stroll upon the frozen deep—there occurred that unparalleled act of cruelty which renders the case of the Arran stowaways unique in our criminal annals. The deed is succinctly set forth in a dozen words by the writer of the letter already quoted:

The stowaways got a biscuit apiece, and were ordered to go ashore.

Land was not visible to the naked eye, but the captain alleged that he could see it by means of his spyglass. "There were," he assured the boys, "houses and people dwelling in them not so far away." Alternatively, they could make for another vessel, the Myrtle, also embedded in the ice, a mile or two from where the Arran lay fast—this at least was true—and might there obtain food. They must leave the ship, as he, the master, had not provisions enough to carry them all to Quebec. The distance between the Arran and the coast was by the crew variously estimated as from 8 to 20 miles. The mate, taking a rosier view of the boys' prospects, put it at 5.

Picture to yourself, good reader, the situation of these hapless youngsters, ragged, barefooted, starving, and further reduced by long-continued ill-usage. The piercing cold of that dark northern clime, the wide white waste of the icefield, stretching as far as the eye could reach to the invisible horizon—and four of them were children of 11 and 12! Not even the fertile and resourceful invention of modern Nazi specialists in barbarism could contrive a more devilish act of cruelty. The wonder is that any of the victims survived to tell the tale, and that only two perished under the dreadful ordeal.

The letter before referred to caused great consternation in Greenock, where the relatives of the missing boys, who knew not what had become of them, were horrified and furious to learn of their ill-treatment. The whole community, we are told, spoke of nothing but "the boys on the ice," and wrath was kept warm for the return of the *Arran* to her home port, when a reckoning could be had with the perpetrators of the alleged atrocity. When, on the evening of Thursday, 30th July, the ship came up the Clyde and neared the quay, those aboard could see that a hostile crowd awaited her arrival. No sooner was she moored than several men leaped on board to take summary vengeance on the two officers, who, apprised of their intention, prudently sought safety in the cabin. The police were sent for to protect them from the popular fury, but the crowd was not dispersed till 11 o'clock that night.

Next day the captain and the mate were taken before the Sheriff, charged with assault, and with "cruelly and maliciously compelling one or more of Her Majesty's lieges to leave a ship while said ship was embedded in ice at a considerable distance from land, to the imminent risk and serious and permanent injury of their persons." It was not then known to the authorities that two of the children had died as the result of the accused's inhuman action. Both men were committed for trial, bail being refused. Meanwhile the Procurator-Fiscal had telegraphed to the police at St. John's, Newfoundland, from whom he learned that five of the boys had reached the shore, that four were still at St. George's Bay, that Bernard Reilly, the eldest, was gone to seek work at Halifax, Nova Scotia, and that little Hugh M'Ewan and Hugh M'Ginnes (each aged 11) had lost their lives on the ice. As the result of this information the prisoners were further charged with murder, but this count was afterwards dropped, and the charge reduced to assault, cruel and barbarous usage, and the "innominate offence" of compelling the boys to leave the ship to the danger of their lives.

The return of the survivors to their home port was achieved under conditions very different from those of the outward voyage. The boys were taken by the authorities in a schooner to St. John's, where they embarked in the brigantine *Hannah and Bennie*, belonging to no less important a personage than the

Provost of Greenock and Member of Parliament for that Burgh, which they reached in comfort and safety on 1st October, six months from the fatal hour when they adventured upon the Arran. It was the local Fast Day; and the welcome given them by the crowds awaiting their arrival was something more cordial than that (in the dreadful journalistic phrase) "extended" to their oppressors, then lying in jail to abide the consequences of their crimes.

II

The trial took place in the High Court of Justiciary at Edinburgh, before the Lord Justice-Clerk (George Patton) and a jury, and occupied three days: 23rd, 24th, and 25th November, 1868. The Lord Advocate (Edward Strathearn Gordon), the Solicitor-General (John Millar), and Mr. W. E. Gloag, Advocate-Depute (the future Lord Kincairney), conducted the prosecution; Mr. George Young, Q.C. (afterwards Lord Young), and Mr. Charles Scott, advocate, appeared for Captain Watt; the Dean of Faculty (James Moncrieff, later Lord Justice-Clerk) and Mr. Robert Maclean, advocate, for Kerr the mate.[1] After long debate upon the relevancy of the indictment, objections to the so-called "innominate" charge were repelled, and the trial proceeded.

The first of the boy-witnesses called was James Bryson (16). He told how he and his companions had boarded the Arran at Greenock, and hid in the hold and other parts of the ship. They remained concealed for a day and a night, without food or water. He saw the carpenter battening down the hatches; they [witness and Brand] were down in the hold. Brand knocked up and the hatchway was again opened. Brand and himself were seized with sickness, which lasted 3 or 4 days. He remembered the Arran coming in sight of ice at Newfoundland. He had been scrubbed and flogged before then. It was with the lead line that

[1] The best report of the proceedings will be found in the *Scotsman* of 24th, 25th, and 26th November, 1868. The official report is contained in Couper's *Justiciary Reports*, vol. i. pp. 123–168.

he was flogged. "The mate flogged me when I was sitting on one of the hatches. I was made to take off my jacket, waistcoat, and shirt, leaving only my semmit on. The coil was about ½-inch thick. The mate flogged me for about 3 minutes. The blows were very painful. I cried out in consequence of the pain I was suffering. When I was screaming, the master of the vessel came forward. The mate made me strip off the rest of my clothing. I was then made to lie down on the deck. Both the master and mate were present. Robert Hunter (one of the crew) was ordered to draw water in a bucket; he threw it about me as he was ordered. Several bucketfuls of water were thrown on me. The weather was very cold at the time. It was salt water that was thrown about me. The captain then scrubbed me with a hair broom all over my body. The process occasioned me great pain. The mate then took the broom up and scrubbed me harder than the captain. I made frequent attempts to rise during the operation of scrubbing. When the captain was scrubbing, the mate was standing over me with a rope in his hand, with which he threatened to strike me if I attempted to run away. After the mate had scrubbed me, he handed the broom to Brand and told him to scrub me with it. I could not say whether my body was marked in any way by the scrubbing, or whether the skin was broken. I felt pain during the scrubbing, but not afterwards. After the scrubbing was finished I was made to wash my clothes. I was ordered to the forecastle by the mate. I was naked at the time. When I had been there about an hour my coat and semmit were returned. I suffered very much from exposure. My body had not been dried in any way." The ill-usage continued throughout the voyage.

When the ship reached the icefield, and the captain and mate went "ashore" for a walk, the famished boys started to look for food. "Brand and I went into the cabin to get something to eat. Brand secured some biscuits, and on coming up he told me he had a pocketful and that there was no one there. I went down to get some but could find none. I took some currants out of a keg, because I could get nothing else. I was hungry at the time. I took about a fistful of currants and returned to my work of scraping the deck. The mate was coming up the vessel's side when he saw me coming out of the cabin. He ordered my hands to be tied, and Brand and I were searched. The mate gave the order. Nothing was found on Brand. My pocket was cut on the outside and the currants 'kepped' in a saucer. The captain ordered the currants to be given to the other boys. I was afterwards stripped naked by order of the mate. The captain was present all the time and saw what took place. The mate placed my head on the deck, seized my legs, and held them up to his breast while the captain flogged me. He gave me 15 to 20 lashes. The ship at this time was surrounded by ice, but was not frozen in. I was ordered by the mate to help the boy Currie to scrub the deck when I was stark naked. I was so engaged for about 10 minutes. After sweeping the deck, the mate sent me to the house in the forecastle, where I remained for about quarter of an hour, when I was called out and my semmit was returned to me. I was then placed on the hatch and the mate told me to tell him all that I had done in my life."

Well might Master Bryson have cried aloud with the Psalmist, "The plowers plowed upon my back: and made long furrows."

It will simplify matters if we now hear the other evidence regarding the floggings of Bryson, before we come to the more atrocious episode of the boys being driven from the ship.

David Brand (16) deponed: "I was present when Bryson was flogged. The weather was cold, but I do not think it was freezing. Bryson was very dirty and it was on that account that he was scrubbed. I scrubbed him by order of the mate. It was a hard broom that I scrubbed him with. I was so engaged for about 10 minutes. The mate did not interfere with me while I was brushing him. I stopped when I thought he was clean. 3 or 4 pails of water were thrown upon Bryson, who was crying out during the operation. The mate flogged him after he had been scrubbed. The flogging was continued for about 2 minutes. There were about 30 blows given during that time. I saw marks on his person after the flogging was over. The captain was present during the flogging, but said or did nothing. I saw blood on Bryson's back after the flogging was over. He remained naked after the flogging. I stole some biscuits and a piece of beef out of the cabin to eat. Bryson went in afterwards and took some currants. He was seen by the mate, who ordered him to be searched. The captain afterwards flogged him for about 2 or 3 minutes. The lead line was used to flog Bryson. The captain held him with one hand and flogged him with the other. The mate flogged him after the captain was done. The captain said he would make them go on the ice presently. Hugh M'Ginnes asked the captain what he would do on the ice with his bare feet. *The captain replied that it would be as well for him to die on the ice as in the ship, as he would get no more food there.* Paul was crying bitterly. He cried out 'Oh, my fingers!' I do not know why he cried that out. Paul was the last one that went on to the ice. None of us got any breakfast that morning. We went away from the ship without tasting any food. Some biscuits were thrown overboard after we left the ship—one biscuit to each." This generous dole was in response to the boys' piteous appeal not to be sent empty away.

John Paul (11) deponed: "I went on board the *Arran* the day she sailed. I hid myself in the fo'castle-head and remained hidden all night. The tug was away before I came out. I was poorly clad when I went on board. I had no shoes on and had no clothes except those I was wearing. I took no clothes or provisions with me. There were other stowaways on board. M'Ginnes was clad the same as myself. No shoes were supplied to me on board. I got canvas to make trousers, but it was taken from me again some days after, before I left the ship. It was taken back because I could not get them made. I remember Bryson being scrubbed some days before we left the ship. He was scrubbed with a 'kyar' broom—a hard broom with which they swept the decks. When we were going to be put on the ice I hid myself. I was brought forward, and asked the mate to keep me on board. He said he would have nothing to do with it. When on the rails I was struck by the captain with a belaying-pin, because I would not go on the ice. I was the last to leave the ship. I had had 2 or 3 pieces of biscuit for breakfast that morning and some biscuits were thrown from the ship after me."

Only two of the boys—Reilly and Bryson—were willing to tempt fortune on the ice; the former because he was anxious to get a job ashore, and the latter because for him nothing worse could happen than he had suffered on the ship. Reilly told him the captain said he could see houses on the land through his glass, and Bryson said if that were so he would go too. Brand refused to go over the side, so the captain caught him by the collar of his coat and forced him into the bows. Little Paul had hidden himself in the forecastle. "The captain went in and brought him out," continues Bryson. "Paul went crying to the mate, asking him to keep him on board. He [the mate] said he would have nothing to do with putting us ashore on the ice. He saw what was going on. The Captain followed Paul and told him to go forward. M'Ewan, who was hiding in the galley, began to cry. *The captain said to him that he might as well die on the ice as in the vessel, as he would get no meat on board till he got to Quebec.* Brand and I heard this. We then all went down on to the ice. Reilly went first; I went down from the rails; Paul, M'Ewan, and M'Ginnes came down. Currie remained on board; he had not been asked to go.[1] M'Ewan and M'Ginnes were crying in the ship and while they were getting over, and they continued crying when they got on to the ice. Paul had on a blue coat; he had no shoes. M'Ginnes had bare feet too, and his clothes were all ragged and torn. M'Ewan had boots, and was better clothed than any of us. When we went over the ship's side we had no provisions with us. After we got out on the ice there was one biscuit apiece thrown to us by the mate's order. It was between 8 and 9 in the morning, and clear daylight."

Before following the further fortunes of the castaways we may note two points: first the attitude of the mate. This ruffian had been unceasing in his cruelties to the children throughout the voyage, and it is probable that the plan to drive them from the ship originated in his morbid ferocity; but, as we have seen,

---

[1] Peter Currie (12) had been throughout exempt from the cruelties of the mate, who was a friend of the child's father. Doubtless he escaped his companions' fate by reason of the mate's influence with the captain. He survived to bear witness for the defence at the trial.

he took no active part in this, leaving the captain to carry out the final and most fiendish outrage. Why? Doubtless, in view of the possible consequences of the inhuman deed, he wished, ostensibly, to have no hand in it, so that he might hold himself free from innocent blood. The second is even more amazing: the behaviour of the 22 members of the crew, who looked on, and did nothing to prevent the outrage. They were afterwards to admit that they all "thought it too dangerous to put the boys off," but maintained that it was none of their business; it was not for them to interfere with the captain. Their previous indifference to the brutalities practised upon the lad Bryson is referable (*vide* Mr. George Blake's essay on the case aftermentioned) to "the sea-customs of the period." But surely this is an anachronism; here we are far from the days of Smollett and of Captain Marryat. Be that as it may, let Master Bryson resume his tale.

"We did not see how far the land was distant; we saw a black haze, but nothing else. *I thought I might as well die on the ice as on board the vessel.* We were 12 hours on the ice that day. We found the journey very dangerous. We had gone about 10 or 11 miles before we met with danger; it was near the shore. The ice had been pretty good, but there it was all broken. I fell into the water up to the neck while jumping from one piece of ice to another. We all fell into crevices at various times. We got out the best way we could, each had just to scramble for himself. M'Ewan fell in once and I pulled him out; he fell in a second time and scrambled out himself; the third time he went down and never came up, the ice closed over him. It was hopeless to attempt to save him. . . . Some hours after this happened M'Ginnes sat down on a piece of ice and said he could go no farther. We urged him to come along with us, and said if he did not he knew what would become of him: he would be frozen. He appeared exhausted. No attempt was made to assist him; we had enough to do to assist ourselves, going all day across the ice barefooted. Our clothes were frozen upon us by this time. He [M'Ginnes] had nothing on but his ragged frozen clothes. He was 'greeting.' *We heard his cries a long way behind us although we could not see him. . . .* The captain told us where the *Myrtle* was lying, and said that when we got to her we would get food. He pointed in the direction, telling us to keep by the stern of the *Arran*. We went 300 yards in that direction, and then we thought it better to make for the nearest point of land. We never saw the *Myrtle* all day. We were within sight of the *Arran* when we changed our course."

The end of the icefield was reached that night; they saw the land and houses, but between them and the shore there was a stretch of open water. Bryson, Brand, and Reilly severally tried to ferry across, each on a piece of ice, paddling with a batten and bits of wood they had brought from the ship. The distance was about a mile. A woman saw them from the shore, and a boat came out and picked them up. "The sun was just going down at the time we were rescued."

What more dreadful picture was ever painted than this of the one child trapped by the floating ice, perishing in the icy water, and the other left "greeting" on the ice to be slowly frozen to death?

The cross-examination by Mr. Young was mainly directed to these shocking episodes. "When M'Ewan fell in the third time," said Bryson, "it was about midday. The others were about 100 yards ahead of me at the time; I then ran on. I do not know why none of the rest looked round any more than I did. I looked no more after M'Ewan. M'Ginnes sat down, tired, about 5 miles from the shore. I never stopped; I left him sitting 'greeting.' I heard him for about 100 yards off, I dare say—for about ten minutes; the ice was bad, and we could not go extra fast at that time." They told the people on shore that M'Ewan and M'Ginnes had been left behind. Nothing more was heard of them while the boys remained at St. George's Bay.

David Brand and John Paul corroborated in all respects the story told by Bryson as to what happened, from the time of their leaving the ship until their rescue by the boat. "M'Ewan fell in oftener than any of us," said Brand; "he was the youngest, and weakly and feeble. There was some soft ice at the place which closed over him; I never heard or saw any more of him." As regards the abandonment of M'Ginnes: "The ice was so bad we could not carry him, he could not walk, and we could get no assistance. He appeared to be exhausted; his bare feet were much swollen. He had very little clothes on; his trousers were very ragged and you could see his skin through them." Both boys were unshaken by cross-examination, little Paul quaintly saying, in reply to Mr. Young: "The reason I ran away from Greenock was *for a pleasure sail*. I was comfortable at home. I lived with my mother, but did not tell her I was going. I took the *Arran* to go in because she was a good ship. *I did not know the captain.*"

Of the members of the crew examined, most sought to minimize the cruelty with which the stowaways were treated throughout the voyage; but none could deny the brutalities to which Bryson was subjected, nor the compelling of the children to leave the ship. "Three of the little boys were unwilling to go," said George Henry. "They began to cry when they were asked to go by the mate, and continued to do so when they went away." *By a juryman*—"Why did you not interfere when you thought the boys were going to be placed in such danger?— I had no right to interfere with my master and mate; I was a servant." "If the master or mate had been going to murder the boys, would you have interfered?—There was a chance of their reaching the shore, and some of them did reach it." "Did you ever expect to see them again?—I cannot say whether I did or not." "Did you think they would be drowned?—It was very uncertain to think anything."

William Salton, the ship's-cook, stated that when Reilly told him he was going ashore with Bryson, witness said he would be a fool to do so, because of the danger. "He said he would rather go than stand the abuse." Witness saw the little boys leave the ship, "ordered by the captain and mate to go." Had they remained on board there was plenty of provisions to last till they reached Quebec.

Mrs. Agnes M'Ginnes deponed to her son leaving her and stowing away on board the *Arran*; that he was 11 years of age in April last, and that she had never since heard of him. Mrs.

M'Ewan deponed in like manner regarding her son, who also was 11 years of age in April last; that he was not a strong boy, and that she had heard nothing of him since, except that he had perished.

The Crown case closed with the reading of the accused's declarations. The captain declared that he "invited" the boys to leave the ship and have a run on the ice. "I pointed out to them houses on the shore, and said to them they might have a fine run ashore"! Being interrogated if he forced or compelled the boys to leave the ship, he declared: "I cannot say that I did so; but I, of course, told them to go." He made no inquiries on shore with a view to ascertaining their fate, and did not know what became of them after leaving the ship.

The mate declared that he never caused Bryson to be scrubbed with a hard brush, neither did he ever assault him, or strike him with a rope. He did not force or compel the boys to leave the ship. No inquiry was made as to what became of them.

III

The first witness for the defence was Peter Currie (12), the boy who had enjoyed the exceptional favour of the mate. He told how he saw his companions leave the ship. "He heard the mate say he would wager any man on board £20 they would be back to their dinner." Cross-examined by the Solicitor-General —The boys slid down by a rope; the captain "assisted" them on to the rail. "They were 'greeting' all the time; when they were sliding down, and while they were going away. The captain ordered them to go. I saw one biscuit each thrown to them when they were on the ice. That was all they got. I saw them at breakfast at 8 o'clock; they got half a biscuit. That was all they had since 12 o'clock, dinner-time, the day before." M'Ewan was a weakly boy; witness had seen him spitting blood. M'Ginnes's health was "middling good." He and Paul were barefooted when they left the ship.

Two members of the crew, M'Lean and Thomson, respectively steward and boatswain, deponed that the captain was a kind, quiet man, who seldom interfered with the discipline of the ship: "The mate took everything to do with that." One of them admitted, in cross-examination, "I thought it possible for a man to reach the land on the ice, but not for boys so clad. It was not my place to interfere." The chaplain of the Seaman's Friend Society, Greenock, also gave the captain the highest possible character. He was so well-disposed, especially to boys, "that it was generally believed they liked to stowaway with him on that account"! The parish minister of Ardrossan and four of his parishioners also testified to the many virtues of this exemplary skipper.

The accused James Kerr (the mate), having been again at the request of his counsel interrogated on the libel (indictment), pleaded guilty of assault as libelled, and the Solicitor-General accepted the plea.

IV

The Solicitor-General, in presenting the case for the prosecution, said the evidence which had been given during the trial seemed to him so clear and conclusive that he felt it his duty to ask for a verdict finding the master of the *Arran* guilty of the crime of which he was accused. The mate, who pleaded not guilty in the first instance, had subsequently withdrawn that plea and pleaded guilty to the charge of assault set forth in the libel. He (the Solicitor-General) felt that it was not inconsistent with his duty to accept that plea, and he had therefore withdrawn the charge of culpable homicide in the case of the mate. Although his own personal feelings would lead him to say that he could consistently take the same course with regard to the master as he had been enabled to take with reference to the mate, he felt that the evidence against the master was too strong to warrant such procedure. The case was one of considerable importance. The powers of the master of a vessel were necessarily large, and might be used either for good or evil; and it was just because these large powers might be misused by the men to whom they were entrusted that the jury ought not to shrink from the strict performance of their duty, because it was only by the proper discharge of the functions imposed upon them that the law could be vindicated, and the weak and helpless protected against the strong. The jury had heard the whole of the evidence that had been adduced in this painful case, and it was for them to say whether that evidence had not conclusively established the guilt of the master.

The learned Solicitor-General then went through the main points of the evidence, calling the attention of the jury to the several acts of cruelty, which he submitted were abundantly established. He remarked that, in considering the case against the master of the Arran, the jury would have to determine three minor points: first, whether there was any compulsion used in putting the boys on the ice, or whether they left the ship of their own free will; second, what was the amount of danger attending the journey over the ice, assuming that it was compulsorily taken; and third, what were the consequences that might have been reasonably expected to ensue from a journey undertaken in such circumstances. There could be little doubt, from the evidence the jury had listened to, that the boys were compelled to leave the ship, and that they did not voluntarily quit the vessel on so perilous a journey as that which they had to take; that the journey was one which was full of danger to those who were forced to take it; and with regard to the probable consequences of the act so perpetrated, what other results could have been anticipated than those which were proved to have happened? The whole of the evidence pointed clearly to the fact that the child who sank in the water, the child who was left to perish upon the ice, and the surviving boys who were more or less injured by the exposure and fatigue they were compelled to undergo, owed their deaths and injuries to the culpable conduct of the master of the Arran, by whose orders they were forcibly expelled from that vessel. Indeed, it seemed impossible that the jury could arrive at any other conclusion than that the master had been guilty of the crime of culpable homicide.

With regard to the master's previous good character, he was undoubtedly entitled to all the benefit which that character could give him; but at the same time the jury must not allow this consideration to overbalance the facts that had been proved in evidence.

Mr. Young, in addressing the jury on behalf of the prisoners, said, although he could not regard the case otherwise than as a serious one, he had not been prepared for the long, solemn, and he might almost say pompous address to which he had just listened. The case was undoubtedly of a nature which was calculated to excite considerable public interest, and a charge such as that which had been preferred against the prisoners was sure to arouse a certain amount of popular indignation. But whatever might be the feeling out of doors, it was for the jury to determine the case upon its own proper merits, and he had no doubt that they would succeed in arriving at a just and satisfactory verdict. In order to do this, they would have to sift the whole of the evidence; and he asked them, was it reasonable to suppose that two and twenty grown men, who formed the crew of the ship in which the boys were stowed away, would have allowed the stowaway lads to be compulsorily sent adrift under circumstances which, in their belief, must have been likely to lead to their destruction? It was obvious to his mind that those men did not regard what had taken place when the boys left the vessel in the light in which, for the purpose of the present prosecution, it had been represented.

The assaults which had been charged against the prisoners were the least serious part of the case, and required but few observations. The jury should remember the position in which the master was placed with regard to the stowaways. It was obvious that lads like those who had concealed themselves on board the *Arran* belonged to the very worst class; and although they might not all of them be guilty of theft on board, they at any rate forced the master to provide them with food which was not intended for their consumption. It could hardly be expected that such characters should be sumptuously fed by those upon whom they forced themselves. Neither was it reasonable to suppose that a part of the equipment of a merchant vessel should consist of clothing for stowaway boys. As to the lad Bryson, it was proved that he had contracted exceedingly dirty habits; and that this being the case, it hardly seemed unreasonable that he should be washed—not with a gentle hand, like an infant, but in such a way that the operation should be a lesson to him, and teach him for the future to be more cleanly in his person. That Bryson should also have been flogged was by no means a surprising circumstance when his conduct was taken into consideration; and the jury should recollect it was not alleged that he had been injured by the punishment.

Coming to the most serious part of the case—the sending of the boys on shore—he (the learned counsel) confessed that he could not approve of the course pursued by the master on that occasion; but it was quite another thing to say that the master was guilty of the crime which was charged against him in the indictment. The charge had not been proved by the evidence. The actual state of the matter was this: a few days before the act which led to the more serious charge, the boys had been put upon the ice for the purpose of giving them a fright, and they were afterwards called back and taken on board the vessel again. Subsequently Reilly and Bryson seemed to have entered into an agreement to go ashore, and asked the smaller boys to join them. If the bigger lads were willing to make the attempt, it was hardly right, so far at least as they were concerned, that the captain should be held responsible for permitting them to do it. But the captain was of opinion that the attempt was fraught with some danger; and although he permitted, and probably undoubtedly pressed, the little boys to go along with the bigger ones, he was at the same time under the impression that the boys would return to the ship so soon as they saw the peril attending the journey over the ice. It was not true that the captain had, as was alleged in the libel, dragged the boys from the vessel. That he had permitted them to leave it was not itself a reprehensible act, but he had told the boys they were to return; and after they had left the ship, when he suggested to the mate that the boys should be called back again, the mate replied that they were sure to be back to dinner.

With regard to the charge of culpable homicide, he (counsel) contended that there was no reliable evidence that either M'Ewan or M'Ginnes had perished in that way. With regard to M'Ewan, the only evidence as to his death was that he had plumped into the water and was lost sight of for three seconds by his companion, who then ran on to join the boys in front, and only looked to see whether M'Ewan had got out of the water. It would surprise no one if both M'Ewan and M'Ginnes were to turn up alive and well.

Mr. Young concluded by saying that such things had happened over and over again; and it had been laid down by a learned judge as a broad general rule, that it was not safe for a jury to find the death of a person unless the body was found.

The Lord Justice-Clerk then summed up. His Lordship said that the jury had heard the learned counsel for the prosecution and the defence, and it lay with them to arrive at a just conclusion. In coming to that conclusion they would require to keep in view, and be regulated by, the evidence alone. The main question which the jury would have to consider was whether the prisoners had been reckless and indifferent to human life. They must satisfy themselves whether both the boys were dead. The law said that clear evidence must be adduced as to the death.

The boy M'Ewan was the first to leave the ship for the purpose of making his way ashore. Paul and he fell into the water together. He had a struggle to keep himself clear of M'Ewan, and he saw M'Ewan's face sinking for ever under the ice. Brand said that M'Ewan, in trying to jump from one piece of ice to another, had fallen into the water, when the ice closed over him, and that he was seen no more. The evidence differed there. But the question which the jury would have to decide was whether that was evidence of the drowning of the boy. They could not exact from the public prosecutor the production of the boys' bodies. The question was whether they were left in any reasonable doubt that the boy was drowned. If they considered it a conclusive fact that he might have escaped, it would be an element in the case.

They had next to consider the case of the boy M'Ginnes, whose death arose from positive exhaustion and inability to move onward to the point which he wished to reach. He was left there by his companions, who were endeavouring to effect their own escape. The jury must judge whether he also escaped or was at present alive. They would bear in mind that the boys set out on a perilous journey.

Was it, then, the fault of the pannel that these boys lost their lives? Was he free from culpability or not? Were the two boys—neither of whom was then 12 years of age—forcibly driven out of the ship against their will by the prisoner at the bar? His Lordship considered that they were compelled to leave the ship by reason of threats, and by the exhibition to one or other of them of physical force. These unfortunate children could not act according to their own desires or inclinations—a very small share of compulsion on the part of a man in authority was sufficient to make them do things against their will. Bryson, Brand, and Paul deponed that they were compelled to leave the ship. Doubtless they were told that Currie was sent to the mate to announce their intention of leaving the vessel, and that M'Ewan was a party to that arrangement. Bryson said that he was not; he said—"Reilly and I were willing to go." But so far as the testimony of Bryson was concerned, M'Ewan was not willing. Brand was of the same impression, and so was Paul. His Lordship thought that the jury had an overwhelming mass of evidence before them to the effect that these boys did not desire to leave the ship, but were forced to do so. He did not believe that the boys had been induced to leave the vessel to play and then return. Bryson and the others had given positive evidence to say that the captain had forced the boys to leave, declaring that they had better die on the ice than on board the ship.

After going over the evidence of Brand and Paul, his Lordship said it proved that force was exercised by the captain towards the boys to make them leave the vessel. His Lordship proceeded to comment on the indifference shewn by the captain as to the fate of the boys. Two witnesses had deponed that the captain said, loud enough for the boys to hear him, that if they found the road difficult, they were to return; but it had been proved that none of the boys ever heard such an expression made use of. But assuming the expression to have been used, was it a situation for boys of 11 years of age to be put in by the captain?

After reviewing the evidence as to the flogging and scrubbing of the lad Bryson, his Lordship said that, if the jury believed that death had been occasioned by the captain's authority or instrumentality, they would come to the conclusion as to his guilt. His Lordship concluded by saying that the case was a very important one—the first of the kind that had come before the tribunals of that Court. It was perfectly right that the matter should have been investigated; and he had no doubt but that the jury would give a decision in accordance with the facts of the case.

The jury retired at twenty minutes to three o'clock, and after an absence of thirty-five minutes returned to Court with the following verdict: "On the two charges of assault the jury are unanimously of opinion that the captain is not guilty; that he is guilty of the charge of culpable homicide; that he is guilty of compelling the boys to leave a British ship; but that, on account of his previous good character, they recommend him to the leniency of the Court"! The jury found the mate guilty of assault, according to his own confession.

The Dean of Faculty then addressed the Court in mitigation of the sentence of the mate, arguing it was impossible to maintain discipline on board a ship unless there was the power of chastisement in the hands of the superior officer. He pointed out that Bryson was not in the slightest degree injured, except for a time, and concluded by reminding the Court that his client had been four months in prison.

Mr. Charles Scott said that he had intended to address the

Court in behalf of his client (the captain), but after the recommendation of the jury he would not do so.

The Lord Justice-Clerk then sentenced Kerr, the mate, to four months' imprisonment, and Watt, the captain, to eighteen months' imprisonment.

This result was received by the audience with loud hisses, and we who read the tale today would doubtless wish to associate ourselves with that expression of indignation at the astounding lightness of the sentences, which manifestly fail, in the Mikado's famous phrase, "to let the punishment fit the crime."

V

For the subsequent history of the survivors and their persecutors I am indebted to the valuable account of the facts furnished by Mr. John Donald of Greenock, in his entertaining volume entitled: *The Stowaways and Other Sketches: True Tales of the Sea* (Perth: 1928). "Reilly," the author tells us, "went to Halifax, N.S.; Bryson emigrated with his father and family to America, where James obtained employment as a street-car conductor; Peter Currie died of consumption about two years after he came home; John Paul became a foreman riveter and removed to Itchen, Southampton, where he died some years ago; David Brand proceeded to Townsville, North Queensland, where he founded the flourishing engineering firm of Brand, Dryborough & Burns, and died suddenly and unexpectedly in the month of November, 1897. . . .

"Soon after leaving prison, both Watt and Kerr quickly got to sea again as master and mate respectively—in different vessels, of course. The former is said to have died at Pensacola, a year or two after his release; but Kerr served for many years as a shipmaster before retiring to rest ashore. He died over twenty years ago."

Those sufficiently interested in this strange story are recommended to consult Mr. George Blake's brilliant study of the case: "Stowaways of the *Arran*," in his engaging epic of the Clyde, *Down to the Sea* (London: 1937), by which blessed volume my attention was first directed to the subject. "So they passed into the night, one and all," he finely concludes, "and beyond that question we would all have asked of them—if, above the rumble of the Philadelphia streetcars, over the clangour of iron on iron, or through the beat of the Coral Sea they did not sometimes hear, and with terror, the cry of a child greetin' on the ice of the North Atlantic?"

Note.—THE BOYS IN THE MINCH

History is apt to repeat itself. Since re-telling this old tragedy of the sea I have attended a recent trial which, in ruthless disregard for human life, presents some similar features. On 4th October, 1938, two Grimsby trawlers, *Buckingham* and *Carisbrooke*, were anchored in Bayble Bay, near Stornoway, in the Isle of Lewis. They were sheltering from a north-west gale which had blown hard all night. The weather, even in the bay, was boisterous, with an off-shore wind and a rough sea. In the dusk of the evening five lads, whose ages ranged from 15 to 22, put off from the village of Upper Bayble to beg for fish—a common practice of the islanders. They went out in a 10-foot rowing-boat, which normally required four oars, though they took but two, with which they rowed in turns. The boat was sharp-pointed at bow and stern and had then no rudder. The boys made for the *Buckingham* as the nearer ship, but before they reached her she weighed anchor and stood out to sea. So they decided to try the *Carisbrooke*, which lay farther out, half a mile or so from the shore. With difficulty they got alongside, breaking two thole pins, used as rowlocks, in the process, and, having got alongside the trawler, fastened their boat by her painter. Almost immediately the boat broke adrift, so the skipper had reluctantly to take up his anchor and manoeuvre his ship to recover it. When this was done it was found that one of the oars was lost. Another was provided, also a bit of a soap box and a knife to make new thole pins.

Now this unnecessary trouble and delay, just as he was about to leave for the fishing-grounds, was very grievous to the skipper. Four times, in terms at once forcible and foul, he ordered the boys into the boat, but they were afraid to go. It was now dark, and to row back in the teeth of wind and sea would be both difficult and hazardous. The skipper, they said, might as well throw them overboard—it was "murder." Finally, they asked him to tow them in; a rope was passed from the ship to the boat, the boys embarked and the towing began, the trawler's engines running dead slow. While the vessel was turning towards the shore all went well, but no sooner did she straighten out upon her course than the men in charge of the rope saw that the boat was in imminent danger of being swamped. The mate shouted to the engine-room: "Ease it down, or else you'll lose the boat!" and was going to the wheelhouse to warn the skipper when someone cried out: "The boat's gone!" The trawler's lights were switched on, and after a search the boat was found, water-logged, with the youngest boy clinging to her. The rest were seen no more, and their bodies were never recovered.

The skipper, F. G. Thomsett, was charged with the culpable homicide (manslaughter) of the four lads in the High Court at Edinburgh on 15th February, 1939, before the Lord Justice-Clerk (Lord Aitchison) and a jury. The young survivor told his piteous story, and every member of the crew examined bore witness to the manifest peril of the venture, and said that not one of them would have entered the boat under the conditions on which the boys were compelled to do. They described the skipper as "mad" with anger. The accused stated that his own ship being in danger he had no time to bother about the boat, and it never occurred to him to take the boys inshore to sheltered water instead of leaving them to take their chance. His attitude was that he did not invite them aboard, and they might get back as best they could. The jury, having considered their verdict for 15 minutes, found the accused guilty, and the judge sentenced him to 8 months' imprisonment. A factor in his condemnation was the very different behaviour of the skipper of the Buckingham, to which that afternoon another boatful of boys had put out. Not only did that more humane master give the earlier "customers" fish, but he towed their boat *alongside* until he saw them safely ashore. The appearance and demeanour of the two men in the witness-box afforded a significant contrast, which, doubtless, was not lost upon the jury.

KILLING NO MURDER;

Or, Diminished Responsibility

Physicians are like kings—they brook no contradiction.
The Duchess of Malfi, Act V. Sc. ii.

I

THE KING'S PARK MURDER

THE ANCIENT SANCTUARY of Holyrood, embracing an area some
five miles in circumference, of old afforded a refuge from importunate creditors to such debtors as preferred rheumatism
acquired within its bounds, to jail fever contracted in the Tolbooth. Now known as the King's Park—the name changes according to the Sovereign's sex—this fair champaign, unique
adornment of a capital city, is dominated by the majestic bulk
of Arthur's Seat. Over against this rise the long ramparts of
Salisbury Craigs, whither, you remember, Reuben Butler re-
sorted on the morning following the Porteous Riot, and among
whose rocks Deacon Brodie's partners hid the tools employed
by them in their abortive raid on the Excise Office. Between
the mountain and the Craigs lies the deep valley of the Hunter's Bog, and high up on the steep hillside, extending from St.
Anthony's Chapel to the foot of the cleft called the *Guttit
Haddie* (which, being interpreted, signifies eviscerated had-
dock), winds among a wilderness of whins the narrow track
with the picturesque name of the Piper's Walk. Of this inconsiderable pathway there will presently be more to say.

While the old-time criminous denizens of the Park were commonly those unable or unwilling to pay their just and lawful
debts, it has been in bygone days the scene of violence and
bloodshed. The Duke's Walk, running from the Palace of Holyrood House to Abbeyhill, was once a popular pitch for duellists,

and many a pretty quarrel has been settled there by the arbitrament of steel or lead. At the northern end of the road may yet be seen in the grass verge of the footway a little heap of stones, still known as Muschet's Cairn in memory of one Nicol Muschet, who in 1720 murdered his wife near this place, a crime immortalized by Sir Walter Scott in *The Heart of Midlothian*. Muschet, a dissipated young Edinburgh surgeon, having wearied of his long-suffering spouse, attempted, in conjunction with divers unconscionable and vile associates, basely to compass her disgrace and death. These abominable schemes miscarried; and finally the miscreant severed at one blow the nuptial knot and the poor creature's throat. It is pleasant to record that he was well and truly hanged and that his principal abettor was declared infamous and banished.[1]

Two centuries later the peaceful amenity of the Park was affronted by another murder of a very brutal and savage type, which, because of certain medico-legal peculiarities, make it worth while briefly to consider. Strangely enough, four years after there was perpetrated in Edinburgh, near another hill, Corstorphine, a further crime of similar character, presenting a curious resemblance to the other, but even more revolting and inhuman. In each case the victim was a young woman, horribly done to death in circumstances of extreme atrocity, by a young married man with no apparent motive to commit the crime; in each the murderer, while admittedly sane, escaped his doom on the ground that he was alleged to have been subject to fits, tendering by his counsel in the course of the trial a plea of "Guilty of culpable homicide" (manslaughter), which was accepted by the Crown, to the saving of his neck and the perplexity of Justice.

(1)

On Wednesday, 21st March, 1934, within the High Court of Justiciary at Edinburgh, the diet was called against Alexander

[1] Those caring to hear more of this dreadful business may consult a further account of the deed and the doer in *The Riddle of the Ruthvens* by the present writer, under the title of "Nicol Muschet: His Crime and Cairn."

Toomey. The Lord Justice-Clerk (the Right Hon. Lord Aitchison) presided; the Crown case was conducted by the Lord Advocate (the Right Hon. W. G. Normand, K.C., M.P., now Lord Justice-General) and Mr. T. M. Taylor, Advocate-Depute; Mr. D. Oswald Dykes, K.C., and Mr. A. M. Prain, advocate, appeared for the defence.

The charge upon which the accused was indicted ran thus: "That on 23rd or 24th January, 1934, in Holyrood Park, Edinburgh, at a part to the south-east thereof known as Hunter's Bog and near to a pathway known as the Piper's Walk, you did assault Rachel M'Millan, otherwise known as Rita M'Millan, then residing at 36 West Bowling Green Street, Leith, Edinburgh, and did strike her upon the head and body with your fists or with a blunt instrument, and did tie her hands together with a piece of blue material, and did place two pieces of blue material round her neck and over her mouth and a necktie round her neck, and did tie the said pieces of blue material and the said necktie tightly round her neck and did strangle and asphyxiate her and did murder her." Annexed to the indictment were lists of 16 productions (exhibits), chiefly medical reports and articles of clothing, and 19 witnesses, "all in Edinburgh."

The accused, a slightly built young fellow of respectable appearance, was placed in the dock, and after smiling to someone in the gallery, calmly awaited the issue of the day. His counsel intimated a special defence: "That the accused pleads Not Guilty, and specially that on the date that he is alleged to have committed the crime libelled he was insane or in such a state of mental weakness as to make him irresponsible for his actions." One member of the jury stated that he had certain scruples as to serving. "Do I understand," asked Lord Aitchison, "that if the evidence in this case should justify a verdict of murder, you would not be prepared to return that verdict?" "Not so long as capital punishment is the law of this country," replied the conscientious objector, who was thereupon excused. The trial then proceeded.

The first witness for the Crown was Mrs. Catherine Rich, 36 West Bowling Green Street, Leith, who stated that she let a bedroom in her house to women lodgers. One, Helen King, had lived there for some time with a female friend; when the latter left in the beginning of January, she asked to be allowed to bring another girl to share her room. This was Rita M'Millan, who came on the 14th. She said she was a waitress at a dance club, the Havana, and went out to work as a rule between 8 and 9 at night, returning between 4 and 5 in the morning. She was in good health and of a cheerful disposition. On Tuesday, 23rd January, she left about 7.30; witness never saw her alive again. Next day she learned that the dead body of a girl had been found in the King's Park, and later at the City Mortuary she identified it as that of Rita M'Millan.

Helen King (25), who described herself as an unemployed waitress, stated that she was a friend of the deceased, with whom she had lived in the High Street for five months, and told how it was arranged that they should lodge together at her new rooms. So far as witness knew she had no employment. About 8 o'clock on the evening in question witness and Sarah Westwood, another lodger, chanced to visit the Suburban Bar in the Fleshmarket Close, where they saw the deceased with some girl friends. The accused came in and joined the party, and after divers small whiskies and light ales, he invited Rita to go out with him. About 10.15 witness and Westwood, in pursuit of further refreshment, sought the Olympia Café, 86 Leith Street, for supper. There they found Rita and the accused enjoying a high tea: the girl had fish and chips; the man, bacon and eggs. They seemed to be on very friendly terms. The last witness saw of them was at 10.45, when she and her friend left to go home. Rita did not come back that night, and next day witness learned of the finding of the body, which she later identified. She now recognized certain articles of clothing as those worn by the deceased on the night of her death: a coat and beret; an undervest and silk slip; a pair of knickers and a pair of garters; the belt of a frock, a piece of tape, a pair of stockings, a handkerchief, and a pair of shoes. All these things Rita had on when she last saw her alive. Shewn pieces of blue material, witness said they were bits of the blue dress Rita was wearing that night; the handbag and purse produced were also her property. Shewn a black necktie with a grey stripe, she said it was like the tie worn by the accused that night. As regards the accused's condition on the evening of 23rd January, the Lord Advocate asked her: "Did it appear to you at any time that night that he was not able to understand what he was saying or doing?" "He was quite normal," replied the witness. She admitted, in reply to Mr. Dykes, that the accused had had a drink. "Was that having any effect upon him?—Not so far as I could see." She was certain that another tie, produced by the defence, now shewn to her, was not that which Toomey was then wearing. Rita's handbag contained a powder-puff, lipstick, and money—witness did not know how much. She was wearing some blue beads which belonged to witness. The Lord Justice-Clerk: "When you last saw Toomey that night was there anything odd in his manner?—Nothing at all. Or his speech?—No, nothing. Or his behaviour?—No, nothing."

Mrs. Sarah Westwood (25) stated that she was a married woman, living apart from her husband. Three months before Rita M'Millan's death witness shared lodgings with her in the High Street. She said she was working in a café, the whereabouts of which witness did not know. When Toomey invited Rita to go out with him that night he said it was "to some other bar for a drink." When witness saw them later in the café they were both sober and seemed on friendly terms. Toomey was then wearing a tie like that produced by the Crown. Witness denied that she and Rita were earning their living on the streets.

Joseph Ingman, manager of the Suburban Bar, Fleshmarket Close, said he had known the accused by sight for three years. He was in the public bar at 7.15 on 23rd January and ordered a light ale. About 9 o'clock witness saw the accused upstairs with three women, in whose company he had never seen him before. [Witness identified King and Westwood.] At 10 o'clock the accused and one of the girls left the premises. Neither was under the influence of drink, and he saw nothing odd or strange about their demeanour. Frank Adamson, barman at the public-house, gave corroborative evidence. Jean Edwards, waitress in the Olympia Café, 86 Leith Street, identified the accused as having supped with a girl whom she knew well by sight. Witness thought they were under the influence of drink, "but not much." They were quite friendly.

Mrs. Bridget Millar, 90 Holyrood Road, stated that the accused was her nephew. On 24th January, about 12.30 a.m., she, having gone to bed, was awakened by a knocking at her door. "I asked who was there, and the reply was, 'Alick Toomey.'" She asked him what was the matter, and he said that he had struck a girl in the King's Park. Witness said, "Don't be silly. Go home." He asked her to go up to his mother's, and went away. He was only two minutes in her house. He seemed very strange in his manner, his eyes were glassy, and she was rather frightened. She told her husband, who remarked, "He'll be drunk." Later they decided to go to the mother's house, 48 High Street, where they informed that lady of what had happened. She was much alarmed, and accompanied witness and her husband to the accused's house, 15 Leith Street Terrace. It was then about 2 a.m. They found him going to bed. His mother asked him what he had done, and he repeated that he had struck a girl in the King's Park. Her husband bade him go to bed. They then sought counsel of Patrick Toomey, the accused's brother, who lived at 24 Montrose Terrace, and it was thought well to inform the police, lest the girl might be lying unconscious in the Park. This was accordingly done. The accused was not a frequent visitor at her house, but she met him occasionally at his mother's. She once saw him in a fit, on the day his brother was being buried. Cross-examined—Witness had heard of the accused having similar attacks, in one of which he was taken to the Infirmary. In reply to the Court, the accused sometimes had difficulty in pronouncing words. In the seizure at the funeral there was a twitching of the arms. She noticed the same twitching when he came to her door that night.

David Millar, husband of the previous witness, corroborated as to the midnight call. When witness went to the accused's house that night he appeared to be dazed and his eyes were glazed. He was sober. Witness had seen the fit at the funeral; the accused lashed out with his hands.

Mrs. Rose Toomey, 48 High Street, mother of the accused, said he was born on 27th June, 1907. He attended St. Patrick's School. Later he became successively a message boy, a brewery worker, and a miner. He served for a time with the Royal Scots and was discharged; afterwards he joined the Cameron Highlanders under a false name, being again discharged on discovery of the fact. Since then he had been unemployed. He used to leave home for short periods without notice. In 1925 he was found in a fit on the road at Dumfries and was taken to hospital. Thirteen months ago he took a fit in the Cowgate and was treated at the Infirmary. "The doctor said if he did not stop taking liquor it would stop him." The fits followed upon his taking drink, because he was not accustomed to it. He had not been drinking heavily during the past two years; she had only seen him drunk once: "at the New Year time"—in Scotland a privileged season. Cross-examined—she had never seen her son in a fit. There were times when he was strange and stuttered in his speech. He married in 1932. As a child he was delicate and had been in hospital.

Patrick Toomey, shoemaker in Leith, brother of the accused, corroborated. In cross-examination he said that some five years before, his brother took a fit in the common stair in which they lived. He was then in the Cameron Highlanders. He was kicking and frothing at the mouth and had to be held down for an hour, when he was taken to the military hospital at the Castle. He had seen the accused in smaller fits, once in the house when he had lost his temper. The tie produced for the defence was that which his brother was wearing on the night in question. In reply to the Court, witness never knew of any doctor attending the accused for fits.

Detective-Constable Donald M'Culloch stated that on the morning of 24th January Patrick Toomey called at the Central Police Office and gave certain information, as the result of which the accused was arrested. He was then in bed, asleep.

At the Police Office, having been duly cautioned, he made a voluntary statement, as follows: "I met a girl in the Suburban Bar on the night of the 23rd. After having several drinks with her we left the bar about ten o'clock and went from there to a café in Leith Street. We had supper in the café and went to the King's Park, entering at Holyrood at 11 p.m. We turned to the right and went along by the High School cricket ground. We stood along the railings for about half an hour." The statement went on to explain that the accused had proposed to have immoral relations with his companion and asked how much she wanted. The girl said her fee was ten shillings, but her admirer would only go the length of half a crown, which he tendered for her acceptance on the amazing grounds *that he was a married man and was unemployed!* This offer the girl declined, and made an observation which annoyed him. "I struck her a blow on the face," concluded the statement. "She started to scream, and I ran away and left her clinging on to the railings at the side of the cricket ground." (This is a very inadequate account of his proceedings, as wc shall find when we hear what was the condition of the body.) Questioned as to the identity of the missing girl, Toomey said: "I know her only as Rita. She stays in West Bowling Green Street." Thereafter the officers searched the Park in the vicinity of the railings of the cricket ground, but found nothing to support the accused's statements; so they returned to question him further. "I will take you to where the girl is," said he. Witness took him in a car along with two other detectives to the King's Park. When they entered the Park the accused asked to be taken to the south end of the Radical Road—the famous path which skirts the base of Salisbury Craigs. "Come along this way," he cried, and the party went about 100 yards northward up the Road, and by his direction turned into an old quarry and climbed over the rocks into the Hunter's Bog till they reached a bunch of whins. There Toomey halted, with the remark: "If you find the coat you will find the girl." Witness went in the direction the accused indicated. "I made a search, and among the whins I found a coat, and immediately afterwards, the body. The accused had led us to within 25 yards of the spot. The body was lying on its right side, face downwards, with the arms underneath. It was practically nude and obviously dead. The time was ten minutes to seven and it was quite dark." The accused was then taken back to the Police Office, and Dr. Douglas Kerr, Surgeon of Police, was driven by witness to the place where the body lay. Photographs were taken, and the body was removed to the City Mortuary. When it was lifted up, a piece of blue cloth was seen to be tied around the neck, and underneath it was protruding part of a man's necktie. Witness identified the necktie produced as that tied round the dead girl's neck. Her hands were crossed in front of the breast and bound together with a piece of blue cloth similar to that tied round the neck. There were also found nearby a coat and hat, stockings, and other garments which had been stripped off the body, and in a whin bush a handbag, empty save for a halfpenny. On the accused being searched there was found upon him a handkerchief, stained with blood and having adhering to it small particles of grass. When charged with murder the accused replied, "I have nothing to say." He appeared in no respect abnormal, was quite sober, and spoke with perfect clearness, nor did he complain of any loss of memory. Witness saw nothing about him or what he said to suggest that he had not been in full possession of his senses that night.

Cross-examined—After his first fruitless search witness again saw the accused, who was anxious to know if the girl had returned to her home. He remarked, "Someone must have been with her after I left her." Witness found near the body an empty purse and a powder-puff, but did not find any blue beads. (These beads were never found; probably their string was broken in the struggle, and they were scattered among the whins.)

Detective-Constable Alexander Telfer gave corroborative evidence regarding the information received at headquarters and the visit to the King's Park. Detective-Inspector John Sheed identified the several articles found near the body, also the clothes worn by the accused: a suit and three shirts, together with the handkerchief having blood and grass upon it. Witness saw nothing unusual in the accused's appearance, except that he was very pale.

Dr. Sydney Smith, Professor of Forensic Medicine in the University of Edinburgh, stated that on the instructions of the Procurator-Fiscal he performed, with the assistance of Dr. Douglas Kerr, a post-mortem examination on the deceased, the result of which was embodied in a Joint Medical Report, dated 24th-25th January, 1934, from which the following particulars appeared:

"The body was that of a young adult woman, naked except for a petticoat and singlet, which were pulled up over the shoulders. The hands were tied together tightly at the wrists with a piece of blue material, tied in a reef knot. Around the mouth and throat was a blue ligature, tied in a double knot on the right side. This passed first round the neck, then over the mouth, then again round the neck. Below this was another blue ligature, which was tied very tightly around the mouth with two turns, and forcing the tongue firmly against the hard palate and the back of the pharynx.

"Under the first ligature there was a man's necktie, tied tightly round the neck twice with the knot in the front, deeply compressing the tissues of the neck and forming a groove just above the thyroid cartilage.

"The body was in a state of complete rigor mortis and the surface shewed marked signs of post-mortem discoloration. The face, ears, and hands shewed deep congestion of the tissues. The left eye was blackened, and the tissues round it and round the left cheek were contused and swollen. Blood was issuing from the nose and mouth. There was a large bruise over the chin extending to both sides of the lower jaw, but particularly to the right.

"There were a number of scratches and small abrasions on the back and front of the body and on the limbs, apparently due to the body rolling over thorns or bushes. There was blood and grass on the palms and surface of both hands." Certain lacerations of the private parts were also noted.

"From the above examination," concluded the report, "we

are of opinion that death was due to asphyxia, due to the pressure exerted by the ligature round the neck, and to the closure of the upper air passages by the ligature in the mouth pressing the tongue upwards.

"We are further of opinion that the deceased received severe blows upon the face, chin, and mouth shortly before death, and that a blow from a blunt object or heavy pressure had been inflicted upon the private parts shortly before death."

Professor Sydney Smith also read a second report by himself and Dr. Douglas Kerr respecting certain stains found on the clothing of the accused. All the stains were due to blood of human origin.

Cross-examined—The amount of blood found on the accused's clothing was very small. "The blow on the face might be quite disconnected with the strangulation which was the cause of death?—I should say the blows on the face were delivered just shortly before death. How shortly?—It is impossible to say. An hour or two?—I should not say an hour or two. I think less. You examined the body about seven hours after death. Are you in a position to say that some of these bloodstains were not the result of injuries a couple of hours before death?—It would be difficult to say."

Dr. Douglas Kerr, Surgeon of Police, Edinburgh, gave corroborative evidence and concurred in the reports as true.

Dr. David Henderson, Professor of Psychiatry in the University of Edinburgh; Physician-Superintendent, Royal Edinburgh Hospital for Mental Disorders; and Physician-Consultant in Psychiatry to the Royal Infirmary, Edinburgh, stated that in accordance with instructions received from the Procurator-Fiscal, he visited Saughton Prison on 27th and 31st January and made an examination into the mental state of the accused. Witness also interviewed his mother and his wife, who furnished a detailed account of his life-history. The results were embodied in a report, dated 6th February, 1934, which witness now read:

"He was a delicate child, who gradually acquired better health and developed in the same way as the other members of the family. During his adolescence and adult life certain significant features appeared which require mention. He was unstable and erratic, and on several occasions left home and employment without warning, so that he was reported as 'missing.' There is no evidence to shew that he was not perfectly conscious of what he was doing. On two occasions he is stated to have threatened to commit suicide: once by filling the sink with water and stating that he would drown himself; on another occasion four or five years ago, when he threatened to take poison. His mother mentioned a peculiar incident, when on one occasion he tied his little sister into a chair. He has always been subject to fits, which have occurred when he was under the influence of liquor, and for which he was treated, on one occasion at least, in the Royal Infirmary, Edinburgh. About two years ago he is reported as having had another fit, while attending a funeral and not being under the influence of drink.

"The above disorders of conduct have been mentioned in detail, because they have been taken into consideration when estimating the prisoner's mental state.

"The prisoner is a married man, 26 years old, who had a clear realization of his position and knew the charge against him. He was composed in his bearing, co-operated readily in my examination, and gave no evidence of any flagrant mental symptoms. On the contrary, he behaved in a perfectly normal manner, shewed no emotional instability, and denied that he had ever suffered from hallucinations or delusions. He had a clear appreciation of time and place, and his memory was excellent both for remote and recent events.

"Physically, there was no evidence of any organic disease of his nervous system.

"Comment.

"On the basis of the above examination I am of the opinion that the prisoner is of sound mind and is fit to plead."

In reply to the Lord Advocate, witness stated as his definite opinion that the accused was sane. Asked whether he had formed a conclusion with regard to the suggestion of epilepsy, witness said: "I have come to a conclusion, and I have listened to the evidence given this morning. I have not been impressed by the history of the so-called epileptic turns." "If a man suffers from an epileptic fit, loss of consciousness is an invariable feature, and of course, as a result, loss of memory? —Yes. Did he complain to you of any lapse of memory when telling you his story?—No. I think one can fairly and conclusively rule out the possibility of an epileptic fit in these circumstances. There might be a case where a man may be neither mentally defective nor insane, who may yet suffer from diminished responsibility, and I ask you to give the jury your considered opinion whether this man can be said, in your view, to be fully, or only partially, responsible for his actions?—Taking into consideration the whole history of this man from his early years—his ill-health as a child, the fact that he did not do well at school, the further fact that he leaves home impulsively and stays away, and also the fact that on two occasions he has threatened suicide, and that he has been subject to emotional attacks of some kind—I would be willing to go so far as to say there was diminished responsibility. A certain amount of alcohol would tend to lessen the sense of responsibility in a man of this type and to make him more unstable. Apart altogether from alcohol, would you regard the accused as a man of unstable mentality?—I would. With a somewhat narrow margin of self-control as compared with a normal man? —Yes. And in that sense incompletely responsible for his actions?—That is correct. And liable under stress to give way to conduct which a normal man would resist?—Yes."

Cross-examined by Mr. Dykes—Epilepsy was an exceedingly common cause of crimes of violence. "If these attacks were not epileptic, can you suggest what they were?—They might be merely hysterical or emotional." Re-examined—There was nothing to suggest that the accused had suffered from any of these complaints on the night of 23rd-24th January. By the Court—"Assuming it were proved in this case that the accused did commit the acts set forth in the indictment, speaking from the medical point of view and on your responsibility as a mental specialist, would the accused in your opinion be wholly or only partly responsible?—Only partly responsible. Is that your considered judgment?—It is, my Lord."

Dr. William M'Allister, Bangour Mental Hospital, described three visits paid by him to the accused in Saughton Prison on 26th January, 6th February, and 9th February respectively, and read the report of his several examinations. Witness failed to find any evidence of abnormality, except that, according to accused's own statement, he had suffered from epilepsy from childhood. "The account of the 'epileptic' seizures," continued Dr. M'Allister, "was by no means typical. . . . These seizures were invariably associated with drink." Witness found nothing in the accused's condition to warrant the suggestion that he suffered from epilepsy. The description of the "fits" was unlike epilepsy. There was no suggestion that on the day of the tragedy, or at any time near that date, the accused had had a "seizure." With a view to clearing up the question of epilepsy, however, witness proposed to see him again at intervals, and to furnish a further report. This witness did on 20th and 27th February. On neither occasion was he able to elicit any indication of mental disorder. On the contrary, on both examinations he found the accused perfectly lucid and able to discuss matters quite rationally. He conducted himself correctly in every respect. "I am of opinion," concluded Dr. M'Allister, "that the 'fits' from which Toomey alleged that he suffered, whatever their character may have been, were not epileptic. . . . My conclusion is that the accused is now sane, and I am unable to find any evidence that he was insane at the time of the alleged murder." Witness was, however, of counsel with Professor Henderson that the accused's responsibility was limited and impaired.

(2)

So soon as Dr. M'Allister had left the box Mr. Dykes, addressing the Lord Justice-Clerk, said: "After anxious consideration of the very important evidence that the Crown has so properly led as to the mental condition of my client, I venture to tender to the Court a plea of Guilty of culpable homicide."

The Lord Advocate: "In view of the medical evidence I feel I am not only justified, but that it is my duty to accept that plea. Your Lordship will appreciate that I have given the possibility of such a plea being tendered my anxious consideration. My acceptance of the plea is not grounded on any idea that the crime is other than a brutal and cruel one, but simply upon the ground that according to the testimony of very able medical men, who have had the fullest opportunity to arrive at a considered opinion, this man cannot be treated as a man whose responsibility is equal to that of a normal man. It falls within the well-known category in our criminal law, so far as murder is concerned, of a man whose capacity is limited and partial, and who, though neither insane nor mentally defective, is yet in a state bordering on mental deficiency. I accept the plea."

The Lord Justice-Clerk, addressing the jury, said: "The accused, through his counsel, has tendered a plea of Guilty to the crime of culpable homicide, and the Lord Advocate has accepted that plea. In that situation I must ask you to return a formal verdict of Guilty of culpable homicide."

The Clerk of Court then asked the jury's assent to the following verdict, which they duly gave: "The jury unanimously find the accused Guilty of culpable homicide in terms of his own confession."

In passing sentence his Lordship addressed the prisoner as follows: "Alexander Toomey, you have pleaded Guilty to a very terrible crime. You brutally assaulted this young woman, and you took her life. It was a cruel, cowardly, and inhuman crime. The life of a prostitute is as precious in the eyes of the law as the life of any other person, and but for the evidence that you cannot be held fully responsible for what you did, you would have been convicted of murder. In view of the medical evidence the Lord Advocate has, in my opinion, acted rightly and mercifully in accepting your plea. It is essential in the public interest and in your own interest that you should be confined for a long period. Having regard to the terrible atrocity of your crime, I cannot limit the sentence to less than that you be detained in penal servitude for the term of fifteen years."

The accused received his sentence unmoved, and before being taken from the dock to the cells below, he turned and had another look up at the gallery. On the application of his counsel the Lord Justice-Clerk granted permission for him to see his wife and child before he was removed to prison.

Here endeth the first murder. We shall hear a great deal more about this doctrine of diminished responsibility when we come to the second crime. Meanwhile we may note that in the judgment of both the eminent specialists called by the Crown, the accused was perfectly sane and in full possession of his faculties; that the alleged "fits" from which he and his relations said he had suffered, were certainly not due to any known form of epilepsy, and that in none of them had a doctor been called in to attend him. ·

(3)

Persons curious in criminology will find an account of the scientific aspects of the case in Professor Henderson's learned —and for the mere laymen, bewildering—book, entitled, *Psychopathic States*, p. 56 (London: Chapman & Hall, 1939). After perusal of this perturbing work I have grave doubts whether I myself ought any longer to be at large! We learn that the prisoner—this was not disclosed at the trial—"had previously been in the hands of the police for (1) theft and (2) housebreaking." "Here, then," observes the erudite author, "we have a strange case, a so-called motiveless murder, which is best understood in terms of his psychobiological development. The story is that of a young man of poor physique and turbulent disposition who, episodically, throughout his career had exhibited aggressive conduct, finally resulting in murder.

. . . Incidentally, the above case illustrates that in Scotland in cases of capital crime we are returning to the doctrine of 'partial insanity,' but the term 'partial' is being used in a different sense from formerly. In the past 'partial' was used to designate a form or type of mental disorder, a monomania; now it is being held as synonymous with mitigating circumstances."

Still, despite these esoteric and recondite theories, I am old-fashioned enough to think that here the accused, in Lord Braxfield's famous phrase, would have been "nane the waur o' a hangin'."

II

The Murrayfield Murder

For the experienced reader mention of murder in Murrayfield will recall the pleasure derived from old perusal of R. L. Stevenson's delectable tragi-comedy, *The Misadventures of John Nicholson*, and he will see again in memory's glass "the house at Murrayfield—now standing solitary in the low sunshine, with the sparrows hopping on the threshold and the dead man within staring at the roof—and now, with a sudden change, thronged about with white-faced, hand-uplifting neighbours, and doctor bursting through their midst and fixing his stethoscope as he went, the policeman shaking a sagacious head beside the body." The house itself, familiar to the novelist's youth, is real enough and still stands among the hollies of its high-walled garden; but the murder is a murder of the mind, conceived by him as an appropriate happening in such a scene: a spot with Ambrose Bierce's "suitable surroundings."

Curiously, in 1813 a horrid murder was in fact committed in the near neighborhood, when an old man was killed and robbed by two young ruffians on the Edinburgh-Corstorphine road, a quarter of a mile from Coltbridge, a little to the westward of the road below "Belmont," leading to Ravelston Dykes, now Ellersly Road—an unusual homicide of which I shall presently furnish an account. Here and now, however, I will have my hands quite full enough in dealing with the latest atrocity of which Murrayfield has been the theatre.

(1)

It is a strange coincidence—and an additional link between the two cases—that while the first we see of the King's Park murderer is when he knocks at his aunt's door in the small hours and tells her, "I have struck a girl in the Park," the first appearance of the Murrayfield murderer is equally dramatic. At 10.45 on the morning of Sunday, 7th August, 1938, a young man entered the West End Police Station in Torphichen Place, Edinburgh, and announced to the officer on duty: "I killed a woman last night in 'Ormelie,' in Corstorphine Road. The body's in the grounds. It's Sir William Thomson's house. He's on holiday."

The man was James Boyd Kirkwood, thirty years of age, a gardener by trade, who lived with his wife and child at 5 Roseburn Street, and was then employed to tend the grounds of "Ormelie," the mansion belonging to a former Lord Provost of Edinburgh. Examination of the house by the police left no doubt that a bloody and ferocious crime had in fact been perpetrated therein, and a search of the grounds disclosed, buried in a grave which had been dug in a potato patch in the garden, the dead body of a young woman. It was identified as that of Jean Ronald Powell, who lived at 10 Roseburn Place, and was employed as an assistant in a Haymarket dairy. Following upon this discovery, Kirkwood was arrested on the charge of murder and was in due course committed for trial.

Tuesday, 8th November, was the appointed date. Much local interest had been aroused by the dreadful circumstances of the crime, and despite the wet weather, a long queue began to form in the Parliament Square several hours before the doors of the High Court of Justiciary were opened to the public. The Court was crowded throughout the proceedings and many were unable to obtain admission. The Lord Justice-Clerk (the Right

Hon. Lord Aitchison) presided; the Solicitor-General (Mr. J. S. C. Reid, K.C.), assisted by Mr. L. Hill Watson, K.C., and Mr. R. H. S. Calver, Advocates-Depute, conducted the prosecution; the Dean of Faculty (Mr. W. D. Patrick, K.C., now Lord Patrick), and Mr. A. M. M. Williamson, advocate, appeared for the defence. With such a personnel and a crime so singular, one looked forward to a trial of exceptional interest. As a matter of fact it proved one of the most ineffective of the many to which it has been my lot to listen. This was due to the manner in which it was handled, not to the intrinsic quality of the facts. The accused, a powerfully built young man of average height, whose left arm was crippled by infantile paralysis, was seated in the dock between two police officers. He surveyed attentively the crowded Court-room and listened to the proceedings with complete composure, occasionally addressing to his official guardians some comment upon the evidence. A special plea was intimated by his counsel: "The pannel pleads Not Guilty, and further, that at the time of the acts charged he was insane and not responsible for his actions."

The terms of the indictment were as follows: "James Boyd Kirkwood, prisoner in the Prison of Edinburgh, you are Indicted at the instance of the Right Honourable Thomas Mackay Cooper, His Majesty's Advocate, and the charge against you is that, on 6th or 7th August 1938, in the dwelling-house known as 'Ormelie,' Corstorphine Road, Edinburgh, occupied by Sir William Thomson, you did assault Jean Ronald Powell, 10 Roseburn Place, Edinburgh, and did strike her on the head with a hammer or other blunt instrument, and did thrust the shaft of said hammer into her private parts to her severe internal injury, and did murder her." Annexed to the indictment were lists of 99 productions (exhibits) and 39 witnesses for the Crown. The jury included four women; but its composition was of no importance, its functions, by reason of the course adopted, being merely formal.

The first witness called was James M'Donald Powell (35), brother of the dead woman, who stated that he was employed as a warehouseman and lived at 6 Baxter's Buildings, Holyrood

Road. On Sunday, 7th August, he identified his sister's body at Edinburgh City Mortuary. Jean was a little older than witness. Both their parents were dead, and for a time she had lived in an orphanage; later she was in domestic service, and at the date of her death was employed in a dairy. She lodged with one Mrs. Swan. Witness saw his sister practically every week-end. She was always in good health and spirits, and led an orderly life. She had once been engaged to be married, but the engagement was broken off. Witness never heard of her knowing anyone named Kirkwood, neither did he himself know the accused. He identified two signet rings and a wristlet watch, found on the body, as those which his sister habitually wore.

Mrs. Lucy Swan, 10 Roseburn Place, stated that Jean Powell had lived in her lodgings for about a year. She worked from nine in the morning till six in the evening, and on Saturdays till one o'clock. She was a most respectable girl. A week before her death she told witness she had an appointment with somebody at two o'clock on Saturday at the corner of Roseburn Terrace. She did not say with whom the appointment was made. After having her dinner that day, Jean left the house shortly before two o'clock; witness never saw her alive again. She now identified, as produced, a red hat, a green coat, a frock, a belt, and a pair of shoes, all which the dead girl was wearing when she left to keep her fatal tryst.

Robert Bell Watters, 34 Roseburn Street, a waiter in a public-house at 59 Roseburn Terrace, stated that he knew the accused as an occasional customer. The last time he was in the shop was on Saturday, 6th August, about two o'clock in the afternoon, when he came in and spoke to another man for a bit, and then the pair went out, returning immediately with a girl whom witness had never seen before, but whose body he subsequently identified at the City Mortuary. [Witness now identified in Court the other man, of whom we hear nothing further.]

Alexander Watt, 15 Watson Cresent, a scavenger in the employment of Edinburgh Corporation, stated that he knew by sight the accused as the gardener employed at "Ormelie."

He passed him daily while he, witness, was on his beat. They talked to each other now and again. On the morning of the murder accused invited witness into the grounds of "Ormelie"; the house was closed and empty, but the accused had the keys and took him in by the back kitchen to a room in which there was a wireless. Witness remained about ten minutes. The accused was not very bright that morning. By the Court—"What do you mean by that?—He was never very cheery. There was nothing special about him that attracted my attention."

John Walker, Sergeant in the Edinburgh City Police, stated that he had never seen the accused until 10.45 a.m. on Sunday, 7th August. He entered the station at Torphichen Place, went straight up to the counter and said, quite calmly, "I killed a woman last night in 'Ormelie' in Corstorphine Road—Sheena Powell. The body is in the grounds. It is Sir William Thomson's house. He is away on holiday. She works in Dempster's Dairy." Accused was not excited. "He had a suspicion of a smile on his face." Witness warned him to say nothing more about it in the meantime, and rang up the Central Police Office to send an officer from the C.I.D.

Detective-Sergeant David Newberry stated that on Sunday, 7th August, in consequence of instructions received, he went to "Ormelie" in company with Detective-Lieutenant Sheed. The garden gate was locked, but he scaled it and opened a side door, admitting his companion. They went up to the house and found the front door locked. The garage door was open, the key being in the lock. They went through the garage to the rear of the house and searched the outbuildings, greenhouses, etc., but found nothing. He noticed a mark, as of something having been dragged along, on the cement pathway leading to the garden. Near the toolhouse he found a spade, with fresh soil adhering to the upper part. "On crossing a potato patch where there had been some young potatoes growing, I noticed some of the shaws half buried in the soil. This, of course, was a thing no gardener would do. An area of 16 to 18 feet had been disturbed. I secured a spade from the toolhouse and commenced digging round about this freshly turned piece of soil. After about an hour's digging I came upon a lady's stocking, which I now identify. Continuing, I came upon the leg of a woman." He communicated his discovery to the Procurator-Fiscal and to the Surgeon of Police and waited until they arrived on the scene. When these gentlemen, accompanied by a police photographer, came, the digging was resumed, and presently the naked body of a young woman was unearthed. This was photographed in situ, and after its removal the grave also was photographed. It, the grave, was 3½ to 4 feet deep. The head was wrapped in a piece of canvas, and there were also found in the grave bits of torn underclothing. On each hand was a signet ring, and on the left wrist a watch, which had stopped at 5.22. The keys of the house having been obtained, witness entered by the back door, accompanied by the Fiscal, the police surgeon, a fingerprint expert, and other officials. Very extensive bloodstains were seen, extending from the back door to the main staircase, which was also stained with blood. On the first landing was a pail, containing brownish soapy water, and a scrubbing-brush. The carpet was blood-stained; both it and the floor had been washed. At the end of the lobby leading to the music-room was found a washing-cloth, and at the foot of some steps a bundle, a hammer, and a piece of soap. Asked as to the condition of the hammer, witness said: "It was very badly bloodstained all over, and had several hairs sticking underneath the split portions of the wood near the head." The bundle was wrapped up in a sofa cover from the music-room. It contained a lady's coat, a pair of shoes, a hat, a suspender belt, pieces of knickers, a pair of gloves, a handbag, and two sofa cushions. There was blood upon the cushions. On entering the music-room witness saw at once that someone had been washing and cleaning up the place. The carpets had been moved to one side. The condition of the couch attracted his attention: the corner nearest the window was very badly bloodstained. That coincided with the stains on the sofa cushions found outside on the landing. On a table were a bottle of sherry, three tumblers—two whole and one broken—a foreign coin, and a box of matches. Witness then described how he took possession of certain articles of clothing at the accused's house and of the clothes he was wearing when arrested. On being charged and formally cautioned at the Police Station, accused made no reply.

Dr. Douglas Kerr, Surgeon of Police, stated that he was present in the grounds of "Ormelie" when the body was unearthed and immediately examined it after its removal from the grave. The woman had been dead approximately 21 hours; his examination was made at one o'clock, so she died about 4 p.m. the previous day. Next day, in the City Mortuary, assisted by Dr. Ogilvie, witness made a further examination of the body and prepared a report, which he now read. The injuries found are too horrible and shocking for transcription. The head was completely shattered. Shewn the large heavy hammer found beside the bundle in the corridor, witness said it was a most likely instrument to have inflicted the injuries. Tremendous violence must have been used. Other and even more revolting injuries had been inflicted with the shaft of the hammer; these were caused before death. With regard to the accused's clothing, spots of blood were found upon his shirt. They were due to spurting. If he were not wearing his coat and waistcoat, and was striking the woman on the head, after the first or second blow blood would spurt; or when he drew the hammer back to strike, some drops of blood might be thrown off. By the Court—"As regards the head injuries which you found, you say that tremendous violence must have been used. Can you say whether there had been a series of violent blows? —There must have been at least seven blows. Four of them caused fractures of the skull, the others were glancing blows. I think the woman was lying on her back in the corner of the sofa and moving her head about, trying to dodge the blows, and these just made a glancing blow, instead of a direct one like the others."

The next witness was James Kirkwood, the accused's father, who stated that his son was born in September, 1907. His first illness was at the age of four, when he suffered from infantile paralysis, which permanently affected his left arm. At the age of 17 or 18 he began to take fits, which continued to recur for three or four years, sometimes as many as three or four in one day. He was terribly strong when in a fit, on one occasion wrenching the bars of an iron bedstead. In September, 1925, he was treated for fits at Glasgow Royal Infirmary, and after that the fits were less frequent. The last time he had a fit, so far as witness knew, was in 1928, when he was found lying unconscious on the road. At home he worked on witness's farm until 1932, when he left to become a gardener. He married in 1934. Witness only once saw his son the worse of drink.

Up to this point the learned Dean of Faculty had not put a single question in cross-examination of any witness, but he now proceeded to cross-examine this one. In none other of the many murder trials attended by me have I seen counsel for the defence refrain from cross-examining the Crown witnesses. Doubtless the learned Dean had, as we shall see in the sequel, good reason for adopting so unusual a course, whereby the prosecution was, to some extent, defeated and the safety of his client's neck assured. Witness said that when the accused began to take fits they were living at Inverkip, where he was attended by Dr. Taylor of Skelmorlie, who had since died. Sometimes his fits lasted for three hours, and he might have three in one day. When he was 17 or 18 he wandered away from home and was found in Port Glasgow. In 1927 the family removed to Dunfermline. His son left, saying he was going to join a ship at Bo'ness; but they learned he was found unconscious on the road in Bishopton, near Glasgow. He never had anything to do with the sea. About 1930 his son obtained some arsenic from a local chemist; he said he wanted it to kill weeds in a garden where he worked; witness became alarmed and informed the police. His son frequently complained of headaches, for which he took aspirins. By the Court—"When these turns you have told us about came on, did they do so suddenly, or were there any warning signs that the fits were coming on?—No. There were no warning signs." It is noteworthy that while this witness in giving his evidence was visibly affected, his son in the dock exhibited no feeling whatever.

Professor Henderson, of the Chair of Psychiatry in Edinburgh University, the distinguished alienist whom we have already met in the King's Park case, stated that, as instructed by the Procurator-Fiscal, he visited the accused in Saughton Prison on 20th August. Witness chanced to have seen him some three years before in Edinburgh Infirmary, when treated for poisoning—an attempted suicide. Accused recognized him at once. They had a long conversation. He was quite composed and did not shew any emotion. He had no hallucinations or delusions; his memory was intact and his intellectual faculties were well preserved. Witness came to the conclusion that he was then sane. "A person who has suffered from infantile paralysis has a sense of differentiation from his fellowmen," said witness; but that would not affect his sanity or responsibility. Witness had come to the conclusion that the fits, as described, were epileptiform. A person's mentality and character might be altered by the occurrence of such fits. From the interview, and from the history of the case prior to 6th August, witness considered that the accused was sane at that date. Although there was no evidence of the man having had a fit for eight years, witness regarded the history of his former fits important. The Solicitor-General—"Can you offer any definite opinion as to whether, when his crime was being committed, the perpetrator was able to appreciate what he was doing?—I consider that he was able to appreciate what he was doing."

Cross-examined by the Dean of Faculty—If there was a long-continued subjection to epileptiform fits, some deterioration of mental capacity would be likely. A person was apt to become, and to be, more irritable and unstable emotionally than would otherwise be the case. Such people were inclined to be moody and morbid in their outlook; they might not have the full responsibility which a normal person has for his actings. "You may examine such people day after day, and say: 'These people are sane; they are not certifiable'?—Yes." Under stress or emotion they might act in an irresponsible manner; their responsibility has become diminished. When witness saw the accused in the Infirmary he was suffering from atropine poisoning, taken in the form of eye-drops, which he had swallowed during a domestic quarrel, remarking to his wife: "That will finish me."

Re-examined by the Solicitor-General—Witness was satisfied that the accused was an epileptic and had an epileptic constitution, and that he was a man who, in any circumstances of any emotional value, was unlikely to act with the same judgment, reason, and foresight as one who did not so suffer. "Can you explain to me in what way this man's self-control differs, in your view, from the self-control of a hasty and ill-advised, but nevertheless fully sane person?—I can only point to the fact that in this man we have a history of years that he suffered from epileptic fits, and in these circumstances that he differs from the type of individual you have drawn. Did the circumstances of the attack have any influence with you? We were told that there must have been no fewer than seven violent blows with the hammer, probably while the man was holding the woman's neck with his other hand?—I think that would be an indication of the point I have stressed." By the Court—"But might not a sane man commit a crime of that kind?—Yes; but he is less liable to commit a crime of this kind than a man so suffering." Witness did not suggest that the crime was committed while the man was subject to an actual attack. There must be permanent deterioration of his mind, independent of the onset of an attack. He assumed that something happened in that room to start off the man's violent behaviour. By the Court —"If he was insane when he committed the crime, it would be a mental derangement associated with epilepsy. Other forms of mental derangement could be ruled out absolutely. It was a temporary attack. At the present time the man was perfectly sane and normal." With regard to the legal doctrine of diminished responsibility, looking to this man's undoubted epileptic history, witness would not think it safe to proceed upon the view that at the time of the crime he was a fully responsible person. There would be a condition of mind falling short of insanity that, medically, would diminish his responsibility. That was witness's considered judgment.

Dr. Ivy Mackenzie, a Glasgow mental specialist, stated that

he examined the accused in September and had a long conversation with him. He was perfectly clear in his answers; witness could find nothing abnormal in his intellectual or emotional condition, and was of opinion that he was then quite sane. Having learned the medical history of the man, witness thought his fits were of an epileptic character. One was entitled to assume that at the time of the crime he was under the influence of epilepsy, and was irresponsible. On the whole facts as disclosed, witness thought that *when the assault was committed, the assailant was suffering from a definite fit or seizure.* By the Court—"Can you say more than that the circumstances of the crime are consistent with its commission during an epileptic attack?—Yes, that is what I say. Is it not very much in the region of conjecture as to what the man's condition was at the time?—It would also be conjecture to say he was perfectly sane when he did it."

The Dean of Faculty, in concluding his cross-examination, asked: "Then am I to take it that your true view of this case is that having regard to the circumstances of the crime, the brutal character of the attack, the perverted sexual character of the attack, and to the epileptic history, the only conclusion you can draw is that the crime was committed under the influence of an epileptic seizure?—Yes, I think so." By the Court—"I understand your conclusion to be that whatever the degree of his responsibility may be, you cannot hold him as a fully sane man at the material time?—No, certainly not. That is my considered judgment as a medical man."

(2)

Dr. Mackenzie having left the box—

The Dean of Faculty. My Lord, in view of the evidence that has emerged, and in view of the information which I myself have in my possession as to this man's medical history, I feel justified in tendering a plea now that he was of diminished responsibility, and therefore tender a plea of culpable homicide.

The Lord Justice-Clerk. I understand there is no question as to his sanity now?

The Dean of Faculty. None whatever, my Lord.

The Lord Justice-Clerk. You say he is able to plead now?

The Dean of Faculty. Entirely.

The Solicitor-General. In view of the evidence, I feel bound to accept that plea.

The Lord Justice-Clerk. I will need to put it to the accused himself.

The Dean of Faculty. If you please, my Lord. We have explained the whole thing to him before.

The Lord Justice-Clerk. James Boyd Kirkwood, under this Indictment, which charges you with the crime of murder, are you prepared to plead quilty to the crime of culpable homicide?

The Accused. Yes, my Lord.

That plea was accordingly recorded and signed by the accused. One noticed that in doing so he used only his right hand and did not raise his left arm, the book being supported on the rail of the dock by the Clerk of Court. His Lordship thereupon directed the jury to return a formal verdict, which they did as follows: "The jury unanimously find the pannel [prisoner] Guilty of culpable homicide in terms of his own confession." The Solicitor-General having moved for sentence, the Lord Justice-Clerk, addressing the accused, said: "James Boyd Kirkwood, you have pled Guilty to a most appalling crime. You inflicted terrible injuries upon this woman; you took her life, and afterwards you buried her body. That was a terrible crime. It is quite impossible for me to assess what the precise degree of your responsibility is, but the only sentence I can pronounce upon you that can in any way be commensurate with the crime you have committed, and adequate in the public interest, is that you be detained in penal servitude for life." The accused, who heard his sentence apparently unmoved, was then taken to the cells below, where he was permitted to see his father before going to prison, and the Lord Justice-Clerk having thanked and discharged the jury, the Court rose.

(3)

One might have expected that Kirkwood, in view of the atrocious nature of his crime and the fact of his admitted sanity, would deem himself fortunate in that he saved his neck. Tried in the good old days by Lord Braxfield or Lord Deas, he would infallibly have been the subject of diminished vitality. But the convict thought otherwise, and dissatisfied with the severity of his sentence, presented to the High Court of Justiciary an application for leave to appeal against it, under the Criminal Appeal (Scotland) Act, 1926. That Court is empowered, if it sees fit, as well to increase as to reduce a sentence; but although wellnigh every criminal convicted of serious crime automatically appeals, I know of no instance in Scotland where a sentence has been increased. Thus the appellant, having everything to gain and nothing to lose, enjoys a fresh run for his money; the Crown is put to needless trouble and expense, and the time of the Court unnecessarily wasted.

The case was called on 15th December before a Court consisting of the Lord Justice-General (Lord Normand), and Lords Moncrieff and Carmont. Mr. Gordon Stott, advocate, appeared for the appellant; Mr. Hill Watson, Advocate-Depute, for the Crown. Kirkwood occupied his old seat in the dock, between two prison warders, and listened to the proceedings with his wonted composure. The Court was again crowded, shewing the public interest which the case aroused.

Counsel's submission was that in view of the whole circumstances of the case, and in particular of the mental condition of the appellant as established at the trial, the sentence was not only excessive, but so much so as to be in itself a miscarriage of justice. Evidence was given at the trial on behalf of the Crown by two experts in mental diseases. Professor Henderson stated that at the time when he examined him the appellant was sane, and was of opinion that he was sane on 6th August, the date of the crime, and able to appreciate what he was doing. That was somewhat qualified by a later statement by the same witness, who said he was satisfied that Kirkwood was an epileptic and one who, in circumstances of emotional stress, was unlikely to act with the same judgment, reason, and foresight as a person who did not so suffer. In his opinion Kirkwood was not a fully responsible individual. Dr. Mackenzie was of opinion that the crime was committed under the influence of an epileptic fit, and that the accused could not be held as a fully sane man at the time of the crime. In view of these facts, counsel submitted, the sentence was one of appalling severity. With regard to the protection of the public and any precaution to that end, that must not be allowed to take the form of the oppression of any individual, particularly one whose mental condition was like that of the appellant. Doubtless the day would come when such a sentence· in the circumstances would be regarded as barbarous.

Mr. Hill Watson said that probably what weighed with the presiding Judge at the trial was the extraordinary brutality of the crime, and in addition, the medical evidence was clear that this man was of a type who might indulge in crime of that nature without any warning, and one who was most dangerous to the public.

The Lord Justice-General intimated that the case would be sent for consideration of the whole Court (thirteen Judges).

On 23rd January, 1939, the final hearing of the appeal took place in the High Court before eleven Judges—the trial Judge (the Lord Justice-Clerk) did not sit, and Lord Pitman was indisposed. Their Lordships, in their splendid Justiciary robes of scarlet and white, presented on the Bench a most impressive sight. The prisoner was as composed as ever, and the Courtroom crowded as before. Mr. G. R. Thomson, K.C., and Mr. Gordon Stott appeared for the appellant; the Solicitor-General and Mr. Calver for the Crown.

Mr. Thomson, having dealt with the facts of the case with which we are already familiar, said that following upon the medical evidence, a plea of culpable homicide on the ground of diminished responsibility was accepted by the Crown. The learned counsel proceeded:

At this point, accordingly, effect had been given to what is now an established doctrine of the law of Scotland, namely, that a measure of irresponsibility, short of insanity, alters and reduces the quality of the crime. That was the effect of the tendering and accepting of this plea.

But this doctrine of diminished responsibility has a second effect and a second function. It mitigates the punishment which falls to be awarded. The function of the Court, in the light of this doctrine, as I understand it, is to endeavour to assess how much of the crime is due to responsibility and how much is due to irresponsibility, and then to inflict a sentence that is commensurate with the responsibility.

How, then, did the presiding Judge approach the problem? His Lordship in passing sentence said:

It is quite impossible for me to assess what the precise degree of your responsibility is, but the only sentence I can pronounce that can be in any way commensurate with the crime you have committed, and adequate for the public interest, is that you be detained in penal servitude for life.

Counsel submitted that it was his Lordship's function as Judge to endeavour to make that assessment. As regards the reference to the public interest, he maintained that there was no warrant for the view that a man who committed a crime, and turned out to be an epileptic, should be shut up for life. In reply to questions from the Bench, counsel said that the man was being sentenced to penal treatment to provide against the public danger and not as a punishment for his crime. Counsel then described at length, and illustrated by authorities, the development of the doctrine of diminished responsibility and its effect upon the punishment to be awarded. The Lord Justice-General pointed out that in the present case the matter of diminished responsibility was already taken into consideration when the Crown accepted the plea of culpable homicide. His Lordship also said that he was not surprised that the presiding Judge had found it impossible to assess the degree of diminished responsibility and translate the result into terms of punishment. That was a divine task, not a human one.

Without calling on the Solicitor-General to reply, the Court reserved judgment.

On 10th February the eleven Judges met to pronounce judgment. The opinion of the Court, which was unanimous, was read by the Lord Justice-General. After complimenting counsel on their arguments at the two hearings, his Lordship said that the appellant's counsel argued that the Court was bound to assess the guilt and misfortune of the pannel, and that in this case the presiding Judge had failed to do so. Secondly, he said that the protection of the public was not a relevant consideration for a Judge in imposing criminal penalties. And thirdly, he said it was unfair and oppressive to pass an indeterminate sentence on the appellant because of his mental condition, and that such a sentence would prejudice any prospect of his restoration to a normal mental condition and normal responsibility. "I think," said his Lordship, "that there is no doubt'that the defence of impaired responsibility is somewhat inconsistent with the basic doctrine of our criminal law: that a man, if sane, is responsible for his acts, and, if not sane, is not responsible. It is a modern variation of that basic doctrine, justified in each case by medical testimony directed to the special facts of that case. The mental weakness, or weakening of responsibility, is regarded by our law as an extenuating circumstance, and it has effect as modifying the character of the crime, or as justifying a modification of sentence, or both." When the jury had, under the presiding Judge's direction, given effect to that extenuating circumstance by reducing the crime from murder to culpable homicide, the Judge had still to consider whether it should have further weight when he was imposing sentence. The presiding Judge had stated that he found it impossible to make assessment of the degree of responsibility, and his Lordship could find no material evidence on which such assessment could have been made. With regard to the separation of the pannel's own protection from that of the public, his Lordship, having reviewed the respective authorities cited, observed that when a pannel was convicted of a crime committed under an impulse which he was less able to resist than the normal man, and when there was evidence that the impairment of his powers of resistance might come into play after a long interval, during which there had been no premonitory signs of danger, and when the crime had been one of atrocious ferocity, the protection of the public against its repetition was specially relevant. With respect to the effect of an indeterminate sentence on the appellant's future, his Lordship was satisfied that the prisoner's mental and physical condition would be carefully considered and treated, and would be reviewed from time to time by the proper authorities. "There is nothing that would justify us in interfering with the sentence," concluded the Lord Justice-General, "and I think that the appeal should be dismissed. That is the opinion of the whole Court."

(4)

As a layman who has known one or two cases of epilepsy, I was much struck by the demeanour of the prisoner, as well during the trial as at the two hearings and the dismissal of his appeal. It was admitted that his last recorded fit was in 1928. I had opportunity to watch him closely on those four occasions, and I have never seen anyone more cool and collected, or presenting less sign of that "emotional instability," which, in such trying circumstances, one so afflicted might have been expected to exhibit. A man apparently more master of his feelings it were difficult to conceive. His imperturbable composure was never shaken. Indeed, he seemed to stand the strain better than some of those officially concerned in the proceedings; and what "circumstances of emotional value" more powerful can be conceived than to be tried for one's life?

In considering these (and other) cases one is surprised at the small part played in the tragedy by the person who may be termed in a sense the leading lady of the drama. The slaying is done "off"; she is dead and done with. And amid all the fuss and concern for the fortunes of the slayer, but scant respect is paid to the fate of his hapless prey. Here, we have two strong, healthy young women both wantonly butchered in the heyday of life, the one elaborately strangled, the other brutally battered to death, and each, *while yet alive*, subjected to a further nameless outrage. Pace the psychiatrists, and at the risk of being deemed unduly sentimental, I confess to feeling for the unfriended victims more sympathy than for the interesting executors of their so hideous doom.

PIECES OF EIGHT;

Or, *The Last of the Pirates*

There be land-rats and water-rats, land-thieves and water-thieves—I mean pirates.
The Merchant of Venice, Act I. Scene iii.

I CANNOT REMEMBER how early in life I began, as the phrase is, to form a library. My favourite books were those known as fairy tales, but I was also very partial to pirates and stories of mutiny and murder on the high seas, with plenty of blood and treasure and walking the plank, that picturesque contrivance for the disposal of unwanted passengers.

By the time I came of age, although I was then avidly devouring the glamorous novels of the 'Nineties, the shelves of my modest bookcase—I had started collecting in my nursery days—still held my dear assemblage of fairy tales, with which, despite my newly acquired manhood, I was loth to part. One blank there was, which ought to have been filled by a well-beloved, blue-clad volume, to wit, *Giant-Land: The Wonderful Adventures of Tim Pippin*. That much-prized possession had once been borrowed by a rascally boy, falsely calling himself my friend, who notwithstanding indignant and repeated protests, refused to return the volume, on the manifestly feigned pretence that he had lost it. At all events it was lost to me. And although many years afterwards, when a responsible parent, I managed to procure another copy, ostensibly for the benefit of my progeny, it proved to be but an indifferent reprint, on inferior paper, the plates much worn, and in a binding that blushed redly for its own shortcomings. I never felt that it really and truly represented my old love. Further disenchantment awaited me in the fact that while my boys were perfectly polite about it, I could see that the immortal Tim failed somehow, for them, of his appeal. A more recent reprint, in which the delectable illustrations are photographically reproduced, was even less satisfying. But I may yet pick up a copy of the first edition, unless all such were read to bits by appreciative youngsters long ago.

I also retain what I flattered myself to be a complete set of the works of Mr. Knatchbull-Hugessen, who later, to my young bewilderment, wrote under the style and title of Lord Brabourne. There they were, and are, from *Stories for My Children* to *Ferdinand's Adventure*; a goodly company as any youngster could desire. They may even be of some material as well as spiritual value, seeing that many of them are illustrated by the inimitable pencil of Ernest Griset, who must surely have studied Art in Fairyland. Most prized of all, by reason of being my first love, was Holme Lee's *Fairy Tales*. I have the book still, and unless old affection blinds me, I esteem it one of the best and most original of its kind ever written for the delight of deserving childhood.

Why such masterpieces should have been suffered to go out of print, and have to be sought for like Elizabethan quartos, I cannot tell. I know not what form of intellectual pabulum is nowadays provided for the sustainment of our young. Doubtless they would find but little savour in these old-fashioned feasts, which I was wont to devour with gusto. For the drone of no aeroplane ever disturbs the silence of the Forbidden Forest; the Granite Castle is innocent alike of sanitation, wireless and central heating; and there are neither tubes nor escalators in the Underground City. Tuflongbo's journey, while beset by most engaging perils, does not expose him to the common daily risk of being slain or mangled by some ruthless or incomplete motorist. Even more damning than such defects, the heroes and heroines of these tales are, like the angels, refreshingly unconcerned with Sex, whether in its physical, fictional, or filmic aspects. Fancy a modern child's amusement at this account of Tuflongbo's birth—a variation on the time-honoured cabbage motif—as furnished by his naïve biographer. It appears that he was the child of one Mulberry, "a distinguished member of the

Royal Society of Wiseacres," whose reputation for profound learning procured for him the post of tutor to the infant son of the reigning Queen of Sheneland.

It was during one of his official visits to his royal pupil that his beloved wife, the bright and fanciful Lupine, while wandering in the heat of the afternoon under the pleasant shadow of the garden trees, found their wee, drowsy dot of a baby fast asleep on the curled and crinkled leaf of a parsley-bush. A serviceable little fairy-nurse sat over-against him, fanning the rays from his face and singing a lullaby, while a perfumed zephyr hovered round the spray and rocked the quaint cradle in time to the tune. . . .

"Take him; he is not glass—he won't break," said the fairy-nurse; "he belongs to you and Mulberry."

One would like to have heard Mrs. Gamp's opinion of these irregular proceedings, particularly her comments on the proficiency of the fairy-nurse and her remarks upon the unqualified assistance of the zephyr.

The ravishment of my first *Tim Pippin* had at least one wholesome result: thus early was I taught, by dire experience, the salutary lesson *never to lend a book*. Twice only did my resolution falter, with effects that but tended to confirm it. A school friend of mine fell sick, and I lent him a bound volume of the *Boys of England* journal—the robustious forerunner, in the 'Seventies, of the *Boy's Own Paper*—containing that most thrilling and attaching tale: "Alone in the Pirates' Lair," of which a word or two presently. It says much for my regard for that boy that I parted even temporarily with such a treasure. My poor friend died, and after a decent interval I applied to his legal representatives for restitution of my property, only to be told that as his illness had been infectious, everything he had handled was destroyed. So I lost both my friend and my book.

It, the work in question, concerned the voyage of "the good ship, *Titania*, homeward bound from Canton, and laden with a costly cargo," when first we sight her, "lying at anchor off the Ladrones," and told how she was taken by the cruel and blood-thirsty pirate chief, Don Pablo, who was, in the Court-circular phrase, "accompanied" by that romantic figure, Donna Inez, "a most lovely lady," most unhappy in her love, and whose machinations were subsequently foiled by the resourceful young hero, Jack Rushton, dreadfully referred to throughout the tale as "the mid."

The other experience, in itself inconsiderable, but markedly suggestive of the danger of lending, was this. I was very fond of *Dick Rodney, or the Adventures of an Eton Boy*, by that admirable romancer, James Grant, author of *The Yellow Frigate*, *The White Cockade*, and other works, dear to discriminating youth, in which there figures a diabolic mariner, named Antonio el Cubano, whose fiend-like deeds used agreeably to curdle my young blood. "By his tawny visage and coal-black beard, his long scarlet sash, in which a sheathed knife was stuck, and also by the rings in his ears, we recognized him as a Spanish seaman." And in a very short time he started to let loose hell upon the unfortunate company of the ill-fated brig *Eugénie*. Well, I lent this inestimable narrative to another schoolboy chum. In the course of time, and with no little difficulty, I succeeded in reclaiming it from him, and was pained to find that certain of its immaculate pages—I was ever particularly nice as to the condition of my books—were stained and defiled by the insertion, as a book-marker, of a dried fragment of red herring, which yet remained *in situ* to testify the horrid fact! This was the last straw; I have not again lent a book.

And now, if your patience be not exhausted by perusal of the irrelevant reminiscences of this superfluous prologue, I can promise you as a reward of your indulgence a true story of piracy and murder, strange and direful as conceived in any romance of the sea. For here you have a schooner, bound for the Brazils, laden with a rich cargo and great quantity of specie in Spanish dollars, commanded by an Englishman, and manned by a mixed crew of seven; the murder of the captain and steersman by two devilish foreigners, the mate and cook; a cabin boy, who in the end, like Jim Hawkins, was to save the situation by his pluck and bring the mutineers to justice; the attempt to suffocate the honest hands, the seizure of the ship, and the scuttling of her in the wild Hebrides; the landing on a lonely island, the burial of the treasure on the beach; the capture of the murderers, their trial and conviction at Edin-burgh, and their execution on the Sands of Leith, theirs being the last trial for piracy in Scotland—these surely are matters to furnish forth a stirring story of the deep. Further, in none of the collections of trials known to me is any account of the case included, and it would be a pity were an affair so interesting to lack commemoration. The source from which my narrative derives is an admirable report of the proceedings by Alexander Stuart, "Clerk to the Trial," published at Edinburgh in 1821.

I

On 26th November, 1821, before the High Court of Admiralty at Edinburgh, began the trial of Peter Heaman and François Gautier for the crimes of piracy and murder.

From the portentous circumlocutions of the indictment on which they were charged the following facts emerge. The schooner *Jane* of Gibraltar—owner, Moses Levy; Thomas Johnson, master—sailed from her home port on 19th May, 1821, bound for Bahia in the Brazils. She had on board specie to the amount of 38,180 Spanish silver dollars, shipped by certain merchants in Gibraltar and consigned to divers signors overseas. Her cargo included 20 pipes of sweet oil; 34 bales of paper; 98 barrels of beeswax; and 15 bags of aniseed. The pannels joined the ship at Gibraltar; Heaman as mate and Gautier as cook, the other members of the crew being James Paterson, Peter Smith, David Strachan, and Johanna Dhura, *alias* John Hard, together with the cabin boy, Andrew Camelier. It was alleged that in seven degrees north latitude, and five days' sail to the west of the Canaries, the pannels did shoot the captain in the head with a musket, and completed their work by beating him savagely with the butt end thereof, and that they then attacked and slew by similar means the seaman James Paterson, and caused the bodies of their victims to be cast into the sea. This for the piratical purpose of seizing and taking possession of the ship and of the specie and other cargo aboard. They next confined Smith and Strachan in the forecastle, by fastening down the hatchway, "and did attempt to suffocate the said two persons by smoke," and did thereby succeed in terrifying them into assisting in the plan to seize the vessel and cargo. The pannels then steered for the coast of Scotland, where they intended to appropriate the proceeds of their villainy, and the ship having arrived off the island of Lewis on 21st July, 1821, she was scuttled by them, whereby she was lost and driven ashore. They landed the specie and cargo near Swordale, for the purpose of secreting and carrying off the same; but upon the information of the cabin boy they were apprehended, and taken before the magistrates at Stornoway and thereafter before the Sheriff of Edinburgh, when they were duly committed for trial.

The diet was called before the old Admiralty Court, which was abolished in 1830. Sir John Connell, advocate, Judge-Admiral, presided; the Lord Advocate (Sir William Rae of St. Catherine's), assisted by John Hope and Duncan McNeill, advocates-depute, instructed by the Crown Agent (Adam Rolland, the friend of Sir Walter Scott), conducted the prosecution; Thomas Maitland and Archibald Hope Cullen, advocates, appeared for the defence. (Hope afterwards became Lord Justice-Clerk; McNeill, Lord President; and Maitland, a judge, with the judicial title of Lord Dundrennan.) No objection was offered to the relevancy of the indictment; the pannels pleaded Not Guilty; and a jury of fifteen Edinburgh merchants was empanelled. Gabriel Surenne, George Street, teacher of French, was appointed as interpreter for Gautier, who knew not English.

The first witness called was the cabin boy, Andrew Camelier, who stated he was aged 18, a native of Malta, and had been four years at sea. He joined the *Jane* at Gibraltar, where the schooner was manned; the crew consisted of six men, besides witness and Captain Johnson. The pannels were respectively shipped as mate and cook. Witness slept in the cabin, in a bunk aft of the captain's: "when in bed their heads were near each other, there being only a plank between them." Heaman, the mate, also slept in the cabin, but on the other side. The rest of the men slept in the forecastle. Strachan and Dhura formed the captain's watch; Smith and Paterson the mate's; but Smith hurt his foot and was laid up, so Gautier took his place. Some seventeen days after they sailed, the captain, who had been on watch, came down at midnight to the cabin and went to bed. The boy was then in his bunk, and shortly fell asleep. The mate, the cook, and Paterson were on the watch.

The boy was awakened by a shot. So near was it, that it seemed to be fired into the captain's bed. There was no light in the cabin. He ran instantly up on deck. The first thing he saw was the mate striking with the butt end of a musket at Paterson, who was crying out. He was felled beside the main hatchway, and the mate continued to strike him. The captain then rushed up on deck; he was holding his hand to his head, which was bleeding, and cried out: "What is this? what is this?" The boy said he thought that the mate was "fighting" with Paterson. At that moment the cook "caught" the captain and struck him down with the butt end of a musket. As he lay groaning on the deck the mate struck him on the belly with his musket. The mate then went forward and called the men on deck. Dhura came up first, and Strachan wished to come also; but the mate had an axe in his hand "and desired him not to come upon deck," so he stayed below with the injured Smith. The mate took Dhura aft, the boy remaining on the forecastle. Presently he was called aft and ordered to help in throwing the bodies overboard. "The deponent [witness] was crying at this time, and was not able to give much assistance." Dhura, too, seemed to be frightened. The dead body of Paterson, with an iron weight attached to his foot, was cast overboard, as likewise was that of the captain, "who did not appear to be quite dead when he was thrown overboard." After the captain was struck down, the boy said to the mate: "Don't kill me!" to which the murderer answered: "Very well."

That night the mate made the hatches fast on Smith and Strachan, and nailed them down in the morning. The murderers, averse, as appears, from further bloodshed, hit upon the ingenious device of asphyxiating the two men imprisoned in the forecastle. They lit a fire in the cabin with a tar barrel, and made in the forward bulkhead two holes, whereby the smoke would enter the forecastle. The boy was ordered to prepare a paste of flour and water, with which the hatchways, cabin door, and other crevices were anointed to prevent the smoke escaping save by the holes. The fire was kept up for two nights and a day, when the mate remarked to the cook that he supposed the men were now dead. When the hatches were opened, however, Smith and Strachan were found to be alive, though, not unnaturally, "down-hearted." They were given some food and the hatches were again fastened down. Dhura begged the mate to allow the men on deck, and on the third morning this was done; the cook and the mate making them swear upon a Bible, which they kissed, "that they would never say anything about what had happened."

By order of the mate witness cleaned out the cabin; there was blood on the floor, on the seat, and on the captain's bed beside the pillow, which was "all spoiled and the feathers knocked out of it." The bed-clothes were brought on deck and thrown overboard. Witness was then told to wash the deck, which was bloody where the captain and Paterson had lain. The cook shewed him a musket ball, "a little flattened, with blood on it," which he said had fallen from the captain's head. Captain Johnson was a quiet, kind, and good-tempered man; he had no sort of quarrel with any of the crew before he was killed. Witness never saw him drunk. There were six muskets on board; after the murders two were kept and the others thrown overboard. The casks containing the dollars were opened by the mate, Dhura, and Strachan—the cook was then at the helm—and the bags in which the dollars were packed were put below the bulwarks. The casks were burnt.

The ship's course was changed and she was headed for Scotland. The mate was now captain, and the cook mate. The first land they made was the island of Barra. Heaman, dressed in the dead captain's green coat, attended by Smith and Strachan, went ashore in the ship's boat. They returned with a larger boat, which they said they had bought from the inhabitants of the isle, the mate explaining that they would land the money in that boat later. They then set sail from Barra and made for Stornoway. Off that coast the ship was scuttled and abandoned, while the crew, taking their booty with them, started for the shore. "After they were aboard the boat they counted the dollars, partly by hand and partly by measuring with a tin pot." Each received six thousand three hundred as his share of the spoil, such as had belts stowing the dollars therein. Following upon this equitable division, "the boat was broken with driving ashore, and they put the money into the ground, after they got on to the shore, amongst the small stones on the beach." From the wreck of the boat they made a tent, in which they proposed to camp and enjoy a rest from their labours, but presently they received a call from two gentlemen, who took the names of the party, opened the sea chests of the men, except that of the mate, and departed, leaving two persons to attend the castaways. The cabin boy ran after the strangers and to one of them (whom he now identified as Mr. Roderick M'Iver, surveyor of customs at Stornoway) he told the dreadful story of the voyage. He had previously informed Dhura that he intended to disclose the truth at the first opportunity, to which that mariner answered: "Very well."

Witness further stated that after the captain was killed, the mate and the cook compelled the others to help to navigate the vessel. The accused shared between them the captain's belongings, including his gold watch, chain, and seals, and his green coat, all of which witness identified as produced. Of the ship's papers, some were burnt and some thrown overboard, with pieces of iron attached to sink them. "The fire which the deponent has mentioned to have been kindled by the mate, was made on the floor of the cabin, just inside the door, a large piece of wood from one of the casks and the copper in which they cooked their victuals being placed under the fire, to prevent it from burning the floor." There was no stove in the cabin. He did not see the captain offer any violence to Paterson.

Mr. Maitland's cross-examination failed to shake the evidence in chief, but elicited a few additional particulars. The smallness of the stage on which the tragedy was played is shewn by the fact that the *Jane* was but fifty tons burthen; that the captain's bed had no mattress, but a bit of sail and blankets; and that there was no window in the cabin, but two small holes from the deck to admit air. On the night of the murder there was very little wind. When witness was wakened by the shot he saw a flash, but it was so dark he could see no person. He ran up on deck without looking at the captain's bed. He was sure there was no one at the helm.

David Strachan, aged 19, corroborated the previous witness as to the events preceding the mutiny. He stated that after the schooner sailed, he frequently heard conversations about killing the captain and taking the money which was aboard. Heaman, the mate, first broached the subject. He said that he did not wish the crew to take part in the murder: "there was one man on board who would do it, if they would take a share of the money." Strachan, Smith, and Paterson, when the project was mentioned to them, said they would have nothing to do with it. Heaman often recurred to the subject when witness was on the watch with him, and urged that the thing should be done. Strachan warned the captain of the purposed plot, but mentioned no names. The captain said "that the Frenchman [Gautier] was not so stout as to reign over them all." He heard no more of the matter until the fatal night. Strachan and Dhura were on watch with the captain from 8 o'clock till 12 on the night he was killed. When the captain left the deck he appeared to be sober. The two pannels and Paterson then took the watch; Smith, who should have shared it, was below, having cut his foot. Witness went to bed and to sleep. He was awakened by Paterson crying out: "O Lord! O Lord!" Heaman came to the hatchway and called down: "All hands on deck to shorten sail." All those below turned out except the injured Smith. When Dhura went up, the mate, who had a hatchet in his hand, prevented him from going on deck, and also forbade witness to do so, saying that he [Strachan] had given information to the captain. The hatches were battened down upon them. In the course of the forenoon smoke began to come into the forecastle, continuing for some two or three hours; a second smoke attack was afterwards made, which lasted even longer. The two prisoners were wellnigh suffocated. They got neither bread nor water during their confinement, though they called out repeatedly for same. After two days and one night the hatches were opened; Strachan was called up by Heaman; Gautier tied his hands behind his back and lashed him to the studding-sail boom, which was lying on the deck. Dhura gave him a glass of brandy and bade him keep up his heart. The invalid Smith was then brought on deck. The mate told them that the captain and Paterson had been killed. He offered them sufficient bread and water and a share of the money, if they would take the smaller boat and leave the ship. This offer they declined, on the reasonable ground that they would never reach land. Whereupon Heaman ordered them below again, and the hatches were replaced. Next day witness was allowed on deck, and was informed by Gautier that he must die: "You go in the sea," was the Frenchman's facetious phrase. Heaman was at the helm, and to him Strachan appealed for mercy. The mate said if he would swear secrecy his life would be spared, and sent him below to get his Bible, upon which he took the oath required of him. Thenceforth witness was at liberty. He described how the dollars were brought on deck, the ship's papers destroyed, and the vessel headed for the Orkneys. They spoke another schooner, when Heaman hoisted the American flag, and in answer to the stranger's questions, said that his ship was the Rover, thirty days out from New York, bound for Archangel. Witness corroborated as to the arrival off Barra, the purchase of the big boat, the scuttling of the Jane, the landing near Stornoway, the division of the dollars—which witness thought unequal, as Heaman got more than his just share—the coming of the custom-house officers, and the subsequent disappearance of the cabin boy, who was pursued in vain by the mate: "Captain Shadewell of New York," as he named himself to the natives, returned empty-handed; "he said he had got a fright, having been chased, and that he had thrown away his coat and waistcoat and his watch." That night they were all apprehended in the tent which they had erected on the shore. Witness identified as Captain Johnson's property the watch, chain, and seals found upon the cook, also the several weapons before mentioned. The cross-examination was negligible.

Peter Smith, aged 19, told how he shipped on the *Jane* at Gibraltar. Some time after she sailed, Heaman said "that he wished to put away with Captain Johnson to get the dollars, and that he would carry the ship to a place where they might be landed in safety." Paterson and Strachan were present and the three seamen were invited by the mate to join in the plan, but they said they wished to have no hand in it. Excepting the captain, the mate was the only one aboard who understood navigation. Heaman frequently visited the men's quarters in the night and urged them to mutiny, but none of the crew would agree. Heaman then dropped the subject and nothing happened till the night of the murders. The captain, Strachan, and Dhura were on watch till midnight, when the seamen came down and went to bed. Witness had cut his foot a week before and was unable for duty. About two or three o'clock in the morning—Heaman, the cook, and Paterson being on the watch —witness was awakened by Paterson running forward, crying: "Murder, murder! God Almighty save my soul, for I am murdered now!" The mate called all hands on deck to shorten sail; the others went up, but witness could not do so. Next day the hatches were battened down on him and Strachan, and an attempt was made to suffocate them by smoke from the cabin, through two holes bored in the bulkhead. After two nights and a day of this treatment they were allowed on deck. The cook said to Strachan: "You go in the water," and Strachan asked what was to become of Smith, to which the cook replied: "All the same." They appealed to the mate to spare their lives, which he consented to do, provided they would swear upon the Bible never to reveal what they had heard or seen. He then informed them that the captain and Paterson had been killed and their bodies cast overboard. After the course had been altered they spoke the *Lark*, of Canterbury, to whom the mate reported that he was the captain and had sailed from New York. "The mate directed them to say, if they should be boarded by any vessel, that they had been robbed by pirates, and that from their own knowledge they had no dollars on board." All the crew helped to work the ship from fear of the mate and of the cook: "if he [witness] had not done so he would not have been alive this day." The course of the voyage, the scuttling of the schooner, the adventure of the boats, and the landing of the dollars, "a part of which was buried and a part retained in their chests," were described all over again. At Barra the mate gave himself out to be Captain Rogers, of the *Rover*, from New York; at Lewis he called the ship by a different name, and said he was the owner's son. He explained that the captain and one of the crew had gone to Liverpool, and that their ship had struck on a rock and broke in pieces. Captain Johnson's trunk had his name upon it in brass nails. These witness removed by order of the mate, and covered the top with canvas, under which the marks were still plainly visible. About ten minutes elapsed between the time when Paterson cried out and Dhura went on deck when called by the mate. Cross-examined by Mr. Maitland, the muskets were usually hung on a bulkhead in the cabin; witness had put the captain's pistol in order for him a week before he was killed. He [Smith] did not see either the muskets or the pistol on deck the day or evening of the murder.

Johanna Dhura, *alias* John Hard, stated that he was 24 years old. He corroborated the evidence of Smith, Strachan, and the cabin boy as to the happenings before 7th June, when the captain met his death. He had shared that night the captain's watch—Johnson was then quite sober—and the watch was taken over by the mate, the cook, and Paterson, the cook having taken Smith's place. He was awakened by a "hollowing" in Paterson's voice, but did not hear what was said, as he slept "so far back." A little after Heaman called down: "All hands to take in sail." He went on deck; Heaman was at the hatch with an axe in his hand and would not permit Strachan to come on deck, "but desired him to keep down." He saw neither Paterson nor the captain on deck, but heard moaning as he was going aft, and having been sworn to secrecy with the rest, Heaman shewed him the bodies of the captain and Paterson, and bade him help the cook and the boy to throw them overboard. The boy was frightened and crying, and the cook "gave the best hand in doing so." He heard groans from the captain's body as it was cast into the sea. The cook tied weights to the feet to sink them. He was ordered to help the boy to wash the deck; it was so dark he could not see whether there was blood there or not, but next morning he found the soles of his feet were bloodstained. The cabin was cleaned up by the boy. Witness described the attempt "to smoke the lads below." They were kept there two nights and a day, when Strachan was allowed on deck; Smith's foot was very bad, and he was confined to his hammock. They were sworn like the others at the binnacle and kissed the Bible. When the *Jane* was off Lewis Heaman ordered witness to go below and make a hole in the bottom; as he did so he got the boy to keep a look-out, fearing that the mate might shut down the hatches on him while the ship was sinking. He also spoke to the dividing and burying of the dollars near Stornoway. After the custom-house officers' visit the cabin boy was missing; he had often heard him say that he would give information the first chance he had. Witness never heard anyone on board the ship say that the captain had killed Paterson. Neither the mate nor the cook shewed any hurt the morning after the captain's death. Cross-examined, when he saw the bodies on coming aft, they were lying at some little distance from each other and opposite ways. They lay on the starboard side of the deck; one of them under the boat and the other close to the side of the vessel.

Hugh M'Neil, son of Donald M'Neil of Watersay in Barra, spoke to the coming of a schooner in June last. The captain came ashore and went to the house of witness's father, with whom he dined. He called himself Rogers, and said he was come from New York, and bound for Archangel. He landed part of his cargo of beeswax and oil, and bought a boat from the islanders. He wore a green coat. The pannel Heaman was very like the man, but he would not swear he was the same.

Roderick M'Iver, surveyor of customs at Stornoway, stated that having heard in July last that a vessel, supposed to be a smuggler, was at anchor near Stornoway, he sent four of his men to find out what she was up to, and followed himself. They saw nothing of the ship, but found a large boat on the shore, and six men belonging to it, who had pitched a tent there. One of these, the pannel Heaman, said he was mate of the brig *Betsy* of New York, which had been lost off Barra Head. He and the captain had quarrelled, and the latter had gone off in the ship's boat with five men for Liverpool. He and the remainder of the crew had taken another boat and tried to reach the mainland, but were driven ashore where they then were. The brig, he added, was owned by his father. He gave his name as George Shadewell. Witness searched the men's sea chests, and found dollars in them all. He took a list of their names; "but it rained so fast that the names were obliterated as soon as written"—a genuine bit of local colour. Witness left two of his men in charge of the castaways. When he reached the top of the cliff, which overhung the beach where the boat lay, he was joined by the cabin boy, who had followed after him, and the boy told him that the mate and the cook had murdered the master and a seaman named Paterson, and seized the ship; and he described the circumstances of the crimes. Whereupon M'Iver sent back two more of his men, with orders to rouse the country folk, and if the strangers attempted to escape, that they should stave in the boat and bind the men with cords. He then proceeded to Swordale with the boy. The boy told him that there was a further quantity of dollars hidden in the men's hammocks and still more buried on the beach; and next morning, the whole party having been secured, a search for the dollars resulted in the finding of 31,211, "as near as the deponent can recollect."

John Murray, tenant in Melbost, said he was one of those

who saw upon the shore a boat and six strange men. He was present when M'Iver, having searched their chests, went home. A sailor boy followed him, and the pannel Heaman sent two of the others to bring him back. Heaman remarked to witness that the boy was "foolish," and did not care what he said or did at times—"nor though he struck a man." The mate, however, appeared very anxious when his men returned without the lad, and himself set out in search of him. Meeting with no better success the mate came back, "without any of his clothes except his trousers and his drawers," explaining "that he had met two men, and had thrown away the rest of his clothes and his watch."

Kenneth MacIver, tacksman of the farm of Tolsta, said that at 6 o'clock on the morning of 23rd July he saw a schooner lying on her broadside in the water, 50 or 60 yards from the shore. Her topmast had been carried away. The coast was rocky and it was blowing hard; "it blew harder still towards the afternoon, when the vessel was driven to pieces." She did not seem to have been long water-logged. Pipes of oil, beeswax, bales of paper, and some jars of olives were washed ashore from the wreck. She was schooner-rigged, and coppered; shallow, but of great length. Tolsta, where she went ashore, was 10 or 12 miles from Swordale.

Abraham Levy Bensusan, of Goodman's Fields, London, stated that Mr. Moses Levy of Gibraltar was a correspondent of his house. He, Moses, was owner of a schooner named the *Jane*, and on 21st May witness was instructed by him to effect an insurance on the vessel's cargo, which he did, the policy being dated 11th June, for £1800. The voyage insured was from Gibraltar to Bahia and any other ports in the Brazils. He identified certain bills of lading, bearing to be signed by Thomas Johnson as master of the *Jane*.

George Robertson, of Great Winchester Street, London, spoke to a policy taken out with his firm, dated 11th June, on specie on board the *Jane*, for £3375.

This concluded the evidence for the Crown, and the case closed with the reading of the pannels' judicial declarations at

Stornoway, before his Majesty's Justices of the Peace for the county of Ross, and at Edinburgh, in presence of the Sheriff-Substitute of that city.

II

Peter Heaman declared that he was 35 years of age. He shipped as mate on the *Jane*, which was brig-rigged fore and schooner-rigged aft, "and would carry from 90 to 120 tons." (He was probably better versed in tonnage than the cabin boy, who put it at 50.) Her cargo included 38,000 dollars, contained in bags which were stowed with sawdust in casks. From the time that the vessel left port there were frequent conversations among the crew about the money. Such conferences occurred at every meal-time and on every watch, as there was opportunity. "Paterson said the best plan would be to make the master walk on shore on a plank." The captain was dissatisfied with the cook's methods "in making the victuals ready"; upon which occasions Gautier, resenting the aspersion on his art, was wont "frequently to swear in French and sometimes in Spanish, which displeased the master, who threatened to blow his brains out with a pistol." Strachan was at the helm on the night of 6th June and told the captain of the intended mutiny, whereupon the captain said "he would revenge, either when he got to port or on the first opportunity." At 3 or 4 o'clock in the morning of the 7th, the captain came on deck in his night-shirt, with a loaded pistol, and mistaking Paterson, who was at the helm, for the cook, "blowed his brains out." The cook was forward, on the look-out. On hearing the shot he came aft; "and the captain, finding that it was not the Frenchman he had shot, began to strike him with the pistol, saying he wished it was loaded for his sake." The captain got him down on the deck. Witness had taken the helm. All the crew struck the captain; he saw them "all over each other in a cluster." Dhura, the cabin boy, and the cook threw the bodies overboard. When all was over, the whole crew came aft and asked the declarant what was best to be done. He advised that they should proceed on the voyage, and say nothing about what had happened. This he did to keep the peace among them. Smith and Strachan proposed to make for the north of Scotland, where they could buy a boat and so get ashore, and scuttle the ship at sea. To this they all agreed. On the 20th they put into Watersay Bay, in Barra, where declarant bought from a fisherman a boat, for which he paid 12 guineas; and from another, a sail for £5. These were paid in dollars "from the common stock." His account of their further adventures does not differ from that which we have heard from the crew, except that he denied having given any orders; everything was done after consultation among the whole ship's company. Being interrogated why, seeing that he messed with the captain, he did not inform him of what was passing among the crew, he replied that the captain was a very passionate man, and he was afraid of the consequences.

On his subsequent examination at Edinburgh Heaman declared that he never proposed to Smith, Strachan, or Paterson to kill the captain and seize the treasure. When the captain's body was thrown overboard, the boy said: "There you go to hell, you ——! You will never plague me more." The boy seemed to him to be the most blood-thirsty of the lot. When the light came he observed that the boy was all over blood. There was a great deal of blood upon the deck; he therefore entreated the men to wash the deck before daylight, "otherwise it would be a horrible sight." (One would hardly have expected him to be so sensitive.) He himself did not leave the helm till 7 a.m. No one ever prevented Smith and Strachan from coming on deck, the hatchway of the forecastle was not closed down, and no attempt was made to suffocate anyone there.

François Gautier, a native of Havre-de-Grace, aged 23 years, said he never heard any talk among the crew as to killing the captain and seizing the cargo; he did not understand their language. Only the mate spoke French. "It was jocosely mentioned that if they could lay their hands on the money, they would all be men of fortune." With regard to the silver barrels, "he knew it to be money from the captain's conversation with the mate, and from the captain desiring him to fry six eggs, as he had been throng counting the money." The captain could speak a few words of French. Having heard from Dhura that Paterson had said: "they should lay a plank over the ship's side and tell the master to walk over it," the declarant very properly made answer "that it was wrong of them to entertain such ideas." He thought the captain "was afraid of what happened," as he had been told by Strachan something about the proposed seizing of the silver. As for the alleged mutiny, he told the same story as the mate. The captain came on deck with a pistol and shot Paterson dead at the wheel; he next attacked the cook; the others came to his rescue and rushed upon the captain, whose intention, the mate said, was to kill them all. The captain was drunk while on the watch, "and he took a further dose before he turned in." After his death nobody was confined in the forecastle and no fire was lighted in the cabin. The mate, as knowing navigation, was entrusted with the command of the ship. "In other respects they were all as brothers." The boy threw the dead bodies overboard, remarking, of the captain's: "You will swim well. I shall suffer no more from you." The declarant never had any quarrel with the captain, though he sometimes found fault with the manner of the cooking, but he, the cook, never answered back, as he could not speak English. The mate took the helm after Paterson fell, and therefore was not among those who attacked the captain. The bags with the dollars were put into the boat when the ship was sunk, and were divided equally among them, "and the mate got a few bags from the rest as a present." After the boat came ashore they buried the dollars on the beach.

This closed the case for the Crown, and the pannels' counsel having stated that they had no evidence to adduce for the defence, the Lord Advocate addressed the jury.

III

His Lordship observed that as this important and certainly not uninteresting trial had already lasted sixteen hours, he would be as concise as the circumstances of the case would permit. They were called upon to judge in a case which occurred many thousand miles distant from the nearest corner of this kingdom; the crime committed in a vessel not belonging to this country nor in any way connected with it; the accused owing no allegiance to this country, yet brought here to be tried. Such was the jurisdiction of that Court. The accused had the benefit of counsel who displayed ability and zeal in their defence, and as one of them was a foreigner, it was satisfactory to know that the French consul was in Court, watching in his interest the proceedings. The prisoners were charged with the crimes of piracy and murder. Piracy could be committed either by the crew of one ship taking another ship, or by the crew of a particular ship appropriating the ship in which they sailed. The latter crime was more heinous than the former, as it involved a breach of trust. Such acts had been held to infer capital punishment. His Lordship then reviewed the facts proved in this connection: the seizure of the ship, the altering of her course, the stealing of the dollars. When she was scuttled and the crew left her, they had not calculated on the nature of the cargo, which kept her afloat until she was driven ashore on the island of Lewis and broke up. Unable by reason of the wind to reach the mainland, the crew were forced to land on the same island, and as their boat was damaged they had to camp upon the beach. The first thing they did was to bury in the sand the treasure they had stolen, in order to conceal it. The wreck of the ship attracted attention, the boat was discovered. The surveyor of customs had told of his visit to the castaways, and how he was followed by the boy, who disclosed the truth of the situation. It was clear to demonstration that not only the ship, but her cargo, was carried off by the prisoners at the bar, and that in order to deprive the owners of their property they sank the vessel and attempted to secure the most valuable part of the cargo. "This being proved, and acknowledged by themselves, I cannot see what defence can be set up for them. I must leave them the full advantage of the defence whatever it be, as I cannot comprehend its nature. Gautier admitted that he joined in the mutiny, agreed to come to Scotland, and took his share of the dollars. Heaman, after the captain's murder, commanded, and directed the voyage—he being the mate, whose duty it was to prevent such an offence. Therefore against each and both the crime of piracy was proved."

With regard to the more foul and atrocious charge—that of murder—it was proved by the four seamen examined that the suggestion of seizing the ship came from the mate; he was continually proposing that the specie be taken and the captain murdered. He said he did not inform the captain of the plot because the master was a passionate man, yet all the witnesses concurred that Captain Johnson was a quiet, good-tempered man, who quarrelled with no one. The cook merely said that he was found fault with for his cooking. It was proved, and even admitted by the mate, that Strachan did warn the captain the night before he was killed. His Lordship then examined the evidence of the murders, as proved by the cabin boy and the other hands: the shooting of the captain, and the battering of Paterson to death. As to the smoke test applied to the men in the forecastle, he thought the design was to frighten, rather than to murder them. The oaths were administered to cover the facts which the pannels feared might come to light. "You see how little confidence perpetrators of crimes have in each other. None of them could trust themselves [sic] to sleep below; each was afraid of the consequences that might happen to him if he slept." The pannels' account of the affair—how the captain came on deck and blew out Paterson's brains by mistake, attacked the cook, and was set upon by the whole crew—was contradicted in express terms by all the witnesses. Should it be argued that these were *socii criminis*—accessories to the crime—in so far as helping to carry off the specie, and therefore not entitled to credit, that objection could not be taken to the cabin boy. He slept beside the captain and they did not wish to trust him, so he was told nothing of the plot. What he afterwards did, he did upon compulsion; and at the first opportunity he disclosed what had happened. As regards the rest, they were driven to obey the mate. He was the only one who could navigate the ship; if they confined him they were unable to sail her, and what then would become of them and the vessel? Nothing could have been fairer or more consistent than the evidence and manner of these witnesses. No men could have looked the pannels in the face as they did, had they been endeavouring falsely to swear away their lives. Even assuming that their declarations were true, Gautier was art and part with the whole crew in murdering the master, Heaman said he was at the helm; but his presence, in the circumstances of the case, made him also an accessory. He was in command, the captain being dead; according to his own story he looked on at the murder and did nothing to prevent it; therefore he too was art and part in the crime. But the statement was incredible. The more the evidence was weighed the plainer it became that the testimony of the boy and of the other men contained the real and true state of the facts. However, if they, the jury, had any doubt as to that, the pannels were entitled to the benefit of it; but he felt it his duty to demand from them against both prisoners at the bar a verdict of Guilty.

Mr. Maitland then addressed the jury for the defence. After some general observations as to the atrocity of the charges—which, instead of exciting indignation against the pannels, ought rather to make the jury turn a most jealous and scrutinizing eye upon the evidence—he said that he would not follow the course adopted by the Lord Advocate, but would consider the crimes together. If there was no proof of murder there could be none of piracy. The Crown case was that the affair began by murder, the object of which was piracy. The defence rested entirely upon an impeachment of the credibility of the witnesses. The vessel was manned by eight persons—a captain, a mate, and six seamen. The prosecution asked them to believe, not only that the two prisoners at the bar devised the plan of murder and piracy, but that it was carried into full and perfect execution by them. It would not do for his Lordship to implicate the others, for all his witnesses claimed to be guiltless. They maintained that what they did was the result of terror and compulsion. He, counsel, proposed to shew the gross improbabilities presented by the Crown case, of which the first was that such a scheme could have been carried into execution by two out of eight persons. Strachan said that he informed the captain that there was mischief brewing in the ship. "You have thus this nefarious scheme mooted to the crew, talked of, discussed, argued about, originating solely with the two men at the bar, everyone on the ship against it but themselves: and finally a communication made to the captain of what was going on. If this had been true, what would have happened? The very reverse of what occurred here. There was the captain, who knew the peril that impended over him; he had six out of eight of his crew with him, and only two to subdue. Yet instead of taking any steps to secure his own safety, he silently allows matters to proceed to a crisis. In the perfect knowledge that his own murder had been planned, he allows the intending assassins to remain at liberty, and refuses the means of securing his safety when they are offered." The third improbability was the alleged mode by which the captain was murdered. According to the cabin boy they had retired to rest, and in the dead of the night some person unknown, armed with a musket, came down the companion-way, the cabin being in total darkness, and fired a random but fatal shot at the captain in his bed. It was impossible to conceive a more clumsy mode of perpetrating the crime, or one which afforded less chance of success. An immediate alarm in the ship was inevitable; yet the jury were asked to believe that Gautier, to whom the deed was directly imputed, committed it when he had no friend on board except the mate. The next improbability concerned the murder of Paterson. He was not said to have been killed as preparatory to the murder of the captain; Gautier shot the latter before assailing Paterson; but the natural course would have been to kill Paterson first. He was at the helm, and it was impossible for Gautier to enter the cabin without exciting his notice. His destruction should, in the circumstances, have preceded that of the captain; but all the witnesses, with consistent improbability, say that was not so. It was remarkable that the firing of a musket in so small a vessel should have been heard by no one but the boy. But the most incredible part of this incredible tale was the story of the attempt to smoke the two men to death. The prosecutor could not get off by saying it was only intended to frighten them. The Crown case required that there was a deliberate intention to put them to death. Counsel then proceeded to pour contempt upon the alleged fire kindled in the cabin, which produced smoke without flame. "Why smoke them at all?" said he. "You are asked to believe that the pannels were not very nice in accomplishing their objects. They are represented as men familiar with bloody purposes and still bloodier actions, and if they had intended to put these witnesses to death, they would never have taken such a ridiculous and inefficacious mode of carrying out their purpose." If such a fire was in fact kindled, those who lit it ran the most eminent risk of setting fire to the ship and destroying themselves in the middle of their misdeeds. The account given by Strachan and Smith of their imprisonment and release was equally absurd and unbelievable.

"Follow this ill-fated vessel and her crew through all their disastrous course. In the wild ocean, on the desert shores of Barra, among the habitations of men, these witnesses, with pure hands and innocent hearts, were spellbound by the pannels at the bar, and compelled reluctantly to participate in the perpetration of the most atrocious crimes. Their whole conduct is accounted for by the exertion of an influence altogether supernatural on the part of the prisoners. Gentlemen, if you can for a single moment go into such a notion as this, I may shut my lips, for I can never hope to aggravate its improbability by any statement of mine." Not the least improbable of all the improbable statements they were called upon to credit was the pretended reliance of the prisoners upon the efficacy of an oath taken by four men to whom they had just set the example of murdering their captain and a fellow-seaman. Counsel then examined at length the evidence of the witnesses, making the most of such minor discrepancies as were to be found therein. They had ample opportunity to arrange their story, and what they stated on their judicial examination he did not know: their declarations were buried in the bosom of the public prosecutor. They made no disclosure of what had happened, either at Barra or at Lewis. "These immaculate witnesses, with pure hands and innocent hearts, as if all their faculties had been paralysed and all their energies deadened by the spells of an enchanter, maintain an inviolable silence, and reject various opportunities of making that disclosure upon which they wish you to believe they had long before determined." The "disclosure" which the boy at last made, was extorted from him by the terror of immediate detection and from a base hope of saving himself by sacrificing his companions. The Crown theory that the crew were concussed and terrified by the pannels could be turned against them; his unfortunate clients were concussed and terrified by the majority of the crew. While, in the circumstances of the case, he did not seek a verdict of Not Guilty, he did, looking to "the fearful obscurity" in which it was involved, ask them to return one of Not Proven.

The Judge-Admiral then proceeded to charge the jury. The crime of piracy was, he said, proved against the pannels by their own declarations. It was proved by the Lewis witnesses that the pannels were found there in possession of the specie; that on being questioned they gave a false account of the vessel and of themselves, pretending that their ship had been wrecked, and making no mention of the dollars that were hid in the sand; and by the anxiety of Heaman when the boy escaped, and the search made for his recovery. If he were guilty of piracy, so also was Gautier, for they acted all along in concert. With regard to the objection that the witnesses were *socii criminis*, they all remained on the ship, helped to sail her where she was carried, and took a share of the plunder. Did they accede voluntarily or did their accession proceed from force and fear? There was no one on board the vessel but the four witnesses and the two pannels; so that as to the force, there was only their own evidence. The jury had seen and heard them, and must judge as to their credibility. None of them seemed to his Lordship to be of that bold and determined character which must be possessed by those who engage in such a crime. The boy, in particular, seemed to him to be as candid a witness as ever appeared in a court of justice; he was modest in his manner and his statements were consistent and distinct. As to the others, there seemed to be no reason to disbelieve any one of them. It was admitted by all hands that Thomas Johnson, the master, and James Paterson, one of the crew, lost their lives by violence on the 7th of June. The question was: Were the pannels the guilty actors, or art and part only in the murders? If they, the jury, believed that the pannels were the principal agents in the piracy, that formed a strong presumption against them in regard to the murders. Again, if they believed the four witnesses told the truth about the piracy, that raised a strong presumption that they were telling the truth about the murders. If the story told by the pannels in their declarations was neither proved nor probable, the account given by the witnesses must be accepted as true. They had heard a great deal from counsel as to the improbability of the latter, but what could be more incredible than that of the pannels?—the captain going to bed at midnight, and between 3 and 4 o'clock in the morning starting up, and with a pistol in his hand, rushing to the helm and shooting the steersman, with whom he had no quarrel! As to the cook, though there had been words about his cooking, who could believe that the captain, a quiet man of good character, and entrusted by a Jew with a valuable cargo, would have murdered him on the spur of the moment? Having shewn how the statements of the crew were, so far as possible in the circumstances, corroborated by the material facts of the case, his Lordship observed that if he had expressed himself more strongly than he should have done, they must pay no regard to what he had said, except in so far as it accorded with their own deliberate judgment.

On the conclusion of the charge at 6 o'clock in the morning of Tuesday, the 27th, the jury were enclosed and the pannels carried back to prison. At 2.30 p.m. they returned to Court with their sealed verdict, which unanimously found both pannels Guilty of the crimes libelled. The Lord Advocate having moved for sentence, the Judge-Admiral addressed the pannels at length upon the heinousness of the crimes of which they had been convicted, and the circumstances of peculiar aggravation attending their commission. "If the law of this country permitted a punishment greater than death to be imposed in any case, that punishment would be inflicted on you." His Lordship, however, had to be content to adjudge the pannels "to be carried from the Bar back to the Tolbooth of Edinburgh, therein to be detained, and to be fed on bread and water only," as provided by a humane statute of King George the Second, until Wednesday, 9th January, 1822, and upon that day, between 9 in the morning and 12 noon, "to be taken furth of the said Tolbooth to the Sands of Leith within floodmark, and there to be hanged by the neck upon a gibbet by the hands of the common executioner until they be dead, and their bodies thereafter to be delivered to Dr. Alexander Monro, Professor of Anatomy in the University of Edinburgh, to be by him publicly dissected and anatomised in terms of the said Act."

IV

The *Edinburgh Evening Courant* of 29th November, 1821, in reporting the trial, remarks: "The prisoners are respectable looking men, with no trace in their features to indicate minds capable of planning and executing crimes of so horrible a nature as those for which they have been tried. Heaman's countenance, in particular, has a very superior cast. During the whole proceedings he was very attentive. Gautier received the most unremitting attention from M. Surenne, a French gentleman who was sworn as interpreter." The *Scots Magazine* for January, 1822, informs us: "Heaman is a native of Sweden, but came to England when a boy, and has since belonged to Sunderland. He is married, and his wife, with several children, were in the Outer Session-House during the trial. Gautier is a Frenchman, and has a wife somewhere in Spain." The *Courant* of 10th January, 1822, gives the following account of the last act of the tragedy:—

Execution of Peter Heaman and François Gautier for Piracy
and Murder

Yesterday these two unfortunate men were executed on a platform on the Sands of Leith, within high-water mark, for the crimes of piracy and murder, pursuant to the sentence of the High Court of Admiralty.

Between 8 and 9 o'clock the Magistrates and their attendants proceeded from the Council Chamber in carriages to the New Jail, where a detachment of the 3rd Dragoon Guards had arrived. About half past 9 o'clock the great gate of the Prison was thrown open, when the procession proceeded in the following order:—   .

A detachment of Cavalry.

A large party of Police.

The City Officers with their halberds.

Three carriages, in the first of which were the four Bailies of the City in their robes with white gloves and white staves. In the second were two gentlemen in attendance on the Magistrates, and the Reverend Mr. Wallace, a Roman Catholic Clergyman. In the third were the Reverend Dr. John Campbell, one of the Ministers of the City, and the Reverend James Porteous, Chaplain of the Jail.

A cart with a seat on the upper end on which the criminals sat.

The whole was closed with another party of the Police, who also surrounded the cart, and a party of Dragoons.

The procession proceeded in this manner from the Jail along the Regent Bridge, down Leith Street, Leith Walk, and Constitution Street, to the platform which was erected at the bottom of the street, on the sands, about 50 yards from the north-west corner of the Naval Yard, and was guarded by a Company of the 41st Foot. At the bottom of Leith Walk the Admiral and Resident Magistrates of Leith, fell into the procession immediately after the carriage in which were the City Magistrates.

Immediately upon ascending the scaffold, the 51st Psalm was given out by Dr. Campbell and sung, in which Heaman seemed to join with the utmost seriousness while Gautier, kneeling, was assisted in his devotions by the Clergyman who attended him.

Upon the psalm being completed Dr. Campbell addressed the spectators in a manner most telling and impressive and well adapted to the solemn and melancholy occasion. In the course of his address the Dr. observed that he was instructed by Heaman to acknowledge in the most public and unqualified manner his participation in the crime for which he was about to suffer, the fairness of the trial and the justice of the sentence which had been pronounced.

Heaman then came forward and, bowing to all around him, spoke for a short time. He cautioned all who heard him to take warning from the melancholy situation to which his crimes had adduced him, to abstain from bad company, his associating with whom and disregarding the principles and precepts of our holy religion had been the means of bringing him to his untimely end.

Dr. Campbell then offered up a most impressive prayer during which Heaman kneeled.

During the time that Dr. Campbell addressed the spectators as well as while he engaged in prayer and during the short time that Heaman spoke, Gautier was engaged with the Clergyman who attended him in acts of devotion according to the forms of their religion, in which he seemed very earnest and which continued a short time after Dr. Campbell had concluded his prayer.

The devotional exercises over, which were conducted throughout with much fervour and solemnity, the unfortunate men shook hands with the Magistrates and Clergymen around them, and mounted the fatal drop. While there, Heaman prayed aloud most fervently for some time. Heaman's last words were—"Lord Jesus receive my soul," upon pronouncing which he shook hands with Gautier and then dropped the signal, when they were launched into Eternity.

The behaviour of both the criminals was decent, resigned and penitent. They were dressed in coloured clothes, Heaman in a brown jacket and white trousers and Gautier in a brown coat. The procession moved at a slow rate down Leith Walk, and as Heaman passed the crowds collected at the corners of the different streets and lanes and the people at the windows, he stood up uncovered and bowed respectfully. Gautier seemed absorbed in thought and remained seated, taking little or no notice of anything around him. He appeared weak, and for some time was supported by a man on the platform.

The crowd of spectators was immense, particularly on the Sands, being little short of from 40–50,000 but, owing to the excellent manner in which everything was arranged, not the slightest accident happened.

During the execution the great bell of South Leith Church tolled. After the unfortunate men were cut down their bodies were conveyed under an escort of Dragoons to Dr. Monro's class-room for dissection pursuant to their sentence.

Some additional particulars concerning the Last of the Pirates is furnished by the *Scotts Magazine* for February, 1822. "Gautier was twenty-four years of age, a Frenchman and a Roman Catholic. He had a wife living somewhere in Spain. Heaman was about thirty-six years old; he was born in Carlscrona in Sweden, but came to England when a young boy, and had been employed from his early years in the seafaring line. During the last war he had been many years in a French prison at Longwy, where he married a woman, who, with three or four children, now reside in Sunderland.

"It is forty years since a similar execution took place on Leith Sands, namely, that of Wilson Potts, on the 13th February, 1782. Potts was captain of the *Dreadnought* privateer of Newcastle, and was convicted before the Admiralty Court of having plundered the *White Swan*, of Copenhagen, of four bags of dollars. He was recommended to mercy by a majority of the jury, because it was in proof that he had committed the crime while in a state of intoxication, and had, on coming to his senses, taken the first opportunity of returning the money to its owners." Captain Potts' lines were much harder than those of Mate Heaman.

.   .   .   .   .   .

On perusing this tale of the ill-fated *Jane's* last voyage, one is struck by the youthfulness of the honest hands. Camelier, the cabin boy, was but 18; Strachan and Smith, 19; Dhura, 24. Even Gautier, the diabolic cook, was only 23 or 24; and Heaman, the bloody-minded mate, 35 or 36. The latter, being wellnigh double the age of the others, was obviously throughout the evil genius of the crew.

These dim and dusty figures are "plain" indeed when compared with the lively "coloured" company of a more famous schooner, the *Hispaniola*. Yet I think that Long John Silver would have approved the cook, with his playful phrase: "You go in the sea"; and that Israel Hands would have perceived in the murderous mate a choice and kindred spirit.

THE BOY FOOTPADS;

Or, More Murder in Murrayfield

The lawyers are bitter enemies to those in our way. They do
not care that any body should get a clandestine livelihood
but themselves.   *The Beggar's Opera.*

IN LOOKING through a volume of the old *Scots Magazine*—that
admirable journal, which cries aloud for a general index—one
cannot fail to light upon something that interests, amuses, or
instructs. Every subject in the heavens above and in the earth
beneath and in the waters under the earth (from balloons to
diving-bells) finds a place in its brave pages. Art, literature, and
law; historical affairs and domestic intelligence; politics and
poetry; characters, anecdotes, and correspondence; matters topi-
cal and topographical; births, marriages, and deaths; and beyond
all, in my esteem, reports of criminal trials. Such a heading as
"Horrid Murders" lightens agreeably the heaviness of articles
like "Account of Marble Quarries in the North of Scotland,"
or "General View of the Principles of Pantomime"; and from
the mine of solid information provided, one recovers, with patience, an occasional gem.

For example, in the book now before me (being volume 75,
for the year 1813), my expert eye encounters (at page 475)
this attaching notice:

ATROCIOUS MURDER

On the 12th of May, between nine and ten o'clock in the
evening, Mr. William Muirhead, smith in Calton, Edinburgh,
was robbed and murdered on the road from Corstorphine to
Edinburgh, a little to the westward of Coltbridge. Next day,
John M'Donald was apprehended on suspicion of committing
this horrid crime, and on the 15th, James W. Black was also
apprehended for the same offence. They were soon afterwards

indicted, and on the 7th of June stood trial before the High Court of Justiciary, the particulars of which are given in a preceding part of this number.—Page 429.

And sure enough, on turning up the page referred to, I find there, and in the nine succeeding pages, an adequate report of that interesting trial.[1] The case, though by no means a cause *célèbre*, is worth recalling for divers reasons: it adds a new item to my collection of Edinburgh crimes, and it is remarkable for the precocious depravity of the youthful perpetrators, who, in the words of the presiding Judge, "after making systematic preparation in providing themselves with deadly weapons, coolly and deliberately sally forth to the public highway, with the diabolical and premeditated purpose, not only of robbing of their property, but of embruing their hands in the blood of, their unoffending fellow-citizens, if they should give them even the slightest 'salute'," conduct which his Lordship well described as exhibiting "a degree of savage barbarity altogether unparalleled in the annals of the world, that was indeed sufficient to make us ashamed of human nature itself, if it did not in fact appear more characteristic of demons than of men." But then the Lord Justice-Clerk spoke according to the dim lights of his day, and could have no conception of the immense progress in brutality to be achieved by professors of modern Nazi doctrines and practice, as applied to the gentle arts of spoliation and murder.

Additional interest attaches to the case from the fact that, as recorded in the obituary notice of the murderers, "the circumstances attending their execution were quite unprecedented in this part of the kingdom": *they were hanged upon the very spot where the deed was done.*

I

On Monday, 7th June, 1813, before the High Court of Justiciary at Edinburgh, took place the trial of John M'Donald,

[1] The proceedings are also reported in the *Edinburgh Advertiser* of 8th June, and in the *Edinburgh Evening Courant* of 10th June, 1813.

painter, and James Williamson Black, slater, for murder and robbery. The Lord Justice-Clerk (Boyle) presided, the other Judges being Lords Meadowbank, Gillies, Succoth, and Pitmilly.[1] The Lord Advocate (Archibald Colquhoun), assisted by H. Clephane, advocate, appeared for the Crown; James Simpson and Samuel M'Cormick, advocates, for M'Donald; and John Tawes and Andrew Gillies for Black. The charges against the pannels, as set forth in the indictment, to which both pleaded Not Guilty, were, briefly, that on the evening of Wednesday, 12th May, on the road leading westward from Coltbridge to the village of Corstorphine, they attacked William Muirhead, blacksmith, residing in the Calton, Edinburgh, and discharged at him a pistol loaded with slugs, one or more of which passed through his heart and occasioned his death; after which they robbed him of his silver watch. "The trial excited great interest," says the Edinburgh Advertiser. "The Court was crowded in every part, and many persons could not get access. M'Donald was 19 or 20 years of age, and Black only 18. Both were slenderly made, and very youthful in their appearance." No objection being made to the relevancy of the indictment, the prosecutor adduced his proof.

The first witness was William Muirhead, blacksmith, son of the deceased, who, being sworn, deponed that he resided in his father's family. On 12th May last there was a meeting in the Calton of the Trade Corporation, to which his father belonged, but which his father said he did not mean to attend, as he meant to take a walk in the country. He accordingly left the house between the hours of six and seven in the evening. Witness waited up for him till midnight, when he became uneasy, "thinking that some persons whom he knew might have persuaded him to go to another meeting," and then went out to seek him, "leaving his sister in bed, and a candle burning." When he returned he was told that two gentlemen had called, who wanted to see him, and "left word that somebody wished to impose on his father." He immediately went out again to seek his brother-in-law, James Brown, whom he met about the

[1] Books of Adjournal, Justiciary Office.

middle of Leith Wynd, and who told him that his father was murdered. They went together to the Guard-house, where they saw the body of the deceased. Witness then went home to inform his sister of what had happened, "and got a table-cloth to cover him." His father was 73 years of age. The body had a wound on the left breast and was "very bloody." Deceased had a silver watch, which the deponent saw him wearing when he left the house that evening. It had appended to it a steel chain and a brass seal, which witness now identified as produced.

James Brown, last-maker, a son-in-law of the deceased, stated that he and Mr. Muirhead were members of the same Corporation. On 12th May he attended a meeting thereof; deceased was not present. Between twelve and one o'clock he was called out of the room by Bailie Johnston and Captain Brown of the City Police, who told him that his father-in-law had not come home. Witness said he might have gone to another meeting, and went out to seek him; but when half-way down the Calton Hill they informed him that the old man was murdered and that his body was then in the Guard-house. They went there, and saw the body "quite dead." It had a large wound in the breast, measuring four inches by two and a half. Going home, he met young Muirhead in Leith Wynd, who begged for God's sake to tell him the worst, as he was prepared for it. Witness told him his father was "actually killed." They watched the body in the Guard-house all next day, "to prevent improper visitors being admitted." The body was inspected there by surgeons on Thursday, and again on Saturday in the deceased's own house. On the second occasion, witness saw three balls taken out of the body, one quite flat, which one of the surgeons wrapped in a piece of paper and put in his pocket.

Robert Young, writer, stated that on 12th May he travelled from Glasgow to Edinburgh in the *Telegraph* coach, leaving that city at four o'clock and arriving at eleven that night, "which he believes is later than usual." About half a mile on the west side of Coltbridge he saw a man lying face-downward on the road. The coach was stopped; witness got out, and on examining the body found a large wound on the left breast, with a great deal of blood on the footpath below where the man was lying. On the waistcoat being opened, "the wound appeared so large that a man could have put his three fingers into it." The pockets of the deceased were examined by the guard, but neither watch nor money was found in them; only two keys, which were replaced. It was then about ten o'clock, and bright moonlight. Leaving the body where it lay, the coach proceeded to Coltbridge, where the alarm was given.

Adam M'Coul, servant to Mr. Lindsay, Coltbridge, stated that he was desired by his master to take a cart and bring in the body of a man, who was said to have been found west of the road to Ravelston, a quarter of a mile from Coltbridge. He did so, and conveyed the body to the West Port police office, whence he was desired by Captain Brown to carry it to the City Guard, which he did, when it was laid up on a kind of board or bench in the Guard-house. Witness saw the wound, which was very large. The body was put into the cart about a quarter past ten.

Dr. Farquharson, physician in Edinburgh, stated that on 13th May he was called in to inspect the body of the deceased. It lay in the back room of the Guard-house, which was dark, and from the amount of coagulated blood covering the wound, he could only examine it generally. He put his hand into the wound, which was very large; and on pressing forward one of his fingers he felt a hole through the heart, which he thought sufficient to have caused death. On the 15th witness made a further examination, together with Mr. Andrew Inglis, surgeon, in the deceased's own house. The wound was in the left breast, of a triangular shape, about four inches and a half long on the one side, three and a half on the other, and two and a half at the base. Three bullets were taken out of the body, two complete and one flattened and shattered; these were sealed up and delivered to the Sheriff, with a report of the post-mortem, which witness now read. "The heart was holed through, as also the left lobe of the lungs." He identified the bullets as shewn to him. Andrew Inglis, surgeon, examined, corroborated, and concurred in the medical report.

Helen Binny stated that she lived with her mother, who kept an alehouse at Coltbridge. In the beginning of May two lads came to the house one evening between six and seven, and called for a bottle of porter. One of them—Black—she had seen before and now identified. She shewed them into a room, where they sat an hour over their porter—which witness thought suspicious; and on looking through a hole in the door "she saw Black tying something tight round his middle." He thrust some object into his left breast and pulled his coat down on it. "The other lad [M'Donald] who was leaning on the table looked at him and winked." They then went out, after calling for a gill of whisky, the big one (M'Donald) paying the reckoning, 11d. They walked westward out of her sight. Some time later she went down to the bridge over the Water of Leith, where, between nine and ten, she heard two pistol shots. She was standing on the bridge and her brother was fishing below when she heard the reports: "there was no time between them." The lads had left the house between nine and ten. The Glasgow coach came up about half an hour after she heard the shots; an alarm was given and a cart sent to bring in the body. Witness was positive as to Black, having known him for five years, but could not swear to M'Donald.

John Binny, brother of Helen, corroborated her as to the coming of the two lads and their consumption of liquor. He knew Black by sight, but had never seen the other and could not swear that M'Donald was that person. While they were refreshing themselves in the sitting-room, witness "went out to the fishing in the water, close by Coltbridge." There he remained, with what success is not recorded, until a quarter to ten. While he was fishing he heard two shots fired, "first one crack and then another, just as hard as they could fire them." The sound came from the westward and seemed at no great distance. It would then be about half-past nine. Witness had gone to bed when the Glasgow coach came in with the news that a man had been murdered. He arose, dressed, and went to Mr. Lindsay's to get a cart sent to fetch the body. Having done so, he went in to Edinburgh and informed the police of what had happened, giving them a description of the persons who had been at his mother's house that day. He saw the body brought in at the West Port and deposited in the Guard-house.

Margaret Smith, tenant-in Coltbridge, stated that on Wednesday, 12th May, two lads came to her house between six and seven, and asked whether she sold spirits. She replied that she did not, "but they would find them next door, over the bridge." They went eastwards. Witness lived westward of the bridge. She identified the prisoners as the lads in question. At ten minutes after eight they came back and asked what o'clock it was; her son, a little boy, looked and told them. They continued to lounge about for some time and at nine o'clock they went away west; the bigger (M'Donald) first, the shorter one waited a little and then went after him. Witness said, loud enough to be heard by them, "it was a pity they were not followed, as she thought they had some bad intentions." They walked west very hard. When the Glasgow coach came past half an hour later, she told the guard she suspected two young men, "one of whom had a halt."

Alexander Muirhead, tenant in Corstorphine, stated that as he went into Edinburgh that evening he met and passed on the road two lads, going westwards. On his return from town about half-past eight he met the same two lads, coming eastwards, "a little on this side of the road which leads to Ravelston" (now named Ellersly Road), and was jostled by them, but passed on his way and went straight home. It would be about half-past nine when he passed the foot of the Ravelston road, and there was then no dead body lying thereon. As he was entering his own house in Corstorphine the *Telegraph* coach went by. A little below the Ravelston road and "Belmont" he met an old man named Muirhead, coming towards Edinburgh, whom he knew as a smith in the Calton. He had a staff in his hand and was quite sober; witness stopped and spoke to him, asking whether he was not afraid to go into Edinburgh alone. The old man answered No; it was a fine night and he had no fear, upon which they parted and went their several ways. This was some 200 yards distant from the place where he had met the lads going east. Witness heard no shots fired; the wind was in the west.

William Inglis, butcher in Corstorphine, stated that going home that night about eight or nine he met the two lads near Ravelston "entry" (Ellersly Road). A good many people were on the road at the time. Witness recognized one of them and called: "Hallo, Black, is that you?" and went on. He did not see them again.

George Dechmont, one of the sheriff officers for the county, stated that he was present at the examination of the prisoners before the Sheriff. He afterwards went with another officer, John Auld, and the accused M'Donald in a coach to a place on the Queensferry road, to which the prisoner directed them. "They went by Blackhall, and turned up the road leading to Ravelston quarry.[1] They came to a crooked tree, and Auld and the coachman went to a wheaten field, while he remained with M'Donald in the coach, and searched the ridges, where they were informed by the prisoner the pistols were hid; and in one of the ridges, to which they were directed by the prisoner, they found the pistols stuck in the ground. Auld gave the pistols to the witness; M'Donald marked them with a knife by his desire; and witness delivered them to the Sheriff." He now identified the weapons as produced. John Auld, his fellow-officer, examined, corroborated.

John Kyle, clerk to John Muir, late hardware merchant, in the Royal Exchange, being called, was objected to by counsel for the defence, as not being clerk to Mr. Muir at present; but he stating that he had only ended his engagement on Saturday last, and was a clerk at the time the indictment was served, the objection was not persisted in. Witness stated that on Monday the 3rd, or Tuesday the 4th of May, a young man came into the shop when witness was in the back-shop, and going into the fore-shop he found the shop-boy, or apprentice, shewing the

---

[1] Long a favourite of mine; but I have failed to find either the crooked tree or the wheat-field, which, in the course of time and nature, have long since vanished. The house of "Belmont" still survives above the first bend of Ellersly Road.

customer pistols. Witness said the price was 22s. the pair; the young man said he could only give 16s. This being refused, he offered 17s., then 20s., both of which being also refused and he saying he could not give more, witness agreed to let him have them for 21s. The lad then offered 19s. Witness stuck out for 20s., whereupon he went to the door and returned with another lad, and got the two pistols for 20s. Witness believed that the prisoners were the same lads, but would not swear to them—"is pretty certain they are the same, but he could not positively say"—a mental attitude with which those acquainted with the ways of witnesses are only too familiar. The pistols now shewn to him were similar to those he sold, but witness would not swear to them, the shop mark having been rubbed off; "but he thinks them the same."

Before this witness left the box, the Lord Justice-Clerk admonished him that if in future he should deal in such dangerous weapons, he ought to be extremely careful how he sold them, especially to persons of the appearance of the prisoners, as, however the event of this trial might turn out, it must be a matter of serious regret to him to think that he may possibly have furnished weapons from which consequences similar to those under trial might have ensued.

John Bruce, apprentice to David Tait, hardware merchant, being called, counsel for the pannels objected to his evidence, as he was wrongly designed apprentice to Mr. Tait, and not to Mr. Muir, he (counsel) having then in his hand an indenture, binding witness to Mr. Muir, upon which there was no transfer of service. Mr. Tait, being called, deponed that Bruce was not his apprentice; that he had been merely "left" in the shop by Mr. Muir; and that witness considered him at liberty to leave whenever he chose. He paid him his weekly wages, and told Mr. Muir he had no intention of keeping him, as he expected a person from London. Bruce was then examined. He stated his age as 16, and said that he was Mr. Muir's apprentice and not Mr. Tait's; he was only with Mr. Tait for a while, till his nephew came from London. On being asked whether he understood that the time he served with Mr. Tait was to be consid-

ered in his indentures with Mr. Muir, witness said he thought
so, if Mr. Muir agreed. He had described himself as apprentice
with Mr. Tait, but to Mr. Muir.

Counsel on both sides having been heard upon this nice
point, the Lord Justice-Clerk expressed regret that so delicate
a question had at present been urged, as it involved a point of
law of great importance. "The plurality of the Judges thought
the designation sufficient, as it enabled the pannels easily to
find out the witness by inquiring at Mr. Tait's. On the other
hand, it was agreed that the law was: that where a witness was
so designated as even possibly to occasion a mistake, he was im-
properly designated. A witness was not to be sought after by a
chain of inquiry, but cited by direct, positive information; and
the objection in the present case ought to be sustained." The
objection being by a majority of the Court repelled, the witness
was examined; but as he proved unable to identify either the
pannels or the pistols, there had been much ado about nothing:
the mountain had not even produced a mouse.

John Ormiston, solicitor-at-law, stated that on the morning
of 15th May he was consulted by Mrs. Watterson, residing in
the Cowgate. She asked his advice how to get rid of certain
police officers, who had applied for a warrant to search her
house and that of her son-in-law, Robert Graham, for the purpose of recovering a watch. Witness advised her to procure the
watch and bring it to him, which she did. Witness handed
the watch to the Procurator-Fiscal, and now identified it as
produced.

Mrs. Jean Watterson stated that some police officers came to
her house to search for a watch, on which she went to Mr.
Ormiston to ask his advice. "As her man was coming home, she
wanted the police officers sent away." As advised by Mr. Ormiston she went to her son-in-law, who, she understood, had given
stockings and shoes in exchange for a watch; she got it, and
gave it to Mr. Ormiston "not half an hour after." It was a silver
watch like that now shewn to her.

Robert Graham, shoemaker in the Cowgate, shewn a watch,
identified it as that referred to. On Thursday evening, 13th

May, two lads, whom he now recognized as the prisoners at the bar, came to his house and asked him if he could mend a shoe. Witness said he could do so, "always when at home, but in summer he travelled the country, selling goods, and did not mend shoes." They then asked what kind of goods he sold, and he said stockings. He offered a pair at 2s. 6d., which M'Donald agreed to take; also a pair of shoes, which, as they fitted him, that young gentleman also took. But, remarking that he had not enough money on him to pay for them, he said he would leave his watch as a pledge, and would return in half an hour with the cash. He and his companion accordingly left, taking the goods with them; but witness saw them no more until shewn them in the Police Office. The watch was No. 67; he did not notice the maker's name. It had no chain or seal. Witness was certain it was the very watch produced in Court. On going to Leith he took the watch with him in hope of meeting the lads. Returning, he met his mother-in-law coming to seek him; she told him the police had been "after" the watch. He gave it to her, and bade her for God's sake give it up directly.

Andrew Inglis, serjeant-major of the Edinburgh City Police, stated that in the beginning of May a person came to the office with information that a man had been murdered. At two o'clock in the morning Captain Brown desired him to go out to the place where the murder was said to have been committed, and try to find any weapons, such as pistols, etc., with which the crime might have been perpetrated. A quarter of a mile past Coltbridge witness saw a great quantity of blood on the road, on examining which he noticed something glittering. He took it up and found it was part of a steel chain; he also found a seal and a button, all of which he now identified. Three men came up, one of whom was the deceased's son-in-law, who recognized the chain and seal. Witness made inquiries at Corstorphine and Coltbridge regarding any suspicious persons seen in the vicinity. So soon as he heard of two lads, of whom one had a lame leg, thick lips, and black hair, he knew immediately that it was the prisoner Black, whom witness had often seen at the police office—in what capacity is not recorded. Next day he accompanied Captain Brown to the spot, and narrowly examined the adjacent wall to see whether it bore any marks of bullets, but could find none. Witness could easily have known shotmarks, having been over 24 years in the army.

David Arthur, edge-tool maker, son-in-law to the deceased, identified the watch, which the old man had got from Mr. Gibson, Black Bull Inn, Calton. He also identified the chain. John Gibson, vintner, stated that at the end of last harvest he and the deceased exchanged watches. The one now shewn him was that which he gave to Mr. Muirhead; witness saw it in his possession the day before he was murdered. William Lockhart, watchmaker, Canongate, stated that he cleaned deceased's watch on 26th December, 1812. He identified the watch, chain, and seal.

Robert Adam, clerk to Mr. Edmonstone, hardware merchant, West Bow, stated that he knew the prisoner M'Donald as an occasional customer. He bought shot from witness once or twice. The last time he did so was in the beginning of the week of the murder, when he asked for the shot he had got formerly—"swan or Bristol large shot." He made no mention of his purpose, nor did witness ask him. Shewn a paper containing shot brought from the Sheriff-Clerk's office, witness said it was the same kind as supplied by him to M'Donald. The balls extracted from the body were of the same size. "Swan shot is marked with 2 B's, all of the large shot."

William Rae, Sheriff-Depute of the county, and James Wilson, Sheriff-Clerk-Depute, proved the several declarations of the prisoners, as freely emitted by them when in their sober senses. The pannels' declarations were then read. These documents are sufficiently remarkable to be given at length. It is manifest that the young declarants were born before their time, and were equally unfortunate in their age and country. In those dark days not only were their brilliant gifts wholly unappreciated by their contemporaries, but the authorities rewarded their achievement with a gibbet. Had they been privileged to be subjects of some enlightened Totalitarian State, how different would be their lot! Their precocious depravity and ruthless savagery would win for them an honoured place among the choicest spirits of that happy land, and their memorial would be writ for all time in the bright blood of their victims.

In his first declaration, emitted on 14th May, M'Donald denied all knowledge of the murder and robbery. He admitted that he and Black were at Coltbridge on the afternoon of that day, and had a drink at a house there; but he maintained that they returned to town by eight o'clock. In a second declaration of the 15th he stated that his former declaration was "erroneous," and that he now wished to tell the truth. Warned by the Sheriff to be careful what he said, as that functionary could not assure him of safety, "he persevered notwithstanding in his resolution to tell the truth." Which, it appeared, was this. He and Black went out that evening with the determined purpose of robbing some person. After they had waited for a time the deceased was seen approaching from the westward. Black asked him "what was the clock," and the old man having held out his watch for them to see, Black made a snatch at it and broke off the chain. "Immediately thereafter Black fired his pistol, by which Mr. Muirhead was brought to the ground. Then he, M'Donald, also fired his pistol, but in such a manner as to do no damage. Thereafter Black rifled the body, and they made the best of their way up the road which leads to Ravelston [Ellersly Road], and hid the pistols at the end of a ridge in a wheat-field."

Black also made two declarations. On 17th May he, like M'Donald, denied all knowledge of the crimes; but next day, being duly warned, he expressed a desire to make a clean breast of the whole facts. On the Monday before the deed was done M'Donald and he went out on the Musselburgh road with intent to commit a robbery. They found no opportunity of doing so, and accordingly spent the night in Musselburgh. Next day they visited Haddington, and returning from that town in the evening, met a gentleman on horseback, whom they deemed a suitable subject for their purpose. So M'Donald attempted to seize his bridle; but the gentleman, having clapped spurs to his horse, got past him, M'Donald firing his pistol after him without effect. On the day of the murder they went out on the Coltbridge road on a robbing expedition, "M'Donald alledging it was a good opportunity, being the market-day; and having proposed the Coltbridge road on account of the easy escape that could be made up the road leading to Ravelston. After waiting some time, a person carrying a bundle [the witness Alexander Muirhead] was seen coming from the westward, and him they determined to attack"; but most fortunately for him he got past, after having been jostled off the footpath. It was thereupon resolved to attack the first person who came up, and to shoot him if the smallest resistance were made. Presently the old man Muirhead approached, and the murder and robbery were effected. But Black's version of the deed differed notably from that of his associate. He averred that *M'Donald* made the snatch at the watch, and shot the old man, "having first threatened to blow his brains out," to which the venerable victim mildly made answer: "Oh no, my man, you'll surely no' do that." Whereupon the other fired his pistol and shot him dead upon the spot.

I think there can be little doubt that Black's is the true version of the tragedy, for M'Donald was manifestly throughout the leading spirit and the greater villain. It is characteristic that he should seek to lay the blame of the crime on his confederate's shoulders.

The Crown case was here closed, and no evidence was led for the defence. The speeches of counsel and the charge of the learned Judge are not reported; but we read: "The jury were addressed by the Lord Advocate for the Crown, and by James Simpson, Esq., for M'Donald, and John Tawse, Esq., for Black; after which the Lord Justice-Clerk summed up the evidence, when the jury were inclosed, and desired to return their verdict on Tuesday, at two o'clock."

Accordingly on that day, 8th June, the jury returned their verdict, "all in one voice finding the pannels Guilty." The Judges then delivered "at considerable length" their several opinions regarding the enormity of the pannels' guilt, and ex-

pressed their astonishment that in a country so long distinguished for knowledge and virtuous conduct so many instances
of youthful depravity had lately occurred, and their fear of
being obliged to revert to "those more striking and awful pun-
ishments which our law enjoins."

The Lord Justice-Clerk, in passing sentence, observed that he
entirely concurred in what had been so properly and eloquently
said by the Judges who preceded him. Addressing the pannels
his Lordship, having reviewed the circumstances of the crimes
charged and complimented the jury on their verdict—"the
justice of which was most manifest not only to the Court, but
to every person who heard the evidence," remarked that after
what had been said as to the heinousness of the crimes, he did
not propose to add more than to declare that of all the cases
within his personal experience, or of which he had either
heard or read, that of the pannels' seemed the one of the most
marked atrocity and attended with the least palliation. That
persons of the early years of the pannels should, as clearly appeared in evidence and from their own declarations, after making systematic preparation in providing themselves with deadly
weapons, coolly and deliberately sally forth to the public highway, with the diabolical and premeditated purpose, not only
of robbing of their property, but of embruing their hands in
the blood of, their unoffending fellow-citizens if they should
give them even the slightest "salute," was a degree of savage
barbarity altogether unparalleled in the annals of the world.
Such conduct was indeed sufficient to make us ashamed of
human nature itself, if it did not in fact appear more characteristic of demons than of men. The case had happily demon-
strated the excellence of that system of police which the inhabitants of the city now possessed. Every one of similar
habits with the pannels must now be convinced that his person is marked, that the eyes of the officers of justice are upon
him, and that however secretly and systematically crimes may
be committed, their punishment will be equally certain and
immediate. His Lordship further observed that, looking to the
unprecedented magnitude of the pannels' guilt, he had

strongly participated in the sentiments expressed by Lord
Meadowbank, and had once thought it was necessary that the
mode of punishment should be no less signal and exemplary,
by their Lordships ordaining them to be hung in chains, that
their carcases and bones might wither in the winds of heaven,
and afford a lasting example to their associates of the just vengeance of the law. But on further reflection he had become
disposed to forgo this procedure, from a consideration of the
uneasiness it must occasion to the innocent neighbourhood,
but from no regard to the feelings of the relatives of the pannels, who seem to have paid so little attention to their conduct.
It was, however, necessary that their punishment should take
place in no ordinary manner, and that they should expiate their
crimes as near as possible to the spot where the blood of that
old and unoffending man, so barbarously murdered, was crying out against them from the ground; and that their bodies
should afterwards be publicly anatomized, and their skeletons
preserved to future ages as monuments of youthful depravity.

His Lordship, tempering justice with mercy, then gave the
young scoundrels much good and godly counsel as to the
means whereby they might escape yet greater penalties in
another world. He had noticed, he observed, with the utmost
horror and regret, the callous and hardened demeanour which
M'Donald had exhibited from the first moment of the trial;
and pointed out that unless he and his associate repented of
their crimes, a punishment ten thousand times more severe
than that now to be awarded would infallibly be pronounced
against them. His Lordship then sentenced both to be executed at, or as near as possible to, the place where the murder
was committed, upon Wednesday, 14th July next, and thereafter their bodies to be publicly dissected and anatomized. The
prisoners were then removed and the Court rose.

"We have never," says the *Edinburgh Evening Courant* in
concluding its account of the case, "witnessed anything so
shocking as the conduct of M'Donald during the whole course
of the trial. He behaved with the utmost apathy, and more
than once interrupted both the witnesses and counsel. He re-

ceived the dreadful sentence of the law with an indifference which excited equal horror and disgust. During the address of the Lord Justice-Clerk he frequently interrupted his Lordship in the most indecent manner; and on the conclusion of the sentence, when his Lordship wished Almighty God to have mercy upon his soul, he loudly replied: 'He will have none upon yours!' Black conducted himself with firmness and resignation."

II

The last public appearance of our young ruffians had a good Press.[1] "The execution of these unfortunate young men," remarks the Scots Magazine, "took place on Wednesday, the 14th of July, pursuant to their sentence by the High Court of Justiciary, for the murder and robbery of Mr. William Muirhead, smith in Calton, on the 12th of May last; and as the circumstances attending their execution were quite unprecedented in this part of the kingdom,[2] the following correct account of the particulars seems worthy of insertion."

The wanton cruelty of the crime, the youthfulness and determination of the criminals, the truculent behaviour of M'Donald at the bar, and the poetic justice of the penalty being paid on the very spot where the deed was done, all appealed largely to the popular imagination and stimulated interest in the final act of the tragedy.

At half-past eleven o'clock on the fatal morning the cart in which the condemned lads were to be conveyed to the place of expiation was brought from the College Yard by the City Guard to the door of the Tolbooth, or prison of Edinburgh, wherein they were confined. A Lieutenant and half a troop of the 7th Dragoon Guards, with 200 men from the Castle garrison, under the command of a Field Officer, took up their positions in the Lawnmarket around the prison. At half-past twelve the four Bailies of the city, preceded by the town officers

[1] Edinburgh Evening Courant, 15th July, 1813; Edinburgh Advertiser, 16th July; and Scots Magazine for that month, pp. 522–524.

[2] NOTE.—Execution at the place of the crime.

and accompanied by their proper attendants, proceeded from the Council Chamber to the Tolbooth. The prisoners were brought out and placed in the cart, and the procession moved on in the following order:

A body of the High Constables.
The city officers, with their halberts.
The Magistrates in their robes, with their staves
of office.
The Rev. Professor Ritchie, Mr. Porteous, chaplain
of the jail, and Mr. Badenoch, a Roman Catholic
clergyman, who attended M'Donald.

THE CART

with the two criminals, who were drawn with their
backs to the horse and the executioner
fronting them.

Another body of the High Constables followed, the whole being escorted by detachments of the 7th Dragoon Guards, of the Norfolk and Northampton militia, and a party of the police.

In this manner the procession marched through the Lawnmarket, along Bank Street, down the Mound, and along Princes Street. At the West End they were met by William Rae, Esq., Sheriff-Depute of the county, and Harry Davidson, Esq., one of his substitutes, with his proper officers on horseback, accompanied by a troop of the Mid-Lothian yeomanry cavalry. Here the Sheriff received the prisoners from the Magistrates, who, with the constables, the dragoons, and the guard from the Castle, returned to the city. The clergymen and other attendants having entered the carriages provided for them, the procession moved on by the Corstorphine road, till it arrived at the place "where the late Mr. Muirhead was found lying, a little more than a quarter of a mile from Coltbridge, and nearly 30 yards to the west of the road which leads to Ravelston."

A gibbet had been erected on the highway, and was so constructed that the feet of the criminals would be suspended above the very spot where they committed the crime. They were then loosed from the cart and brought upon the scaffold; a psalm was sung, and suitable prayers were offered by the Revs. Ritchie and Porteous. Mr. Badenoch, the Roman Catholic priest, also prayed and exhorted M'Donald, "who was of that persuasion."

At twenty minutes to three o'clock the criminals took their stand upon the drop. There for some more minutes "they continued to implore the Divine pardon, Black with a firm voice, M'Donald in one less audible. At last Black, turning round, asked M'Donald if he was ready, and on obtaining an answer in the affirmative (not, however, till the question had been thrice repeated), he grasped him by the hand and kissed him, and exclaiming, 'Lord Jesus Christ have mercy on our souls!' he dropped the signal and they were launched into eternity. Black's body was a good deal convulsed; M'Donald scarcely moved."

After hanging the usual time, the bodies were cut down and put into the cart, and "with the view of impressing the spectators with more awe," they were exposed without any covering, and so conveyed to the College for dissection, in terms of the sentence. The principals, we read, were decently dressed and behaved with decorum and firmness, particularly Black.

The concourse of spectators during the procession was immense, every viewpoint being crowded with people. Great numbers attended the place of execution, "which was on the south edge of a very large pasture inclosure." Unfortunately the weather, as so often happens at outdoor functions in Edinburgh, did its best to spoil the spectacle. "About half-past two o'clock a very heavy rain came on, and as the roads had been previously very dusty, the people who had to return were completely wet and dirty before they reached town." Still, having seen that which they went forth to see, doubtless they were well content with the show. On the other hand, it is satisfactory to know that everything was conducted with the utmost propriety and regularity; "and we are happy to add," says our authority, "that notwithstanding the immense crowd, no accident, that we have heard of, happened, excepting that of an individual who was driven over the side of the Mound by the pressure of the crowd, and received some slight bruises." The roadway of the Mound, connecting the Old Town with the New, as may be seen in contemporary prints, was then unfenced.

I cannot find that the Judge's order that the skeletons of the malefactors should be preserved for the benefit of posterity was implemented. At least, if they were in fact articulated to that end, they have now ceased to be available. The Anatomical Museum in the University of Edinburgh contains the bony structure of one Jock Howison, described as the Cramond murderer and the last criminal whose remains were judicially devoted to scientific purposes. The collection is further enriched by the possession of Mr. William Burke's bones, which rendered such good service in the late owner's partnership with Mr. William Hare, when the firm's business, conducted in the West Port, conferred upon that ill-favoured thoroughfare world-wide fame. But I saw no signs of the other young partners in blood with whom we have been concerned.

Accompanying these gentlemen in their glass show-case when last I visited them, was the skeleton of a young female, purporting to be the framework whereon once displayed, for the delight of the curious in feminine charms, the fair face and form of Mary Paterson, most attaching of Burke and Hare's many victims. But I doubt the authenticity of this relic. Her body was the property of Dr. Knox, the extra-mural lecturer on anatomy at Surgeons' Hall, who had paid the firm £8 for it, preserved it for a time in spirits, and employed divers artists to make drawings of its manifold perfections. I cannot conceive of him disposing of any portion of his so prized purchase, least of all to his hated rival, Professor Monro, the official exponent of their common art. And we know that so soon as suspicion arose of his connection with the murder factory, Knox's first care was to dismember the body of Daft Jamie, upon which he was then lecturing to his class, and to disperse the same among the students, in order to defeat identification. Would he have risked keeping so remarkable and conspicuous a "subject" as the dead beauty? No; however painful to his feelings, personal and professional, the sacrifice of such loveliness might prove, poor Mary would infallibly have to be, in nautical parlance, broken up.

Note.—EXECUTION AT THE PLACE OF THE CRIME

The hanging of our malefactors at the scene of their crime, described in the contemporary Press as "quite unprecedented in this part of the world," in itself afforded a precedent for the execution of other two highway robbers in the following year. These later rascals, who did not go the length of murder, Irishmen named Thomas Kelly and Henry O'Neil, were tried in the High Court of Justiciary at Edinburgh on 19th December, 1814. The third count in the indictment charges them "with attacking, on the 23rd of the said month of November, David Loch, carter in Biggar, then travelling along the road from Briggs of Braid, or Braid's-burn, to Edinburgh, pulling him from his horse, striking him on the head with the butt end of a pistol, to the effusion of his blood, threatening to knock out his brains if he made any resistance, and then and there robbing him of four one pound bank notes, twenty shillings in silver, a twopenny loaf of bread, and a spleuchan or leather tobacco pouch." The first and second charges relate to assaults and robberies committed respectively (1) "upon a cross road near to the farmhouse of Howmuir, in the county of Haddington on 22nd November," and (2) "upon the high road betwixt Dunbar and Haddington, near Hailes houses," on the 23rd, prior to the attack at Braid; the spoil including, in addition to money, the hats, coats, shoes, and gaiters of their victims, as well as a green cotton umbrella! An account of the case will be found in the *Scots Magazine* for January, 1815 (Vol. 77, pp. 26–31).

Although the first two outrages were much graver than the third, the scene of the last was that selected for their expiation. The Lord Justice-Clerk, in passing sentence of death, ordained the pannels to be executed on Wednesday, the 25th of January, "not at the ordinary place, but on the spot at Braid's burn where you committed the assault and robbery upon David Loch." I remember, as a small boy on Sunday walks in Morningside, having my young attention drawn to two stones, set in the middle of the causeway in the old Braid Road, as a memorial both of the crime and of the punishment. So salutary was the lesson thus early inculcated, that since that now distant day I have steadfastly abstained from the commission either of assault or highway robbery!

NICOL MUSCHET:

His Crime and Cairn

"Remember Muschet's Cairn and the moonlight night!"
. —*The Heart of Mid-Lothian.*

TO LOVERS of Jeanie Deans—and every leal Scot should wear
with Dumbiedykes and Reuben Butler the colours of that
plain but admirable heroine—the admonition is superfluous:
they are little likely to forget the circumstances of her mysterious
midnight tryst. Her knights, I believe, are nowadays recruited
mainly from the ranks of the sober middle-aged, who amid
the baggage of the years have retained some relics and re-
membrances of youth; for I am given to understand that the
intelligent young of our time either "can't read Scott" at all,
or only essay the more historical of his tales as (Heaven save
the mark!) a holiday task. This is made matter of reproach
at our rising generation, who are branded by grave seniors as
frivolous and idle-minded, incapable of judgment, their taste
debauched by picture-houses and the orgy of cheap sensation
obtainable at any bookstall. But I sometimes doubt whether in
this regard our children are more blameworthy than were their
wise begetters at the same age, because the best of Scott, which
deals with the manners of his countrymen and the traditions of
his native land, is so supremely good that it takes an experienced
palate to relish the full rich flavour. Were the boys and girls
of his own day bound by the Wizard's spell, and subject to
those enchantments wherewith their parents were enchanted?
I question it; and of a truth some things in the Waverley Novels
that seemed to me as a lad to lack interest, have long since
become a source of wonder and delight. So perfect, for example, are all Sir Walter's legal characters and scenes, one
would think only a Scotsman, and a Scots lawyer, could truly

appreciate their excellence—which says all the more for the discernment of his admirers beyond the Border.

Be that as it may, everyone who has read *The Heart of Mid-Lothian* must recall how Jeanie Deans was summoned by Effie's lover to meet him at midnight at Nicol Muschet's Cairn; how the Rev. Mr. Butler, to whom the message was committed, judged from the unhallowed nature of the spot that he had held converse with the Accuser of the Brethren; and how Jeanie, fearful yet steadfast in her duty, presented herself at the appointed place. What there befell is so dramatically told as to seize the imagination of the dullest reader. The wild figure rising from behind the heap of stones which com-memorates a deed of blood, the girl's sharp temptation to per-jure herself to save her sister's life, the weird strains of Madge Wildfire's warning lilt, echoing among the lonely crags as the pursuers steal upon their prey—these form a picture that lin-gers in the mind long after the book is closed. Sir Walter added a brief note telling who Nicol Muschet was, and why his cairn was regarded with superstitious dread. But, Oliver-like, I always wanted "more." The sinister shadow of the dead murderer stirred a curiosity which the present paper is written to satisfy, so far as may be, and in the hope that other readers have experienced a similar need. Some, perhaps, will be dis-posed to liken my labours to those of Mr. Curdle in his famous pamphlet of sixty-four pages, post octavo, on the character of the Nurse's deceased husband in *Romeo and Juliet*; yet I trust that the result, if less profound, may prove more relevant and instructive.

What we know of Nicol Muschet and his ways, apart from the judicial record of the proceedings against him and his ac-complice aftermentioned, is chiefly derived from his own pen. "The Last Speech and Confession of Nicol Muschet of Boghal, who was execute in the Grass Market of Edinburgh the sixth day of January 1721," contains, as its title-page informs, "a brief Narrative of his Life, his Declaration or Confession be-fore the Lords of Justiciary, a full Account of the Manner of the Contrivance and Perpetration of his Crime; together with Reflections upon the preceding Passages of his life, declaring his Sense of his Sin, and the Lord's gracious Way of Dealing with him during his Imprisonment. All written and signed by his own Hand. Exactly printed according to his subscribed Copy." This is stated to have been signed by the author in the Tolbooth of Edinburgh on the last day of his life, and was printed and sold the same month in a small quarto pamphlet by John Reid "in Pearson's Closs, a little above the Cross." It was later reprinted in post octavo without printer's name or date, and with the addition of certain letters written to and by Muschet, while a prisoner; and was again published in the same form, with a new title-page and no imprint, but "Entered According to Order," and described as "Being one of the greatest and most penitent Speeches ever was Published." A new edition appeared in 1818, printed at Edinburgh for Oliver & Boyd; William Turnbull, Glasgow; and Law & Whittaker, London, and containing, in addition to the former matter, a short preface. Some copies of the quarto pamphlet conclude with a Latin acrostic on Muschet, to which I shall return. There may be other editions of the Confession, but these are all that I have seen. As one not unfamiliar with Scots criminal annals I venture to affirm that they exhibit no instance of infamy more foul than the conspiracy thus unblushingly laid bare.

Of Nicol Muschet's parentage and patrimony no account, so far as I am aware, has hitherto been published, and I have thought it worth while to supply the deficiency. Such particulars as I am now able to give, being somewhat technical, are relegated to a note.* It is sufficient here to state that Nicol was the eldest son of Robert Muschet, owner of the lands of Boghall, lying within the Parish of Kincardine in Menteith, Stirlingshire, and Jean Muschet, his spouse. The date of his birth is unknown, but he was baptised at Kincardine on 13th August 1695. He had the advantage to spring, he tells us, from godly parents, "eminent where they lived for Piety." Fortunately for them it appears that Nicol, though he describes himself as "their only Darling," was not their sole issue. His

* Note I.—Nicol Muschet's Ancestry.

father died when he was a boy just entering the local grammar
school, and he succeeded to the paternal acres in 1st March,
1710. His mother, who was careful to have him trained up "in
the true Presbyterian Principles of Religion," likewise "war'd
liberally on his Literature," and was very diligent to cause him
haunt the company of the godly; whereto, says Nicol naïvely,
"so long as I was in her Sight, I adhered." With regard to
his religious duties, however, he confesses that, like Pharaoh's
chariots, he drove very heavily, and it was with considerable
relief that in the ripeness of time he left home to attend the
College at Edinburgh. He was destined for the medical profession—

> Bred up in Learning, and the Surgeon's Skill,
> Which learns the Way to cure and not to kill,

as his Elegy has it—and having completed the required cur-
riculum, in 1716 became apprenticed to Thomas Napier, surgeon in Alloa. During his student days he lodged, according
to Wilson's *Memorials of Edinburgh*, in the upper flat of the
Auld Cameronian Meeting-house, near the head of Black-
friar's Wynd, the lintel of which bore the inscription, "In the
Lord is my Hope." Despite this pious sentiment the lad began,
as he says, to play the Prodigal, and chose his company "without
ever consulting God or eyeing his Glory." At Alloa the disciple
of Galen continued his wicked courses, though doubtless there
the opportunities offered were fewer than in the capital. "Walking, talking, idle Discourse, reading Plays, Romances or the
like" on the Sabbath day, led to drunkenness, and "other vitious
Practices which the Heat of Youth, by Spate of natural Corrup-
tion, is too apt to fall into." There was little doing in the Alloa
surgery, so Nicol left his master, mostly for want of business,
partly for other reasons unspecified, and returned to his
mother's house, resolving henceforth to live the life of a
country gentleman; but after a few weeks at home his professional zeal was, he avers, rekindled by notice of a dissection at
Edinburgh, and in August 1719 forsaking rural joys he hastened to the city.

On the night after his arrival, while walking on the Castle Hill, he saw at the door of one Adam Hall's house a maid with whom, in his student days, he had some acquaintance. The damsel invited him to refreshment, and over a chopin of ale they fell to discussing old times. Presently they were joined by Margaret Hall, the daughter of the house, whom Nicol had never seen before, and the maid withdrew, leaving her mistress to do the honours. Of Muschet's courting of the hapless Margaret we have only his version, and the allegations he makes against her character, designed to mitigate his own guilt, are countered by the fact that throughout she retained the friendship of her mother-in-law, a good woman. His case is that the girl, as the phrase goes, set her cap at him; yet he asserts that at this their first meeting "she told him a great many things, particularly her Amours with one Andrew Henderson," and conducted herself with a freedom which "wearied" even the brisk young surgeon. On learning that he had not yet found lodgings, she recommended him to the house of John Murray in Anchor Close, whose wife was her friend, promising to call on him there when he was settled. "And truly," says the ungallant laird, "to my sad and lamentable loss, she made me too many Visites." She was, he admits, accompanied on these occasions by another young lady, to whose reputation, however, he is no kinder. So importunate indeed, as he alleges, became the damsels' attentions that he was ashamed and shunned their company. Curiously enough, his next step was to make formal application to Adam Hall for his daughter's hand, and the father, though holding Margaret "not yet fully educate for Marriage," allowed the intimacy to continue.

Muschet was now employed in the shop of Mr. Gibb, surgeon, a position in those days by no means derogatory to his lairdship; and among his boon companions was Archibald Ure, goldsmith in Edinburgh, who hailed from his part of the country. This man, actuated, according to Nicol, by motives of self-interest, pressed him to marry, and generously offered to supply the ring, and anything else his shop could afford, either with or without money. Muschet reluctantly agreed, and on the night of Saturday, 5th September, he and Margaret Hall were made man and wife in the house of John Galloway, tailor in Peebles Wynd, by the Rev. Robert Bowers, an Episcopalian curate, who lodged at the wynd-head, "the Deceast's Father not a little rejoicing, and Archibald Ure and some others being present." In surveying at a later date the course of his career, Nicol severely blames himself for marrying upon so small acquaintance—he had known his bride less than three weeks—a person of whose piety and virtue he had so few proofs. "And how do I regrate my disorderly Method of proceeding in it," he writes, "contrary to the Order and Decency which Christ has appointed in his Church, and the good Laws of Men have established, and my celebrating it with such a Man and in such a Manner as corroborated and approved of the sinful Superstitions of the Church of England, contrary to my Baptismal and National Vows and, I must acknowledge, to the Light of my Conscience also." It is pleasant to note that despite his manifold delinquencies Muschet retained to the last such sound Presbyterian principles. Further, he takes occasion to protest against the wicked calumny, then current, that the sudden ceremony was insisted on by Adam Hall in reparation of his daughter's honour—a much more likely story than that of the bridegroom.

After the marriage the young couple lived for a time with the bride's father on the Castle Hill, but by the following November Nicol, having decided to desert his wife, left her, intending to "improve himself abroad" as a surgeon. He had already quarrelled with the accommodating goldsmith over payment of certain articles of jewellery supplied to his wife— "For I very well understood, tho' too late, his Design in serving me by pretending such Friendship was only for Lucre's sake"—and was busy putting his affairs in order with a view to leaving Scotland, but the appointment of a factor to act in his absence was complicated by the laird's laudable desire to defraud his wife of her legal aliment from his estate.

While these matters were pending Muschet met a man cast by Fate to play Mephisto to our young surgeon's Faust— James Campbell, sometime of Burnbank, then ordnance store-

keeper in Edinburgh Castle, whom Nicol, after enjoying for
some months the advantage of his friendship, forcibly describes
as "the only Viceregent of the Devil." There was an old plea
between Burnbank and Muschet père which behoved to be
settled before the son could leave the country, and over this
business the couple forgathered. Burnbank was a bad lot, and
to his evil communications Nicol ascribes his own downfall;
but, as we shall see, in point of villainy there was not much
to choose between them. A noted gambler and libertine, Burnbank was well known to all the reprobates in Edinburgh by
the familiar sobriquet of "Bankie." Though retaining the
territorial designation, he had in fact sold his estate in 1712
to Colonel the Hon. James Campbell of Burnbank, third son
of Archibald, Earl of Argyll. Burnbank had been in 1714 the
unworthy cause of the Castle losing its ancient right of sanctuary. He was arrested therein for debt, but the Governor,
Colonel Stuart, jealous of the privilege of his fortress, released
the storekeeper, and expelled the messenger-at-arms. The cred-
itor thereupon petitioned the Court of Session, which decided
that the Castle had no privilege to hinder the King's letters,
and ordained the debtor to be delivered up accordingly.

Advised of the matrimonial predicament in which his new
friend had placed himself, Burnbank stoutly combated Nicol's
purpose of absconding, and undertook, for a consideration, by
means of a fraudulent action of divorce, to free him from his
distasteful bonds. Muschet thus describes the unusual nature
of the transaction:— "First having entered into Obligements
one to another, by giving him money to carry it [i.e., the con-
spiracy] on, together with a Bill for 50 Lib. Sterling which he
got for his labour, and by his giving me his Obligement, which
is at present in James Russel, Procurator's, Custody, not to
require any of the said 50 Lib. from me till he procured sufficient Evidence against her." The obligation, embodied in a
formal deed, is sufficiently curious to warrant quotation:—

Be it kend till all men by thir present letters, me, James
Campbell, Ordnance Storekeeper at Edinburgh Castle: Foras-
much as Nicol Muschett of Boghall is debtor to me in three

years rent of his lands, viz. cropt ninety-five, and precedings, and that I have transacted the same for nine hundred merks, Scots money, for which there is bill granted me. Therefore, I hereby declare I am not to demand payment of the said sum untill a legal offer be made him of my discharge of all I can claim of him, and give him up, or offer so to do, all his papers on oath: As also, of two legal depositions, or affidavits of two witnesses, of the whorish practices of Margaret Hall, daughter to Adam Hall, merchant in Edinburgh, and three months thereafter. In witness whereof, I have written, with my own hand, on stamped paper thir presents, at Edinburgh, the twenty-eighth day of November, one thousand seven hundred and nineteen years.

James Campbell.

After much thought devoted to "concerting wicked measures against the Defunct," Nicol wrote in opprobrious terms of Burnbank's dictation a letter to his wife, stating that he had taken horse for London, and that she would never see his face again. "To make it clink the better," they dated the missive from Newbattle, and despatched it by a caddie "to the care of Mrs. Thom, Mercatrix at the Bowhead," where Mrs. Muschet lodged. Their amiable object, as explained, was to cause her to despair, that she might more readily enter into temptation. Meanwhile her husband, in his own phase, lurked in the house of one Alexander Pennecuik, "for present in the Abbay." I shall return to Mr. Pennecuik later. The Abbey was that part of the Canongate east of the Horse Wynd and the Watergate, within the Sanctuary of Holyrood, chiefly occupied by debtors and other persons at odds with fortune. You remember it as affording refuge to Mr. Chrystal Croftangry, in *Chronicles of the Canongate*.

The young wife, believing herself deserted, resolved "to take a Trial of the Country" with her mother-in-law. Doubtless she meant to state her wrongs to that lady, whom it does not appear she had yet seen. Apprised of her purpose, Burnbank did his best to dissuade her, promising to trace the runaway, and to arrange a suitable provision for her maintenance;

"but notwithstanding, she went off with the Carrier." If she distrusted Burnbank, the sequel surely justified her fears. That worthy, receiving notice of her going, "hired one Andrew Shiels, Writer, to pursue her, together with himself," and having obtained a warrant from a county justice, the Laird of Majoribanks, to apprehend her on suspicion of theft, they tracked her to Linlithgow, "travelling all the way under Cloud of Night, being so eager on their pursuit, having taken Horse at the two Penny Custom-house about 11 o'clock at Night." The alarmed lady, aroused from sleep by the writer, "who presented a Baton as Constable to incarcerate her for Theft," was much relieved by the timeous appearance of the friendly Burnbank, to whom she appealed for aid. That gentleman expressed great concern "that any of his Countrymen's Relations, especially such as she, should be so used"; his offer to "bail her to Edinburgh" was accepted by the writer, and the party returned amicably to town, where Burnbank took her to "one Lorn's, at the Back of the Wall," gave her some money, and charged the landlady to let her want for nothing. On reflection, the object of his solicitude must have seen reason to doubt her benefactor's good faith, for in a few days she made her escape, and having hired a horse, reached her mother-in-law's house in safety. So Burnbank, who was a plausible scoundrel, despatched "a considerable long Letter, promising many fair Things," whereby the foolish woman was induced to come again within the scope of her enemies' machinations.

The plot of which she was the destined victim—well described by Muschet as his "hellish Project"—is of an atrocity so shocking as to render any detailed account of it here impossible. It is sufficient to state that Muschet, Burnbank, and Pennecuik, having inspected various houses, selected that of Bailie Smith "in the Abbay" as most convenient for their purpose; that Mrs. Muschet was persuaded to lodge there; that on a certain Monday night in the end of December 1719, Burnbank and Pennecuik induced her to swallow a quantity of laudanum, with brandy and sugar "by way of Stocktoun Drops," whereby she became unconscious; and that Burnbank had "made it his business to provide one John MacGregory, Professor of Languages in the Canongate," to sustain the rôle of Iachimo. Apart altogether from the character of the scheme, two points strike one as remarkable: the choice of a magistrate's house for the venue, and the academic calling of the hired villain.* It is satisfactory to learn from Muschet that the plot failed; "for after we informed our Procurator, James Russel, of all we could do, he told us unless we could Evidence a Tract of Conversation betwixt MacGregory and her either before or after the Fact, we could never make anything of it." For the credit of the profession let us hope that the lawyer was misled, but as he was the repository of the Burnbank "band" above cited, I fear that Mr Russel was "other than a gude ane."

Among the undesirable acquaintances whom the Laird of Boghall seems to have had a genius for acquiring, honourable mention must be made of James Muschet, "Piriwig-maker in Edinburgh," and Grissel Bell, his spouse. This man has been called a brother of the laird, which is clearly a mistake; he may have been, and probably was his kinsman. The wigmaker and his helpmate were in reduced circumstances, and "for a Piece of Money" the couple agreed to further Muschet's dastardly design against his wife, "which James did by carrying Mac-Gregory several Times to her Room at Night, and drinking with her." But Nicol, finding that his instruments were "very indifferent" unless daily supplied with funds, and having incurred considerable expense "both in frequenting Burnbank's Company, hiring MacGregory and sustaining James Muschet and his Family," began to lose heart. Their operations produced for him no result beyond constant appeals to his pocket, and as the procurator's opinion was discouraging, he "intirely gave over that Thought." So the Professor of Languages resumed his more legitimate labours, and the divorce proceedings were dropped.

But Burnbank was not yet at the end of his resources; he advised that the best way to get rid of Mrs Muschet was "to exhibit to her Poison," and that "the only proper hand for it"

* Note II.—Professor MacGregory.

was James Muschet, who, when it was proposed to him, very readily undertook the job. Burnbank recommended the employment of corrosive sublimate as a safer medium than arsenic, "on Account Arsenick both swelled and discoloured." Such knowledge smacks rather of the surgeon than of the storekeeper, and indeed Nicol implies that he himself furnished the poison, for James, fearing that the laird had given him arsenic instead of mercury, consulted a local chemist, who reassured him on the point. Burnbank approved his caution, remarking that people on such enterprises are never too much aware. The mercury, mixed with sugar, was "on a Sabbath Night" duly administered to Mrs Muschet in a dram; she became violently sick, "so that life was not expected for her," and James, "all trembling," reported to his principal, "By God, she has got it now!" But the victim rallied, and the two miscreants sought counsel of Burnbank. They enquired for him at the Castle Gate. "The Porter sent a Man who brought him down," says Nicol, "and we walked a considerable time on the Castle Hill; and Burnbank's Advice was, to continue it, so that when she was rendered very ill with one Dose, another might carry her off; which accordingly was done, but not with expected Success." The lady having become shy of sugar, Muschet put some of the poison in a nutmeg-grater, obligingly lent by Burnbank, with which James pretended to add a zest to her liquor. The grater looked "as if it had been burnt in the Fire by Reason of the Mercury corrosive," when James later presented it to Pennecuik as an interesting souvenir; but the lady still survived. Then James's wife tried her hand with poisoned meal introduced into warm ale, yet without putting a period to the patient's sufferings.

In view of these repeated failures Burnbank proposed to revert to his original plan, with a change of scene to a gardener's house in the suburbs, and with James, "under the name of Mr Stewart, a Country Gentleman not agreeing with the Town Air," in the part for which Professor MacGregory was originally cast. Apparently even Nicol's depravity had its limits, for he opposed the scheme. He had hitherto remained lurking in the background, but now by Burnbank's advice he rejoined his wife, who was still confined to bed, and the poisoning began again, "in Sack and Cinnamon as a Cordial after her sickness," with the husband as ministering devil. "All these preceding Projects failing, Burnbank advised to commit yet more Wickedness," the new purpose being that James should carry the lady to Leith some afternoon, "and drink with her till it were very late," and on their way home drown her in a pond. Burnbank mentioned two places as suitable, both on the north side of the south walk to Leith, "which," says Nicol, "he and I went on a Sabbath Day to see," and approved; but James would not "condescend" to the device. He offered, however, to try an idea of his wife's: to take Mrs Muschet "on pretence of kindness" to the West country, riding on a pillion behind him, and by loosening her pad, to throw her off as they forded Kirkliston Water when in flood. "Burnbank, not thinking this proper, gave advice for James to knock her on the Head and throw her into some Hole without the Town, and immediately thereafter to flee to Paris; which in no Ways he would condescend to." So matters were at a deadlock, and presently the laird fell out with Burnbank "by Reason of his keeping up his [Nicol's] Papers," and the attempts on Mrs Muschet's life were meantime discontinued.

In the spring of the following year, however, the campaign was reopened with fresh vigour. Nicol and his wife, who had recovered from her illness, were living in Dickson's Close, in the High Street, above the Nether Bow, while James and his helpmate occupied a room at the head of the adjacent St. Mary's Wynd. After much debate the conspirators could think of nothing better than Burnbank's last suggestion, namely, "to knock her on the Head when going down Dickson's Closs late to her Room." This course agreed to, in May 1720 the parties "deeply conjured" themselves never to discover the plot, and, undismayed by former failures, set about arranging details. James and his wife were to get twenty guineas for "right executing" the project, for which amount, says Nicol, "he sought my Bill, alledging himself not sure without it." Of this sum

Muschet presently advanced to James one guinea, "which he gave to Mr James Ure, Writer, to give to the Kirk Treasurer," and afterwards "Half a Guinea to bury his Child, with 16 Shillings Sterling to turn his Cloaths, a little before the fatal Accident happened"—a delicate allusion to the murder. James's private recreations seem to have incurred the fine and censure of the Kirk, but the occasion is unrecorded. For the rest, in whatever state his garments were, he had obviously more need to turn his heart. The general plan was as follows:—Mrs James undertook to invite Mrs Muschet to her room of an evening and keep her there till eleven or twelve o'clock, "by affoording her Meat and Drink, and intertaining her with flattering Discourse"; James meanwhile would lie in wait for her return and attack her in the dark entry of the deceased Dickson. That part of the alley which was to be the scene of the proposed slaughter still exists for the satisfaction of the curious. So much for the place, but the instrument was yet to seek. Mrs James borrowed a heavy hammer-head from a neighbour, and James got a piece of wood from a wright in Moutrie's Hill, which he fitted as a shaft to the head, hurting his hands in the process. It was arranged that after the deed he should throw away the head, and take the shaft home and burn it. Several times did Mrs Muschet accept the perilous hospitality of St. Mary's Wynd; "but always when James followed her to give her the Stroke in the dark Closs, some Body going up or down prevented it."

About the time of the harvest the subject of these abortive measures took a much-needed holiday in the country; nothing further could be done till her return, and Nicol, losing hold of hope, proposed that the enterprise should be abandoned. But Grissel Muschet, with a force of character reminiscent of Lady Macbeth, argued, "Is it reasonable, think you, so to do, when my Husband and I have wared so much Time and Pains to accomplish that Design, and in Expectation of our Reward, now to give it over?" The laird yielded to the lady's logic, and the business was resumed by her and James; but Mrs Muschet "wearied to stay so oft and so long in their Room," and they reported that unless Nicol came with her himself, it was not in their power to keep her there so late. This was the beginning of the week before the unfortunate woman was finally disposed off; as in the case of King Charles the Second the ceremony had been unconscionably delayed. For several successive nights her husband performed his hateful office, but fate was still against him. James's landlord would not suffer the guests to stay in his house after ten; James, "waiting her as formerly, some Times did not see her, and some Times was prevented by the People walking in the Closs; and by waiting her so late for some Nights before, was seised with a violent Toothach, which occasioned him to keep his Room for two or three Days." Pity the woes of the assassin, hugging his hammer and counting the hours in that cold black passage, with the shrewd blasts of an Edinburgh October night for company!

Thus far, the only explanation of Muschet's amazing tale seems to be that he was throughout the dupe of his accomplices, who merely pretended to forward his infamous plots so long as money was to be made by them; if not, then surely James was the most inept murderer that ever wielded weapon. It is probable that Nicol himself at length realised this, for, leaving James to nurse his toothache, he decided to take the matter in his own hands: "The Devil, that cunning adversary, suggested to me, being now hardened and also desperate by all the foresaid Plots failing, that it were but a light Thing whether he or I were the Executioner." It chanced that "upon Sabbath was Eight Days before the Fatal Act," Nicol Muschet sat in the Canongate Church, that forbidding barn, hearing sermon. The prelection was upon the Sixth Commandment, of which the minister treated "in a very pathetic manner," displaying the exceeding sinfulness of shedding innocent blood. After sermon the gentleman whose pew Nicol shared invited him to qualify the discourse at Barnaby Lloyd's house in the Canongate, apparently one of the few taverns with which the laird was unacquainted, and whence a week later he was to lead his wife to her doom; "which Concurrence of Circumstances," he observes, "tho' not then regarded by me, now plainly convinces me that in the Righteous Judgement of God these very Means which tend to the deterring of others from Sin, had quite the Contrary Effect on me." He seems to have recognised that he was a hard case.

On Monday, 17th October, Nicol Muschet began the day by borrowing a knife from his landlady, Mrs Macadam. He and James, now happily restored to health, dined together, and meeting with some congenial company, diverted themselves till nightfall. A message was then despatched to Mrs Muschet by a caddie, summoning her to Lloyd's, and after her arrival James went off upon his usual draughty night duty, viz., "to wait her as formerly in the foresaid Closs with the Hammer." No sooner was he out of the way than Muschet, bidding his wife follow him and ask no questions, left the house. Down the Canongate went the silent pair, across the Abbey Close, and passing the Palace of Holyroodhouse, entered the bounds of the King's Park.

Before we accompany them farther it may be well to contemplate for a moment the scene of the ensuing tragedy. The King's Park, although as a royal domain immune from the obscene hands of the speculative builder, could not escape the common lot of things earthly, and that part of it with which we are concerned has seen some changes since Nicol Muschet's time. The ruined chapel of St. Anthony the Eremite yet dominates the Haggis Knowe, and on May Day the damsels of Auld Reikie—if in this degenerate age the fashion be not forgot—may still "weet their een" at his holy well, where it bubbles from its ancient source on the braeside, beneath the majestic bulk of Arthur's Seat, rising unchanged and unchangeable in the track of the devouring years. St. Margaret's Loch below, in whose waters the scene is now reflected, is an innovation, dating only from 1857, and her rival well was brought hither from Restalrig but a few years later. The present carriage road to Jock's Lodge has superseded the oak-shaded footway named the Duke's Walk, once the favourite promenade of James, Duke of Albany and York, when in 1680–81 he kept court at Holyrood; and the modern parade ground has obliterated the enclosure named St. Ann's Yards, together with the

woods and house of Clock Mill, which of old occupied the area
between the Palace and the north-eastern boundary of the park.

As the couple, having left the Abbey precincts, were crossing
St. Ann's Yards, "She weep'd," says Nicol of his wife, "and
prayed that God might forgive me if I was taking her to any
Mischief." She begged him to return, but he said he was bound
for Duddingston, and swore that if she did not go also, she
should never set eyes on him again. So the hapless woman,
who, strangely enough, in spite of all his ill-usage, plainly had
an affection for her husband, went on with him to the end.
When they entered the Duke's Walk she remarked that was
not the way to Duddingston, upon which Muschet said he
would "lead her another Way than the Road thro' the middle
of the Park," i.e. round the eastern flank of the hill, instead
of by the direct path over the Hunter's Bog. They reached the
chosen place, "which was near the east End of the said Walk"
—I shall consider its exact position presently—and there in the
black night, between the Whinny Hill and the deserted fields,
Margaret Hall was brutally done to death. The particulars are
too horrible for recital; suffice it to say that Muschet only
effected his purpose after a severe struggle, and but for his
wife's long hair, by which he held her down, he declares that
he could not have overcome her resistance. I spare the reader the
canting comments of the murderer. His end accomplished, Nicol
fled from the fatal spot, but when he came "near to the Tirlies
at the Entry of the Duke's Walk from St. Ann's Yard," he
bethought him that, despite his violence, his victim might yet
survive; so he returned to "mak' sicker," which done, he again
sought the city by the way he came. The Tirlies are defined in
Pennecuik's *Streams from Helicon* as "The narrow Wicket,
which delivers in To the Duke's Walk" from "Saint Anne's
flow'ry Park." Muschet states that, such was his condition after
the murder, he forgets what further he did and said that night;
but he admits that he boasted of "the horrid Wickedness" to
James Muschet and to his landlady, Mrs Macadam.

The discovery of the crime next morning is set forth in the
depositions of the witnesses at the magisterial inquiry into the

affair. Isobell Stirling, relict of John Steuart, workman in Abbeyhill, declared that on Tuesday, 18th October, about ten o'clock forenoon, being in the Park, she saw at the east end of the Walk a woman lying dead in a very dismal posture, "having her throat cut into the very neck-bone, and her chin cut, and one of her thumbs almost cut off, and found her to be also cut in the breast in several places, and also in the other hand very barbarously, and found some hair in her hand, but could not distinguish the colour by reason of the blood, and saw an Holland sleeve of a man, lying just next to her, bloody, having the letter N sewed with green silk thereon." James Steuart, servant to Widow Bortleman at the Watergate, declared that on the same date he saw at the east end of the Duke's Walk, within the King's Park, a woman lying with her throat cut, and having other wounds upon her, whom he, Robert Bagham, and others lifted from the ground, put on a bier, and carried from thence to the chapel at the Watergate; "and delivered to John Kelso, constable in the Abbey, the bloody sleeve lying by her, having the letter N sewed with green silk thereon." By whom the body was identified as that of Mrs Muschet does not appear.

Meantime Muschet, having consulted with James's wife Grissel, early that morning went down to Leith, where he spent the day "in the House of one James Lumisden, Sailor." After dark he returned to Edinburgh, and met Grissel Muschet by appointment at a close-head within the Nether Bow. She reported that "all Things were very well," and said he might safely go to his quarters; she also told him that she and her husband were determined to perjure themselves for his safety. Relieved by this assurance Nicol ventured out to a tavern near the Cross, but on his return home, finding that his landlady had been carried to the Guard House for examination, he immediately went back to Leith. Next day, Wednesday, 19th October, Muschet, accompanied by Mr Lumsden, came to Edinburgh and had a consultation in the Fleshmarket Close with one Hugh Hay, a writer. The man of law advised that if the laird could stand his trial it was not proper that he should abscond, but if not, he must do what he thought best; so Nicol, no wiser than many another client after a similar experience, withdrew again to Leith to reconsider his position. On Thursday, the 20th, James's wife, perceiving that the game was up, and that she and her amiable consort might now whistle for their twenty guineas, lodged information against Muschet with the magistrates, who sent a party of the City Guard to arrest him; but Nicol, relying on Grissel's loyalty, had left his sailor friend and removed to the house of James's mother-in-law, so that they failed to find him. On Saturday, the 22nd, Grissel, learning that he had taken refuge with her mother, informed the authorities of the fact, and, says Nicol, "came out with a Party about 8 o'clock at Night, with Andrew Jelly, her landlord; and was so well satisfy'd with her certainty of my being there, that she not a little rejoiced in Company of the Soldiers, and all the way she let none pass without asking who they were, fearing my Escape." Clearly a capable person, this Grissel. James, owing to a previous engagement with the Keeper of the Tolbooth, was prevented from joining the party. Apprehended and carried before the magistrates, Nicol denied all knowledge of the crime; but on one of the Bailies giving him a more distinct account of the whole circumstances than he could have done himself, "Conscience, that great Accuser, would keep silent no longer": he confessed his guilt, and signed a declaration to that effect. At this time he said nothing to implicate either Burnbank or James and his wife, nor of the the previous attempts upon Mrs Muschet's life, but confined himself to a brief account of the murder. The prudent James, who had plainly "split" upon his late employer, was released on bail, and retired to the country, where he remained until the laird's trial.

The judicial proceedings of which Nicol Muschet was the occasion are printed from the official records in that valuable little work, *Criminal Trials Illustrative of the Tale entitled "The Heart of Mid-Lothian"* (Edinburgh: 1818), edited anonymously by Charles Kirkpatrick Sharpe. On 28th November 1720 the pannel was placed at the bar of the High Court of

Justiciary, charged with the murder of his wife. The judges present were Lord Royston, Polton, Pencaitland, Dun, and Newhall; the Solicitor-General (Walter Steuart), and John Sinclair, advocate-depute, with Duncan Forbes and Andrew Lauder, appeared for the crown. The libel having been read, the pannel craved the Court to appoint counsel for his defence, and John Horn, John Elphinston, and Charles Erskine were accordingly empowered to plead for him. Several of the above names recur upon the trial of Captain Porteous, sixteen years later. On the 29th the libel was found relevant, "there being no defences proponed thereagainst," and the pannel was remitted to the knowledge of an assize. On 5th December, a jury having been sworn, the pannel judicially confessed and acknowledged the crime of murdering his own wife, as set forth in the indictment, whereupon the jury returned a verdict of guilty; and on 8th December sentence of death was duly pronounced, the pannel to be hanged upon a gibbet in the Grassmarket of Edinburgh between the hours of two and four o'clock afternoon on Friday, 6th January 1721. Owing to the course adopted by the defence no evidence was led, but James and his wife, as good citizens, were plainly ready if required to bear unimpeachable witness for the prosecution. "It seemed good in the Eyes of a just God," says Nicol, in commenting on his trial, "to restrain any of the Advocates from pleading on my Behalf."

No account of the final ceremony has been preserved, but doubtless the miscreant made an edifying end. The expense of his removal, according to a note of the City Chamberlain's outlays on that occasion which has been preserved, amounted to £39, 14s. 8d. Scots.* After preliminary suspension in the Grassmarket, his body was hung in chains, on the Gallow Lee, at Greenside, by Leith Walk, a distinction conferred only upon the most flagrant offenders. When the New Town of Edinburgh was in course of building, the sand for the mortar was taken from the sandhill of which the Gallow Lee was com-

* Note III.—Execution of Nicol Muschet.

posed. It is a pleasant fancy that Nicol's ashes, on the analogy
of Alexander's dust, may yet subserve a useful purpose in helping to uphold our hearths and homes.

After his conviction Nicol Muschet addressed to the Lords
of Justiciary a holograph declaration, printed from the original
MS. in the volume above mentioned; this he afterwards in-
corporated, with some variations, in the public Confession on
which I have so largely drawn. In the later document he amplifies
the narrative of his misdeeds, and indulges in a vein of sanctimonious sentiment if possible more repulsive than his crimes.
He forgives freely and frankly all offences done to him by
Archibald Ure, Burnbank, and the Muschets, whom he describes as the only instigators and ringleaders of his wickedness;
also such evil-disposed persons as had spread reports regarding
his relations with his landlady, Mrs Macadam, his habit of
inebriety, and his attempts to commit suicide while in prison,
all which calumnies he most solemnly repels. He expresses
gratitude to his judges for "mitigating the Pains" of his punishment—perhaps he expected to be broken on the wheel, like
the murderer of the Laird of Warriston; he hopes that his
mother and the rest of her children may be warned by his
example to walk soberly, righteously, and godly, and concludes
with an adieu to this vain transitory world, the stage of sinning
and sorrow—"Welcome Heaven and Eternal Enjoyment!"
Surely James Hogg's Confessions of a Justified Sinner owe
some of their gems to the collection of Nicol Muschet. But
it is always the same story: from the Black Laird of Ormistoun
in 1567, to Hugh Macleod of Assynt in 1831—the greater the
criminal, the more confident his assurance of salvation.

On 21st November the prisoner's mother had addressed to
him from Boghall a long and pious epistle exhorting him to
repentance, but containing nothing to our purpose; and on
5th January 1721, the last day of his life, he received and
replied to a letter from "his Soul's Well-wisher, Alexander
Pennecuik," whose name the reader may remember in connection with what Nicol terms the "Abbay Plot." These letters

were printed as broadsides and circulated at the time, the latter being entitled, "A Gentleman's Letter to the Laird of Boghall, The Day before his Execution, with Boghall's Answer." Pennecuik complains of being imprisoned as accessory to the murder on the strength of Muschet's declaration to the Lords of Justiciary, which he politely describes as "A Volume of Lies"; he conjures Nicol to clear his character and to declare his innocence, and wishes him in return a comfortable death. "You very well know," writes the laird in reply, "you was in Bailie Smith's, which in relation to other Things I could not escape to mention; in doing of which to the utmost of my knowledge, I have done neither you nor any other Injustice, as I am to Morrow to appear before the Supreme Judge." In an interesting paper contributed to the sixth volume of the publications of the Edinburgh Bibliographical Society, the late William Brown gives some account of the two Alexander Pennecuiks, uncle and nephew, both poets and often confused one with another. The uncle, a most respectable writer and doctor of medicine, was the author of *A Description of Tweeddale*, etc.; the nephew wrote *An Historical Account of the Blue Blanket*, also *Streams from Helicon* and other works, of the type euphemistically described in booksellers' catalogues as "curious." He is known to have been of dissipated habits and his end is chronicled by a brother bard, Claudero, as follows:—

> To shun the fate of Pennycuik,
> Who starving died in turnpike-neuk;
> (Tho' sweet he sung with wit and sense,
> He like poor Claud, was short of pence).

Mr Brown. identifies this disreputable writer with the friend and accomplice of Nicol Muschet on grounds which to me seem sufficient. He recognizes the Pennecuik touch in the Latin acrostic, *ab amico quandam conscriptum*, to which I have before referred, as well as in a contemporaneous broadside entitled "Elegy on the Death of Nicol Muschet of Boghall, written at the desire of his friends." The Elegy gives a vigorous sketch of Nicol's career, and tells how, having "drown'd Religion with the Juice of Malt," he compassed his wife's destruction:—

> To take her Life, a thousand Snares are laid;
> Sweet harmless lass, she's ev'ry day betrayed:
> At last, with SATAN, who had form'd the Plot,
> He leads her to the Fields, and cuts her Throat.
> I've plac'd his Sins in such a glaring Light,
> To make the Mercies of the Lord shine bright . . .
> Thus I've perform'd the Office of a Friend,
> Recorded his lewd Life, and pious End.
> O may all Youths take Warning, and conspire
> To loathe polluted Paths, which lead t'eternal Fire.

A further link, unnoticed by Mr Brown, is supplied by the poet's acquaintance with James Campbell of Burnbank, who, as Sir Walter Scott observes, is repeatedly mentioned in Pennecuik's satirical poems.

It was remarked by a reviewer of these narratives on their periodical appearances that my heroes had a habit of getting hanged; but unfortunately neither Professor MacGregory, Pennecuik, nor the Muschet pair was brought to justice for their respective parts in the conspiracy. It is, however, some consolation to learn that Burnbank did not wholly escape punishment. He was tried on 21st March 1721, as appears from an abridgment of the record, printed by Maclaurin in his *Criminal Cases*, upon an indictment charging him with violence, falsehood, and attempt to poison, or being art and part in those crimes, having, together with Nicol Muschet, hatched a most wicked and villainous design of bereaving Margaret Hall of her honour and reputation, and even of her life. The obligation to procure evidence for the deceptive divorce, the fraudulent arrest at Linlithgow, the "hellish project" of the Abbey, and the repeated administration of poison, form the grounds of the charge; nothing is said of the Dickson's Close scheme, or of James Muschet and his wife, though there is a general reference to accomplices. Probably the worthy couple had turned King's evidence, but what proof in support of the libel the Crown adduced is not recorded. For the rest, the facts are those with which the reader is familiar. The jury found Burnbank guilty; he was declared to be infamous and incapable of bearing or enjoying any public office, and was banished to His Majesty's plantations in America, never again to return to Scotland.

Notwithstanding divers ballads upon Burnbank's fate published as broadsides at the time—e.g. his *Sorrowful Lamentation* and last farewell to Scotland, and an *Elegy* on his mournful banishment to the West Indies, from which it appears that in addition to his other offences he had been in use, as ordnance storekeeper, to sell for his own profit the military stores—there is reason to fear that after all his native land was not rid of the ruffian. In 1722, while a prisoner in the Castle, he, and another, George Faichney, got hold of a man named James M'Naughton, whom having made drunk, they burnt "in a most indecent manner," for which outrage both were indicted. So late as 1726 Burnbank was still in the Castle, as may be inferred from a passage in the Wodrow correspondence, and it is probable that he never left the country, but died in confinement. Some further account of him will be found in *The Argyle Papers*, edited by Maidment (Edinburgh, 1834).

A word as to the *locus* of the murder. The exact site is, I fear, not now to be identified, for the existing cairn on the north side of the road, opposite the Keeper's Lodge at the north-eastern entrance to the Park from Meadow-bank, while it commemorates the crime, does not mark the actual place of its commission. The original cairn, raised on the spot in execration of the deed at the time, survived until, as we learn from a footnote by C. K. Sharpe to the record of the trial before cited, "it was removed during the formation of a regular footpath through the Park, suggested by Lord Adam Gordon, then resident at Holyrood-house." This was in 1789, when his Lordship was Commander of the Forces in Scotland. In the 1818 edition of the Confession already mentioned, the anonymous editor states: "The place where the deed was committed is on the north side of the footpath through the Duke's Walk, and within a few yards of the wicket which opens into the highroad from Jock's Lodge to the city. It was long marked by a cairn of stones, raised by passers by, expressive of their abhorrence of the crime, which was removed some years ago, when the footpath was widened and repaired."

Thus the memory of Muschet and his misdeeds was like to have been forgotten, but in June 1818 came forth *The Heart of Mid-Lothian*, and, incidentally, provided for him an imperishable memorial. Attentive readers of the tale will notice that Scott places the scene of the murder "beneath the steep ascent on which these ruins [of St. Anthony's Chapel] are still visible," that is, near the space now occupied by St. Margaret's Loch, and some two hundred yards farther west than the accepted site, but it is probable that he did so for reasons merely romantic, the nature of the ground there being more suitable, from the picturesque standpoint, both for the stalking of Robertson and for his effective evasion of the pursuers.

In 1822 the advent of George the Fourth, of magnificent memory, involved the Duke's Walk in further alterations. From the *Historical Account of His Majesty's Visit to Scotland* (Edinburgh, 1822) I find that the old road was again repaired, "and from the point where it comes in contact with Comely Gardens, to Parson's Green, was diverted to a line more to the southward." Finally, as appears from a passage in the *Edinburgh Weekly Journal*, cited, with a vagueness that defies verification, by James Grant in his *Old and New Edinburgh*, the cairn was restored in 1823, near the east gate and close to the north wall—where it now stands. "The original cairn," he quotes apparently from the *Journal*, "is said to have been several paces farther west than the present one, the stones of which were taken out of the old wall when it was pulled down to give place to the new gate that was constructed previous to the late royal visit." So the coming of that gorgeous Personage was after all of some benefit to posterity. Prior to that august event the cairn is unmarked in any of the numerous plans of Edinburgh which I have examined, but by the following year it became a feature of these, and continues to be so even unto this day.

In the Author's Notes of 1830 Sir Walter writes of the cairn as "now almost totally removed in consequence of an alteration on the road in that place." Probably he was then unaware of its restoration, due to the revived interest in the spot which his novel had aroused. Those responsible for its re-erection would, I take it, place the new cairn as near as possible to the original position, which, as we have seen, had been superseded by the roadway, and was doubtless somewhat farther to the west. A tradition among the park keepers that it stood of old beneath the Haggis Knowe is obviously derived from the romance, and is but another tribute to the power and permanency of the Wizard's spell.

Note I.—NICOL MUSCHET'S ANCESTRY.

On 27th October 1617 Nicol Muschet, second son of David Muschet of Callichat and Janet Henderson, daughter of Mr. Malcolm Henderson, minister at Kilmadock, his future spouse, received from the said David sasine of the lands of Boghall and half of the lands of McCorranstoun, called the Bog of McCorranstoun, in the Parish of Kincardine in Menteith; and failing heirs of the marriage, these lands were destined to Andrew, third son of the said David Muschet— Stirlingshire Reg. Sas., vol. i. fol. 29. Of the marriage there were three sons, David, James, and John, and four daughters, Christian, Janet, Agnes, and Margaret—Ibid., vol. vii. fol. 295; vol. x. fol. 397. David, the eldest son, apparent of Boghall, on 23rd June 1651 was infeft in the six merkland of McCorranstoun, on a charter granted by George Henderson of McCorranstoun with consent of his curators and of Margaret Muschet, his mother—Ibid., vol. ix. fol. 28. He was apparently in the army, for he is designed Captain David Muschet of McCorranstoun—Gen. Reg. Sas., vol. xi. fol. 270. His name frequently appears as pursuer or defender in legal processes, and on 4th October 1692 he was fined £60 Scots for "striking and blooding" Mr. Robert Muschet in Noriestoun—Register of Menteith. On 22nd November 1699 Captain David Muschet granted a disposition in favour of Mr Robert Muschet in Boghall, late schoolmaster at Kincardine, and Jean Muschet, his spouse, of the four merkland of Boghall— Stirlingshire Reg. Sas., vol. xii. fol. 16. Whether Jean Muschet his spouse was Janet, the sister of Captain David, is not known; but our Nicol Muschet, the eldest son of this couple, succeeded to the lands on 1st March 1710—*Ibid.*, vol. xii. fol. 465. The entry in the Kincardine Parish Register on 13th August 1695 recording the baptism of Nicol, son of Robert and Jean Muschet, unquestionably refers to him. His brother James served heir to Nicol on 1st February 1723—*Register of Menteith.*

Note II.—Professor MacGregory.

This singular scoundrel appears to have been at the time a character well known in Edinburgh. There is preserved in the Advocates' Library (*Pamphlets*, First Series, vol. 24) a re-markable broadside of four pages, small folio, entitled "Mr. MackGregory's Advertisement," which is announced as "to be seen in all the Coffee-Houses in Town, and Copies on't are to be had from the Author." The Professor's modest account of his accomplishments proceeds upon the narrative that "Mr. John MackGregory, Licentiat in Both Laws of the Faculty of Angers, having since the Peace of Ryswick at several Courses travel'd over all Europe, and over a part of Asia and Africa, as far as the River Euphrates, the Red Sea, and the Nile, and having had Extraordinary Occasions of Seeing and Observing every Thing Remarkable, both by Land and Sea, in the Orient as well as in the Occident . . . having liv'd at most of the Courts of Europe . . . and being now come Home hither to his own Country, does make Profession of Serving Gentlemen and Ladies by Teaching 'em MODERN GEOGRAPHY and UNIVERSAL HISTORY, in their greatest Latitude, and with All that belongs to them." The syllabus of the course is no less varied than attractive, including as it does the Postage of Letters by Doves from Alexandria to Cairo; the Generation of Chickens in Ovens by the Cofts of Old Cairo; the Catching and Killing of Crocodiles in Pits upon the Banks of the Nile; a true Account of the Creation and Fabric of the World; the Beauty and Harmony of Evangelick Doctrine; the Examples and Characters of Virtuoso Ladies; the Follies and Mis-carriages of Coquets; Seraglios Public and Private; the Variety and Differences of Tongues; the Propriety and Elegancy of Expression; and (more relevantly) French, Italian, High

Dutch and English. Here, surely, was a wondrous feast to tempt the fastidious palate of Auld Reikie! "If, therefore," concludes the Professor, "there be any Gentleman or Ladies, who have a desire to be Tought GEOGRAPHY, and HISTORY, or the LANGUAGES, These are to give Notice, That they may have that Service carefully done them by the said Mr. MackGregory, who is to be heard of at the Exchange and Caledonian Coffee-Houses, and desires, That all Those who have a Mind to Imploy him, may Engage with him before the First of November, being then to begin his Courses, which are from that Time to continue Daily, and be compleated within a Year." It appears further that the indefatigable savant found leisure to write sundry learned works, as "The Geography and History of Mons" (Edinburgh, 1709), and similar volumes dealing with Lille and Tournai. He also published "An Account of the Sepulchers of the Antients, and a Description of their Monuments, from the Creation of the World to the Pyramids, and from Thence to the Destruction of Jerusalem, in two parts. . . . By John MackGregory, LL.L., Professor of Geography and History" (London, 1712).

Note III.—EXECUTION OF NICOL MUSCHET.

Ane note of the Chamberlaine's expense anent
Nicol Muschett.

		lb.	s.	d.
Imprs.	Paid 2 men wairding said Nicol ye night before he was hangit,	oo	16	10
Item.	Wine to ye Minister and ye Bailizes, ...	02	oo	oo
Item.	Ane Coul to ye sd Nicol, . .	oo	08	oo
Item.	Ane knife to cut aff his hand, .	01	10	oo
Item.	Ane tow to hang him, . .	oo	06	oo
Item.	Paid Deacon Gawinlock putting up ye gallows, 6 men, 1 day, .	05	08	oo
Item.	Paid ye Smith for cheinzies, .	24	06	08
Item.	Breid and yill to ye workmen, .	02	oo	oo
Item.	Paid Saunders Lumisdaine ye hangman, ...	03	oo	oo
	Summa est	39	14	08

The original MS. of this curious account of expenses was lent by Charles Kirkpatrick Sharpe to James Maidment, who first printed it in his notes to *The Argyle Papers* (Edinburgh, 1834).

THE ADVENTURES OF
DAVID HAGGART

He hath as fine a Hand at picking a Pocket as a Woman,
and is as nimble-finger'd as a Juggler.—If an unlucky Session
does not cut the Rope of thy Life, I pronounce, Boy, thou
wilt be a great Man in History. —*The Beggar's Opera.*

THE DAY of David Haggart, thief, murderer, and man of letters,
dawned at Edinburgh in 1801, and closed untimely in the same
city in 1821, the year in which died a greater adventurer,
Napoleon. During the short course of his pilgrimage he saw
much of men and manners in many parts of the United Kingdom, his way of life affording a rare opportunity to compare
the administration of justice in vogue in the respective countries. He was convicted time and again of divers minor offences,
on four occasions he contrived to escape from prison, and his
activities ceased only as the result of the fortuitous slaying of
a turnkey at Dumfries. Born too late to take proper rank with
the heroes of the *Malefactors' Bloody Register*, he was yet in
time for Knapp and Baldwin's *Newgate Calendar* and Camden
Pelham's *Chronicles of Crime*; but it is regrettable that Borrow,
who enjoyed the privilege of his acquaintance, found no room
for him when compiling in 1825 the six volumes of *Celebrated
Trials*. This neglect, however, has since been handsomely
atoned by the reception of David, at his own valuation, into the
Valhalla of the *Dictionary of National Biography*, in which he
boasts, with others of our greatest, his memorial column.

Deacon Brodie, the most distinguished Scot among "gentlemen who follow the employment of highway robbery, housebreaking, etc.," left no autobiography. Secure in the eminence
of his fine achievement he was content to base his title to
immortality upon the admiration of his contemporaries, well
assured that future generations would recognise his right. In
his case no such adventitious aid was needed to keep green a
memory so gay and picturesque and gallant: deeds not words

are the foundation of his fame. It is otherwise with the audacious boy who holds in Edinburgh tradition a place but little lower than that assigned to his accomplished forerunner. David Haggart lives by reason of his "Life," written by himself whilst under sentence of death for a crime which in respect of artistry would have failed to satisfy De Quincey, and on its merits could have won for the perpetrator no wreath of posthumous renown. But David was cut off in the heyday of youth, at an age when the great Deacon had barely begun to put forth his first exiguous shoots of evil, and with a knowledge of human nature remarkable in one of so inconsiderable years, he realised that, rascal as he was, he yet was not bad enough to be remembered. No report of his trial had appeared beyond such scant notices as were furnished by the local Press, and a nine days' wonder was insufficient to satisfy his young ambition. The enforced leisure of his seclusion, and the solitude, so favourable to literary labour, of the condemned cell, begat in him a bold idea. He had, in the course of his calling, often occasion to note the transient infernal glory cast upon such of his persuasion as ended their career on the scaffold by the printed appearance of their "Last Speech and Dying Confession," composed by the prison chaplain according to rule, and adorned with the inevitable woodcut. He also knew that the broadsheets conferring this brief apotheosis were not more flimsy and impermanent than the falsehoods embodied in their rude topography. How then if he should write in full an account of his twenty years, not as these were actually mis-spent, but as, with his inverted notion of greatness, he would fain have lived them, which, published in book form at a convenient price, might enable him to palm off upon posterity for the genuine Haggart the David of his romantic dreams?

Hints of this inspiration thrown out to sympathetic friends, but without disclosure of how he meant to manipulate his "facts," met with cordial approval. A respectable Writer to the Signet, his agent at the trial, undertook to see the work through the press and to write a preface. Another worthy member of the Society, who shared the hobby of Mr. Cranium in *Head-*

long Hall, offered for an appendix some curious information respecting his bumps, which the interesting subject, with his tongue in his cheek, conscientiously annotated. Finally, he himself, as Henry Cockburn informs us, drew his own portrait in the Iron Room of the Calton Jail—a charming sketch, doing, we may be sure, the original ample justice—to serve as frontispiece, which, with a facsimile holograph certificate of the authenticity of the entire work, formed most suitable embellishments. In a second edition, which by the way was speedily called for, the head of the portrait was for some reason redrawn by another and yet more flattering hand, but not to the improvement of the plate. I know not who is responsible for the glossary of thieves' slang which further enriches the volume. This, though reprobated by purists, not the least popular of the contents, was rendered necessary on David's inspiration to tell his tale, not in the sanctimonious twaddle of the broadsheets, but in the living cant language of his kind— "penned," as Borrow puts it, "by thy own hand in the robber tongue."

The venture proved an immediate success. The book was devoured by the virtuous; they experienced in its perusal a pleasing thrill, and felt for the nonce vicariously wicked. The interest aroused on all hands was highly gratifying to the criminal classes, who regarded the memoir as their Odyssey. The anathemas of the godly, well meant but arguing a lack of humour, served merely to widen its appeal; if the book were truly damnable, excommunication had the opposite effect. A critic of the 'nineties has pronounced in another connection this dictum: "The morality of art consists in the perfect use of an imperfect medium"; and again, "Vice and virtue are to the artist materials for an art." Judged by these canons David Haggart is justified of his work; and even in an age when Art for Art's sake is become a discredited dogma, one must admit that no better guide to roguery was ever written.

The book, which went forthwith into a second edition, has been repeatedly reissued in various forms—even so recently as 1882 one appeared with the delightful subtitle: "An Edinburgh Fireside Story"; and notwithstanding all efforts to the contrary, it is still accounted a real *document humain*. As such it has been accepted even by so keen a connoisseur in knavery as Mr. Charles Whibley. Could the young author have foreseen the inclusion of his "faked" personality amid the goodly fellowship of *A Book of Scoundrels*, he would have felt that his ingenious labours were not in vain. Yet, after all, the "Life," despite the animadversions of the day and Lord Cockburn's later strictures, is not wholly fictitious: "Some truth there was, but dashed and brewed with lies"; a modicum of straw went to make the bricks of Haggart's monument. He verily was an habitual thief; he did break prison, murder a warder, and pay the penalty appropriate to his deserts. But in reading him we must bear always in mind that his criminous geese are avowedly swans of darkest plumage, and while we discuss with gratitude his bill of fare, let us have ever a ready eye for the salt-cellar.

David Haggart, according to his truculent title-page, *alias* John Wilson, *alias* John Morison, *alias* Barney M'Coul, *alias* John M'Colgan, *alias* Daniel O'Brien, *alias* The Switcher, was born at the farm-town of Goldenacre, near Canonmills, then a suburb of Edinburgh, on 24th June 1801. His father, John Haggart, was a gamekeeper, who, to meet the wants of an increasing family, adopted the additional occupation of dog-trainer, a capacity in which he "was much taken up in accompanying gentlemen on shooting and coursing excursions." A sporting element was thus early introduced into our hero's life. The boy assisted his father on these occasions, and twice spent a season in the Highlands, carrying the bag. We may believe that he was, as he says, "a merry boy"; that the sportsmen took to him, and tipped him more handsomely than wisely. To their thoughtless generosity he attributes his future extravagance. After the manner of his kind he received at home a strict religious training, and his education was entrusted to one Robert Gibson at Canonmills, whose school was later removed to Broughton. David claims to have been always dux of his class, but admits he was sometimes "turned down for kipping." At ten a severe illness interrupted his studies, and on his recovery, being master of the three R's, he was kept at home to help his father. Henceforth experience was to be his teacher, and he lost no time in learning his new lessons.

A bantam cock, belonging to a lady "at the back of the New Town," caught his sporting fancy; and an offer to acquire it legitimately being rejected, he stole the fowl. Rob the Grinder, who also was "led away by birds," has remarked the curious affinity between those innocent creatures and crime. With his next offence, the robbery of a till from a Stockbridge shop, David took his first serious step in his profession. Repentence, he explains, would have been useless: "It was all just *Fate*." In Currie one day for an outing with a chum, Willie Matheson of Silvermills, he captured near that village a pony, on which both boys mounted and made for home. At Slateford, Willie, who was no horseman, fell off; but David rode the prize back to Silvermills, where he concealed it in a hut which they "had formerly built for a cuddie." It was ultimately recovered, much the worse for the adventure, by the owner, a vendor of eggs and butter, who vowed vengeance upon the ravishers; but the good wives of the quarter, with whom David was a favourite, appeased his wrath by purchasing his entire stock.

Passing from these childish follies, we find him, in July 1813, a boy of twelve at Leith races—that sport of our forebears immortalised by Fergusson. "In July month, ae bonny morn," the poet tells us that he encountered upon the like occasion a damsel whose name was Mirth. Our hero, less fortunate, there made the acquaintance of a more potent spirit, and the intoxicated boy enlisted as a drummer in the West Norfolk Militia, then stationed in Edinburgh Castle. He remained with the battalion a year, attaining some proficiency in blowing the bugle, but the red coat so attractive to his boyish eye proved too strait-laced a garment for one of his wayward disposition, and when, in July 1814, the regiment was ordered to England to be disbanded, David obtained his discharge.

To this period belong his parleyings with George Borrow upon the Castle Braes, set forth in the early chapters of *Lavengro*. The parents of the future philologist were living in Edinburgh, where his father, an adjutant in the Norfolks, acted as recruiting officer—perhaps the same from whom on the Links of Leith David took the King's shilling; and George, who was two years David's junior, was prosecuting his studies at the old High School. The rowdy evangelist, as Mr. Lang somewhere terms him, did not publish his reminiscences of Haggart until 1851, and lapse of time must have affected his memory, for he describes David as a lad of fifteen, when in fact the boy was barely twelve, and it may be questioned whether in other respects his portrait is much more accurate than the author's. Readers of *Waverley* will remember the feature of old Edinburgh life called *bickers*, of which in his General Preface Sir Walter gives so vivid an account. Haggart tells us nothing of these mimic battles, but Borrow devotes a chapter to chronicling his own prowess as a leader of the Auld against the New Toun callants. The scene of these conflicts was the grassy slopes by the Nor' Loch, then little better than a grievous swamp, near the ruins of the Wellhouse (vulgarly, Wallace) Tower. On one occasion the valient George, having succumbed to the superior parts of "a full-grown baker's apprentice," was like to be brained with a wheel-spoke. What followed he describes in a single breathless sentence:

Just then I heard a shout and a rushing sound; a wild-looking figure is descending the hill with terrible bounds; it is a lad of some fifteen years: he is bareheaded, and his red uncombed hair stands on edge like hedgehogs' bristles; his frame is lithy, like that of an antelope, but he has prodigious breadth of chest; he wears a military undress, that of the regiment, even of a drummer, for it is wild Davy, whom a month before I had seen enlisted on Leith Links to serve King George with drum and drumstick as long as his services might be required, and who, ere a week had elapsed, had smitten with his fist Drum-Major Elzigood, who, incensed at his inaptitude, had threatened him with his cane; he has been in confinement for weeks, this is the first day of his liberation, and he is now descending the hill with horrid bounds and shoutings; he is now about five yards distant, and the baker, who apprehends that something dangerous is at hand, prepares himself for the encounter; but what avails the strength of a baker, even full-grown?—what avails the defence of a wicker shield?—what avails the wheel-spoke, should there be an opportunity of using it, against the impetus of an avalanche or a cannon ball?—for to either of these might that wild figure be compared, which at the distance of five yards, sprang at once with head, hands, feet, and body, all together, upon the champion of the New Town, tumbling him to the earth amain.

David, having vanquished the incipient baker, rallies the Auld Toun forces, and drives the enemy from the Braes. During the summer holidays that year Borrow spent much time exploring the Castle Rock. One day, as he was negotiating the Kittle Nine Steps, pleasantly commemorated ·in *Redgauntlet*, he spied a red-coated figure seated on the extreme verge of the precipice. Approaching "the horrible edge" he recognised our hero, and thus addressed him:

"What are you thinking of, David?" said I, as I sat behind him and trembled, for I repeat that I was afraid.

David Haggart.—I was thinking of Willie Wallace.

Myself.—You had better be thinking of yourself, man. A strange place this to come to and think of William Wallace.

David Haggart.—Why so? Is not his tower just beneath our feet?

Myself.—You mean the auld ruin by the side of The Nor' Loch—the ugly stane bulk, from the foot of which flows the spring into the dyke, where the watercresses grow?

David Haggart.—Just sae, Geordie.

Myself.—And why were ye thinking of him? The English hanged him long since, as I have heard say.

David Haggart.—I was thinking that I should wish to be like him.

Myself.—Do ye mean that ye would wish to be hanged?

David Haggart.—I wad na flinch from that, Geordie, if I might be a great man first.

Myself.—And wha kens, Davie, how great you may be, even without hanging? Are ye not in the high road of preferment? Are ye not a bauld drummer already? Wha kens how high ye may rise?—perhaps to be a general or drum-major.

David Haggart.—I hae na wish to be drum-major: it were na great things to be like the doited carle, Else-than-gude, as they call him: and troth, he has nae his name for naething. But I should have nae objection to be a general, and to fight the French and Americans, and win myself a name and fame like Willie Wallace, and do brave deeds, such as I have been reading about in his story book.

Myself.—Ye are a fule, Davie; the story book is full of lies. Wallace, indeed! the wuddie rebel! I have heard my father say that the Duke of Cumberland was worth twenty of Willie Wallace.

David Haggart.—Ye had better say naething agin Willie Wallace, Geordie, for, if ye do, De'il hae me, if I dinna tumble ye doon the craig.

I pretermit for lack of space Borrow's moral comments, merely remarking that to record at forty-eight this conversation held as a child of ten is a high tribute to his power of memory.

John Haggart, who had meanwhile removed to the Canongate, sent his returned prodigal again to school. What kind of scholar the ex-drummer made is not recorded. Equipped for a commercial life by a nine months' course of arithmetic and book keeping, he was apprenticed to Messrs. Cockburn & Baird, mill wrights, with good prospects of doing well; but the firm failed, and David was once more without an occupation.

To follow him in any detail through the long-drawn catalogue of his misdeeds, even had space so served, were tedious, and, if Lord Cockburn's judgment be sound, unprofitable. I propose, therefore, only to take a rapid glance here and there at his brave pages, referring the reader who should savour his style to the book itself. Let none such shrink from the perusal because the author happened to be hanged, for, as has been well observed of Wainwright, "The fact of a man being a poisoner is nothing against his prose."

Although, pending his apprenticeship, David by day conformed to the common standard, he had, he tells us, "various adventures in the streets at night"; and his operations were only limited by "want of knowledge of the flash kanes, where I might fence my snibb'd lays." His attention, therefore, was at the outset confined exclusively to "blunt." Thrown idle in April 1817, in less than three months he had greatly increased his experience: "Everything I saw, or heard, or did, was wicked; my nights and my days were evil." He fell, in other than the scriptural sense, among thieves of varied capacity and sex, who found in him an apt recruit. His chief pal was one Barney M'Guire, an Irishman, "a darling of a boy, and a most skilful pickpocket," who carried professional enthusiasm so far as to "do" even his own brother. Under this expert's eye David rapidly completed his education. In August 1817 he went with his mentor to make his début at Portobello races. A man in the crowd, who had been a successful backer, attracted his regard. "There were a good many old prigs keeping an eye on him, but I got the first dive at his keek cloy [breeches' pocket], and was so eager on my prey, that I pulled out the pocket along with the money." Instantly the notes were passed to Barney, and when the victim laid hands on David, nothing was found upon him. The poor man apologised for his mistake, remarking that someone had picked his pocket. The incident cost him £11. After the races were over the pair, accompanied by Barney's young brother, set out by coach for Jedburgh, where they began a tour of the Borders. They spent their time attending the "fairs" (markets) held in the different towns at that season, with the following substantial results: St. James's fair, Kelso, £20; the Rood fair, Dumfries, £17; the inn at Lockerbie, £23; and Langholm fair, £201. The magnitude of the last haul calls for special notice. Among the good folk whose attention was engrossed by the cattle, our friends remarked "a conish cove [gentleman], with a great swell in his suck [breast pocket]." David took one side and Barney the other, while young M'Guire hovered in the rear. David turned back the left breast of the coat over the man's arm; Barney touched him on the right shoulder, saying, "Are these sheep yours, sir?" and young M'Guire "snib'd the lil [stole the pocket-book]," the several acts being simultaneous. The brothers then bolted with the "dumbie," David remaining in sympathetic converse with his victim.

"Picking the suck," he obligingly explains, "is sometimes a kittle job. If the coat is buttoned, it must be opened by slipping past. Then bring the lil down between the flap of the coat and the body, keeping your spare arm across your man's breast, and so slip it to a comrade; then abuse the fellow for jostling you." On the other hand, he observes that the keek cloy is easily picked: "If the notes are in the long fold, just tip them the forks [fore and middle fingers]; but if there is a purse or open money in the case, you must link it [turn out the pocket]." Thus does genius make light of its gifts.

Shortly after the division of the spoil, they saw one John Richardson, a sheriff-officer from Dumfries, who had encountered them in that town, so they hastened away in a post-chaise, leaving word with the landlord that they were off to Dumfries. Next day found them at Carlisle, where they put up, as was their wont, at a good inn, taking their ease after the Langholm coup, and passing the time with cards, dice, and billiards, "besides a number of legerdemain tricks" to keep their hand in. Their luck had temporarily deserted them; an excursion to Cockermouth fair yielded only £3, and an unsuccessful assault with intent to rob "a conish cove who sported an elegant dross scout (gold watch), drag [chain], and chats [seals]," led to the police seizing their luggage and nearly capturing themselves. Having replenished their wardrobes at the expense of a confiding tailor, the party set forth by coach for Kendal. At that fair, "one of the finest horse-markets in England," Barney opened negotiations with a dealer of promising appearance on pretence of purchasing a horse. The man asked thirty-six guineas, Barney offered twenty-eight, and on his rising another guinea the seller, greatly to his discomfiture, closed the bargain. There was nothing to be done but pay the money. Later in the day, however, the misfortune was retrieved by disposing of the animal for £29, but "having lost five per cent. on the transaction," they more than restored the balance by robbing the purchaser of £43. At Morpeth fair, to which they next repaired, they fell in with a "school of prigs" on an outing from York, under the care of one Park, alias Boots. Twice, as these immature practitioners were essaying a pocket, did David's superior powers enable him to intervene and secure the prize, £15 and £17.

By December the pair (for from henceforth we hear no more of young M'Guire) were again in Newcastle, where they found it prudent to take private lodgings in the house of "a Mrs. Anderson in Castle Street," with whom they lived about a month. The lady had three daughters—"very pleasant girls"; and with this family they spent "a jolly Christmas." They passed for gentlemen travelling on pleasure, and would seem adequately to have sustained that rôle, as, sporting white-caped coats, top boots, and whips (!) they escorted the young ladies to theatres and public balls. But even amid such refining influences the Old Adam occasionally showed his hand, and other frequenters of these resorts suffered to the tune of some £70 by reason of his presence.

Perhaps none of our hero's performances has evoked more indignation than his thus dragging into his narrative the names of these inoffensive folk, to whom, as we shall see, he admits being indebted for further hospitality in the future, and much has been written upon the peculiar baseness of his conduct in this regard. Yet, as appears from a letter of 8th August 1821 to the editor of the *Scotsman*, the fact that in all Newcastle there was then no such street as "Castle Street" inspires a hope that the ladies' name was equally apocryphal with that of their local habitation, and that the whole episode existed but in David's too exuberant fancy. The names, however, were suppressed in the second edition of the "Life," which looks as if they belonged to real persons.

In January 1818, having parted from their hostesses with mutual regret, the adventurers removed to Durham. A lonely house on the York Road tempted them to extend their practice; they broke in at a window, overpowered the inmates after a strong resistance, and left the richer by £30. In a day or two they were recognised, arrested, and committed to Durham Assizes, where, having in due course been tried for burglary, they were found guilty and sentenced to death. Our hero was soon engaged in contriving his escape, and after long conference with his fellow-prisoners a plan was resolved on with good hope of success. "We set to work upon the wall of our cell, and got out to the back passage, when the turnkey made his appearance. We seized him, took the dubs [keys], bound, and gagged him. Having gained the back-yard, we scaled the wall; but Barney and another prisoner fell after gaining the top. By this time the down [alarm] rose, and poor Barney and the other man were secured." David was not the lad to leave his benefactor in the lurch. The first use he made of his freedom was to obtain a "fiddlestick" (spring saw) at Newcastle. Returning to Durham with a Yorkshire acquaintance, they were pursued by two "bulkies" (constables), at whom he fired his pistol; one fell— "whether I have his murder to answer for, I cannot tell, but I fear my aim was too true, and the poor fellow looked dead enough"; the Yorkshireman accounted for the other. That night David climbed the back wall of the jail by means of a rope ladder, and conveyed the "fiddlestick" to the expectant Barney, who lost no time in severing the iron bars of his cell window, when the friends were happily re-united. After a brief and unproductive tour in Berwickshire they reached Kelso, putting up at the Crown and Thistle. At the market Barney was caught redhanded by a burly farmer in a felonious attempt upon his "cloys." David rushed to the rescue of his pals, and "a terrible milvadering [combat]" ensued. But the farmer proved "very powerful"; a crowd gathered, and David was forced to flee, abandoning Barney to his fate, which took the form of three months in Jedburgh jail.

Deprived of Barney's friendly company and counsel, David, alone in the dismal February weather, found the colour of life sadly faded; his thoughts reverted to the bright eyes of the Misses Anderson, those "very pleasant girls," and soon his steps turned in the same direction. He was warmly welcomed, and remained with them till June. During his visit Miss Maria became the bride of a local shopkeeper; David himself led the nuptial festivities, and made, he tells us, "a very merry night of it." One evening as he was bringing Miss Euphemia home from the play, she was annoyed by the importunities of a belated reveller, who "mistook the lady for a girl of the town." David did all that, as a gentleman, he could in vindication of the damsel's honour, "and in doing so sunk into his keek cloy, and eased him of a skin [purse] containing nineteen quids of dross" —a superfluous touch, but the "skin" was too much for our Ethiopian. Though upon holiday, David engaged in one or two minor exploits, yielding "thirty-three quid screaves [notes], a dot drag, and two dross chats"; but he felt that he was wasting valuable time, so in June he "took leave of Mrs. Anderson and her worthy daughters, with sincere regret and sorrow at parting on both sides." "Never," he adds with creditable feeling, "will I forget the kindness, and even friendship, of these good people to me"; and, indeed, this domestic interlude remained one of his most agreeable memories. One regrets that he did not go a step further on the right road, and ranging himself, as the French have it, settle down blamelessly with the maiden for life. But that, perhaps, would have been hardly fair to Miss Euphemia.

David returned to Edinburgh, and after sojourning a space with one Train in the Grassmarket, removed to Mrs. Wilson's, East Richmond Street. He was now associated with William Henry, a well-known "snib," and principally engaged upon "the hoys and coreing [shoplifting]," the "cribs" of Billy Cook in the Calton, and of John Johnston at Crosscauseway, affording ready receptacles for their "lays." One night in the High Street, opposite the Tron Church, he met George Bagrie and William Paterson, alias Old Hag, "two very willing but poor snibs, accompanying a lushy cove, and going to work in a very forkless manner." Perceiving their incompetence, David interposed his experienced hand, and the "smash" (silver) was presently "whackt" (shared) at a house in the South Bridge kept by a Miss Gray, who, it is to be feared, was "other than a gude ane." There David met an old apprentice of his father's, having a commission to look out for the lost sheep, and was by him persuaded to return home. Expressing penitence, he was welcomed after the manner of prodigals, and a severe illness for a month confined him to the straight path; but no sooner was he about again than he reverted to his old ways. Certain petty thefts of tobacco and butter led to his committal to the Calton Jail, from which he was released on 18th December upon his relatives finding caution for his appearance when required. He had lost the grand manner, and in company with two young ladies, "both completely flash, as well as game," preyed upon the shop-keepers of the New Town. More than once he was arrested on suspicion, but managed to evade justice. In January 1819, with the assistance of Mr. Bagrie, he stole two webs of cloth from a merchant in Musselburgh; this they hid at the Dumbiedykes, and from it David caused to be made "a greatcoat for a favourite girl of mine," named Mary Bell, who hailed from Ecclefechan. Personally, David seems to have cared nothing for the bravery of bright clothes which so appealed to the heart of Deacon Brodie; he describes himself as becoming very careless and shabby in his dress. Apprehended with this young lady on ac-count of a brawl in a Calton eating-house, and brought before the Sheriff, he was thus addressed by his lordship: "Haggart, you are a great scoundrel, and the best thing I can do for you, to make you a good boy, is to send you to Bridewell for sixty days, bread and water, and solitary confinement." A further charge of watch-snatching in the Candlemaker Row added an-other sixty days to his period of retirement. Released on 23rd July, he hung about Leith and Portobello, sleeping among the Figgate Whins, and doing nothing beyond "petty jobs."

In September he left Edinburgh for Perth fair, where he as-sociated with sundry professional brothers, of whom one was called The Doctor. With these gentlemen he began a business tour in the north, visiting Dundee, Arbroath, and Aberdeen. In consequence of their operations at the races in the Granite City the gang was arrested; three were convicted of theft, David and The Doctor getting two months apiece "for being found among snibs." The magistrate observed that he was "sorry to see sae mony guid-looking lathies gaen on the way we war gaen"; to which David rudely retorted: "You auld sinner, it does not appear so, when you are sending innocent people to Bridewell."

The bailie, who seems to have been a judge of character, replied: "Ye are the warst amang them a'; if I had kent ye better I wad hae gien ye a twalmonth!" The couple were released on 25th November, and set out for Edinburgh by such easy stages that the journey occupied a month, but their depredations en route call for no comment. At Edinburgh The Doctor bought a new hat in a shop on the North Bridge, David the while "forking" a silver snuff-box from the hatter's "benjy cloy." They then honourably paid for the hat and departed. On 25th December they broke into a house in York Place, "opposite the Chapel," where they secured some "wedge-feeders" (silver spoons). David furnishes a complete list of further burglaries committed by him in Edinburgh and Leith, none of which are of special interest. "I generally entered the houses," he says, "by forcing the small window above the outer doors. This was an invention of my own, but it is now common, and I mention it," he thoughtfully adds, "to put families on their guard."

On 1st March 1820, David, along with a lad named Willie Forrest, was apprehended by Captain Ross, of the Leith police, and one of his "bulkies," and after a violent resistance was taken, "streaming all over with blood," to the lock-up. After many examinations, which he describes as tedious, he was committed for trial. "But on the evening of the 27th of March, having obtained a small file, I set to work and cut the darbies off my legs. I then, with the assistance of the irons, forced my cell door, and got into a passage. I then set to work upon a very thick stone wall, through which I made a hole, and got into the staircase just when twelve struck." The outer wall, however, proved too strong for him, so he unbarred the door of the debtor's room and liberated his friend Forrest to assist in the work. Their joint efforts were successful in removing a large stone, and by 5 A.M. David had regained his freedom. Through Leith Links and past Lochend they ran to Dalkeith without stopping, and only remaining long enough in that town to steal twelve yards of superfine blue cloth, left for Kelso. From thence, covering, for David, familiar ground, they reached Dumfries, where our hero was delighted to meet again his old pal Barney

M'Guire, whom he had not seen for over a year. It is apparent from his narrative that to his association with that master mind is due the marked superiority of his earlier offences, for since his association with Barney ceased in 1818, we must admit a regrettable falling off in quality and style. With Barney, then, he started for Carlisle, in good hope of rising to the old level of achievement; but, alas! no sooner had they reached that town than Barney was "pulled" by John Richardson, the sheriff-officer, and David was once more bereft of his support. Poor Barney went to Botany Bay for fourteen years. "He was a choice spirit and a good friend," says David, regretfully; "I had no thought and sorrow till I lost Barney."

Haggart and Forrest were retaken next day, brought back to Edinburgh, and committed for trial at the High Court on 12th July. Charged with eleven specific acts of theft, two of reset, one of housebreaking, and one of prison-breaking, the pannels pleaded guilty to the whole charges except reset; evidence was led, and the jury found them guilty of theft, generally, but the housebreaking charge not proven. This verdict was objected to by the defence as inapplicable to the libel, and the Court ordered informations. Before the hearing, however, Haggart had escaped; and on 5th April 1821, the Court, after awarding sentence of outlawry against him, repelled the objections stated in arrest of judgment (*Decisions of the Court of Justiciary, 1819–31*, No. 10).

Meanwhile, in Dumfries jail, to which he was restored, our hero made acquaintance with two other prisoners, a boy Dunbar, who had just got seven years, and a man M'Grory, then under sentence of death. With them he formed a plan to overpower and gag the turnkey, Thomas Morrin, in the absence of the head jailer, secure his "dubs" (keys), and make their escape. A stone, obtained from another prisoner, was tied in a piece of blanket for use as a weapon. The morning of Tuesday, 10th October, was fixed for the attempt. They were put as usual into the Cage, an "open-railed place, one storey up in the side of the jail, where the prisoners go for fresh air." There they found one Simpson, who, although he was to be discharged the next day, agreed to share their enterprise. Unfortunately, two ministers called for the condemned man, and M'Grory was locked into his cell with them. The others cut through their irons with an improvised file, and David concealed himself in a closet at the head of the stair. Dunbar then called Morrin to come up and let out the ministers. David thus describes what followed:—

He came up the stair accordingly with a plate of potatoe-soup for M'Grory. When he got to the top, he shut the cage door. I then came out upon him from the closet, and the pushing open of the door knocked the plate out of his hand. I struck him one blow with the stone, dashed him downstairs, and without the loss of a moment, pulled the dub of the outer jiger [door] from his suck. I gave only one blow with the stone, and immediately threw it down. Dunbar picked it up, but I think no more blows were given, so that Morrin must have received his other wounds in falling. I observed Dunbar on the top of him, riffling his breast for the key, I suppose, which I had got. Simpson had a hold of Morrin's shoulders, and was beating his back upon the steps of the stair. I rushed past them, crossed the yard as steadily as I could, pulled the dub from my cloy, where I had concealed it, and opened the outer jiger. It was sworn upon my patter [trial] that I had the dub in my fam [hand] when I passed through the yard, but this neither is, nor could be true, for it would have let all the debtors see what I was about. Besides, I well remember that upon getting to the top of the outer stair, I sunk into my cloys with both fams, not being sure, in my hurry, into which of them I had put the key. Some of the witnesses, on my trial, also said that I was bareheaded at this time, but this was not the case, for I had Dunbar's toper upon me.

He gives an exciting account of his escape from the town, and his ingenuity in baffling his pursuers, headed by John Richardson. As he lay next day hidden in a haystack he heard a woman ask a boy, "If that lad was taken that had broken out of Dumfries Jail." The boy answered, "No, but the jailer died last night at ten o'clock." So now David knew that henceforth he was sealed of the tribe of Cain. When the coast was clear he left his lair, and changing clothes with a scarecrow in an adjacent field, "marched on in the dress of a potatoe-bogle." That night, concealed in a hayloft, he heard the farm lads discussing his prowess: "He maun be a terrible fallow," said one. "Ou, he's the awfu'st chield ever was," said the other; "he has broken a' the jails in Scotland but Dumfries, and he's broken hit at last." Thus even in his own time was David privileged to behold the genesis of the Haggart myth. At Carlisle he found refuge with a lady friend who furnished him with "blone's twigs" (girl's clothes), in which, travelling only by night, he reached New-castle, where he again changed his dress. "Blowen," I am given to understand, is the spelling preferred by purists. On this oc-casion he had the decency to avoid the Andersons; but one day he passed in the street another old friend, John Richardson, a rencontre which caused his return to Edinburgh. In the coach he made acquaintance with a Mr. Wiper, who invited him as his guest to the Lord Duncan Tavern in the Canongate.

It is interesting to note that before they parted company the friends spent a pleasant evening at "Mrs. M'Kinnon's, on the South Bridge," a name memorable in the annals of Edinburgh crime. Of this lady, who followed David to the scaffold within two years, there would be something to say were the subject less infragrant.

After a brief stay at Jock's Lodge, the fugitive crossed the Firth in a Fisherrow boat, and was landed at Cellardyke. In sailor's clothes he wandered about Fife, replenishing his purse by sundry successful thefts; but Edinburgh, "where danger was most to be dreaded," drew him back: he took ship for New-haven and re-entered the capital. The first thing that met his eye was a police bill, offering a reward of seventy guineas for his apprehension; so he turned again to the North, and falling in with James Edgy, a well-known Irish "snib," began a course of robbery in the Highlands which proved almost as productive as the old days with Barney. Concluding their tour in Glas-gow, Edgy embarked on board the *Rob Roy* steamboat at the Broomielaw, and David joined the vessel at Erskine Ferry, *en voyage* for Ireland. At Lamlash Bay, in Arran, they put in to land a passenger, Provost Fergus of Kircaldy, who had recognised our hero, and afterwards communicated the fact to the police. Of this, however, David had no suspicion at the time, otherwise, as the Provost went ashore "in a black night," he could "easily have put him under the wave." They reached Belfast on 30th November 1820.

With Haggart's Irish experiences I have no space to deal, but must hasten on to the catastrophe. He realised a profit of upwards £230, and in the course of his adventures again broke prison at Drumore. Caught stealing notes from a pig drover at Clough fair, and committed to Downpatrick Jail, he was tried on 29th March 1821, convicted of felony, and sentenced "to lag for seven stretch." He inveighs bitterly against Irish "justice." Removed to Kilmainham Jail, David at once set about organising an escape, but the plan, betrayed to the authorities, miscarried, and all he got for his trouble was "a bat with a shillela" on the right eyebrow, the mark of which he carried to his grave—no long journey. Presently there arrived on the scene his old enemy John Richardson, who, inspecting the prisoners in companies of twenty, quickly spotted his man. David's denial of his identity was of no avail, and after the necessary formalities he was taken back to Scotland.

He records, in capitals and with much complacency, how on the night the coach arrived at Dumfries it was met by thousands of people with torches, "all crowding for a sight of Haggart the Murderer." As, heavily ironed, he entered the prison, he passed over the spot where, six months before, he had struck the fatal blow—"Oh, it was like fire under my feet!" Examined by the Sheriff, he refused, he says, to answer any questions, and in due course was transferred to Edinburgh for trial. His comment upon the evidence of the Crown witnesses is brief: "I was fully as wicked as they made me"; but he still maintained that he never meant to kill the turnkey. Convicted and sentenced to death, he took comfort in the reflection that one born to be hanged cannot be drowned.

Leaving David's veracious history, we find the fullest reports of his trial at Edinburgh on 11th June 1821 in the *Edinburgh Weekly Journal* (13th June), and the *Courant* (14th June).

An abridged account is given in the *Scotsman* (16th June). The Lord Justice-Clerk (Boyle) presided, the Solicitor-General (Wedderburn), J. A. Maconochie, and John Hope appeared for the Crown; Henry Cockburn and Thomas Maitland, for the defence. The pannel, charged with the murder of Thomas Morrin by giving him several severe blows on the head with a stone, which fractured his skull, having pleaded not guilty, and no objections being taken to the relevancy, the prosecutor adduced his proof. It was proved by the surgeons who attended Morrin during life, and made the post-mortem examination, that deceased had received five wounds on the left side of his head, one of which, above the eye, was two inches long, and penetrated to the bone; that death was due to fracture of the skull; and that the injuries might have been inflicted with the stone produced. Several witnesses swore that Morrin before he died stated that "David Haggart had done it." The principal witness for the Crown was John Simpson, of whom we have already heard. He gave substantially the same account of the affair as David, except that he denied having himself laid hands on the deceased. He saw Morrin attacked either by Haggart or Dunbar, but could not say which of them struck the blows, "being in a puzzle." Vainly did Mr. Hope endeavour to get the witness up to his precognition. Simpson, though he admitted seeing the deed done, swore that he knew not who did it; whereupon Hope moved the Court to commit him for prevarication. The judge, however, while describing his evidence as "unsatisfactory," would not go that length.

In the ballad which he composed after his conviction, "just to show that my spirit could not be conquered," David had a dig at Simpson—

> My life by perjury was sworn away,
> I'll say that to my dying day.
> Oh, treacherous S——, you did me betray,
> For all I wanted was liberty.

No witnesses were called for the defence. The Solicitor-General, in addressing the jury, pointed out that it was not necessary to prove that the mortal blows were given by the prisoner at the bar. It was sufficient to prove that he was concerned in the crime. The deceased had told several persons that "David Haggart had done it," and there was no one else in that part of the jail but Haggart, Dunbar, and Simpson. The latter had obviously not told all he knew, but what had been wrung from him was of greater importance. On the whole case there could be no doubt of the prisoner's guilt. Cockburn, for the defence, in a speech reckoned "ingenious," took the line that the murder was committed by Dunbar, who, curiously enough, had been sent to transportation before the trial at which his evidence must have been most material. No weight attached to what Morrin said before he died, as he was not then in a state to give any reliable testimony. It was an extraordinary circumstance that the prosecutor should move to have his chief witness committed for prevarication, and yet maintain that so far as it went his evidence was good. He asked for a verdict of not proven. The Justice-Clerk having summed up, the jury, "without retiring or hesitation," unanimously found the prisoner guilty, and the Court sentenced him to be hanged on 18th July, his body to be given to Dr. Alexander Monro for dissection. Such was then the ultimate fate of the condemned.

The trial, we read, "occasioned great anxiety, the Court and avenues leading to it being crowded throughout the day." The prisoner, who is described as "prepossessing," preserved the greatest composure during the proceedings, and heard his sentence unmoved. This was duly carried out on the appointed day, "at the usual place of execution, head of Libberton's Wynd," in presence of an immense and sympathetic crowd. David, "decently dressed in black," met his doom with "calm serenity," and on the steps of the scaffold, "turning to the multitude, he earnestly conjured them to avoid the heinous crime of disobedience to parents, inattention to Holy Scriptures, of being idle and disorderly, and especially of Sabbath-breaking, which, he said, had led him to that fatal end."

The efficacy of this exhortation must have been somewhat weakened by the publication, a few days later, of the famous

"Life," advertised as containing "an Account of his Robberies, Burglaries, Murders, Trials, Escapes, and other remarkable Adventures." price 4s., and written rather too racily for edification. The editor, George Robertson, W.S., explains that his task was undertaken with great reluctance, but having acted as agent for the pannel he did not think himself justified in refusing a request so anxiously pressed upon him. He excuses the levity of his author's tone on the ground that it was impossible for the unfortunate youth faithfully to record the thoughts and actions of his past life in other than his familiar language—which seems to imply his own belief in the verity of the narrative. The proceeds of the sale were to be devoted to David's aged parent and to charity. I find, on research, that Mr. Robertson was admitted a member of the Society in 1819; he acted as Sheriff-Substitute at Portree from 1829 to 1844, and died in the latter year at the age of fifty-one. In the fad of George Combe, W.S., who furnished the phrenological appendix, David found an unexpected means of further self-advertisement. Judged by his "bumps" he proved as bold a blade as he could desire. On one point, however, he gave the expert a bad fall: Mr. Combe held him indifferent to the attractions of the sex; the warmth of David's repudiation in his "Remarks" upon this article must have been, for him, painful reading. His further observations on the cerebal development of our hero and of Mrs. M'Kinnon are published in the *Transactions of the Phrenological Society* (Edinburgh, 1824). The philosopher makes a comparative analysis of the characters of his two involuntary subjects, deduced by him from their "bumps," and illustrated by certain grim engravings of their respective heads, as shaved to facilitate the application of his art after the owners had no further use for them.

Combe married a daughter of Mrs. Siddons. Before doing so he examined her head, and consulted Spurzheim. Luckily her anterior lobe was ascertained to be large; and as the lady had a fortune of £15,000 and was six years his junior, the scientist risked the step, with, it is recorded, the happiest results.

The "Life" was reviewed in the *Scotsman* (28th July) and in the *Scots Magazine* (August 1821); the former objected to its publication on moral grounds, but the latter expressed strong doubts not only of its propriety but of the author's good faith. It appeared, "from certain documents," that David's adventures in England were "about as authentic as the travels of Munchausen." On 18th August was published at 1s. *Animadversions and Reflections* upon the "Life," described in the advertisements as "an Antidote to a Book calculated to contaminate Society," which sufficiently indicates its purport. The anonymous author deals with David very solemnly, and the effect is depressing. A list of thefts of money alone, compiled from the "Life," brings out a balance in his favour of £912 on the four years' trading.

The veil was finally withdrawn by Henry Cockburn, who both in his *Journal* and *Circuit Journeys* gave, after many days, his reminiscences of his strange client. "He was young, good-looking, gay, and amiable to the eye," says his lordship, "but there was never a riper scoundrel—a most perfect and inveterate miscreant in all the darker walks of crime." A presentation copy of the book, containing "a drawing of himself in the condemned cell, by his own hand, with a set of verses, his own composition," was all Cockburn got for his exertions at the trial. "The confessions and the whole book," he states, "were a tissue of absolute lies—not of mistakes, exaggerations, or fancies, but of sheer and intended lies. And they all had one object: to make him appear a greater villain than he really was." But this, as we have seen, is too sweeping a charge; and where I have been able to check the hero's statements, as in the matter of his two trials at Edinburgh, I have found them borne out by the facts.

David wanted to die a great man, at the head of the profession of crime—Scotland's Jack Sheppard. A strange pride, Cockburn thinks. Robert Louis Stevenson, however, has noted that the ground of a man's joy is often hard to hit, but he adds that to miss the joy is to miss all. "In the joy of the actors lies the sense of any action. That is the explanation, that is the excuse."

And that, for example, is the true key without which the false
"dubs" of Deacon Brodie are insignificant as the Lantern-Bearers' hidden light. Let it serve for the epitaph of David Haggart.

Note.—"Mrs M'Kinnon."

Years after I had done with David Haggart, I was moved
to commemorate this lost lady of old years in "The Strange
Woman" (*Glengarry's Way and Other Studies*, Edinburgh:
1922). Mary M'Kinnon kept what she euphemistically called
"a licensed tavern"—there is a briefer and more accurate term
—at No. 82 South Bridge, Edinburgh. In 1823 she was tried
for and convicted of the murder, with a table knife, of one of
her clients. The case has certain remarkable features justifying
narration. Still later, on the happy acquisition of a portrait by
Charles Kirkpatrick Sharpe, drawn from life in the Calton
Jail, I ventured to write a playlet on the subject: "Mrs
M'Kinnon At Home" (*Rogues Walk Here*, London: 1934).

THE FATAL COUNTESS:

A Footnote to "The Fortunes of Nigel"

> Right: they are plots.
> Your beautie! O, ten thousand curses on't!
> How long have I beheld the devill in christall?
> Thou hast lead mee, like an heathen sacrifice,
> With musicke and with fatall yokes of flowers,
> To my eternall ruine.
> —*The White Devil.*

AS A LOVER of Elizabethan drama in general and of John Webster's splendid contribution to it in particular, I have often wished that fine poet had written a play on the murder of Sir Thomas Overbury. We know less of Webster personally than about any of his great contemporaries; the dates of his birth and death are both conjectural, and indeed the only definite dates in his life are those on the title-pages of his plays. But from these it is plain that the action of this dark tragedy must have gone forward before his living eyes. In 1612 he published *The White Devil*, and in the following year his elegy on the death of Prince Henry; in 1623, *The Duchess of Malfy* and *The Devil's Law Case*. Now, the poisoning of Overbury in the Tower, the scandalous divorce, and the amazing marriage all occurred in 1613, while the trial of Somerset and his countess for the murder took place in 1616. Probably, however, none of the dramatists then ransacking the universe for subjects was bold enough to tackle the intriguing matter thus lying ready to hand. King James was too exclusively King James for anyone to run that risk. The Overbury business, as M. de la Boderie remarked of the Gowrie affair, was "a little aromatic, and told different ways"; the good King's connection with it could not be handled with impunity.

For the *dramatis personæ* there is his Most Sacred Majesty King James the First and Sixth. James was much more than the mere pedantic pantaloon of *The Fortunes of Nigel*: he was "the wisest to work his own ends that ever was before him." [1] He was also the son who abandoned to her fate his mother Mary Stuart; the kinsman who held his cousin Arabella captive till she went mad and died; the prince who repaid England's debt to Raleigh by spoliation, imprisonment and death; the guest who caused his boy hosts the Ruthvens to be butchered in their own house, and immured their child brother in the Tower for forty years; the friend who, Judas-like, betrayed his discarded Pythias with a kiss. There is the King's favourite himself, Robert Carr, that sumptuous young Scot, who rose from pagedom to peerage, became the virtual ruler of England, and fell from place and power for love of a wicked woman. There is the Lady Frances Howard, beautiful and evil, for whom I had nearly borrowed a title from Marston: "The Insatiate Countess"; corrupt as Webster's own Vittoria, merciless as the Marquise de Brinvilliers. There is Sir Thomas Overbury, scholarly and subtle, the real power behind the imposing figure of the Favourite, sacrificed despite his craft to a Court intrigue and the fury of a woman scorned. These are the principal parts; for minor characters we have Mistress Anne Turner, wise woman and bawd; Doctor Forman, a knavish necromancer; Paul de Lobell, a French apothecary; Sir Theodore Mayerne, his Majesty's physician; the Earl of Northampton, Lord Privy Seal; Sir Thomas Monson, Master of the Armoury; and Sir Gervase Elwes, the Lieutenant of the Tower. Bishops, bravoes and panders, poison-mongers and magicians, supply the chorus.

Here surely was a company which ought to have appealed to Webster. But he would bear in mind how in 1604 his friends Chapman, Marston and Ben Jonson had been cast into prison, and hardly escaped mutilation, for a playful allusion to ubiquitous Scots and a line in parody of the Royal accent; [2] and if his knowledge of Scottish history extended so far, he would re-

[1] Memorandum by Sir George More, who succeeded Sir Gervase Elwes as Lieutenant of the Tower.—*Archæologia*, vol. xviii.

[2] *Eastward Hoe!* Act III. Sc. iii.; Act IV. Sc. i.

call how in 1601 a sheriff officer was hanged at the Cross of Edinburgh by Royal command, for having at a public roup inadvertently exposed the King's portrait upon a nail in the gibbet, the gibbet itself being condemned to the fire.[1] So we cannot wonder if Webster hesitated to use the Great Oyer of Poisoning as material for that "true drammaticke poem," that "sententious tragedy," in which he might have immortalised the facts, and we must be content to digest as best we may, with what illustrative sauce we can provide, the plain, substantial fare set forth for us by the laborious Howell.[2] Strong and solid meat this, not comfortably to be compassed by queasy stomachs. But I have thought that a glance at the menu, a mere epitome of the feast, though pretending to no critical or culinary value, might in these days of substitutes prove more easy of assimilation.

"Oh! it was a naughty Court," this Court of King James, as pictured for us in the pages of contemporary annalists; even a naughtier than that of his Merrie Grandson, and a much more vulgar. A monarch who knew not soap neither regarded water, and whose other personal peculiarities were equally objectionable; who accepted the dedication of the Bible, and wrote the curious letters to his beloved "Steenie." Curled and scented minions who ruled their doting master, and dispensed Court favours like so many small kings. Fine ladies, whose faces, plastered with paint, seemed mere masks; imperfectly acquainted with the Decalogue, clause seven, and for whom "the holy estate of Matrimony made but a May game." A new nobility, parasitic, prodigal and rapacious; "Faith and Honesty and other good acts little set by," and, generally, a moral tone comparable only to that of the Cities of the Plain. "O the Court, the Court!" exclaimed Mrs. Turner, who certainly was no purist. "God bless the King and send him better servants about him, for there is no religion in the most of them, but malice, pride, whoredom, swearing, and rejoicing in the fall of others. It is so wicked a

[1] Pitcairn, *Criminal Trials*, ii, 351.
[2] *State Trials*, ii. 786–862; 911–1022.

place as I wonder the earth did not open and swallow it up. Mr. Sheriff, put none of your children thither."[1] This, to be sure, was after her own conviction of similar backslidings, when her point of view had undergone a change.

Who killed Sir Thomas Overbury? That he was the victim of a murderous conspiracy, and that the Countess did her best to poison him, for which attempts Weston, Mrs. Turner, Elwes, and Franklin suffered death, is not disputed. But some authorities have held that there was another and a deeper plot by which the crime was actually effected, a plot conceived by King James himself and carried out by his French physician Mayerne, through the venal apothecary Lobell; Somerset and Northampton, Monson and the doctors, being cognizant of both enterprises, while the Countess and her bungling agents were made scapegoats for the more capable and distinguished criminals. Thus, according to the familiar formula of Elizabethan drama, there was both plot and underplot in the same play. The whole business is complicated and mysterious beyond the common puzzles of history; compared to this farrago of obscure and double motives, witchcraft and poisons, the affairs of Gowrie and of Sir Edmund Berry Godfrey are but the machinations of children, and the Gunpowder Plot a parlour riddle. If it was in fact of the King's contrivance this is unquestionably James's masterpiece, but the trail is too skilfully confused to afford the satisfaction of bringing it home to him.[2]

The curtain rises upon a "Masque of Hymen," written by Ben Jonson and designed by Inigo Jones, presented, on 5th January 1606, before their Majesties and the Court at the marriage of Robert Devereux, Earl of Essex, with the Lady Frances Howard. The maskers, played by courtiers, included, appropriately enough, certain characters representing Perverse Affections, afterwards routed by Reason; but as the contracting parties were children of fourteen and thirteen, Reason had less to do with the matter than family ambition. The bridegroom was

[1] Amos, *The Great Oyer of Poisoning*, p. 221.
[2] See A. C. Ewald's admirable study of the case, "A Perished Kernel," in his *Stories from the State Papers*, 1882, ii. 42–72.

the son and successor of Elizabeth's unlucky favourite; the bride, a daughter of Thomas Howard, Earl of Suffolk, Lord Chamberlain, and grandniece of Henry Howard, Earl of Northampton, Lord Privy Seal. These noblemen were respectively son and brother to that Duke of Norfolk, of Elizabeth's subjects

> . . . not the first who found
> The name of Mary fatal,

who lost both heart and head for love of a captive queen. The marriage, though binding in law, was limited to the ceremony: even the Court of King James saw the impropriety of carrying matters further; so the bridegroom was straightway sent abroad to learn the art of war, while the bride, like Diane de Castro, returned to her dolls. What the children thought of it all is not recorded.

The next scene is the Tilt Yard at Whitehall; the time 1607, the occasion, a grand tilting match arranged by splendid Sir James Hay, "a Scotch man and a Favourite of the King's," at which his new page, just arrived from France, was to carry his device to the Sovereign, "according to the custome of those pastimes used." The fortunate youth thus distinguished owed his preferment to his nationality and good looks. He was one Mr. Robert Ker—*anglicè* Carr—son of Sir Thomas Ker of Ferniehurst in Roxburgh, an old adherent of Queen Mary and a man of weight in Scotland. The lad was "about twenty years of Age; a comely personage, mixt with a handsom and Courtly garb." [1] As bearing his master's shield he rode proudly up to the dais, his unusual grace and beauty struck all beholders; and James, "whose nature and disposition," Lord Clarendon suavely observes, "was very flowing in affection towards persons so adorned," shared the general interest.[2] Just as the handsome page was dismounting to perform his office, his horse started and threw him, breaking his leg in the fall. His Majesty, graciously concerned, sent to ask who he was, and learning that he

---

[1] Wilson, *Life and Reign of King James*, 1653, p. 64.
[2] Authorities for the "amiable weakness" of his Majesty in this regard are cited by Harris, *Life of James I.*, 1753, p. 69, n. (HH).

was Scots and a Ker, remarked that he himself had when in Scotland a page of that name, "which this proved to be." So by Royal command the injured lad was lodged in the palace and his hurt attended by the King's mediciners. His Majesty took the greatest interest in the case, daily visited the patient throughout his illness, taught him Latin every morning (which no doubt contributed not a little to his rapid convalescence), and upon his happy recovery appointed him a Gentleman of the Bed-chamber.

It was soon known throughout the Court that the office of King's Favourite had changed hands. "Then the English lords, who formerly coveted an English favourite, (and to that end the Countesse of Suffolke did look out choyse young men, whom she daily curled, and perfumed their breaths,) left all hope, and she her curling and perfuming, all adoring this rising sun, every man striving to investe himselfe into this man's favour, not sparing for bounty nor flattery." [1] The estimable matron above mentioned was afterwards rewarded for her pains by becoming the mother-in-law of the successful candidate.

Henceforth Robert Carr's fortune was assured. The King could refuse him nothing, "even unto the half of his kingdom"; and for an unprecedented time he was privileged to bask in the sunshine of the Royal favour. The gilded rungs of the ladder by which he was destined to climb so high may here be noted: he was knighted in 1607; created Viscount Rochester, 1611; private secretary to the King, 1612; Knight of the Garter, Baron of Brancepeth, Earl of Somerset, and Lord High Treasurer of Scotland, 1613; Lord Chamberlain and Lord Privy Seal, 1614. His influence was paramount. "No Suite, no Petition, no Grant, no Letter, but Mr. Carr must have a hand in it; so that great rewards are bestowed upon him by Suitors, and large sums of money by his Majesty, by which means his wealth increased with his favour, and with both honour, for worth and riches dignify their owners." [2] The ugliest business in this connection was the forced sale to the Favourite in 1609 by the King's com-

[1] Weldon, *Court and Character of King James*, 1651, p. 64.
[2] *Truth Brought to Light*, 1651, p. 8.

mand of Raleigh's rich manor of Sherborne. The moving protests against this infamous transaction made by Sir Walter from his dungeon were without avail. "I maun hae the land, I maun hae it for Carr," was the judgment of the second Solomon: such was the justice of James the Just. But although his Majesty did not scruple thus to despoil the public treasury and even to plunder private persons to gratify his new fancy, there were limits to his extravagance. "He was very liberall," says Weldon, "of what he had not in his owne gripe, and would rather part with 100. li. hee never had in his keeping then one twenty shillings peece within his owne custody." Everyone knows the story of how Lord Treasurer Salisbury sought to open the King's eyes to the magnitude of his prodigality by piling on a table in his view £5000 of the £20,000 for which he had given an order to Carr; and how James, sobered by the sight of the great pile of gold, at once restricted the gift to that amount.

While the nobility of England, headed by the haughty Howards, contended for the Favourite's favours, there were two members of the Court who refused to bow the knee to the new Baal: Queen Anne and Henry, Prince of Wales. His Majesty's "dearest bedfellow," as James inelegantly and inaccurately termed his consort, living in separate state and holding her own Court at Denmark House, had long since given him up as a bad job. Her complacency increasing with her bulk, she merely shrugged her ample shoulders at the Royal ongoings and went her own way. She was no Isabella to cope with the King's Gavestons and Spensers, though she had found her Mortimer, if all tales are true, in the Lord Pembroke. But the case of Carr was more than even her good nature could tolerate, and she hated him heartily. The Prince was mentally, morally and physically so unlike his Royal sire as to give some colour to contemporary scandal. A lad of brilliant promise, graceful, accomplished, intelligent and generous-hearted, an ardent patriot and a lover of arms, he was the hope of England and the people's idol. Strangely enough in so corrupt a Court, his morals were irreproachable. Small wonder that the King, envious of his popularity and virtues, looked but coldly on this paragon son, and that there was little love lost between them. "No one but my father would keep such a bird in a cage," said the Prince, of Raleigh whose pupil and admirer he was. Naturally detesting the Ganymedes whom the King delighted to honour, Carr's phenomenal rise and influence especially provoked Prince Henry's hostility, and the two young men were openly opposed. Indeed so strained were their relations that the Prince is said on one occasion "to have strook him on the Back with his Racket." [1]

Behind all these conflicting interests and animosities there was one inconspicuous figure whose hands held many of the strings. Thomas Overbury, squire's son, Oxford graduate, law student and man of letters, was one of those people so aptly described by the Tichborne Claimant as having "plenty brains and no money," for whose benefit persons conversely endowed are specially created. Upon a voyage of pleasure to Edinburgh, he had there made acquaintance with Robert Carr, who accompanied him on his return to England. The intimacy continued, and in 1608 by the Favourite's good offices Overbury was appointed a Gentleman of the Household and graciously knighted. [2] Sir Thomas and his friend in combination made a powerful pair, the intellectual gifts of the one supplementing the material advantages of the other. But for Overbury's prompting the beautiful and brainless Favourite could never have sustained, politically, the part he was called upon to play. "The voice was the voice of Jacob." Overbury became his second self, wrote his letters, coached him in statecraft, and "devilled" for him to such effect that Sir Robert Carr won golden opinions for his unexpected ability. And the Queen, who despite her complaisance was no fool, disliked Sir Thomas Overbury even more than she did the Favourite.

The curtain rises for the entrance of the heroine. Frances, Lady Essex, pending the return of her young husband from abroad, had "come out," and was now in the enjoyment of

[1] Osborne, *Traditionall Memoyres*, 1658, p. 119.
[2] "I ken the man weel; he's one of my thirty-pound knights."—*Eastward Hoe!* Act IV. Sc. i.

those privileges to which her rank and beauty entitled her. "The Court was her Nest, her Father being Lord Chamberlain; and she was hatched up by her Mother, whom the sour breath of that Age (how justly I know not) had already tainted. . . . And growing to be a Beauty of the greatest Magnitude in that Horison, was an Object fit for Admirers, and every Tongue grew an Orator at that Shrine." [1] As to her character, she is described as being "of a lustfull appetite, prodigall of expence, covetous of applause, ambitious of honor and light of behaviour." [2] These attributes would not of themselves have sufficed to render their possessor conspicuous in Court circles, but the charms of the youthful debutante won for her a conquest of the first importance. Contemporary authorities concur in stating that the Prince of Wales, whose coldness had hitherto withstood the fire of so many fine eyes directed upon him, succumbed for a time to the wiles of the bewitching Countess, "set on" to the seduction of his Highness by her crafty granduncle, Northampton. Old heads are seldom found upon such young and lovely shoulders; regrettably for the success of that nobleman's schemes his charming relative, casting prudence and family interest to the winds, fell desperately in love with the Favourite, the all-powerful rival of the House of Howard. That so vain a man as Carr appreciated the distinction of being wooed by the Prince's mistress goes without saying, yet the position, though flattering, was not without its drawbacks. Meetings were difficult and dangerous, Carr had no talent for correspondence, and a confidant was required to carry on the intrigue if it were to escape the prying eyes of the Court. So His Majesty's adviser was fain to consult his own more gifted counsellor, with the happiest results. Overbury's subtle mind revelled in the occasion; he undertook the whole management of the affair, and actually wrote his friend's love letters! [3] The pen that drew the famous *Characters* must have done its work well; the letters, had they been preserved, would be interesting reading. But in

---

[1] Wilson, p. 56.
[2] *Truth Brought to Light*, p. 9.
[3] Winwood, iii. 478.

spite of all precautions some word of his siren's perfidy reached the Prince's ear, and he availed himself of the first opportunity to break with her. "For dancing one time among the Ladies, and her Glove falling down, it was taken up, and presented to him by one that thought he did him acceptable service; but the Prince refused to receive it, saying publickly, 'He would not have it, it is stretcht by another.' This was an aggravation of hatred betwixt the King's Son and the King's Friend." [1]

And then to the Countess, smarting under this open affront and fearing to lose her hold on Carr in consequence of the scandal—"for dishonest Love is most full of jealousie"—at Christmastide 1609 came my Lord of Essex from the Low Countries to claim his girl-bride. The Earl was now a grave young man of eighteen, "of a mild and courteous condition," whom foreign service had made older than his years. To his amazement and dismay his wife refused to live with him. "Yet notwithstanding, the Earle retained her with him, allowed her honorable attendance, gave her means according to his place, shewed an extraordinary affection, endeavouring rather by friendly and faire perswasions to win her, than to become supercilious over her." [2] Finding her unamenable to reason he invoked the authority of her parents, and in the end she was compelled to accompany her husband to his house of Chartley in Staffordshire, where, doubtless with an ill enough grace, she ostensibly accepted the duties of her position.

The scene changes to Hammersmith, the abode of the wise woman, Mrs. Turner. The widow of Dr. George Turner, a reputable physician, this lady, "of a low stature, faire visage, for outward behaviour comely," was, as our authority frankly states, "little lesse than a flat Bawd, by which means shee is made apt to enter into any evil action, to entertain any motion, be it never so facinorous." [3] Scott used some of her more presentable features for his portrait of Dame Ursula Suddlechop. To this experienced matron Lady Essex applied for guidance in her two

[1] Wilson, p. 56.
[2] Truth Brought to Light, p. 10.
[3] Ibid., p. 13.

pressing needs: how to confirm Carr's love for her and repel that of her husband. The case lay somewhat outside the cunning woman's practice; she deemed it wiser to consult a specialist, and recommended one Dr. Simon Forman "that dwelt at Lambeth, being an ancient Gentleman, thought to have skill in the Magick Arts," by whose aid she had already benefited in a personal affair of the heart.[1] This expert undertook—like old Trapbois, for a consideration—to "inchant" the Earl and the Favourite; and to that end he supplied the Countess with certain phallic emblems, fashioned in wax and lead, together with divers powders to be administered to the respective patients. But despite the exhibition of these mystic drugs the Earl's affection for his wife persisted and the Favourite was as far off as ever. "I cannot be happy so long as this man liveth," wrote the Countess from Chartley to her "Sweet Turner"; "therefore pray for me, for I have need, but I should be better if I had your company to ease my mind. Let him [Forman] know this ill news. If I can get this done, you shall have as much money as you can demand: this is fair play." [2] To the venerable magician, her "Sweet Father," she wrote complaining of the inefficacy of his charms: "My Lord is lusty and merry, and drinketh with his men; and all the content he gives me is to abuse me, and use me as doggedly as before. I think I shall never be happy in this world, because he hinders my good and will ever, I think. So remember, I beg for God's sake, and get me out of this vile place." Subscribing herself "Your affectionate loving daughter," she adds in a postscript: "Give Turner warning of all things, but not the lord [Carr]. I would not have anything come out for fear of the Lord Treasurer [Salisbury], for so they may tell my father and mother, and fill their ears full of toys." [3]

Whether by the potency of the wizard's spells or because

[1] She had given to Sir Arthur Mainwaring, a gentleman of the Prince's suite, one of Forman's prescriptions, "which wrought so violently with him that, through a storm of Rain and Thunder, he rode fifteen miles one dark night to her House, scarce knowing where he was till he was there."—Wilson, p. 57.

[2] *State Trials*, ii. 931.

[3] *Ibid.*, ii. 932.

the country began to bore him, as in his domestic circumstances is not unlikely, the Earl decided to return with his wife to town. Sir Robert Carr was now my Lord Viscount Rochester, and a mightier man than ever. The intrigue was resumed in the winter of 1610–11, and as regards the Favourite's attachment Lady Essex had no reason to complain of the magician's failure: an "inchanted Nutmeg," given to the Viscount in his drink, had proved most efficacious; but "really to imbecillitate the Earl," in Wilson's phrase, seemed beyond the art of magic. It appears from the evidence of the servants in the subsequent divorce case [1] that for the next eighteen months the Earl and Countess followed the Court and visited at sundry great houses, including her father's at Audley-end in Essex, apparently on the common footing of man and wife. On 6th November 1612 Prince Henry died after a brief illness, whether due to poison or typhoid fever has been disputed. In the popular belief Rochester and Northampton were responsible for his taking off, and a horrid suspicion even attached to the King himself as being accessory to the crime.[2] But though my admiration for James is by no means blind, I cannot believe him capable of murdering his own son. The Prince of Wales thus removed from his path, the Favourite was now well nigh omnipotent. The infatuation of Lady Essex for him was such that their clandestine connection no longer satisfied her: she must be his wife before the world; yet his power, great as it was, could not put asunder those whom God was understood to have joined. The resources of sorcery had been exhausted in vain; there remained a shorter and a surer way.

In February 1613 a certain wise woman named Mary Woods, dite "Cunning Mary," being apprehended for theft, told the Suffolk justices a curious tale. She said that Lady Essex had given her a ring and promised her £1000 if she would furnish for the Earl's consumption a poison that should not act for three or four days. Finding herself unequal to the responsibility,

---

[1] State Trials, ii. 789–794.
[2] The evidence is discussed by Mr. Andrew Bisset, Essays on Historical Truth, 1871, pp. 357–410; cf. The Great Oyer of Poisoning, passim.

"Cunning Mary" repented and left London. The affair, as savouring of scandalum magnatum, was promptly burked, and we cannot know how much truth lay at the bottom of the wise woman's well.[1] It is probable that the miscarriage in the matter of "Cunning Mary" arrested the Countess in her more deadly purpose. Her next design was to obtain a divorce on the ground of nullity. As the marriage had subsisted for six years and the parties had lived together for three, it says much for her Ladyship's assurance that she should now boldly announce that she had never in fact been a wife at all, while her unblushing claim to maidenhood, in view of her relations with Prince Henry and the Favourite, is even more brazen. Rochester advised with Northampton, who thought well of the scheme and undertook to put it before the lady's parents and to sound his Majesty on the subject. Lord and Lady Suffolk were fully alive to the advantages of an alliance with the Favourite, and the savour of sculduddery and divinity attaching to the case appealed peculiarly to the Royal palate.[2] But though the proposed proceedings received the imprimatur of these high personages, an unlooked-for obstacle arose.

Sir Thomas Overbury, the Viscount's alter ego, was suffering from swelled head. He had all a ventriloquist's contempt for the puppet whose strings he had so long controlled, and did not always take the trouble to conceal it; he enjoyed the reputation of a successful author, and numbered Ben Jonson among his literary cronies at the Mermaid; he was tired of carrying messages to Hammersmith, interviewing wizards, and arranging assignations in Paternoster Row, where Mrs. Turner when in town resided; and he began to see that not only was this liaison endangering his patron's future prospects but—a matter of more importance—was imperilling his own. He had disliked and distrusted Lady Essex from the first; when, therefore, he

---

[1] Gardiner, History of England, ii. 169 n.; Gibb, King's Favourite, 1909, pp. 126–129.

[2] It is curious that James should have been twice mixed up with the marriages of his favourites to women who divorced their husbands for impotency. Cf. the case of the Countess of March and James Stewart, Earl of Arran.— Fraser Chronicles, Scottish History Society, xlvii. 178–182.

learned that Carr actually proposed to marry her so soon as a disgraceful and fraudulent divorce could be obtained, his resentment knew no bounds. To have the fool he had made appear as wise before men waste time and substance on a worthless woman was bad enough; to let him make her Viscountess Rochester was beyond bearing. Once my Lord had so unscrupulous a helpmate, Othello's occupation would be gone indeed. So Sir Thomas spoke his mind to his patron, and in the pungent phrase of which he was master added to his gallery of *Characters* a new portrait in prose: "The Mistress made A Wife." Their relations had been for some time less cordial than of yore, owing to the arrogant behaviour of Overbury; the Viscount, "being a little netled in his affection, grows something harsh, and Sir Tho. having been heretofore excepted at, with these kind of contentions grows so much more carelesse, answers word for word; so that from fair and friendly speeches they grow to words of anger, and either to crosse the other." [1] In the end the breach between the friends became complete.

Rochester, as is the way with weak natures, could not keep his troubles to himself; he hastened to his mistress, and into her delicate ear poured all the injurious epithets which Sir Thomas had applied to her. From that moment Overbury's doom was sealed; thenceforth the Countess, like Queen Mary, studied revenge. She saw that by proclaiming a tithe of what he knew of her intrigues with Prince Henry and the Viscount, and of her attempts upon her husband's health and life, Sir Thomas could render the divorce proceedings abortive and blast her reputation even in such a Court as that of King James, so she convinced her lover that at all costs the mouth of this dangerous witness must be stopped. One of the Queen's gentlemen, Sir David Woodes, between whom and Overbury "there was some discontent," was offered by the Countess £1000—this being, as appears, the customary fee for such an operation—to assassinate Sir Thomas. She also promised to reconcile Woodes with Rochester, "his greatest enemy." But Sir David declined to act without the Viscount's express war-

[1] *Truth Brought to Light*, p. 33.

rant, so the affair went no further. Carr, at his trial, admitted knowledge of the plan.[1] Northampton and Rochester evolved a subtler scheme. They decided to approach his Majesty, as the fount and source of justice. A word of the common report that, whilst Rochester ruled the King, Overbury ruled Rochester, was all that was required to rouse into action the Royal authority, of which James was morbidly jealous. The post of ambassador "into Flanders, to the Arch-Duke (some say, into France),"[2] was offered to Sir Thomas, who begged to be excused: he had no wish to leave his own country. The King, furious at this flouting of his sovereign will, on 21st April 1613 committed Overbury to the Tower "for a matter of high contempt." What induced so clever a man to resist the King's command and thus to rush upon his fate? In this predicament Sir Thomas had turned to his former friend for aid. It is probable that if Overbury had accepted his banishment Rochester would have been content to let him go, but finding him unwilling to do so he, doubtless at the instigation of the Countess, advised him to resist the Royal order, well knowing what the consequences would be.[3] At all events, as we shall find, the prisoner complained bitterly of his betrayal.

And now the stage is clear for the bill of divorcement. With the infragrant details of that "Devil's Law Case" it is fortunately unnecessary to deal—the curious reader will find them elsewhere, and much good may they do him, but the main facts of the shameless business must be related, in order rightly to appreciate what followed.[4] Early in May a family council was held at Whitehall to discuss the procedure to be adopted, Northampton and Suffolk representing their fair relative, while her husband's interests were confided to Lords Southampton and Knollys. Essex, though no longer desirous of retaining the lady, would admit nothing to prejudice his own remarriage, and without his concurrence the case was hopeless; so the Howards

---

[1] *State Trials*, ii. 982.
[2] Wilson, p. 67. Other authorities say, Russia.
[3] Gardiner, ii. 177–8, *n*.
[4] *State Trials*, ii. 785–862.

had to rest satisfied with a modified plea of impotency *quoad hanc*, to which the Earl to be rid of his wife consented. His Majesty, highly approving of this nice distinction, on 16th May appointed under the Great Seal a Royal Commission to try the cause. Among the ten members nominated was Dr. George Abbot, Archbishop of Canterbury, whose situation was as invidious as that of the one righteous man in the wicked cities; the rest were mostly creatures of the King. The depositions of the witnesses were taken on 2nd June, and the more the Archbishop heard of the case the less he liked it. The Countess had the audacity to maintain by her counsel that her husband was bewitched; how Mrs. Turner, if she attended the hearing, must have enjoyed that touch! But even this impudent assertion is surpassed in effrontery by the testimony adduced in her behalf, for "seven noble women," headed by the Countess of Suffolk, her mother, solemnly declared on oath that, notwithstanding her varied experiences, Lady Essex "remained a Virgin uncorrupted." If the other great dames were, morally, of Lady Suffolk's complexion their evidence would present few difficulties; but there is another explanation, more creditable to the matrons' honour. Modesty had prescribed that the Countess should appear before them veiled. "One mistris Fines, near Kinswoman to old Kettle, was dressed up in the countesses cloathes, at that time too young to be other then *virgo intacta*, though within two years after, had the old ladies made their inspection . . ."— but here our authority becomes somewhat too Jacobean to be followed further.[1] The proof was inadequate even for a packed tribunal, and the case being closed, it was found that the Commissioners were equally divided.

His Majesty was highly incensed; the Archbishop upon his knees begged with tears to be released from his distasteful task, but to no purpose. James was determined that the case should go on; and in defiance of justice and precedent his Majesty adjourned the proceedings till 18th September, adding to the Commission the Bishops of Winchester and Rochester,

[1] Weldon, p. 81.

prelates upon whom he could depend to take their law and gospel from the Defender of the Faith. Then the good Archbishop addressed to the King a letter setting forth arguments scriptural and patristic in support of his opinion, and deprecating the power of Satan to produce the results alleged.[1] James replied at great length, with vast display of learning and a fine appreciation of the physiologic problem which the case presented. Having corrected the Archbishop's divinity, he concluded thus: "I will end with our Saviour's words to St. Peter, *Cum conversus fueris, confirma fratres tuos;* for on my conscience, all the doubts I have yet seen are nothing but *nodos in scirpo quœrere.*"[2] But despite all the pressure his Majesty could bring to bear upon him, the stout old bishop stood firm. He has left on record an elaborate account of the matter, showing how far to pleasure his Favourite King James was prepared to tamper with the laws of God and England.[3] On 25th September, by seven votes to five, the Commissioners pronounced for the nullity of the marriage, and Lady Essex was free of her bonds. By express command of his Majesty the "acute and honourable minority" were forbidden to state the grounds of their decision.

"Of the conduct of James," observes Mr. Gardiner, "it is difficult to speak with patience. . . . Nothing could well have been more prejudicial to the interests of justice than his meddling interference at every step, which did even more harm than the appointment of the additional members."[4] Indeed, none of that monarch's many arbitrary acts did so much to widen the breach between the throne and the people as his behaviour in this connection. For these things were not done in a corner; the four-months' trial had been followed with the public interest always attaching to a *cause célèbre.* The godly were disgusted, the profane intrigued, but the cause of the Favourite had triumphed and his Majesty was content. The

[1] *State Trials,* ii. 794.
[2] *Ibid.,* ii. 802.
[3] *Ibid.,* ii. 805–860.
[4] *History,* ii. 173.

son of the Bishop of Winchester, whose pious zeal for the
Head of the Church had contributed so largely to the happy
issue, was knighted, and for the remainder of his days was
called Sir Nullity Bilson, in remembrance of his father's
prowess. Well might Sir Walter Raleigh write, shortly before
his death:

> Go, tell the Court it glows,
>   And shines like painted wood;
> Go, tell the Church it shows
>   What's good, but does no good.
>   If Court and Church reply,
>   Give Court and Church the lie.[1]

On 11th November my Lord Viscount Rochester was created
Earl of Somerset, and on 26th December his magnificent nup-
tials with the Lady Frances Howard were celebrated in the
Chapel Royal, in presence of their Majesties and the whole
Court. Old Northampton gave away his grandniece, and the
celebrant was that very Bishop of Bath and Wells who seven
years before had married the lady to Lord Essex. The bride,
appropriately robed in white, wore her beautiful hair unbound
—the insignia of maidenhood.[2]

>   O these golden nets,
> That have insnared so many wanton youths!
> Not one, but has been held a thread of life,
> And superstitiously depended on.[3]

The irony of the situation was not lost upon the Courtiers.
The honeymoon over, the noble pair took up house in London,
having acquired the magnificent mansion of Sir Baptist Hicks
at Kensington.

On 15th September, ten days before the judgment which
paved the way for this Ahab festival, with its Court masques
and revels, its City triumphs and banquets, and its cataract of

[1] *Raleigh's Works*, ed. Birch, ii. 396.
[2] Such was then the custom of virgin-brides. Cf. *The White Devil*, Act
IV. Sc. i.
[3] *The Insatiate Countesse*, Act V. Sc. i.

costly gifts, Sir Thomas Overbury died miserably in the Tower. After her failure with the Queen's gentleman Lady Essex, abandoning the assassination motif, took counsel with her trusty friend Mrs. Turner as to the best means of wreaking vengeance upon her enemy; "protesting that she was never so defamed, neither did she ever think that any man durst have been so saucy as to call her whore and base woman, and that to Rochester her only hope, and with an impudent face; but Overbury, that Negroe, that scumme of men, that devill incarnate, he might do any thing, and passe either unregarded or unpunished." [1] The wise woman was greatly shocked at the insults offered to her benefactress; rather than the slander should escape "shee would be his Death's man herself." She was of opinion "that to poison him was the onely way, and that with least suspect; but then the party that should doe it was to seek, for he must bee no ordinary man, [but] some Apothecary or Physitian, that might temper the poison rightly to take effect according to their mind." [2] Death had deprived them of the services of the venerable Dr. Forman, and of Dr. Gresham, his colleague and successor. "After long study" one Richard Weston was selected—he had been the late Dr. Turner's assistant, and enjoyed the widow's confidence. For a reward of £200 he undertook the job.

Sir William Wade, the Lieutenant of the Tower, was a model governor. No visitors, letters or messages were allowed to reach the prisoner; but as this did not suit the conspirators' plans the Royal authority was invoked to dismiss him, and his post was given to Sir Gervase Elwes, a more complaisant gaoler. Somerset was afterwards charged with initiating this friendly move. Lady Essex next procured, through Sir Thomas Monson, the Master of the Armoury, the appointment of Weston as gaoler to the prisoner. Meanwhile Mrs. Turner had introduced her fair client to Dr. James Franklin, dwelling near Doctors Commons, "a man of a reasonable stature, crookshouldered, of a swarthy complexion, and thought to bee no

[1] *Truth Brought to Light*, p. 37.
[2] *Ibid.*, p. 38.

lesse a witch then the two former, Forman and Gresham," [1]
who furnished the ladies from time to time with "the strongest
poison he could get for Sir T. Overbury," viz. aqua fortis, white
arsenic, mercury, powder of diamonds, lapis costitus, great
spiders, and cantharides, "wherewith he might languish away
by little and little." [2] It now only remained to exhibit these
remedies, and her Ladyship's purpose would be achieved.

The campaign seems to have opened on 6th May, when
Weston received from Mrs. Turner in a vial "certain yellow
poison, called Rosalgar," with a view to its insertion in the
prisoner's broth.[3] With the vial in one hand and the captive's
supper in the other, Weston unwelcomely encountered the
Lieutenant of the Tower. "Sir, shall I give it to him now?" he
whispered. The poisoner was either a tyro in his art or he
strangely overestimated the Lieutenant's complaisance, for Sir
Gervase "terrified him with God's judgments"; but perceiving
the good effect of this commination, "drank to him" to en-
courage his repentance.[4] It is singular that the governor of a
gaol, having detected an attempt upon a prisoner's life, should
content himself with preaching a sermon and drinking the
would-be murderer's health. Doubtless Sir Gervase knew that
high interests were involved, for had not the great Lord Privy
Seal called personally to commend the prisoner to his vigilance? Whether or not this poison was actually administered,
Weston told Mrs. Turner that he had given it to Overbury,
upon whom it "wrought very vehemently"; he accordingly
demanded his reward. "The man is not yet dead," replied the
cautelous dame; "perfect your work, and you shall have your
hire." [5]

On 5th June Rochester sent to Overbury a letter containing
a white powder. "It will make you more sick," he wrote, "but
fear not; I will make this a means for your delivery, and for
recovery of your health." Overbury took the powder, "where-

[1] *Truth Brought to Light*, p. 43.
[2] *State Trials*, ii. 941, 947.
[3] *Ibid.*, ii. 917.
[4] *Ibid.*, ii. 938.
[5] *Ibid.*, ii. 917.

upon his sickness grew more violent and his languishment
increased." [1] If, as Somerset at his trial alleged, this powder was
harmless, his sending it under such toxic conditions was unfortunate as being open to misconstruction by the froward.
With the benevolent intention of giving variety to the prison
fare, both Rochester and the Countess were in the habit of
sending from their respective tables wine, tarts, and jellies for
the prisoner's use. One of Lady Essex's accompanying communications to the Lieutenant has been preserved:—

> I was to bid you say that these tarts came not from me; and
> again, I was bid to tell you that you must take heed of the tarts
> because there be *letters* in them, and therefore neither give
> your wife nor children of them; but of the wine you may, for
> there are no *letters* in it. Sir T. Monson will come from the
> Court this day, and then we shall have other news. [2]

At the subsequent trial her Ladyship, examined as to this
document, "Saith, That by *letters* she meant poison." Dr.
Franklin, in his confession of 16th November 1615, gave the
following remarkable account of the methods employed:—

> Sir T. never eat white salt but there was white arsenick put
> into it. Once he desired pig, and Mrs. Turner put into it lapis
> costitus. The white powder that was sent to Sir T. in a letter
> he [Franklin] knew to be white arsenick. At another time he
> had two partridges sent him from the Court, and water and
> onions being the sauce, Mrs. Turner put in cantharides in-
> stead of pepper; so that there was scarce anything that he did
> eat but there was some poison mixed. For these poisons the
> Countess sent me rewards; she sent many times gold by Mrs.
> Turner. She afterwards wrote unto me to buy her more poi-
> sons. [3]

The power of Overbury's constitution to withstand this
toxicological bombardment recalls the endurance of Nicol
Muschet's wife in similar trying circumstances; but the defence

---

[1] *State Trials*, ii. 917.
[2] *Ibid.*, ii. 989.
[3] *Ibid.*, ii. 941.

in both cases suffered severely. Sir John Lidcote, Overbury's brother-in-law, asked Rochester for leave to visit the prisoner, which, as it could hardly be refused, my Lord obtained from the King. Lidcote found him "very sick in his bed, his hand dry, his speech hollow." He instructed Sir John to write his will. As Lidcote was taking leave the prisoner asked softly "whether Rochester juggled with him or not?" but the Lieutenant, who was present, heard the whisper and interfered.[1] From his sickbed the unhappy man wrote repeatedly to his false friend, upbraiding him with his treachery. These letters may be read in the report of Somerset's trial. Their bitter, scornful tone must have been wormwood to the haughty Favourite, while the threat of reprisals was well calculated to make a galled conscience wince.

Is this the fruit of my care and love to you? Be these the fruits of common secrets, commons dangers? As a man, you cannot suffer me to lie in this misery; yet your behaviour betrays you. All I intreat of you is, that you will free me from this place and that we may part friends. Drive me not to extremities, lest I should say something that you and I both repent. And I pray God that you may not repent the omission of this my counsel, in this place whence I now write this letter.[2]

Overbury's last letter, written shortly before the end, after five months' captivity, shows that his eyes at length were fully opened to the extent of Rochester's "jugglery." "You owe me for all the fortune, wit, and understanding that you have," he writes; and then proceeds scathingly to expose his friend's cynical and perfidious conduct, from the time "you had won that woman by my letters" till, by following Carr's treacherous advice, "I was caught in the trap." He has written at large "the story betwixt you and me," which he has sent under eight seals to a safe friend; "and if you persist still to use me thus, assure yourself it shall be published. Whether I live or die, your shame shall never die, but ever remain to the world, to make

[1] *State Trials*, ii. 985.
[2] *Ibid.*, ii. 979.

you the most odious man living." [1] Needless to say, this narrative was never forthcoming; at whose instance it was burked is not hard to guess, but that it would have thrown a flood of light upon the whole dark business is certain.

The result of this turning of the worm was seriously to alarm the plotters. There was a rumor that Overbury was about to be released, and they feared that "they all should be undone." The Countess sent for Weston "and was very angry with him that he had not dispatched Sir Thomas." Weston replied, with reason, that the failure was more his misfortune than his fault: he had given him poison "that would have killed twenty men." [2] There, for the time, the matter rested.

If there be one point clearly established as to the character of King James it is his implacable vindictiveness; he never forgave or forgot. Now as we know from Sir Ralph Winwood, Principal Secretary of State, that "such a rooted Hatred lyeth in the King's Heart towards him [Overbury]," [3] it says much for his Majesty's good nature that at this crisis he should have commanded his own private physician, Sir Theodore Mayerne, to undertake the case. Mayerne was at the top of the professional tree, a fowl of finer plumage than those obscene night-birds Drs. Forman, Gresham and Franklin. He had been physician to Henry IV. of France, and after the assassination of that prince in 1610, came to London on James's invitation. That his Royal master rated his services highly appears from the fact that his official salary was £400, that of the Lord Chief-Justice of England being but £258, 6s. 5d. [4] He had presided over the last illness and death of the Prince of Wales. Mayerne was too grand a man personally to attend Overbury; he merely acted as consultant, leaving the patient in charge of an apothecary named Paul de Lobell, who "dwelleth near the Tower in Lyme Street," and had married a sister of

[1] State Trials, ii. 980.
[2] Ibid., ii. 948.
[3] Winwood to Southampton, 6th August 1613. The grounds of his Majesty's disfavour were jealousy of Overbury's influence with the Favourite, and of his reputation as a man of letters.
[4] Abstract of His Majesty's Revenew, 1651, pp. 39, 49.

Mayerne. The great doctor's written prescriptions in Overbury's case, "containing 28 leaves or pieces of paper, great or small, which is all the phisick that this examinant ministred to him," were handed by Lobell to Lord Chief-Justice Coke at his examination on 3rd October 1615. Among the three hundred examinations taken by Coke in connection with the affair of Overbury—portions only of a few were used at the trials, the rest being suppressed—this of Lobell was discovered and published by Professor Amos,[1] but the prescriptions, like Overbury's narrative, never saw the light. It would be instructive to know their contents. From another suppressed examination—that of Weston—we learn that the Lieutenant of the Tower gave strict orders "that none should come thither but the former apothecary [Lobell] or his man, and that no other came at any time, or gave any clyster to Sir Thomas Overbury." [2] From the evidence in the printed trials and from the suppressed examinations it clearly appears that the prisoner's end was finally compassed by means of a clyster or enema of corrosive sublimate, given him on 14th September, of which after great agony he died on the following day, and that this injection was administered by the "boy" or assistant of Lobell. Now, it is a curious fact that according to the published reports of the trials of the seven persons severally charged with the murder, Lobell, instead of appearing at the bar, was twice produced as a witness; at Weston's trial merely to state that on 3rd July he gave Sir Thomas a bath, "and saw his body very exceeding fair and clear," whereas after death he found it "full of blisters and so consumed away as he never saw the like"; [3] at Somerset's trial, to state that when he first attended Overbury on 25th June he found him "ill," and on three subsequent occasions Rochester asked him how Overbury did, to which he answered "he was very sick." [4] Not a single question was put to Lobell about the clyster, or as to the cause of

[1] *Great Oyer of Poisoning*, p. 167.
[2] *Ibid.*, p. 180.
[3] *State Trials*, ii. 922.
[4] *Ibid.*, ii. 986.

death, nor did the name of the great Dr. Mayerne, as the newspapers say, transpire! But in the MS. account of Somerset's case discovered by Amos, Lobell said that on the third occasion Rochester "willed him to write to Dr. Maiot [Mayerne's name is variously spelt] concerning physick to be given Overbury."[1] This part of his evidence was, for some reason, suppressed in the official report of the trial.

There was much relief in many quarters at this happy issue out of a tight corner. The Lord Privy Seal announced the news to Rochester, his "Sweet Lord," with a ghoulish glee reminiscent of Knox's genial mention of the deaths of Cardinal Beaton and the Queen Regent. To the Lieutenant of the Tower he wrote: "If the knave's body be foul, bury it presently [immediately]; I'll stand between you and harm. But if it will abide the view, send for Lidcott and let him see it, to satisfy the damned crew."[2] The same day, "in post haste at 12," Northampton wrote again to Elwes:—

> Fail not a jot herein, as you love yr. friends; nor after Lidcote and his friends have viewed stay one minute, but let the priest be ready; and if Lidcote be not there, send for him speedily, pretending the body will not tarry.[3]

So at long last Sir Thomas lay in his resting grave, and the Countess was avenged of her enemy. Death is always a costly business for the survivors, but Overbury's demise entailed unusual expense. Weston's account amounted to £180; Dr. Franklin, who had been retained at the modest figure of "2s. 6d. a day for boat-hire, and 10s. a week for diet," claimed an annuity of £200; Mrs. Turner's price being above rubies, she valued her services accordingly; her "toothless maid, Trusty Margaret," Stephen, her manservant, and Mrs. Horne, her Ladyship's own woman, "being acquainted with the poisoning," had all to be squared; and Lobell's "boy" got £20.[4]

---

[1] *Great Oyer of Poisoning*, pp. 116, 140.
[2] *Ibid.*, p. 173.
[3] *Ibid.*, p. 174.
[4] *State Trials*, ii. 926, 942.

Murder by deputy, as appears, is in one sense at least a "paying" game.

. . . .

Two years pass and the curtain rises for the Fourth Act. Enter Chorus. The great Lord Privy Seal has gone to join Sir Thomas among the shades,[1] and my Lord of Somerset reigns in his stead. The Overbury affair is forgotten, unless the Earl and his Countess chance to talk over old times, or when the necessities of Mrs. Turner, "Trusty Margaret," and the rest compel them to remind their noble patrons of former services. But the prisoner of the Tower has taken away with him more than his false friend's secret. The Favourite has lost much of that ability by which he was so long distinguished; his flair for statecraft is sensibly abated; he is become sullen, irritable and overbearing, and he bullies his affectionate master unconscionably. James's hurt protests make pathetic reading. At this juncture the Courtiers—those vigilant readers of the stars—predict the advent of a new planet. Mr. George Villiers, a charming young gentleman from the country, comes to Court, finds favour in the Royal sight, and with classical fitness is appointed the King's cupbearer. A knighthood, a place in the Bedchamber and a pension of £1000 a year, presently follow; it is common knowledge in the Palace that the wind has changed. These things do not improve the Favourite's temper; he quarrels with the graceful Ganymede and treats his Majesty more rudely than ever. He is too proud to learn mankind's hardest lesson. Sir Thomas, among the shades, rubs phantom hands as he watches Nemesis shuffle the cards.

. . . .

In the autumn of 1615 a rumour reached England from abroad that Overbury had met his death by poison. "The Apothecaries boy that gave Sir Thomas the Glister, falling sick at Flushing, revealed the whole matter."[2] Trumbull, the British agent at Brussels, having got wind of this confession, informed Secretary Winwood.[3] The Secretary, who hated the

[1] Northampton died on 15th June 1615.
[2] Wilson, p. 80.
[3] Weldon, p. 95.

Favourite, realised the importance of the discovery and went warily to work. Taxed by him with complicity in the murder Sir Gervase Elwes admitted knowledge of the attempt, which he claimed to have thwarted. Winwood then laid the facts before the King, who directed that the law should take its course: it was impossible that the affair could be hushed up. At this stage the only persons implicated were Weston, Mrs. Turner and the Lieutenant. James sent for Lord Chief-Justice Coke and the other judges, and charged them with the investigation. "Kneeling down in the midst of them," says Sir Anthony Weldon, who was then at Royston, "he used these very words":—

My Lords the Judges, it is lately come to my hearing that you have now in examination a business of poysoning. Lord, in what a most miserable condition shall this kingdome be (the only famous nation for hospitality in the world), if our tables should become such a snare as none could eat without danger of life, and that Italian custome should be introduced amongst us! Therefore, my Lords I charge you, as you will answer it at that great and dreadfull day of judgment, that you examine it strictly without favor, affection, or partiality; and if you shall spare any guilty of this crime, God's curse light on you and your posterity: *and if I spare any that are found guilty, God's curse light on me and my posterity for ever!*[1]

In view of the future fortunes of the Stuart dynasty this imprecation is striking. The incident recalls that other occasion when, after the slaying of the Ruthvens at Perth, James knelt upon the bloody floor, "assuring himself that God had preserved him from so despaired a peril for the perfecting of some greater work behind to His glory"—doubtless the punishment of Overbury's murderers.

Coke had a keen scent for plots; he went into the affair with equal industry and gusto, taking no fewer than three hundred examinations, as Mr. Attorney-General Bacon heard him say.[2] Weston, repeatedly examined, after much prevarication told all he knew; Mrs. Turner and her company of rogues were laid

[1] Weldon, p. 100.
[2] Spedding's Bacon, xii. 302.

by the heels. The enquiry had left no doubt as to the complicity of Lord and Lady Somerset; but though, in Weston's metaphor, Coke's net had thus caught the little fishes, he felt unequal to landing the great ones without assistance. At his request, therefore, the Lord Chancellor (Ellesmere), the Duke of Lennox and the Lord Zouch were associated with him as Royal Commissioners.[1] His hands thus strengthened, Coke summoned Somerset for examination. The Favourite was with the King at Royston; furious at the Chief-Justice's presumption, he refused to submit. "Nay," said his Majesty, "thou must go then, for if Coke sends for me I must go too." [2] Weldon, who was there at the time, gives a graphic account of their parting—on Friday 13th October, an ill-omened date—which is too characteristic of King James to be omitted:—

> The Earle of Somerset never parted from him with more seeming affection than at this time, when he knew Somerset should never see him more; and had you seen the seeming affection (as the author himselfe did) you would rather have believed he was in his rising than setting. The earle, when he kissed his hand, the king hung about his neck, slabbering his cheeks, saying, "For Gods sake, when shall I see thee againe? On my soul, I shall neither eat nor sleep until you come again." The earle told him, on Monday (this being on the Friday). "For Gods sake, let me," said the king, "shall I, shall I?" then lolled about his neck. "Then for Gods sake give thy lady this kiss for me." In the same manner at the stayres head, at the middle of the stayres, and at the stayres foot. The earl was not in his coach when the king used these very words (in the hearing of four servants, of whom one was Somersets great creature and of the Bed-Chamber, who reported it instantly to the author of this history), "I shall never see his face more." [3]

Wilson adds that "he said it with a smile." [4]

The first thing Somerset did when he reached London was

[1] The Chancellor, as Solicitor-General, had helped to bring Mary, the mother of James, to the block; Lennox had lent his support to the King's version of the Gowrie tragedy; Zouch had lately supplanted Somerset in the office of Warden of the Cinque Ports.

[2] Wilson, p. 81.

[3] Weldon, pp. 102, 103.

[4] Wilson, p. 81.

to send, by virtue of his possession of the Privy Seal, a pursuivant to secure Mrs. Turner's papers, then in the custody of a lady friend. He also burnt his own letters to Northampton, having previously entrusted Sir Robert Cotton with those he had received from that nobleman and from Overbury, to which he had affixed false dates.[1] These facts seem hardly compatible with a clear conscience. Unluckily, Mrs. Turner had retained, presumably for purposes of blackmail, the more compromising letters of the Countess, together with the esoteric images made by the late Dr. Forman, and these were already in Coke's hands. When the Commissioners learnt of this abuse by Somerset of his authority, they ordered the arrest of the Earl and the Countess, who on 18th October were severally committed to ward.

What Sir Edward Coke called the Great Oyer of Poisoning opened the following day with the arraignment of Richard Weston at the Guild Hall.[2] According to the admissions of Elwes and of Weston, Lobell and his boy were the actual murderers. The boy was beyond the jurisdiction of the Court, but Lobell was waiting in the witnesses' room. Why was not he indicted? Was the Lord Chief-Justice so ignorant of the law as to bring to trial an accessory, before a verdict had been obtained against the principal? Upon these points the research of Mr. Amos among the suppressed examinations throws a singular light. One Pomler, a French apothecary, deposed that "at the commendation of Monsr. Maierne to the King," Lobell was appointed "to minister such physick" as Mayerne should prescribe for Overbury. Edward Rider deposed that while the enquiry was proceeding he had a talk with Dr. Lobell:—

[Lobell] speaking very hardly against those that went about to prove Sir Thomas to be poisoned, saying that the clyster which they pretend was the cause of his death (for which his son was called into question) was prescribed unto him by Mr. Doctor Magerne, the King's doctor, and that his son had made it according to his directions (not once speaking of his man

[1] *State Trials*, ii. 979, 987.
[2] *Ibid.*, ii. 911–930.

to have any hand in it); and used very reproachful words, saying that our English doctors were all fools.[1]

Lobell further remarking "that there was never a good
doctor in England but Magerne," Rider drily rejoined that
he had heard in Paris that Mayerne was indeed a braver
courtier than a doctor. Meeting Lobell and his wife a week
later, says Rider,

> I told him that I heard it [the murder] was done by an
> apothecary's boy in Lime Street, near to Mr. Garret's, speaking
> as if I knew not that it was his son's boy that did the deed;
> and Mrs. Lobell standing by, hearing me say that he dwelt by
> Mr. Garret and that he was run away, she, looking upon her
> husband, said in French, "Oh, mon mari," &c. that is, "Oh!
> husband, that was William you sent into France"—(or to that
> effect), whom she said was his son's man; whereupon the old
> man, as it seemed to me, looking upon his wife, his teeth did
> chatter as if he trembled, which stroke me also into a quandary
> to hear her say so.[2]

Questioned further as to this boy, Lobell said he had sent
him away with a letter of introduction to a friend in Paris,
from which Rider conjectured "that he indeed did know the
cause of his departure." It is highly suggestive that in these
proceedings Mayerne's connection with the case was never
mentioned at all, and that his agent Lobell, under the generic
guise of "an apothecary," was kept as much as possible in the
background. Coke was in constant touch with the King
throughout the enquiry; the inference is that this Mayerne-
Lobell business was by Royal command deliberately burked.

Another remarkable feature of these trials, strangely foreign
to modern practice, is that the Lord Chief-Justice who presided
had himself got up the Crown case, and admitted only such
evidence as told against the accused. What would our sensitive
sentimentalists, who clamour for the reprieve of red-handed
murderers, have said to this?

[1] *Great Oyer of Poisoning*, p. 169.
[2] *Ibid.*

Great trouble was caused by Weston's refusal to plead to his indictment, which at that date operated in bar of trial. Finally he was induced to do so; according to Coke, at the instance of the Holy Ghost, but more probably by threat of the *peine forte et dure*, to which his continued obstinacy exposed him. Lord and Lady Somerset were represented as the authors of the murder, which was said to have been accomplished by Weston's administration of poisons supplied by them; but Coke laid it down as law that no matter what the poison or how employed, Weston could be convicted upon that indictment. Thus directed, and in the absence of any legal defence, the jury had no difficulty in finding the prisoner guilty. He was hanged at Tyburn on 25th October.

The trial of Mrs. Anne Turner took place at the King's Bench on 7th November.[1] The conviction of Weston made it comparatively an easy matter to secure that of his accomplice. The Countess's correspondence, and Dr. Forman's magical parchments and molten images, were exhibited in evidence against her. When these evil toys were produced in Court, "there was heard a crack from the scaffolds, which caused great fear, tumult and confusion among the spectators and throughout the hall, every one fearing hurt, as if the devil had been present and grown angry to have his workmanship shewed by such as were not his own scholars, and this terror continuing about a quarter of an hour, after silence was proclaimed the rest of the cunning tricks were likewise shewed."[2] The wise woman was found guilty and suffered accordingly on 9th November.[3]

Sir Gervase Elwes was next brought to trial at the Guild Hall on 16th November, charged with "the malicious aiding, com-

---

[1] *State Trials*, ii. 929–936.

[2] *Ibid.*, ii. 932.

[3] "Mistress Turner, the first inventress of yellow Starch, was executed in a Cobweb Lawn Ruff of that colour at Tyburn, and with her I believe that yellow Starch, which so much disfigured our Nation and rendered them so ridiculous and fantastic, will receive its Funeral" (Howell's *Familiar Letters*, 1st March 1618). Had she done no worse than introduce starch into England, Mrs. Turner deserved her doom.

forting, and abetting of Weston." [1] The Lieutenant, an educated gentleman, put up a good fight, and was like to have been acquitted, but the Chief-Justice "drew out of his bosom" a confession made to him that morning by Franklin, who alleged that he had read a letter from the prisoner to Lady Essex containing the words, "Madam, The scab is like the fox: the more he is cursed, the better he fareth," with other similar sentiments inferring his complicity in the crime. But apart from Franklin's statement there was nothing proved against Sir Gervase worthy of death. He was certainly in league with Northampton, and had signally failed in his duty to denounce Weston, but that was all. Elwes was executed on Tower Hill on 20th November.

Dr. James Franklin was tried at the King's Bench on 27th November upon the same indictment as Weston. [2] On his own confession he was found guilty and sentenced to death. He was hanged on 9th December at St. Thomas a Waterings, [3] and made an edifying end. After his conviction, Franklin darkly hinted "that there were greater persons in this matter than were yet known," and that other deaths than Overbury's had been compassed: "I think next the Gunpowder Treason, there never was such a plot as this." With reference to the King's appointing "an outlandish physician [Mayerne] and an outlandish apothecary [Lobell] about the late Prince, deceased [Prince Henry], therein," said he, "lyeth a long tale." [4] And did not Mrs. Turner at Whitehall "shew to Franklin the man who (as she said) poisoned the Prince, which he says was a physician with a red beard [Mayerne]"? [5] These allusions—or illusions—so powerfully impressed the Chief-Justice, that he communicated them to the King, who was naturally unwilling that they should be followed up. But Coke had got this plot business on the brain, he saw poison in every bush.

[1] State Trials, ii. 935–948.
[2] Ibid., ii. 947–948.
[3] Marks, Tyburn Tree, p. 180.
[4] Great Oyer of Poisoning, pp. 227–229.
[5] Spedding's Bacon, xii. 289.

When, however, the case of Sir Thomas Monson was called before him on 4th December,[1] Coke adjourned the diet "till further order be taken." His Majesty, having personally considered the evidence, had decided that the prosecution be dropped. Coke was "mad he could not have his will of Monson." "There is more against you than you know of," he told the accused. James resented Coke's revival of the old scandals about Prince Henry's death; as Wilson remarks, "the Lord Chief-Justice's wings were clipt for it ever after," and he was removed from office within the year. Sir Thomas was soon set at liberty. The quality of mercy was not his Majesty's most conspicuous attribute; why then did he let off Monson, of whom the prosecutor, Sir Laurence Hyde, the Queen's attorney, at the trial said, "I have looked into this business, and I protest, my Lord, he is as guilty as the guiltiest"? Weldon's story, that James feared Sir Thomas meant to say something dangerous, is disbelieved by Mr. Gardiner.[2] Of the diversions of Monson's home circle Weldon draws a curious picture, which would have charmed M. Zola, and exhibits in a strange light domestic manners at the good King's Court.[3]

On her arrest Lady Somerset was ordered to be warded within her own house at Blackfriars or "at the house of the Lord Knollis, near the Tilt Yard," whichever she might prefer. She elected for the former, and there on 9th December she gave birth to a daughter.[4] When on 27th March she was removed to the Tower her chief anxiety was lest she should be confined in Overbury's lodging; her Ladyship was afraid of ghosts. She was given Sir Walter Raleigh's room, whose tenant was then sailing upon his last adventure, which was to end on Tower Hill.

The trial of Frances, Countess of Somerset, held in Westminster Hall before the Lord High Steward's Court on 24th

[1] State Trials, ii. 949–952.
[2] Weldon, p. 112; History, ii. 345 n.
[3] Weldon, pp. 107, 108.
[4] The Lady Anne Carr, afterwards Countess of Bedford, and mother of William, Lord Russell, who suffered in connection with the Rye House Plot.

May 1616, Sir Frances Bacon, His Majesty's Attorney-General, conducting the prosecution,[1] ought to have been the most interesting of the series; but the Countess upon her impeachment pleading guilty, the drama was practically enacted as a "Dumbe Shew," that favourite device of Elizabethan playwrights. This must have vexed the great and eager audience who had paid handsomely for admission: "£50 were given for a corner that could hardly contain a dozen."[2] Of Bacon's "Charge by way of Evidence," which he had intended to deliver if the case went on, the best report is given by Spedding.[3] "Forman's book was shewed," in which the wizard had noted particulars of his clients' cases. "There was much mirth made in the Court upon the shewing this book; for the first leafe my Lord Coke lighted on, he found his owne wife's name."[4] Asked whether she had anything to say in mitigation of judgment, the Countess replied, "I can much aggravate, but nothing extenuate my fault. I desire mercy, and that the Lords will intercede for me to the King." Sentence of death having been pronounced, the prisoner was taken back to the Tower.

The arraignment of Somerset forms the Fifth Act. If the Countess gave the Crown but little trouble it was not so with her noble husband. Bacon had the handling of the case and consulted the King at every step. Coke's judicial pronouncements of the Earl's guilt were much stronger than the proofs, and James was very anxious that Somerset should confess, and throw himself on the Royal mercy. But, perhaps because he had no great faith in that quality, the Earl persistently refused; he preferred the sporting chance of an acquittal. The Attorney-General wrote to the new Favourite, who was naturally much interested in the prosecution of his precursor, "That same little charm which may be secretly infused into Somerset's ear some few hours before his trial, was excellently well thought of by his Majesty."[5] James was at his old tricks; but the case called

---

[1] State Trials, ii. 951–966.
[2] Chamberlain to Carleton, 18th May 1616.
[3] Bacon, xii. 297–305.
[4] Weldon, p. 111.
[5] Bacon to Villiers, 2nd May 1616.

for the exercise of all his vaunted "Kingcraft." Bacon submitted to his Royal master the heads of his intended charge, which, with the King's marginal notes, are instructive reading.[1] Among the things Bacon proposed to prove is "That Somerset, with others, would have preferred Lowbell, the apothecary, to Prince Charles," upon which his Majesty has this "apostyle": "Nothing yet proved against Lowbell." And good care was taken that nothing ever should be. Notwithstanding all the inducements that could be offered, the prisoner continued steadfast in his refusal to confess. He seems to have been satisfied that James would not dare to bring him to the bar, but a visit from the Commissioners disposed of that confident expectation. Seeing that the King meant business, Somerset then threatened that if tried he would make a certain disclosure. That James was seriously alarmed is beyond doubt; the sole question is as to the nature of the secret. What was to be done "if my Lord of Somerset would break forth into any speech of taxing the King"? Bacon arranged with the judges that he should be "interrupted and silenced." [2] To prevent any dangerous disclosure, says Weldon, Somerset at his trial "had two servants placed on each side of him, with a cloak on their arms," who had peremptory orders "if that Somerset did any way fly out on the King, they should instantly hoodwink him with that cloak, take him violently from the bar, and carry him away," [3] and the trial was to go on without him. A curious instance this of what Bacon calls his Majesty's "princely zeal for justice." But the cloak, as we shall see, was not required.

On the night of the Countess's condemnation, Sir George More, who had succeeded Elwes as Lieutenant of the Tower, warned his prisoner to be ready for trial next morning. The Earl "did absolutely refuse it, and said they should carry him in his bed; that the King had assured him he should not come to any tryal, neither durst the King bring him to tryal." [4]

[1] Spedding's Bacon, xii. 286–289.
[2] Ibid., xii. 295.
[3] Weldon, p. 118.
[4] Ibid., p. 115.

Though the hour was midnight Sir George hastened down to Greenwich, where the Court was then in residence and his Majesty in bed. He "bounseth at the back stayres as if mad," and insisted that the sleeping monarch be roused to hear his news. The King fell into a passion of tears: "On my soule, Moore, I wot not what to do!" cried the awakened Solomon. "Thou art a wise man; help me in this great straight, and thou shall finde thou dost it for a thankful master." This he said with other "sad expressions." [1] Promising to do his best, Sir George left the Palace and returned to the Tower at three in the morning. Probably the time had come to try his Majesty's "little charm." Whatever arguments were used proved effectual, for at eight o'clock the prisoner went quietly to meet his fate.

A distinguished audience filled Westminster Hall on 25th May 1616; "more ladies and great personages," says Chamberlain, "than ever I think were seen at any trial." Of the proceedings there are two versions: one in Howell's collection; [2] another, "The Arraignment of the Earl of Somerset," first printed by Amos. [3] In the space at my disposal it is impossible to give any adequate account of the trial; no abridgment would do it justice, and those interested may read it at large in one or other of these forms. (The type of Amos is less murderous than that of Howell.) The prisoner having pleaded not guilty, Bacon rose to deliver his "Charge by way of Evidence." "All the world by law is concluded to say that Overbury was impoisoned by Weston," he told the Peers; "but the question before you is of the procurement only, and of the abetting (as the law termeth it) as accessory before the fact." With reference to the extraordinary intimacy which subsisted between Somerset and Overbury, "I will undertake," said he, "the time was when Overbury knew more of the secrets of state than the Council-table did." He showed how the friendship "ended in mortal hatred on my Lord of Somerset's part,"

[1] Weldon, p. 116. Weldon had this "from Moore's owne mouth."
[2] State Trials, ii. 965–1022.
[3] Great Oyer of Poisoning, pp. 122–159.

owing to Overbury's opposition to the marriage, which drew upon him "two streams of hatred," one from Lady Essex, the other from Somerset. "A third stream" proceeded from the ambition of Northampton, jealous of Overbury's influence. "So it was amongst them resolved and decreed that Overbury must die." He described how Overbury was "trapped" into the Tower, how the appointments of Elwes and Weston were contrived, and what devices were used "to hold and keep him there."

Then must Franklin be purveyor of the poisons, and procure five, six, seven several potions, to be sure to hit his complexion. Then must Mrs. Turner be say-mistress of the poisons to try upon poor beasts, what's present, and what works at distance of time. Then must Weston be the tormentor, and chase him with poison after poison: poison in salts, poison in meats, poison in sweetmeats, poison in medicines and vomits, until at last his body was almost come, by use of poisons, to the state that Mithridates' body was by the use of treacle and preservatives, that the force of the poisons were blunted upon him: Weston confessing, when he was chid for not dispatching him, that he had given him enough to poison twenty men.[1]

In all this Bacon maintained that Somerset was the "principal practiser."

The Attorney-General then adduced evidence in support of his case. The confidential relations between Somerset and Overbury and their falling out were proved by servants of the latter, who spoke to meetings and correspondence between them. Overbury's letters from the Tower showed how he had been "trapped." The Countess's attempt to have him assassinated, of which Somerset admitted knowledge, was proved by the gentleman sought to be employed. The placing of Elwes and Weston was proved by the admissions of Elwes and of Monson to have been effected by Somerset and Northampton: Overbury was committed to the Tower on 30th April; Elwes appointed Lieutenant on 6th May, Weston made gaoler on the 7th. Overbury's father proved that Somerset advised

[1] Spedding's Bacon, xii. 316.

him not to petition the King in his son's behalf lest it should hinder his release; Sir John Lidcote stated that though he at first believed Somerset to be Overbury's friend, he became convinced that he (Somerset) was playing a double game. The strictness of Overbury's confinement was proved by Monson and by Overbury's servant to be by direction of Somerset and Northampton. Somerset's interest in the progress of Overbury's illness was proved by Franklin, Elwes and Lobell. The proof of Somerset's share in the actual poisoning is by no means so clear. Even if guilty he did not need personally to take a hand in the game: the actual slaying might be left to his lady's syndicate of murderers. The only points established against him in this regard were (1) the sending to Overbury in a letter a white powder which made him very ill, and (2) the sending to him of the tarts. Poisoned tarts were certainly sent by the Countess, but there was no proof that those sent by Somerset were poisoned. The destruction and misdating of letters, as proved, was highly suspicious, as also were his repeated attempts to obtain from the King a general pardon in the largest terms, which would have covered his complicity in the murder.

My Lord in his defence admitted the quarrel with Overbury, whose imprisonment he had "plotted" with Northampton to prevent his interference with the marriage; but denied that he desired his death, ever sent him any poison, or knew of the attempts by the Countess and her agents upon his life. As to his tampering with the letters and his endeavours to obtain a pardon before he was suspected, the prisoner had no satisfactory explanation to offer. "His answers," says a eyewitness, "were so poor and idle as many of the Lords his Peers shook their heads and blushed to hear such slender excuses from him of whom much better was expected. The only thing worth note in him was his constancy and undaunted carriage in all the time of his arraignment."[1] The Lord High Steward (Ellesmere) having summed up the evidence, the Peers, after an hour's deliberation, returned a unanimous verdict of guilty, and Somerset was sentenced to death.

[1] Sherburn to Carleton, 25th May 1616.

By no one had the verdict been awaited with more anxiety than by his Majesty at Greenwich. The four letters of James to Sir George More, written shortly before the trial, show his vital concern in the issue.[1] Of his demeanour on the fateful day we have two accounts. The King was "so vital sad and discontented, as he did retire himself from all company, and did forbear both dinner and supper until he had heard what answer the said Earl had made."[2] "But who had seen the King's restlesse motion all that day, sending to every boat he saw landing at the bridge, cursing all that came without tidings, would have easily judged all was not right, and there had been some grounds for his feares of Somerset's boldnesse; but at last one bringing him word he was condemned and the passages, all was quiet."[3] This vivid relation was "told verbatim" to Weldon by Sir George More. The doom pronounced and the secret unrevealed, James was a new man. On 13th July he pardoned the Countess, though the imprisonment in the Tower was not remitted; but the Earl's pardon was delayed by a circumstance typically Jacobean. The King wished to bestow upon the new Favourite the manor of Sherborne, which of old he had wrested from Raleigh, and made Somerset's pardon conditional on his agreeing to give up the estate to his successor; but to this cynical bargain the Earl would by no means consent.[4] So for five years longer he and his wife were kept prisoners in the Tower, till on 18th January 1621 they obtained their release.[5]

What, then, was this tremendous secret that could so shake the majesty of England, and despite the King's solemn oath to the contrary, suffice to save from the scaffold two forfeited lives? Contemporary opinion associated it with Prince Henry's death; but pace Professor Amos, nobody believes that now. Mr. Gardiner thought it was something connected with the

---

[1] Great Oyer of Poisoning, pp. 471–476.
[2] Sherburn to Carleton, 31st May 1616.
[3] Weldon, pp. 118, 119.
[4] Gardiner, ii. 363.
[5] State Trials, ii. 1004. His formal pardon was not granted till 1624, a few months before the King's death.

Spanish pensions; if so, the relation of effect to cause seems scarcely adequate.[1] In the judgment of one so deeply versed in the secret history of the time as the author of *The Fortunes of Nigel*, it related to the intimacy between James and the Favourite. "The fatal secret," writes Sir Walter, "is by some supposed to refer to the death of Prince Henry; but a cause yet more flagitious will occur to those who have remarked certain passages in the letters between the King and Buckingham, published by the late Lord Hailes."[2] Scott notes, too, "the strange letter written by the disgraced favourite to James, in which he [Somerset] obviously claims merit for not having discovered some infamous secret," which, he remarks, "probably relates to the secret practices of the monarch himself."[3] But this was a secret that Somerset shared with "Steenie" and the other minions, and as such was no secret at all. It rather appears to me that his Majesty himself supplies the clue. In one of his letters to Sir George More, already cited, James writes:—

It is easy to be seen that he [Somerset] would threaten me with laying an aspersion upon me of being in some sort accessory to his crime . . . I pray you to urge him, by reason that I refuse him no favour that I can grant him, without taking upon me the suspicion of being guilty of that crime whereof he is accused.[4]

If James was privy to Somerset's plot for destroying Overbury, the matter is plain enough; and of the King's significant susceptibility to such suspicion the passage above quoted affords ample proof. It seems unlikely that Somerset should make so grave a charge without some grounds; but as to this we have no certainty, and his Majesty, like lesser rogues, is entitled to the benefit of the doubt.[5]

By an ingenious refinement of cruelty the fallen Favourite

[1] *History*, ii. 362 n.
[2] *Somers' Tracts*, ed. Scott, ii. 488 n.
[3] *Ibid.*, ii. 233 n, 355 n. Cf. Sir Walter Scott's notes, pp. 262 *et seq.*
[4] *Great Oyer of Poisoning*, pp. 474, 475.
[5] Mr. Ewald, however, is satisfied of the King's guilt, as also are Professor Amos and Mr. Bisset, *op. cit.*

and the partner of his shame were, in terms of their release, compelled by Order of Council to live together at Lord Wallingford's Oxfordshire seats, Grays or Cowsham, "and remain confined to one or other of the said houses, and within three miles' compass of either of the same."[1] Thus, says Wilson, "holding their lives by a Lease of the King's Will, living in a private and obscure condition," they spent the wretched residue of their days. "That Love that made them break through all Oppositions, either by her declining to some new Object—as was the common rumour—or his inclining to reluctancy for the Old, grew so weak that it pined away; and they lived long after, though in one House, as Strangers one to another."[2] For them life must have been as terrible as for Thérèse Raquin and her lover Laurent, with the dead man between them. The Countess escaped first, dying in 1632, sixteen years after the trial, at the age of thirty-nine. Of her last illness and death Wilson paints a ghastly picture; it had been better for her had she made a decent end at Tyburn.[3] The Earl, lagging superfluous on the stage, survived till 1645. Even then he was only fifty-three. From King Charles, who always hated him, he received no countenance. He had lived to see the splendour of Buckingham quenched suddenly in blood. Perhaps he envied "Steenie" the swift blow that finished his career; compared with his own long-drawn punishment, Felton's knife would seem almost merciful.

[1] State Trials, ii. 1005.
[2] Wilson, p. 83.
[3] Ibid.

PHYSIC AND FORGERY:

A Study in Confidence

> "Friend Plain Talk, that epitaph will do very well. Nevertheless, one short sentence is wanting." Upon which, Plain Talk said it was too late, the chiselled words being so arranged, after the usual manner of such inscriptions, that nothing could be interlined. "Then," said Old Prudence, "I will put it in the shape of a postscript." Accordingly, with the approbation of Old Plain Talk, he had the following words chiseled at the left-hand corner of the stone, and pretty low down:
> "The root of all was a friendly loan."
> HERMAN MELVILLE: *The Confidence-Man.*

WHEN I WAS A SMALL BOY in Edinburgh the Sunday afternoon walk with my people was a weekly institution. We were Scottish Episcopalians—unlovely label—and as such free to enjoy fresh air and exercise even on the Sabbath. My Presbyterian contemporaries lived under a sterner rule. After a solid mid-day meal, they either dozed away the day of rest over an old volume of *Good Words* or were haled, flushed and irritable from the feast, to indigestive slumber at afternoon worship. I remember once, while summering with Free Kirk friends at the easterly fishing-village immortalised as the scene of the incomparable *Lantern-Bearers*, being an enforced partaker in these postprandial rites. The sermon, as I recall it, was upon an episode in the career of Abraham, involving his dealings with a damsel named Keturah, a subject as to which my maturer judgment suggests that the preacher was unhappily inspired. But it was not the backsliding of the patriarch that moved me, so much as the intriguing appellative of his handmaid; the name struck me as somehow ludicrous, and its frequent recurrence in the discourse, with a prolonged emphasis on the second syllable, soon reduced me to a state of suppressed laughter such as only youthful blood-vessels could safely have withstood. This unseemly levity of mine, painful to my good hosts, was by them imputed to my prelatic upbringing.

Sometimes our hebdomadal strolls had for their objective a certain suburban cemetery, a well-ordered dormitory of the dead, commanding from its terraced heights a wide and pleasant prospect. But I was not interested in the view; I liked the tombstones, and never ceased to marvel at their chaste design and infinite variety. Here were no harsh and grisly emblems of mortality, such as affright the young visitor to our city graveyards, no grinning skulls and cross-bones, no skeleton Deaths with painfully realistic darts. These Victorian Angels were perfectly genteel and ladylike, yet I thought their marble pinions but ill-adapted for celestial duties. The fat stone Doves, too, that perched so substantially upon tablets dedicated to the smaller tenants, how did they contrive to wing their lapidary flights? Although I was told that all the inhabitants were now on an equality, I chiefly regarded those who were handsomely housed in massive and imposing structures, preferring them to the occupants of meaner monuments. I had never heard of Mr. Shandy and knew nothing of his theory of names, but the inscriptions on the headstones appealed to me, and for the more striking and suggestive I would invent appropriate legends. Certain graves that in later years I visited with interest— those, for example, in which the victims of Dr. Pritchard and of M. Chantrelle await the calling of their testimony at the Great Assize—I then passed by unnoticed; but there was one that caught my fancy by reason of the arresting name of its proprietor: Dionysius Wielobycki. Who was he, this man of alien race, and why did he lie here among these kindly Scots under a designation so outlandish?[1] Surely some story must attach to such an one: a mysterious story was, to speak medi-

---

[1] The full text of the inscription is as follows: "In Memory of / Dionysius Wielobycki, M.D. / Born in / Byten, Volhynia, Poland / in 1813 / Died in Edinburgh / 16th November 1882 / Erected by / Lady Felice / Baroness Wielobycka."

cally, indicated; but I was at a loss to find any that satisfied me. And behold, in the fullness of time I chanced upon the veritable tale, which if less sinister than my young imagination conceived, is yet sufficiently curious to justify recital.[1] The year 1857 is notable in the judicial annals of Scotland as that in which Lord Advocate Moncreiff contended for ten summer days in the Justiciary lists with Dean of Faculty Inglis, before Lord Justice-Clerk Hope as umpire, the stake being the life of Madeleine Hamilton Smith, of attaching memory. Everyone knows how the splendid advocacy of Inglis saved the fair neck of that engaging pannel from the noose which Justice had prepared for it, an escape merited at least by the owner's coolness and pluck. Fewer students of these matters are aware of an earlier duel in January of that year between those two great counsel before the same judicial referee, when the brilliant powers of the Dean were exerted in vain and the Advocate secured a conviction. But a middle-aged physician who had forged a patient's will was plainly a less inspiring client than a beautiful damsel of nineteen who, with a skill and perseverance beyond her years, had freed herself by scientific means from an embarrassing entanglement. It has been said, I know not on what authority, that the Justice-Clerk being notoriously a good judge of feminine charms, the Dean advised Miss Madeleine, who had a neat foot and an undeniable ankle, to keep those assets well in view of the Bench at the trial, the crinoline of that day affording, as may be seen in old pages of *Punch*, special facilities for so alluring a display. The advice of counsel was followed with the happiest results for all concerned. That the turn of an ankle may powerfully affect its owner's fate we have further proof in the case of Thomas Griffiths Wainwright who, as Hazlitt relates, when asked how he had found it in his heart to poison Helen Abercromby, his gentle and confiding sister-in-law, replied with a shrug of his sensitive shoulders:

[1] No separate account of the case, so far as I am aware, was ever published. For the facts, as narrated, I have relied on the reports of the trial in the contemporary press: *Scotsman*, 10th January 1857; *Edinburgh Evening Courant*, 9th and 10th January 1857; and the official record in Irvine's *Justiciary Reports*, ii. 579–583, 1858.

"Upon my soul, I don't know, unless it was because she had such thick ankles!" In the present case, however, poor Dr. Wielobycki, for all the good *his* ankles could do, might as well have had a pair of wooden legs. "A bonny lass," observed that profound philosopher, Mr. James Ratcliffe, à *propos* of Effie Dean's chances of acquittal, "a bonny lass will find favour wi' judge and jury, when they would strap up a grewsome carle like me for the fifteenth part of a flea's hide and tallow, damn them!"

Born, as we learn from his tombstone, at Byten, Volhynia, Poland, in 1813, Dionysius Wielobycki, a political refugee from that explosive little country, came to this country in 1839. He took his degree of doctor of medicine at Edinburgh in 1843, his thesis being "On Plica Polonica." His brother, Severin, who had graduated at the same university in 1841, was in practice in London. These facts appear in the medical directories and registers of the day[1]; from the evidence at the trial we know that Dionysius, before settling in Edinburgh as a homeopathic physician, spent some months in Hawick. Pursuing in the pages of old Edinburgh directories his professional and social progress, we find the first trace of him in 1846, when his address is given as No. 25 Montague Street, on the south side of the city. By 1849 he had risen to a New Town residence, No. 59 Queen Street, where he lived till 1851, when he removed to No. 55, of which he became proprietor. There he was living at the time of his arrest in 1857. For the next fourteen years the bearer being, as Cousin Feenix would say, "in another place," the name of Dr. Wielobycki disappears from the Edinburgh Directory; but in 1871 he turns up again at No. 3 George Square, where apparently he resumed practice, until he retired for good in 1882. After that date his permanent address is the Grange Cemetery.

The Polish doctor was, as appears, a popular physician with a large practice, yielding him on an average £1200 a year—in those days a handsome income. As a homeopathist and a Knight of the Golden Cross (*Virtuti Militari*) he cut a con-

[1] Communicated by Professor Harvey Littlejohn.

spicuous figure in the medical circles of the city. But although a fashionable physician, the Doctor was not above casting a professional fly in suburban waters, and none of his fine patients, as we shall see, had such an influence on his fate as an obscure family in Portobello.

In 1852 there flitted to that watering-place from Galashiels an aged woman named Mrs. Darling, with her three surviving children, Thomas, Margaret, and Isabella. The reason of their removal was, they alleged, twofold: because the town boys threw, presumably according to the season, stones and snowballs at their door, and because they disliked the advent of the railway. So in Rosefield Place, a row of quaint cottages off Brighton Place, hard by the station, our emigrants, unmolested by the more civilised youth of Portobello and indifferent to the proximity of passing trains, found at No. 1 a peaceful haven. The mother falling sick, the great Dr. Wielobycki was summoned from town; but despite the fact that, to the high satisfaction of the neighbours, the carriage of that distinguished practitioner might daily be observed in their sequestered quarter, the old woman, unconscionably, did not recover. Her three children were all well-stricken in years; Isabella, the youngest, was sixty. She appears to have been the only one of any mental capacity, and that to but a limited extent. It was her custom to write their letters, and even to sign their names for them when required. The management of their affairs had long been in the capable hands of Mr. William Rutherford, writer in Galashiels, who looked after their investments, and through whom they received the income. "When they left Galashiels," says that gentleman, "they had £4200, and a house in Edinburgh, which they sold for £375." Their old age was thus comfortably provided for, and so thrifty were their habits that they contrived to save out of income some £50 per annum. They were simple, homely folk, and in all business matters relied on Mr. Rutherford, in whom, justly, they had absolute confidence. On their removal to Portobello he continued to act for them as before.

It was therefore with considerable surprise that on 19th November 1855 Mr. Rutherford received from Thomas Darling a letter, written by Isabella, withdrawing their whole business from his agency in favour of "a gentleman who will in a few days open a correspondence on the subject." This was followed on the 24th by a letter from Dr. Wielobycki, intimating that by request of Thomas he had undertaken the sole management of the family's affairs, and telling him to forward any cash in his possession, to realise the investments, and to deliver the title-deeds of the house in Salisbury Street, Edinburgh, all as belonging to his clients. Mr. Rutherford went at once to Portobello to learn the reason for this extraordinary step. There he was told that "they [the Darlings] wished to put all their money into the hands of one gentleman," who had promised them a higher rate of interest. The financial expert in question was, he ascertained, Dr. Wielobycki. Mr. Rutherford pointed out the impropriety of a physician intromitting with his patients' monetary matters, and said that however competent he might be in his own profession, Dr. Wielobycki was not a man of business and should not be employed as such. But no argument he could use availed to affect their faith in the Doctor's flair for finance, and not unwarrantably rather sore, Mr. Rutherford proceeded to Edinburgh to interview the pecuniary scientist. Interrogated as to his intentions, Dr. Wielobycki stated how he proposed to administer the trust: "He could get 10 per cent. from a Scotch Duke on heritable security." Mr. Rutherford replied that the accommodating nobleman must be a very needy one, as 3½ per cent. was the current rate of interest on such loans. The Doctor then amended his statement: the borrower was "not a Scotch Duke, but a Scotch Duke's factor." Struck by something equivocal in the good physician's manner, Mr. Rutherford with prophetic insight remarked, "I believe you are quibbling; you are going to deceive these people!" Whereupon the Doctor "got into a great passion and said he was a Pole and a gentleman," and Mr. Rutherford left the house. On 12th December he received from Thomas Darling, in Isabella's handwriting, a letter ordering him, in threatening terms, to send all their money to Dr. Wielobycki without further delay. The adoption of this minatory tone to a trusted friend of old standing bespoke, in the fullest sense of the term, an alien influence.

Mr. Rutherford, who had only hesitated in his clients' interests, agreed to give up the agency, but stipulated that he would not deliver the cash and securities except to a respectable agent. The Doctor then employed Mr. F. H. Carter, accountant in Edinburgh, to arrange the transference, and there for the time the matter rested.

Thomas Darling died in April 1856. By his will, which had been prepared by Mr. Rutherford, he left his property to his two sisters, Margaret and Isabella. Though Mr. Rutherford, after handing over the papers, etc., held no further communication with Portobello, he continued to act for the children of two deceased Darling sisters, Janet and Helen. On 16th October Margaret died intestate, so he wrote to Mr. Carter, intimating a claim on behalf of his clients to participate in their aunt's succession, and asking for a state of her affairs. Dr. Wielobycki, having learned of this claim, wrote to Mr. Carter on 27th October that he had consulted Isabella, who begged him to get an opinion from the best counsel as to its validity. "Please also," he wrote, "to disregard all remonstrances and demands made by Mr. R. on you or me until the opinion of our counsel is obtained." Mr. David Wight, W.S., was accordingly instructed by Mr. Carter to prepare a memorial for the opinion of the Solicitor-General (Edward Maitland) and of Mr. Graham Bell, advocate, as to whether under the settlement of Thomas, Isabella succeeded to Margaret's whole estate, or whether the claim of the dead sisters' children to a share was good. On 3rd November each of the learned counsel delivered an opinion in favour of the children's rights.

Tuesday, 4th November, is an important date in the case. On that day Dr. Wielobycki called upon Mr. Wight at his office, No. 11 Young Street, and introduced himself as the bearer of a letter from Miss Isabella Darling, addressed to Mr. Wight, in the following terms:—

1 Rosefield Place, Portobello.
4 November 1856.

Sir,—Being informed by Mr. Carter, accountant, that you are employed by him to ask the opinions of a counsel regarding the validity of my late brother Thomas Darling's disposition, which was made in favour of my late sister Margaret and myself, with a right to equal shares of his property; and knowing that Mr. Rutherford, writer, of Galashiels, not finding in Mr. Carter's office my late sister's will, which I have found amongst her papers and which is written in her own handwriting, dated 21 August 1856, has shown unscrupulously intentions to annoy me by bringing forth presumptuous claims of some of his clients, I beg you therefore to suspend all further proceedings with the counsels, and inform Mr. Rutherford on the subject without delay.—Sir, I am yours,

ISABELLA DARLING.

Two things struck Mr. Wight: the peculiarly apt discovery of the will, and this business-like communication from a person of Isabella's condition. Dr. Wielobycki then triumphantly exhibited the deed itself, which was as follows:—

I, Margaret Darling, residing at No. 1 Rosefield Place, Portobello, having along with my younger sister, Isabella Darling, by the disposition of our late brother Thomas Darling, a full right to the possession each of one half of his property left us by him, and for the love, favour and affection which I bear to my sister Isabella, dispone, give, and bequeath her solely and to the exclusion of everybody else, all goods, effects, debts, furniture, subjects, and property of every description which may belong to me at the time of my death: In witness whereof I have subscribed these presents, written by myself, at Portobello this twenty-first day of August, eighteen hundred and fifty-six.   MARGARET DARLING.

Mr. Wight rubbed his eyes: here was an illiterate old woman who could frame a settlement in technical terms as well as if she had been bred a Writer to the Signet! He describes as suspicious his attitude towards the document, which he handed back without remark to Dr. Wielobycki, who asked him to communicate to Mr. Rutherford the fact of its discovery, conform to Isabella's instructions. On the 6th the Doctor returned with the will for the purpose of having it recorded, and it was sent by Mr. Wight to the Record Office. On the 10th Mr.

Rutherford came to Edinburgh to inspect the lucky *trouvaille*, which he examined at the Register House and at once pronounced to be a forgery of Margaret's writing by Isabella—he was familiar with their respective hands. Later, while in Mr. Wight's office discussing the deed, the two lawyers were joined by Dr. Wielobycki who, despite his triumph, was disposed to be magnanimous, and greeted Mr. Rutherford with effusion. But that gentleman declined his proffered hand. "He asked me what I wanted," says Mr. Rutherford, "and I said I wanted money. He said, 'We all want money, if we could get it; but you can't get it, for there's a settlement.' I said, 'The settlement is a base forgery,' and I accused him of having something to do with it. He said it was not in his handwriting, and I said I knew that as well as he did; but I said, 'You have had a great deal to do with this document, and so much have you had to do with it that I think it is very likely both you and Miss Darling will be punished.'" "Are you aware that you put yourself and this poor woman in the position of both being transported?" is Mr. Wight's version. Whereupon the Knight of the Golden Cross (*Virtuti Militari*) rejoined, "Do you mean to frighten me?" There is a venerable and flowing-bearded proverb which asserts that every man at forty is either a fool or a physician; it was the misfortune of Dr. Wielobycki to figure in both capacities. He dropped the will like a red-hot cinder and proceeded to discuss terms for the settlement of the children's claims. Mr. Rutherford insisted on £1500, being two-thirds of Margaret's estate, and the Doctor undertook to see Isabella and advise her to settle the matter on that footing. After Mr. Rutherford's departure Mr. Wight remarked that the will must have been drawn by a lawyer, but the Doctor explained that he had himself furnished Isabella with a form. He left Mr. Wight under the impression that he was privy to the forgery.

On the 11th Dr. Wielobycki called to say that Miss Darling agreed to pay, and Mr. Rutherford was informed that the enemy had capitulated. "On the Monday afternoon," says Mr. Wight, "he admitted he had been accessory to the fabrication.

I said sneeringly, 'You must have got a will made in your own favour!' and he said he had already got one." This document, as afterwards produced, was as follows:—

I Rosefield Place, Portobello.
2 May 1856.

Dear Sir,—It having been our late brother's Thomas Darling's and our own sincere wish during his life to entrust you with a full management of our money affairs during our lives, we now jointly beg and authorise you to take care of our funds henceforward and all along by investing them in your own name according to the best of your means and disposition to me and my sister Margaret, both of us stating hereby solemnly the express wish of our late brother Thomas Darling as well as our own wish and will of the whole of our funds and property to become yours after our death.—We are, etc.

MARGARET DARLING.
ISABELLA DARLING.

To Dr. Wielobycki,
    55 Queen Street, Edinburgh.

In addition to its other remarkable features, this "will" presents the further peculiarity of having been written by Isabella to Dr. Wielobycki's dictation after the death of Margaret.

On 12th November Dr. Wielobycki met by appointment Messrs. Rutherford, Carter, and Wight at the latter's office, and stated that he had been empowered by Miss Darling to settle, subject to payment of the debts due by the deceased, which was deemed reasonable. Asked what these debts were, the Doctor presented a note of his fees for medical attendance on Margaret, amounting to £231. After some debate it was agreed that the professional labourer was worthy of his hire, and Mr. Rutherford said he would accept £1200 in full of his clients' claims, for which the Doctor gave his own cheque on the Royal Bank.

A bird of the air must have carried word of the matter to the authorities, for on 13th November Dr. Wielobycki received from the Procurator-Fiscal a pressing invitation to call at his chambers and to produce the settlement of Margaret Darling.

'The Doctor returned the citation, endorsed by him as follows:—

> Dr. Wielobycki has been suddenly called to Glasgow professionally this morning at 5 o'cl. & was obliged to start by the first train 7.30—has nothing to declare further, but that the document wanted was demanded back by Miss Darling & it was destroyed by herself—as it was of no use. Dr. W. will however call if wished on his return from Glasgow. Friday, 7 a.m.[1]

Arrested on 27th November on a charge of forgery, Isabella made upon examination what is popularly termed a clean breast, and the good physician's game was up. On 3rd December the polite breakfast tables of Auld Reikie were startled by the following announcement in that morning's papers:—

> APPREHENSION OF DR. WIELOBYCKI.— We understand that Dr. Wielobycki, a homeopathic physician in extensive practice, residing at No. 55 Queen Street, has been lodged in jail for further examination on a charge of having some concern with a forged will, which it is alleged has since been destroyed. It is stated that Dr. Wielobycki had attended professionally two old ladies, Misses Margaret and Isabella Darling, residing at Portobello, and that some time ago they had given into his hands on loan at interest the whole of their property, amounting to about £4000. This property their brother, Mr. Thomas Darling, left equally between them, but to the survivor in fee; the effect of this provision being that had one of them died before him, the other would have been entitled to the whole property, but as he died first, it vested equally in the two sisters. Miss Margaret Darling died recently without having made a will, and her share of the money would have fallen to Miss Isabella and to the children of two sisters who resided in Galashiels but who have been dead for some time. The allega-

---

[1] One would fain have hoped that the Doctor had been called in to consult with his ingenious colleague Dr. Pritchard; but, alas, that notable physician did not commence practice in Glasgow until 1860. The fact that he was a homeopathist need have been no obstacle, as Dr. Pritchard would have met Beelzebub in consultation if money were to be made by doing so, and Dr. Wielobycki was not, as we shall find, unduly scrupulous where cash was concerned.

tion is that a will was fabricated by which the whole of the property was left to Miss Isabella, Dr. Wielobycki still retaining the charge of it. On the will being shown to the parties interested they declared it to be a forgery, and it is stated that it has since been destroyed. We learn that the surviving Miss Darling is about to raise a civil action against Dr. Wielobycki for the recovery of her portion of the money.[1]

From the accuracy with which the facts are set forth we may assume that this paragraph was inspired.

The Doctor's last voluntary appearance at the Sheriff Court was after Isabella had been committed for trial, when he found bail for her to the extent of £300, which he paid by his own cheque. One is reluctant to examine too closely the motive which prompted Dr. Wielobycki to this generous act, but it must be borne in mind that the money was really Isabella's, and that as he did not know that she had already, as the phrase is, given him away, he doubtless hoped to prevail upon her to keep silence regarding his connection with her unlucky chirographic experiment. But his own arrest precluded the possibility of any further consultations with his old patient. A search at No. 1 Rosefield Place and No. 55 Queen Street resulted in the discovery of certain documents, which were taken possession of by the police; the Doctor was apprehended, and having been judicially examined, was committed on the charge.

Now Lord Advocate Moncreiff, as he afterwards explained to the jury, was in a position of some difficulty with regard to the prosecution of the accused persons, by reason of the peculiarities which the case presented. The forged document had been destroyed; if the two parties concerned in the forgery were placed at the bar, it would be no easy matter to bring the crime home to them, and the result might well be that both offenders would escape punishment.[2] So in the exercise of his learned discretion his lordship, considering the relative posi-

[1] *Scotsman*, 3rd December 1856.
[2] A similar dilemma beset the public prosecutor in the historic case of Burke and Hare; but in that instance Lord Advocate Rae was forced by the circumstances to proceed against the less guilty couple—if there be degrees in blackness—who refused to turn King's evidence against the baser pair.

tions of the accused, elected to put the doctor in the dock and the patient in the witness-box.

On Thursday, 8th January 1857, the High Court of Justiciary, Edinburgh, was crowded by a refined audience, vastly intrigued by the development of what is known nowadays as a society sensation. The Lord Justice-Clerk (John Hope) presided, accompanied on the Bench by Lords Handyside and Deas. Lord Deas was not conspicuous for straining the quality of mercy; and though his neck was in no danger, the Doctor must have been relieved to find the amiable Justice-Clerk, and not that Draconic senator, was to be the arbiter of his fate. Dr. Wielobycki's manner throughout the two days' proceedings was marked, we are told, by firmness and composure. The prosecution was conducted by His Majesty's Advocate (James Moncreiff), assisted by Mr. Donald Mackenzie, Advocate-Depute; the Dean of Faculty (John Inglis), with Messrs. Miller and Thomson, advocates, appeared for the accused. The pannel was charged with forging and uttering as genuine a testamentary deed, as set forth at great length in the cumbrous indictment of the time. It was drawn by Mackenzie[1] who, associated six months later with Moncreiff in the prosecution of Madeleine Smith, also framed the indictment upon which that captivating damsel was tried. After a detailed narration of the facts with which the reader is already familiar, the charges, briefly stated, were as follows: (1) on a day between 24th October 1856 and 5th November 1856, forging, or causing to be forged, or assisting Isabella Darling to forge a will purporting to be written by Margaret Darling, and adhibiting her signature thereto; (2) on 4th November 1856, within the chambers of David Wight, W.S., uttering the said will as genuine, well knowing it to be forged, that it might be founded on as setting aside the rights of the next of kin; (3) on 6th November 1856, in the same place and to the same party, uttering the said will as aforesaid, in order that it might be recorded as a probative writ; (4) on 10th November 1856, in the same place, uttering the said will

[1] Donald Mackenzie (1818–1875), afterwards Lord Mackenzie; Advocate-Depute, 1854–58, 1859–61; Sheriff of Fife, 1861; Bench, 1870.

as aforesaid to William Rutherford, with intent to defeat the claims of his clients; and (5) on 13th November 1856, within the house at Rosefield Place, tearing, burning, or otherwise destroying the said forged will, as affording evidence of his guilt in the premises. The pannel having pleaded Not Guilty to these charges, and no objection being taken to the relevancy of the indictment, the case went to trial.

The first witness for the Crown was Sheriff Hallard, who had judicially examined the prisoner and taken his declarations. Two Sheriff-officers spoke to the arrest of Isabella Darling and of Dr. Wielobycki, and identified certain documents found in their respective houses. Mr. Rutherford was then called, and in reply to the Lord Advocate, described his dealings with the Darlings prior to the advent of Dr. Wielobycki, his supersession as their agent by that expert, the invention of the will, his repudiation of that fallacious document, and the settlement of his clients' claims, all as before narrated. Cross-examined by the Dean of Faculty, he thought the will occupied a page and a quarter; it was written on a large sheet of letter-paper. He did not remember whether it was signed on the first page. Isabella was in the habit of writing letters for Thomas, but not for Margaret. She was the most active member of the family and put herself more forward than the others. He had known them for twenty years. When he gave up the agency their money was all invested; £500 on heritable, and the rest on personal security. They were not on good terms with their nephews and nieces. Thomas's settlement gave the two sisters all his property. At their first interview Dr. Wielobycki was very much excited; witness was not in the least so. "I thought he was going to deceive these people; and I said it would turn out to be a swindle, meaning that he would swindle them. He was much annoyed and excited. He did not order me to leave the house." Re-examined, witness said he paid to Mr. Carter £3400 of the Darlings' money.

Mr. Carter, examined by the Lord Advocate, said he was employed by Dr. Wielobycki to get the Darlings' money from Mr. Rutherford. Witness told him he must have Thomas's personal authority to do so, and the Doctor wrote, that if it were really necessary, "I could give you a drive in my carriage" for that purpose. On 17th June 1856 Isabella Darling wrote again, telling him to pay £1600 to Dr. Wielobycki, which he did. Asked how the sum was to be invested, the Doctor said, "on heritable security in Glasgow." On 28th June he received from Dr. Wielobycki a letter in these terms:—

Dear Sir,—Misses Darling of Portobello have requested me this evening to say that they will be much obliged to you to get all the money due to them from the rest of the creditors collected without delay, as they have now an opportunity of getting it invested on more advantageous terms, or to deliver the papers and documents to me to employ a sharper agent, if you find any difficulty in dealing with Mr. Rutherford of Galashiels. I shall call at your office about it on Monday morning; and to give satisfaction to Misses Darling, who are anxious to get clear of the lawyers fast, please to prepare a final account with them for the management of their affairs by you hitherto, for their perusal.

"Before retiring on the 'int," in the Billickin's polished phrase, Mr. Carter paid over to Dr. Wielobycki certain further sums, being the balance of the Darlings' money in his hands. Witness then described the demand made after Margaret's death, and the production of her will by the Doctor on the very day that counsel had advised in favour of the claim. When he heard of the discovery, he asked Dr. Wielobycki whether the will was holograph and explained to him the meaning of that term; the Doctor replied that it was so. Cross-examined by the Dean, witness said he received in all on behalf of the Darlings £3918. On 13th May 1856 he paid Dr. Wielobycki £120, 15s. for medical attendance on Thomas; on 18th June, £1600; on 9th July, £500; and on 31st July, £450. The will was written and signed upon a single page—a half-sheet of foolscap. Re-examined, in addition to the sums mentioned, witness paid direct to Isabella a further £750, which he afterwards learned she gave to Dr. Wielobycki, who got altogether £3420. The Doctor wrote to Isabella that "it was bold and improper in

Mr. Carter to take any further steps without consulting me."
Dr. Wielobycki told witness that the Darlings had "a horror
of lawyers," and would not see one except in his presence.

Mr. Wight, in reply to the Lord Advocate, told how he was
consulted as to the effect of Thomas Darling's settlement and
instructed to obtain opinion of counsel thereon; how Dr.
Wielobyski introduced himself on 4th November, armed with
Margaret's will and the letter from Isabella intimating its discovery; and described the subsequent history of that document
so far as known to him. Cross-examined by the Dean, Mr.
Wight said that whenever he saw the will he remarked,
"'Surely, Doctor, this must have been prepared by a man of
business? Did you give Miss Darling a copy of it?' He said, 'I
had a copy of a will.'" It was written and signed on one page
of blue foolscap, which it nearly filled. Personally, he knew
nothing of the Darlings' handwriting. The first time he saw the
will it was not "backed up"; on the second occasion it was, and
in the same hand as the body of the document.[1] Witness told
Mr. Rutherford that Dr. Wielobycki admitted he had "participated in the fabrication," and the Doctor complained of his
having done so.

Dr. Wielobycki's own holograph settlement, found in his
repositories, was then put in. It bore the fateful date of 4th
November 1856—which, by the way, must have been a busy
day for the Doctor—and is chiefly important as being identical
in legal phrasing with the terms of the forged will.

Isabella Darling, examined by the Lord Advocate, described
the deaths of her mother, brother and sister, and the transference of their whole property to Dr. Wielobycki. "The Doctor
told us we would get better interest for our money if he had
it." At this stage the Lord Justice-Clerk informed the witness
that as she had been called for the Crown, anything she might
say as to her own share in fabricating the alleged will could
never be used against her. Thus assured, Isabella resumed her
tale.

---

[1] This posthumous endorsement forms a curious instance of automatic
writing from "beyond the veil."

After I heard the opinion of the lawyers in favour of my sisters' children, some communication took place between Dr. Wielobycki and me as to making a will for my sister [Margaret]. I said to the Doctor I was sorry it had happened so, and I thought there would be no harm in writing a will for myself on a simple piece of paper. He said at first he thought it would be as well not to do it; but then he went in with me. The Doctor wrote a scroll of it for me and on the same night he said he would write a shorter scroll. This was some time after my sister's death. I think we had spoken of doing it before. The scrolls were written in my house in Portobello. Dr. Wielobycki left me both scrolls and I copied one of them and signed my sister's name to it. I burned the scrolls. When I saw the Doctor afterwards, I told him what I had done, and he said he would see if it would do.

The will as set forth in the indictment was that which she wrote from the Doctor's scroll. He dictated to her the letter written by her to Mr. Wight announcing the discovery. Dr. Wielobycki, approving of her handiwork, took the will and the letter away with him. "The next thing I heard from him was that it would not do": Mr. Rutherford said it was in her handwriting, not Margaret's. In these regrettable circumstances the Doctor advised her to give up £1200 to the nephews and nieces, "and there would be no more about the will." But here, as we have seen, the good physician's diagnosis was at fault. He gave her back the document, which she burned after the settlement with Mr. Rutherford. "He [the Doctor] told me the Fiscal had been inquiring about it, and he asked several times if the Fiscal had been at me. He appeared to be anxious; and he told me to be sure never to mention his name, but to say it [the will] was made between my sister and myself." The joint settlement of 2nd May 1856 by Margaret and herself in favour of Dr. Wielobycki was written by her to the Doctor's dictation after her sister's death, the signature of Margaret being appended by her. "The Doctor sat by my side telling me what to write, word for word. I never wrote a letter except at his dictation." Though she had given her whole fortune to her medical adviser, she only received one quarter's interest on her money: £45, from which the Doctor deducted £20 "for his trouble in lending it out." He carried away all their savings in cash: £159 in half-crowns; £13 in crowns; £2, 10s. in florins; £18, 10s. in shillings; £5 in sixpences; and £172 in notes: in all £370. She also gave him the £750 paid over to her by Mr. Carter. She got no receipt or acknowledgment for any of these sums. Cross-examined by the Dean, she said that Mr. Rutherford was always honest and faithful; they were not dissatisfied with him. "We were told by the Doctor it would be much better to have a private gentleman to manage our affairs than a writer or man of business." With regard to her habit of writing to the Doctor's dictation, she said she could not express herself properly unless directed by a learned man. She put Margaret's name to the will in favour of Dr. Wielobycki "to make it stronger: two names were better than one." As to the forged will, she said, "I did not think I was committing forgery. As it was on a simple piece of paper and without witnesses, I thought the law would not take hold of me." She knew that but for the will her nephews and nieces would have got the money. She had never said it was hard that the Doctor should be imprisoned on a charge he had nothing to do with: "the Doctor was the cause of her making the will." When apprehended she at first denied all knowledge of the affair, but afterwards told the whole truth, as she had now done.

After some formal evidence as to the recording of the will, the giving out of an extract, and the return of the principal to Mr. Wight, James Milroy, law clerk, examined, said he was a patient of Dr. Wielobycki. On 4th November he met him in Elder Street. The Doctor asked whether a will dealing with movable property required a stamp? He answered, no. The Doctor then asked whether any particular form of words was necessary? He replied that any words clearly expressing the intention of the party would be sufficient. The next question was, did it need to be witnessed? "Yes," said Milroy, "unless it is holograph"; and he explained the meaning of that term. Fortified by this legal opinion the Doctor went his way—presumably to Portobello. At this stage the Court adjourned.

When the trial was resumed next morning but one witness remained to be called for the prosecution: the borrower of the £1500. This turned out to be one Mr. Hernuelwicz, a Glasgow merchant and, as appears, a compatriot of the Doctor, who had represented him to Mr. Rutherford as a "Scotch Duke." He described how the loan was negotiated, the security for which was taken in favour of Dr. Wielobycki. The declarations of the prisoner were then read. In the first, emitted on 27th November, with regard to the Glasgow loan he said he had intended to assign the bond to Miss Darling, when the buildings upon which it was secured were completed. Isabella never consulted him about making a will for Margaret. He never dictated anything to her, nor did he leave any paper for her to copy. When Isabella produced the will he made no inquiries; it was no business of his. The letter she wrote to Mr. Wight was her own composition; he had nothing to do with it. He denied that the conversations sworn to by Mr. Wight ever took place. When cited to appear before the authorities he gave back the will to Isabella and saw her destroy it. She was a weak-minded person, who required to be guided and managed. She and Margaret often declared their intention to leave him their money, but he always resisted such proposals. In a second declaration of 28th November he again denied that he had ever given to Isabella scrolls of any letters; but on being shown several such scrolls in his own handwriting, he admitted the fact. As to the joint will by the sisters in his favour, he said that he might have furnished a scroll of it at their request.

The case for the Crown being closed, certain evidence was given for the defence regarding the prisoner's bank accounts, of which he kept two, from which it appeared that all payments were made in his own name and that there was on each a balance at his credit. A coal merchant and a builder gave evidence regarding a Feu Charter in Miss Darling's favour, obtained on the prisoner's instructions, of a piece of ground at Whitehouse Loan, Edinburgh, on which a villa was being built. On cross-examination it appeared that Isabella denied liability, and that the Doctor was held liable for the price: £720. An official of the Register House proved that Dr. Wielobycki bought his house, No. 55 Queen Street, at Whitsunday 1851, and that there was no incumbrance on the property; and an accountant, who had examined his books, said that the Doctor's professional income for the year 1855 was over £1200. An Edinburgh merchant, a dweller in Leith Walk, a Hawick manufacturer, and the keeper of a temperance hotel, severally testified that to their knowledge the prisoner was a man of strict integrity and the highest honour, benevolent, and the reverse of mercenary; they had seen nothing to shake their confidence in him as an honest and upright person. This closed the case for the defence.

The Lord Advocate [1] addressed the jury on behalf of the Crown. He began by referring to the peculiarities which the case presented: the position of the prisoner; the fact that the forged document could not be produced, because it had been destroyed; and the further fact that the hand which forged the writing was that of a person who, instead of being charged with the offence, appeared to give evidence against the prisoner. In secret crimes it often happened that an attempt to bring all the offenders to justice resulted in their escape, and it was in his lordship's discretion to accept the evidence of a party who otherwise might have stood in the dock instead of in the witness-box. The evidence in this case was divisible into three parts: (1) the real or documentary evidence, about which there could be no doubt, including the judicial confessions of the prisoner; (2) the oral evidence, other than that of the accomplice; and (3) the evidence of the accomplice herself. The first was of the highest importance, apart from a single word spoken in the witness-box. The prisoner, a medical man in very large practice, involved himself in the pecuniary affairs of his patients, wrote out draft letters for them, conducted their negotiations, got their whole means into his hands and transferred them into bank in his own name. In the investment of their

---

[1] James Moncreiff (1811–1895). Bar, 1833; Solicitor-General, 1850–51; Lord Advocate, 1851–52, 1852–58, 1859–1866, 1868–69; Dean of Faculty, 1858–1869; Lord Justice-Clerk, 1869–1888.

money he consulted no solicitor, they received no voucher for it, and his creditors could have swept off every penny. Their confidence in him was unbounded, nay, almost incredible. So completely was he master of their minds that they actually allowed him to take the savings of many years, accumulated in half-crowns and shillings, amounting to upwards of £300. There was also the very singular and startling fact that he held in his hands a document, purporting to be signed by Margaret and Isabella, making over to him at their death the whole of their property.

> So that this medical attendant, not content with having received into his own hands the whole funds belonging to this family, not content with having them invested in his own name, took from these ladies a document constituting him their heir. That a man standing in his position should, without the intervention of a law agent, have permitted this to be done was a matter which required no comment; but that document being in his possession, the jury would see at once that not only was he the custodier of the funds, but that he had also the strongest possible interest in their ultimate destination.

Before Margaret Darling died the prisoner consulted Mr. Carter as to the effect of Thomas's settlement, saying she would make a will if the money would not otherwise go to Isabella. So Dr. Wielobycki knew then that no will had been made. After her death, when he heard of Mr. Rutherford's claim, he was in great agitation and wanted an opinion of counsel. It was plain that at that time no will could possibly have existed. The opinions, both unfavourable, were received on 3rd November; on the 4th Dr. Wielobycki came up from Portobello with the alleged will and the letter from Miss Darling. No one could believe that it had been written by herself. It contained words of legal import not used in her brother's settlement; where did she get them? Among the documents found in the prisoner's house was a will in his own handwriting, dated 4th November, in which the very same words were employed. This proved not only that Dr. Wielobycki had a form of will, but one that was verbatim that used by Miss Darling. They had heard what was the prisoner's conduct when the will was repudiated by Mr. Rutherford: he at once negotiated for a settlement, recommended Miss Darling to pay, and when cited by the authorities to produce the will, took it to Portobello and saw Miss Darling destroy it. Were these the acts of an honest man? Without one word of oral evidence the forgery was proved. As to where the guilt really lay, let them remember the great interest Dr. Wielobycki had in the property, that he must have known the will was not made by Margaret, that he tried to pass off the forged deed as genuine, and the moment it was challenged, withdrew it, paid the claims, and saw it destroyed. With regard to the oral evidence, other than that of Miss Darling, his lordship referred to the conversation spoken to by Mr. Milroy as showing that the prisoner was investigating the subject. He then examined at large the evidence of Messrs. Rutherford, Carter, and Wight, emphasising the importance of the prisoner's confession to the letter. Upon this branch of the case, as upon the former one, he was entitled to ask for a verdict of guilty. But the proof did not end there. The deed having been destroyed, it had appeared to his lordship that some further light must be thrown on the matter, and the only question was, should that light be obtained from Dr. Wielobycki or from Miss Darling? In the circumstances of the case—looking to the station of the prisoner and his means of influence, the fact of that influence having been used, the position in which the property stood, and his relation to Miss Darling in the event of her death—his lordship had no hesitation whatever in reaching a decision. If Dr. Wielobycki were guilty, it was one of the most flagrant cases of abuse of position, as well as breach of law, that had come under his notice as public prosecutor. He had accordingly placed Miss Darling in the box. No doubt her evidence was to be received with suspicion, but he would leave it to the jury to say whether, in view of the other evidence before them, they had the slightest hesitation in accepting her story as substantially true. If Dr. Wielobycki did try to dissuade her, his guilty knowledge was proved; when she gave him the

will he must have known that it was forged. The whole chain
of events so hung together as to lead them unquestionably to
the conclusion that the prisoner was guilty of the charges made
against him.

The Dean of Faculty[1] then addressed the jury for the defence. The materials of which the Crown case was composed
were, he maintained, extremely worthless. He could not sufficiently admire the skill with which the Lord Advocate strove
to disguise the absolute necessity under which he felt himself
in accepting the evidence of an accomplice. Such a course
would never have been adopted had it been possible otherwise
to establish the charge against the prisoner at the bar.

For thirteen years he had practised as a physician in Edinburgh, and had enjoyed an excellent and constantly increasing
practice. He had made money, besides being in the receipt of
a very good income; he had purchased the house in which he
lived in Queen Street, and he had a comfortable balance at
his bank account. He was distinguished among all who knew
him as a person not only of undoubted probity and high
honour, but as a man distinguished for benevolence on the
one hand, and for the absence of any special love of money on
the other. Such a man, as regarded personal character and
position in life, was about the most unlikely man to engage in
the commission of an offence such as he was now charged
with.

It was said that he was interested in Miss Darling's estate; but
the whole amount to be gained by the crime was only £1200,
which he hoped to receive on the death of a person not much
older than himself, a sum equal to a single year's income; and
for this he had plunged all at once into this vortex of crime
and guilt. It was incredible; but on what sort of testimony were
they asked to believe it? There was real evidence of his acquaintance with the Darlings, who, having great confidence in
him, entrusted him with the management of their affairs. Even

---

[1] John Inglis (1810–1891). Bar, 1835; Solicitor-General, Lord Advocate,
and Dean of Faculty, 1852; Lord Justice-Clerk, 1858; Lord Justice-General
and Lord President, 1867–91.

if the jury thought his conduct in this regard improper, were they to conclude, because there was some suspicion of a forged will, that he must be the author of the fabrication or have any necessary connection with it? It was alleged that £3670 of the Darlings' money found its way into his hands; but it was given him for investment, he had invested it, and every shilling of it was extant: £2000 lent in Glasgow, £1200 paid to Rutherford, £300 to bail out Miss Darling, making £3500, and leaving only £170 in Dr. Wielobycki's hands, to meet which he had property of much greater value. What a commentary was this on Mr. Rutherford's story that all the money had disappeared! It was all perfectly safe, and whether or not it was discreet of Dr. Wielobycki to invest it in his own name, there had been no deception. The Dean then referred to the rooted and strong enmity against the prisoner which characterised the conduct of Mr. Rutherford throughout. When he insisted on knowing how the money was to be invested, Dr. Wielobycki told him a cock-and-bull story about a "Scotch Duke," because he was disgusted with Mr. Rutherford's impertinence and was quizzing him most unmercifully. With regard to the alleged fabrication, it was strange that the prisoner should have set about forging a will before the unfavourable opinion had been received. He showed the will to Mr. Wight on the morning of 4th November, and that forenoon he had some conversation with Mr. Milroy, the suggestion being that he thus learned how to make the forged instrument. "Why, it was made already and in the hands of Mr. Wight, and if Miss Darling was to be believed, it had been in existence for days!" As to the resemblance between the will and Dr. Wielobycki's settlement, what more natural than that, having it in his possession, supplemented by Milroy's hints, he should use it as a model for his own? "It was said that Mr. Rutherford at once pronounced the document a forgery, but coming from the quarter from which it did, it would present itself to him in the most diabolical light; he [the Dean] would not have been surprised if Mr. Rutherford had expected the prisoner to commit murder, and he was not very sure if he had not thought something of that sort." A great deal had been made of Dr. Wielobycki, when accused of being accessory to the forgery, not having denied it; but how could a Polish doctor know the meaning of the term accessory? Why, if he were guilty, did he not put the will in the fire, instead of giving it back to Miss Darling? He may have given it with some dark suspicion in his mind that something was wrong, but with a desire to let her do with it what she thought best for the purpose of screening herself. The Dean then examined the evidence of Messrs. Rutherford, Carter, and Wight, making the most of the discrepancies between their respective descriptions of the will.

All through, the jury would see a spirit of venom in Mr. Rutherford's conduct; he rushed, in a wild-bull fashion, throughout the whole affair; stumbling himself, contradicted by everybody else at every stage of his proceedings, he was a witness entirely unworthy of credit. With his blundering rage on the one hand, and the indistinct recollection and most imperfect articulation of Mr. Wight, who could not give an intelligible account of any one thing that passed, on the other, he [the Dean] thought the jury would be disposed to give no weight at all to their evidence.[1]

If there were other evidence connecting the prisoner with the forgery, then such testimony might be appealed to as affording corroboration, but there was none. What faith could be placed in Miss Darling? The manner in which she expressed herself as to what she had done was revolting. Her statements were no more to be depended upon than if she had no conscience at all, and even in her falsehoods she was inconsistent. Miss Darling, therefore, stood condemned, and without her there was no evidence. That a man of respectable position in society and of the highest character, without need or poverty to drive him to the commission of an offence so grave, and with no adequate motive even as to the amount of money to be gained by it, should all at once, falling from his high estate of

---

[1] From this passage it is plain that the learned Dean was familiar with the maxim current in the law courts of our English neighbours: "No case; abuse the plaintiff's attorney."

honour and integrity, commit one of the basest crimes, was more than any jury could believe. With this declaration of faith—fallacious, as we shall find in the sequel—the Dean, amid loud cheers from the audience, resumed his seat.

The Lord Justice-Clerk [1] then charged the jury. If they should hold that the prisoner, even if he did not suggest the making of the will, yet concurred in the fabrication and furnished the scroll from which it was written, knowing that the signature of Margaret Darling was to be attached to it, that would amount to forgery. The crime, however, was incomplete unless the forged instrument was used and uttered, but if they were satisfied that the prisoner had produced to Messrs. Wight, Carter, and Rutherford this will as genuine, knowing it to be forged, then he was guilty of using and uttering. In view of the fact, which was not disputed, that he had acquired and possessed so complete an influence over these people that they gave into his hands all their money without even a receipt, it was plain that they were very ignorant, facile, and weak-minded persons. The foundation of the charge was that the will was actually forged; and if it was written by Miss Darling, of what avail to disprove that fact were minute criticisms on alleged contradictions between witnesses as to its outward form? It was an extraordinary thing that the will should be produced on 4th November just when it was required, and it was equally remarkable that so soon as it was challenged the whole purpose of it, namely, to secure Margaret's share of the succession, was given up and the will was destroyed. Even without the testimony of Miss Darling, they could not but hold that it was a forgery. With regard to her evidence his lordship observed:—

> She admitted having written the will, and said she had done so from a scroll furnished by Dr. Wielobycki. In a person of such extreme weak-mindedness, stupidity, and irresolution, capable, as the prisoner described, of saying yes or no to anything, there was often combined with that a cunning, narrow-minded,

[1] The Right Hon. John Hope (1794–1858). Bar, 1816; Solicitor-General 1823–30; Dean of Faculty, 1830–41; Lord Justice-Clerk, 1841–58.

selfish desire to promote their own interests, however unscrupulously. This might account not only for her indistinct ideas of right and wrong, but for her absurd notions as to what was punishable and what was not, and might also account for her doing a thing which, if she had known she was liable to be punished for, she would not have done. But all this want of capacity and of moral discrimination did not prove that she was unworthy of credit when she spoke to actual facts that had occurred.

Having read over to the jury the evidence of Isabella and of Messrs. Wight, Rutherford, and Carter, his lordship said the first question was, were they satisfied as to the existence of this forged will? The learned counsel for the defence had not challenged the fact, and they might take it as established. The next point was, did the pannel aid and abet that fabrication? Even if they disbelieved Miss Darling's statement that he supplied her with a scroll, such as he provided for all her other writings on matters of business, did he know it to be forged, and, so knowing, utter it? Was it possible that if he uttered it he believed it genuine? What was his conduct when it was challenged as a forgery? The prisoner had called evidence to prove that he had £600 in bank, owned a house in Queen Street, and earned a professional income of £1200 a year; that he was reputed an honourable, benevolent, and kind-hearted man. To all that they would give due weight. If, on the other hand, they were satisfied upon the proof that, from whatever motive, the prisoner was a party to the fabrication of the will, or that in uttering it he was in guilty knowledge of its being forged, then however unfortunate it might be for a person of such character and standing, no evidence of character could set aside facts proved to their satisfaction. Evidence of character was of great importance, but they all knew, and experience constantly taught them, that they must trust to proven facts as against all presumptions arising from previous good character.

His lordship having concluded his charge, the jury retired to consider their verdict, and after an absence of twenty-five

minutes returned to Court with the following finding: "The
jury unanimously find the prisoner guilty as libelled, but
recommend him to the mercy of the Court."

> LORD HANDYSIDE (who presided, the Justice-Clerk having
> left the Court)—Since you have recommended the prisoner
> to the mercy of the Court, it would be satisfactory to the
> Court to know the ground on which you make the recommen-
> dation.
>
> THE CHANCELLOR (Foreman)—On the ground of his previ-
> ous good character.

The verdict having been recorded, the diet was adjourned till
Monday next at ten o'clock, when sentence would be pronounced. The Court then rose. The prisoner, we read, who
seemed much exhausted by the protracted trial, received the
announcement of the verdict with the same firmness and
composure that had characterised his demeanour throughout
the proceedings. There was evident sympathy with him in the
crowded Court, but an adverse verdict was generally anticipated. A large crowd, unable to obtain access to the Court-
house, awaited the result of the trial in the Parliament Close.

At the sitting of the High Court on 12th January, the Lord
Justice-Clerk and Lords Cowan and Deas upon the Bench,
when the diet was called against Dr. Wielobycki the Justice-
Clerk stated that in consequence of Lord Handyside not having been able to make up his mind as to the punishment to be
inflicted, the Court would continue the diet against the pannel
till Wednesday following.[1] On that day the Lord Justice-Clerk,
having resumed the facts of the case, observed:

> The matter of punishment has been the subject of very anx-
> ious consideration to the Court. The gravity of the case, the
> great importance of the punishment in point of precedent and
> for the end of deterring others from the commission of such
> crimes, and—I won't disguise it—the commiseration arising in
> my mind at the moment of conviction for the situation in
> which the pannel was then placed, as compared with the de-
> scription of his former position in society, and the faint hope

[1] *Courant*, 13th January 1857.

on my own part that, in the opinion of the rest of our brethren, we might find some kind of encouragement for making an exception from the ordinary line of punishment in these cases, induced us to consider the case with the aid of the whole other members of the College of Justice. We found them all decidedly and firmly of opinion that the course of practice and the character of the offence could lead to but one result, and after full consideration I am satisfied that it is the fitting and proper conclusion. Therefore, Dr. Wielobycki, the sentence of the Court is, that you be transported beyond the seas for fourteen years.[1]

The prisoner was then removed from the bar.

The animadversions of the Dean of Faculty upon the character and conduct of Mr. Rutherford aroused strong resentment in the Border country, where that gentleman was held, personally and professionally, in high esteem. Both the *Border Advertiser* and the *Kelso Chronicle* protested against what they considered a flagrant abuse of the licence allowed to counsel, and demanded a public apology, but none was vouchsafed. It appears that the Dean's strictures had incurred a reprimand from the Bench, but neither of the reports of the charge which I have consulted contains any reference to the matter. It seems unfair that the reporters, having recorded the Dean's diatribe, should have omitted the judicial reproof; but John Inglis was a much bigger man than John Hope, and perhaps they were afraid to do so. At a dinner of the Selkirkshire Farmers' Club, Major Scott of Gala, in proposing Mr. Rutherford's health, spoke loudly in his vindication and waxed exceeding wroth with the Dean of Faculty. Mr. Rutherford, in responding, said that though he had been hardly used, the wounds inflicted by his learned censor were but skin deep, and he was none the worse for them.[2]

Despite the doom pronounced against him by the unanimous judgment of the Lords of Justiciary, the Polish physician

---

[1] *Courant*, 15th January 1857. It is said that Lord Handyside, having known the doctor personally, was naturally unwilling to pronounce sentence on his former friend.

[2] *Scotsman*, 17th January 1857.

was not destined to "dree his weird" to the extent prescribed. By the courtesy of H.M. Prison Commissioners for Scotland and England respectively, I am enabled to acquaint the interested reader with the several stations of his punitory pilgrimage. Dr. Wielobycki, apprehended on 28th November 1856, registered as forty-two years of age and as a member of the Church of England, was, as we have seen, sentenced on 14th January 1857. On 16th February of that year, by order of the Secretary of State, he was transferred to Wakefield prison.[1] On 16th December the convict was removed to Lewes prison, where he remained until 13th July 1859, when he was sent to Dartmoor. On 2nd February 1862 he received a full pardon.[2] There is nothing in the prison records to indicate the grounds upon which the pardon was granted; perhaps the Home Secretary, less Rhadamanthine than the Lords of Justiciary, thought five years' penal servitude was in the circumstances of the case a sufficient punishment.

How the Knight of the Golden Cross (*Virtuti Militari*) employed his recovered leisure during the nine years which elapsed until he again became in 1871 a citizen of Edinburgh, I cannot tell. Only two items of his post-penal history survive: he married, according to the inscription on his tombstone, Lady Felice, Baroness Wielobycka; he died, as his obituary notice informs us, at No. 3 George Square, Edinburgh, on 16th November 1882, at the age of sixty-nine, and in the bosom of the Catholic Church.[3]

Whatever good may have been done by Dionysius Wielobycki in the flesh is interred with his bones in the Grange Cemetery; the evil that he did lives after him, as I have occasion to know, in legend. On asking the other day a venerable lady of my acquaintance in Edinburgh whether she recollected Dr. Wielobycki, she replied that she remembered him perfectly as a dweller in George Square; also his noble helpmate: "a

[1] There was at that date no provision made in Scotland for the accommodation of convicts undergoing a sentence of penal servitude.
[2] Communicated by Dr. James Devon, H.M. Prison Commissioner for Scotland.
[3] *Scotsman*, 17th November 1882.

tall, handsome, fair-haired woman." And then my friend added the, to me, novel and surprising statement: "He was hanged for poisoning his wife"! Seeing that the Baroness Wielobycka survived to have a Requiem Mass celebrated in the Pro-Cathedral, Broughton Street, for the repose of her husband's soul,[1] to erect over his remains a marble monument, and to mourn his loss for a season in the connubial mansion,[2] it would seem that my informant's memory is upon this point defective. Wherefore, being a conscientious historian, I am compelled reluctantly to reject as apocryphal this so dramatic conclusion, which much better "fills the bill," as I of old conceived it, than the simple and insanguinary truth. Verily, there is wisdom in the familiar proverb relative to the consequences of giving a dog a bad name.

[1] *Scotsman*, 17th November 1882.
[2] Edinburgh Directory for 1883.

LOCUSTA IN SCOTLAND:

A Familiar Survey of Poisoning, as Practised in That Realm

> Fie on these dealers in poison, say I; can they not keep to
> the old honest way of cutting throats, without introducing
> such abominable innovations from Italy?
> —*On Murder, Considered as one of the Fine Arts.*

IT IS STRANGE that a critic so acute as De Quincey, while ex-
tolling the rude methods of the mere manslayer, should hold
in light esteem the poisoner's delicate and nimble art. Such
attaching cases as that of Miss Blandy or of Captain Donellan
shall never, he protests, have any countenance from him; and
the instance which he selects as a palmary example of the
purest and most perfect style is that of the savage Williams,
who exterminated with a carpenter's maul two whole families
in Ratcliffe Highway. As in the case of other artists before
and since, quantity rather than quality seems to have been
Mr. Williams' note, and his best bit of work was his last—the
hanging of himself in a prison cell with his own braces.

Regard being had to the relatively rare occurrence of poisoning in Scotland, it would appear that De Quincey's view was
largely held by local exponents of the homicidal cult. Possibly the national sense of thrift counted for something in the
matter; drugs were dear and hard to come by, but the meanest
could command a knife. Be that as it may, one of our chief
connoisseurs, King James the Sixth, followed his native bent
in employing the stake, the dagger and the gibbet for the
elimination of such of his Scots subjects as were repugnant
to the Royal pleasure—compare his unnumbered witch-burn-
ings, *passim*, and the butchery of the Gowrie boys at Perth.
Not until His Majesty enjoyed the refining influence of the
Italianate Court of England did Prince Henry eat at Wood-

stock the impoisoned grapes, and Sir Thomas Overbury die lingeringly in the Tower, attended by the King's mediciner, after a liberal exhibition of realgar, mercury, white arsenic, and dust of diamonds. The last named sounds the most attractive, but doubtless it was all one to the patient: "What would it pleasure me," asks the Duchess of her murderer in Webster's great tragedy, "What would it pleasure me to have my throat cut with diamonds? or to be smothered with cassia? or to be shot to death with pearls?" Queen Mary, so amazingly James's mother, a princess, by reason of her French upbringing and natural gifts, infinitely superior to the gang of noble ruffians about her throne, wrote to Bothwell once, deprecating his crude purpose of blowing up her petulant spouse with gunpowder: "Advise to with zourself gif ze can find out ony mair secreit inventioun by medicine, for he suld tak medicine and the bath at Craigmillar." Poison, she wisely implies, would make less noise than powder; but the hint was thrown away upon the rude Borderer, and more than Darnley was exploded at Kirk o'Field.

For the curious in homicidal pharmacy the accounts of early cases preserved in our records are provokingly scant. This is due as well to the ignorance of the amateur practitioner, as to the ineptitude of physicians in failing to detect him in his interesting pursuit. The pioneer of poisoning groped his way, as it were, in a scientific wilderness, where was "nor path nor friendly clue to be his guide," while the professed man of medicine was better versed in the mysteries of the heavenly, than in those of merely human bodies. The first Scots Act to recognise the crime of poisoning as such is that of 1450,[1] whereby all persons are forbidden under pain of treason to bring home poison for any use by which any Christian man or woman may take bodily harm. "But notwithstanding of these words," observes Sir George Mackenzie, "Apothecaries and others do daily bring home Poyson"; indeed, whatever the Legislature might intend, the Statute was practically a dead letter, for he adds, "I find no instances in the Journal

[1] 7 James II. c. 31 and 32.

Books where any have been convict as Traitors upon this account." [1] Thus the provision was of no benefit to poisoners, who suffered on the scaffold the common doom of homicides, without the added distinction of mutilation and dismemberment.

Passing such hazy instances as the suspected poisoning of Margaret Drummond, mistress of James the Fourth, in April 1502, the earliest case of the kind in our records is that of the Lady Glammis. Jean Douglas, grand-daughter of "Bell-the-Cat" and sister of Archibald, sixth Earl of Angus, a lady famous alike for beauty and virtue, had provoked the wrath of James the Fifth by her attachment to her brothers, the banished Douglases, of whom the King had sworn that while he lived they should never find refuge in Scotland. As the only member of her family on whom the Royal hands could be laid, Lady Glammis was rancorously harried by divers criminal prosecutions, and finally, upon false evidence, done to death. Her first husband, John, Lord Glammis, having died in 1527, she had married a Campbell. In 1532 she was indicted for taking the life of her former spouse "per intoxicationem": contriving his death not, as might appear, by driving him to drink, but by means of drugs, charms and enchanted potions. The lords and lairds summoned as jurymen upon her trial, believing her innocent, refused the office; they were fined and the proceedings dropped.[2] Five years later, however, the attack was renewed in another form. One William Lyon, who unsuccessfully had sought her favours, was found to bear false witness against her; in July 1537 she was tried and convicted, upon what evidence we do not know, for conspiring to destroy the King "be poysone," and for treasonably assisting her Douglas brothers.[3] The judges delayed sentence, and represented the case to His Majesty as one meriting the Royal mercy; but James was not inclined to be clement—the law must take its course. So the hapless lady was burnt alive upon

---

[1] *Laws and Customs of Scotland in Matters Criminal*, tit. viii.

[2] Pitcairn's *Criminal Trials in Scotland*, i. 157*, 158*.

[3] *Ibid.*, pp. 187*, 191*.

the Castle Hill of Edinburgh, "with great commiseration of the people, in regaird of her noble blood and singular beautie." [1] Her husband, in attempting to escape from the Castle, fell down the rocks and was killed; her son, the young Lord, was kept a prisoner till the King's death. The traditional belief that Lady Glammis suffered for witchcraft is erroneous: she died a victim to political spite, "as I can perceyve," Sir Thomas Clifford, the English Ambassador, reported to King Henry VIII. at the time, "without any substanciall ground or proyf of mattir." [2] In the following month Alexander Makke, convicted of making and selling poison, and of concealing Lady Glammis' treason, was condemned to have his ears cut off and to be banished for life to Aberdeen. [3] One wonders how the Aberdonians liked the compliment.

During the troublesome reign of Queen Mary her subjects were probably more occupied with politics than with poison, for we find but two cases upon record: Henry and Patrick Congiltoune, for "the cruel Slaughter by Intoxication" of their nephew, in October 1554; [4] and Adam Colquhoune, for the murder of a servant and the attempted murder of his mother and stepfather "by that secret method of Poison or Intoxication," in March 1562. [5] The wicked uncles escaped, but the other practitioner was hanged and his body burnt to ashes on the Castle Hill.

Under the Solomonic sway of King James the Sixth, when evil-doers increased and multiplied and, reversing the divine command, did their best to displenish the earth, poisoning shared in the revival of naughtiness. The popular belief in . witchcraft, which by precept and example that enlightened monarch did so much to foster, rose to unparalleled heights, and the Records of Justiciary for the time abound in witch-trials, wherein charges of sorcery and poisoning are inextricably mingled. An examination of these, however entertaining and

[1] Pitcairn, i. 195*.
[2] Ibid., p. 198*.
[3] Ibid., p. 203*.
[4] Ibid., pp. 368*, 369.
[5] Ibid., pp. 419*, 420*.

instructive, would take us too far; nor does space permit enquiry into the mystery attending the death of the Earl of Atholl, after a feast of "reconciliation" given in April 1579 by his rival the Regent Morton, who was popularly credited with his taking-off. Cases more strictly relevant are that of Helen Cunninghame in January 1579,[1] for "Ministering of Poysoun to William, hir spous," and of Andro Glencorse in February 1580,[2] for "the poisoning of Issobell Staig, his spous." Both were convicted and duly suffered. In December the same year took place the trial of Laurence, Lord Oliphant, for the slaughter of Alexander Stewart, "schot with ane poysonit bullet." He was acquitted.[3] The only other instance of this peculiar form of crime occurred in June 1609, when the turbulent Border baron, John, Lord Maxwell, treacherously slew with two poisoned bullets Sir James Johnstone of that Ilk, who had superseded him as Warden of the West Marches.[4] In neither case is any proof of preliminary poisoning recorded; perhaps it was inferred merely from the symptoms, or from the morbid appearances.

The year 1590 is memorable for the Great Oyer of Witchcraft—the series of trials following upon the Saturnalia at North Berwick, as to which King James was so curious—but the case of Katharine, Lady Foulis, in July of that year, must have occasioned more scandal in Scots society.[5] This lady, a daughter of Ross of Balnagowan and the second wife of Munro of Foulis, was charged with poisoning and witchcraft, the intended victims being her brother's wife and her own stepson; the object, to bring about a marriage between her brother and her stepdaughter. Fortunately matchmaking mothers seldom carry their scheming to such sinister lengths. We are not here concerned with the witchcraft charges, interesting and typical though they are, based upon the dealings of Lady Foulis with certain sorceresses, "haldin and reput rank com-

---

[1] Pitcairn, i. 80.
[2] Ibid., p. 84.
[3] Ibid., pp. 89, 90.
[4] Ibid., iii. 28 et seq.
[5] Ibid., i. 192–201.

moune Vichis in the countrey." These hags, who varied their
necromantic practices by the purveying of poisons, were employed by her ladyship to furnish "ane stoup-full of poysonit
new aill" for the destruction of the young laird of Foulis; but
the lady, having tried its efficacy upon a boy, who only
"thaireftir tuik seiknes," commissioned the making of "ane
pig-full of ranker poysoune," which she sent to her stepson by
his "nourrice." The nurse, unluckily for herself, "taistand of
the samin, immediatlie thaireftir departit—" upon a farther
errand. In connection with the machinations against the Lady
Balnagowan, it is noteworthy that one of the charges contains
the first recorded mention of that venerable and flowing-
bearded excuse for the acquisition of poison—rats. The fallacious use of the word in this relation may have determined
its value for modern slang. Lady Foulis was accused of giving
eight shillings to a man of the congenial name of McGillie-
verie-dam "to pas to Elgyne *for bying rattoun poysoune.*"
While the minor actors were suitably "convict and burnt,"
the leading lady was acquitted: her jury was composed of
local burgesses and family dependants—a characteristic example of justice as administered under James the Just.

Very different was the treatment accorded in the following
year to another gentlewoman, whose estate the good King
coveted for one of his minions. Among the North Berwick
"witches" socially the most remarkable was Euphame Mac-
Calzean, daughter of Lord Cliftonhall, one of the Senators
of the College of Justice. This lady was in June 1591 sentenced
to be taken to the Castle Hill, "and thair bund to ane staik
and burnt in assis, *quick,* to the death," for treasonably conspiring against His Majesty's life by witchcraft;[1] but the
"Dittay" against her contains another interesting charge:
"Item, Indytit of airt and pairt of the poysouning of the said
Patrik Moscrop, your husband, upon deidlie malice contractit
aganis him, the fyrst yeir of your mariage, be gewing to him of
poysoun, and cuist the rest thairof in the closett; quhairby his
face, nek, handis and haill body brak out in reid spottis,

[1] Pitcairn, i. 247–257.

quhilk poysoun wes expellit be his youth." Further attempts convinced Patrick that Scotland was no place for him, so he fled beyond "the seais" and spent the remainder of his days abroad.

In June 1596 the Master of Orkney was tried for conspiring to murder his brother Patrick, Earl of Orkney, by poison at a banquet in Kirkwall. Though King James personally insisted "in persuit" of the Master, and had the Crown witnesses, in order to confession, tortured with a ferocity which, as Mr. Pitcairn observes, "would disgrace the most barbarous tribe of Indians," the prosecution happily failed.[1] A similar result attended the trials, in October and November of the same year, of Alison Jollie in Fala, for poisoning a neighbour with whom she had quarrelled over "ane aiker of land," [2] and of John Boyd, burgess of Edinburgh, for the "slauchter" of a woman by putting poison into the domestic meal-cupboard, on account of "ane deidlie rancour" conceived against her.[3] In November 1601 two men of Brechin named Bellie were banished the realm for mixing poison with dough, "and casting doune thairof in Jonet Clerkis zaird in Brechin for destructioune of fowlis, be the quhilk poysoune they distroyit to the said Jonet twa hennis." [4] Of a darker hue were the deeds for which in July 1605 William Rose of Dunskeith suffered doom.[5] This miscreant with the cooperation of his mistress, Marie Rannaldoche, frankly designed in the record "ane harlot," essayed to murder his wife with "poysonet and tressonabill drinkis," and failing in his purpose, "unmercifullie strangallit and wirreit" her in her bed. As, in addition to murder under trust, he was convicted of stouthrief or masterful theft, reset, adultery and other crimes, Rose must have been a very pretty villain.

No distinction appears then to have been drawn between the felonious administration of drugs to destroy life and the giving of them with curative intent. Thus, in November 1597,

[1] Pitcairn, i. 373–377.
[2] Ibid., pp. 397–399.
[3] Ibid., p. 399.
[4] Ibid., ii. 336.
[5] Ibid., pp. 481–484.

Christian Saidler in Blakhouse, "a wyise wyffe," who had successfully treated sundry patients by prescriptions obtained "frae ane Italean strangear callit Mr. Johnne Damiet," [1] thereby effecting cures "quhilk be na naturall meanis of phisik or uther lawfull and Godlie wayes" could, in the judgment of the authorities, have been performed, was upon conviction "wirreit at ane staik" on the Castle Hill.[2] It seems hard that she should have suffered for the Crown lawyers' lack of faith. So too, in the case of Bartie Patersoune, "tasker in Newbottill," indicted in December 1607 for "ministring, under forme of medecine, of poysoneable drinkis," the alleged murder of two patients is charged along with the "cureing of James Broun in Turndykis of ane unknawin disease," as also the treating of "his awin bairne" and of one Alexander Clerk, the remedy employed in each case being "watter brocht be him furth of the Loch callit the Dow-Loche, besyde Drumlanrig."[3] Upon this point a further illustration of what was legally held to constitute the crime of poisoning is afforded by the case of Issobell Haldane in May 1623, charged with bringing water from the Well of Ruthven, of which she "had gewin drinkis to cure bairneis," one of whom, notwithstanding, died. For these charitable acts she was "brunt" at Perth as a warning to sick-nurses in general.[4]

In November 1609 James Mure of Monyhagen was "dilaitit" for having given to Margaret Wicht in Dalmellington "ane Inchantit drink."[5] This person, a kinsman of the celebrated John Mure of Auchindrayne, "maist willinglie" offering himself to trial, "disassenting fra all continuatioun," and alleging that the charge was "bot maliciouslie inventit aganis him be the said Margaret for hir awin previe advantage"—a defence worthy of his redoubtable relative—was discharged owing to the nonappearance of the "Persewar." Perhaps, knowing the family, the lady thought it more prudent not to press the matter: the Mures were ill folk to go to law with.

[1] Jehan Damyte, the French or Italian priest and wizard who warned Rizzio of his danger.
[2] Pitcairn, pp. 25–29.
[3] Ibid., ii. 535, 536.
[4] Ibid., pp. 537, 538.
[5] Pitcairn, iii. 68, 69.

Leaving these nebulous and fantastic charges we reach solid criminal ground in the case of the Erskines in December 1613. Robert, Helen, Isobel and Anna, brother and sisters, were branches of the godly tree whereof Mr. John Erskine of Dun had been the stalwart trunk. That inveterate Reformer, surviving till 1591, devoted, we are told, his declining years to the moral and religious welfare of his many descendants. Robert and his sisters were probably then too young to profit by the good man's precepts; but if they were a fair sample of the stock, he had his work cut out for him. Their brother David, the last laird of Dun, died leaving two children, on whose behalf the property was administered by a tutor, an office to which the uncle Robert thought himself entitled— doubtless a long minority would present opportunity for pickings. But apart from this grievance, his sisters urged upon him the hardship of being kept out of a fair estate by the survivance of their little nephews. Beyond credibility as it seems, repeated family counsels were held within their house of Logie as to the best way of expediting Robert's succession. The sisters—who might claim kinship with their resolute countrywoman, Lady Macbeth—finding it difficult to screw their less bloodthirsty brother's courage to the sticking-place, approached one David Blewhouse with a proposal that if he could contrive "be sum sinisterous meanis" the extinction of the two young lives standing between Robert and the estate, he should receive part of the lands and five hundred merks in silver. Subsequently Robert himself called upon Blewhouse to homologate the offer, but that gentleman declined to treat. Thereupon the sisters set out one summer evening from the place of Logie, and passing over Cairn-o'-Mount towards Muir alehouse, took counsel with a wise woman, Janet Irving by name, reputed "ane abuser of the people." From this sibyl they obtained "ane grit quantitie of herbis" which, with instructions for use, they carried home to Logie. Robert, sceptical as to the potency of the herbs, personally interviewed the sorceress, who satisfied him that they were "forceable aneuch" for his purpose. So as directed they were steeped in ale for a long space, and the resultant brew was taken by the family party to Montrose, where the children were then living with their mother. After drinking this beverage both boys were seized with pain and violent vomiting, to which the elder presently succumbed, exclaiming with his ultimate breath, and a grasp of the situation beyond his years: "Wo is me, that I evir had richt of successioun to ony landis or leving! ffor gif I had bene borne sum pure coitteris sone, I had nocht bene sa demanet [treated], nor sic wikket practizes had bene plottit aganis me for my landis." Only less immediately fatal was the condition of the younger boy, "off quhais lyfe," says the indictment, "thair is na hoip." This monstrous and sordid crime was fortunately too clumsy to escape detection, so the uncle and aunts were forthwith apprehended. Robert was tried first in December 1613, and having avouched the deed, was beheaded at the Mercat Cross of Edinburgh.[1] His sisters, denying their guilt, were in the following June convicted upon his confession and on the direct evidence of Blewhouse and others. Isobel and Anna shared their brother's doom; Helen, "being moir penitent, thogh less giltie, than the rest," had her sentence commuted to banishment for life.[2] The whole horrid business forms an instructive comment on the state of Scots society in the golden days of "gentle King Jamie."

Hitherto we have walked in the light of the admirable Pitcairn, whose research has done so much to make plain the way of the student of early Scottish crime. Sir Walter Scott wrote in the Quarterly Review for February 1831 an article warmly appreciative of "his patient and enduring toil," but these labours, unfortunately for us, were carried no further than the year 1624; and for subsequent cases, other than such as are separately reported, until we reach the first series of the official Justiciary Reports beginning in 1826, we must rely on those respectively noticed in the treatises of Burnett and Hume, and included in the collections of Maclaurin and Arnot. The Proceedings of the Justiciary Court from 1661 to

[1] Pitcairn, iii. 260–264.
[2] Ibid., pp. 266–269.

1678, published by the Scottish History Society, are so barren in detail as to yield little to the present purpose. The only grain I have been able to glean from them is the case in May 1665 of Margaret Hamilton, relict of Robert Bedford, merchant in Leith, for the murder of her husband, an Englishman, inspired by an intrigue with his friend, a local surveyor. This lady "employed a servant to buy poison," but being, as appears, of an impetuous habit, she anticipated its action "with the canon bullet that she used for breaking of her coalls," accounting afterwards for the deceased's injuries by a pretended fall down stairs. She was very properly beheaded.[1]

From the inadequate data furnished by these early cases it is impossible to tell the nature of the toxic substances employed, while the common conjunction of poisoning and sorcery does not tend to enlightenment; but such indications as there are point to the poisons formerly classed as vegetable. We now come to the first recorded Scottish case in which the poison used is definitely stated: that of John Dick and Janet Alexander, his spouse, convicted in March 1649 of the murder of his brother and sister by poisoning them with arsenic, administered in a loaf or bannock.[2] It is to be noted that, so curiously conservative is the criminal mind, this irritant has since continued the standard medium in homicidal poisoning. That it was early and widely recognised as such in other times and countries appears from its adoption by the classic school of Greek and Latin poisoners. Arsenic was the favourite specific of the Borgias, the famed Aqua Toffana consisted of a solution of arsenic, and to arsenic Madame de Brinvilliers owed her dreadful power. Its deadly properties were well known; it was readily obtainable and as easily administered; and, until in 1836 Marsh discovered his test, there was no certain method for its detection.[3]

An interesting case, disclosing unusual originality of design,

---

[1] *Justiciary Records*, i. 125, 126.
[2] Burnett's *Criminal Law*, p. 9; Hume's *Commentaries*, 1819, i. 284.
[3] Those curious in the poisons of the ancients may consult *Edinburgh Medical Journal*, xxxiii. 315.

in which death was caused by the excessive administration of
drugs not in their nature poisonous, was tried in January
1676.[1] Two menservants, John Ramsay and George Clerk,
were charged with the murder of their master, John Anderson,
merchant in Edinburgh, an old bachelor, wealthy and infirm,
with none to care for him but his hired attendants, who basely
abused their trust by repeatedly robbing him when they had
lulled his vigilance with liquor. The season was "very sickly"—
dysentery raged in the town; there were many deaths, and the
stricken were ignorantly shunned for fear of infection. To
these wicked servants the idea occurred of counterfeiting by
medicine the symptoms of the disease in their master. For
this purpose they consulted in the King's Park a lad named
Kennedy, an apothecary's apprentice, whom they induced to
supply them with certain purgatives, which speedily produced
the desired result. The old man called in his own physician,
who treated him for the common disorder. From Kennedy
they also obtained syrup of poppy, which they mixed with
their master's drink, and when he was unconscious, rifled his
repositories of money and jewels. They next gave him "powder
of jalap and crystal of tartar" to counteract the effects of his
doctor's prescriptions. But whether by the efficacy of these,
or by the strength of his constitution, the old gentleman began
to mend; so the murderers sought from Kennedy a more
potent drug. This the apprentice refused to give them, "saying
that the body would swell, and they would be discovered";
but he advised an increased exhibition of jalap, which they
accordingly mixed in a conserve of roses prepared by the
patient's own apothecary. So soon as they perceived that the
end was near they secured the residue of his valuables, and
"called in the neighbours to see him die." Ramsay and Clerk
were convicted and, confessing their guilt, were hanged at
the Cross; Kennedy, who had furnished the drugs and shared
the spoils, was in the following February indicted as art and
part in the crime. It was ingeniously objected for him to the

[1] Arnot's *Criminal Trials*, 1785, pp. 142–145; Burnett, p. 9; Hume, i.
285.

relevancy of the charge that the Act 1450 on which he was tried applied only to poisonous drugs, not to such as were given medicinally and were not intrinsically noxious. The point was never judicially determined, for before judgment Kennedy was upon his own petition banished for life; but Sir George Mackenzie in discussing the question observes: "The best of Druggs, given in great excess, is Poyson; for Poyson consists in excess of quantity as well as quality, and whatever overpowers our nature is poysonable to us." [1] The only similar case I have encountered is that of William Paterson, tried in February 1815 for the murder of his wife by repeated doses of sulphur, calomel, tartar emetic, jalap, castoroil and other purgatives. At the trial, a surgeon swore that he was asked by the husband for such drugs to dispatch the wife, and when these were refused with the remark that this was tantamount to murder, Paterson replied, "No; it was only helping her awa"! He was acquitted by a majority of one; but his neighbours, taking a different view of the facts, wellnigh lynched him on his return home. [2]

The attempt and not the deed, which confounded Lady Macbeth, also caused some confusion in practice as regards its proper penalty. Thus in the case of David Hay and Dr. Thomson, March 1692, in which an attempt to poison with laudanum was charged along with the actual murder of Hay's wife, the doctor who had supplied the drug was convicted of art and part. Both were sentenced to be hanged, and to have their heads cut off and affixed to the jail of Lanark. [3] In the case of Dr. Elliot and others in January 1694, where the charge was "the designing to use, and the use-making and buying of poyson," coupled with a malignant conspiracy to fix the like crime on two innocent persons, the accused were sentenced to death. [4] When, on the other hand, in January 1728, Walter Buchanan of Balquhan was charged with two attempts to

[1] Laws and Customs of Scotland in Matters Criminal, tit. viii.
[2] Hume, i. 285; ii. 318.
[3] Burnett, pp. 8, 10; Hume, i. 175, 269.
[4] Burnett, p. 10; Hume, i. 167, 175.

destroy Jean Dougal, Lady Branshogel, liferentrix of part of his estate, by giving poison to an unwitting third party to administer to her, the Court found the libel relevant to infer only an arbitrary punishment.[1] The same course was followed on the trial of Janet Ronald in May 1763, for an attempt to poison her sister by mixing with her food verdigris, of which by the timely use of antidotes she recovered.[2] Since the Act 10 George IV. c. 38, however, the attempted administration of poison with intent to injure or destroy life is a capital offence.

The case of Dr. Elliot above cited calls, on account of its unusual features, for more than passing mention. Daniel Nicolson, an Edinburgh writer, had a mistress named Marion Maxwell, and with the view of regularising their connection, he proposed to rid himself of his lawful spouse. For this purpose the pair "seduced" Dr. John Elliot to furnish them with the necessary drugs, which were supplied accordingly by that venal physician. Some difficulty was experienced in administering these, so the parties formed an elaborate and complicated plot for the judicial destruction of Mrs. Nicolson and her sister, Margaret Sands, by fixing on them a design to poison her husband. In pursuance of this scheme Nicolson waited upon the Lord Advocate, Sir James Stewart, to complain that his life was in danger from his wife and sister-in-law, who he said had conceived a groundless suspicion of his infidelity with Maxwell; that they had applied for poison to Dr. Elliot, who, being filled with horror at such a proposal, informed the intended victim; and asking his lordship's guidance in this painful predicament. Summoned before the Lord Advocate, the doctor confirmed the tale, adding that so anxious were the ladies to obtain poison, they would not hesitate to give a receipt for it in any terms he might suggest. His lordship authorised Elliot to supply what was wanted and to take a

[1] Burnett, p. 10; Hume, i. 176.
[2] Maclaurin's *Criminal Cases*, pp. 211–249; Burnett, pp. 9, 10; Hume, ii. 399.

receipt therefor, intending to secure the poison when in Mrs. Nicolson's possession. The conspirators then placed poison in her repositories, where it was duly "discovered" by the Crown officials. Dr. Elliot next produced a receipt in the required form, bearing to be granted by the wife and her sister, who were forthwith apprehended. But public opinion was less blind than Justice; when the story got abroad the known character and conduct of Nicolson and Maxwell and the professional repute of their medical adviser, raised suspicions which in the end led to the unmasking of the plotters. The doctor, under re-examination, collapsed and confessed; and the three malefactors were brought to the bar, charged with forgery, conspiracy, and attempt to poison. The legal objection to Mrs. Nicolson giving evidence against her own husband was ingeniously surmounted by taking her testimony on oath before the Lord Advocate, the Sheriff, and the Clerk of the Privy Council, and producing her deposition at the trial! His lordship's handling of this case goes some way to explain his popular nickname, "Wily Jamie." All three prisoners were convicted and suffered the extreme penalty.

Resuming our chronological survey we find arsenic playing the leading part in a series of cases the first of which, that of William Bisset and Jean Currier, is of June 1705.[1] Jean, Bisset's mistress, bought from an apothecary in Dundee "an ounce of arsenic unprepared," on pretence of killing a dog, and gave it to Bisset, who administered it to his wife by the hand of their maidservant, as a medicine which her doctor had prescribed. The verdict "finds that the powder found in the defunct's stomach, Mary Murray, was the occasion of her death." Although Currier was accessory to, and was indeed the instigator of the crime, and both were convicted, their sentence was merely whipping, the pillory, and banishment.

An interesting departure from the standardized methods of crime occurs in November 1720 in the case of Nicol Muschet, a villain whose name is familiar to readers of *The Heart of*

[1] Burnett, pp. 9, 268; Hume, i. 270, 276; ii. 370.

Midlothian.[1] Before slaying his wife in the King's Park, as commemorated by his cairn, Muschet and his associates made repeated attempts to destroy her by poisoning and other more violent means, from which her amazing immunity might, but for the sequel, lead one to think the lady bore a charmed life. Burnbank, Muschet's infamous friend and adviser, recommended corrosive sublimate as "far less dangerous to meddle with than arsenic, on account arsenic both swelled and discoloured," and quantities of that poison were from time to time administered to the unhappy woman in the sugar she was in the habit of taking with her "dram." As she recovered from the illness thus induced, it was decided to increase the doses, so the conspirators put the poison into a nutmeg-grater, from which they conveyed it into her brandy and ale. But though afterwards the grater looked "as if it had been burnt in the fire, by reason of the corrosive mercury," the patient still survived, and physical force had finally to be employed to terminate her miserable existence. Muschet was sentenced to be hanged and his body hung in chains to the terror and example of others, a penalty reserved for crimes of singular wickedness.

In the case of Nicolas Cockburn in August 1754,[2] a wife was charged with the murder of her husband and stepmother by putting arsenic respectively into their kail (broth) and porridge, to disappoint a beneficial settlement in favour of the mother as a widow. In the husband's case there was no sufficient proof; but on a post-mortem examination of the mother, the surgeons detected in the stomach "a whitish powder resembling arsenic," some of which was also discovered in the bottom of a vessel used by the deceased for food. A paper containing a similar powder, ascertained on analysis to be arsenic, was found in the prisoner's chest. Dundas of Arniston, the future Lord President, who as Justice of the Peace had taken the woman's dying declaration, deponed to her grounds

---

[1] Criminal Trials Illustrative of the Tale entitled "The Heart of Midlothian," 1818, pp. 323–344; Maclaurin's Criminal Cases, pp. 738–741.

[2] Burnett, pp. 9, 544; Hume, ii. 392.

of belief that her stepdaughter had poisoned her. The verdict
was Guilty. In Andrew Wilson's case in August 1755 a man
bought arsenic "for rats."[1] He was seen to put something
from a paper into a mug of ale, out of which his wife drank
and shortly thereafter died with the usual symptoms of poisoning. She expressed strong suspicion against her husband. A
white powder, which was neither analysed nor preserved, was
noticed in the mug and tasted by a witness, who presently
suffered from vomiting, etc. No medical man attended the
deceased, nor was the body opened, and no arsenic was found
in possession of the prisoner, who absconded. He was brought
back, and convicted on trial. The motive alleged for the crime
was the marrying of a younger woman. Like Muschet, Wilson
was condemned to be hung in chains. In two Inverness cases,
M'Coiler in September 1757,[2] and M'Kenzie in 1760,[3] where
the poisons employed were respectively laudanum and arsenic,
the accused were acquitted.

The curious laxity which then obtained in regard to medical
evidence as to the cause of death, and the existence of any
poison in the body of the deceased, is nowhere perhaps more
strikingly apparent than in the remarkable case of Katharine
Nairn in August 1765.[4] I have often wondered why no enter-
prising novelist has laid hands upon her story, such is the
effective quality of the facts, so nice the question of a just
apportionment of the relative guilt and innocence. "Readers of
Mr. J. A. Symond's book on the Renaissance," wrote Andrew
Lang once, "hold up obtesting hands at the rich and varied
iniquities of the Courts of mediæval Italy. But for complex
and variegated depravity the family of Mr. Ogilvy of Eastmiln
could give the Baglioni and other Italian miscreants a stroke a
hole—whatever view you take of the case." Katharine, daughter
of Sir Thomas Nairn of Dunsinnan, married at nineteen, on
30th January 1765, Thomas Ogilvy, laird of Eastmiln of Glen-

---

[1] Burnett, pp. 9, 545.
[2] Ibid., p. 10.
[3] Ibid.
[4] Trial of Katharine Nairn and Patrick Ogilvie for the crimes of Incest and
Murder, Edinburgh, 1765; Twelve Scots Trials, 1913, pp. 106–135.

isla, in Angus, a gentleman in failing health and more than double her age. There lived with them his venerable mother and younger brother, Patrick, a lieutenant invalided home from the East Indies. Alexander, the youngest of the three brothers, was a dissipated surgeon in Edinburgh, on bad terms with his family. A month after the wedding there arrived from that city Miss Anne Clark, a cousin of the Ogilvys, who was, though unknown to her relatives at Eastmiln, a woman of flagitious life, of evil disposition, and Alexander's mistress. He sent her ostensibly to make his peace, but really to work what mischief she could; failing his delicate brethren he was next heir to the property. The first-fruits of her mission were divers rumours regarding the relations of the bride with the young lieutenant, but neither the husband nor the mother paid much heed to their guest's scandalous whispers. The two brothers, however, quarrelled over money matters; the laird referred to Anne's reports, and Patrick, indignantly denying their truth, left the house, refusing to return though pressed by Thomas to do so. Katharine, whose health was then indifferent—she was in prospect of becoming a mother—asked Patrick to send her some salts and laudanum which he had in his sea-chest at Alyth; and having got the drugs he sent them to Eastmiln by Andrew Stewart, his sister's husband, who delivered them to Katharine. Anne then informed the other members of the family that Katharine had told her she meant to poison her husband, and she (Anne), to put her off, had herself promised to procure poison from Edinburgh, but that Patrick had now supplied it. None of them believed her "horrible tale," and no action was taken. Next day, 6th June, the laird, whose ailments had been increasing, became seriously ill, with symptoms of acute gastric inflammation, and a doctor was summoned but arrived too late; Thomas Ogilvy was dead. Five days later, on that fixed for the funeral, Alexander came post from Edinburgh, sensationally stopped the burial on the ground that his brother had been poisoned, lodged with the authorities an information upon which Katharine and Patrick were apprehended, and assisted by Miss Clark—who after the

death had been dismissed by Katharine—entered into possession of the estate. On their trial at Edinburgh on 5th August
for the crimes of incest and murder, the evidence relating to
the two charges was, wilfully or not, confused; the intrigue,
as appears, being inferred from the poisoning, and the poisoning assumed from the intrigue. The proof occupied forty-three
consecutive hours, but of upwards of a hundred witnesses for
the defence only ten were examined, owing to the undisguised
impatience of the jury. To establish the first charge, the
prosecutor relied mainly on the infragrant testimony of Miss
Clark—than whom in such a connection no witness could have
been more competent—and on that of a servant girl who had
been dismissed by Katharine for theft and had sworn revenge.
As regards the second charge, strangely enough, it was neither
proved that the deceased died of poison, nor that his wife
had the means of poisoning him were she "so dispoged."
The medical evidence as to the cause of death was quite
inconclusive—though three surgeons inspected the body, a
post-mortem had been prevented by Alexander—but the awkward fact that Patrick, shortly before the death, did buy half
an ounce of arsenic, "in order to destroy some dogs that
spoiled the game," was clearly proved. The prisoners having
been found guilty on both counts, Katharine, in the picturesque language of the time, "pled her belly" in arrest of
judgment, and sentence was in her case delayed. The conduct
and result of the trial was widely and adversely criticised, and
efforts were made to have the verdict reviewed by the House
of Lords, but this was found to be incompetent. After four
several respites Patrick, protesting his innocence, was hanged
in the Grassmarket. Meanwhile Katharine in the Tolbooth
had given birth to a daughter, who did not long survive. The
night before she was to appear for judgment, having changed
clothes with the midwife, she escaped from the prison. Her
uncle, William Nairn, an Edinburgh advocate, later raised to
the Bench as Lord Dunsinnan, doubtless knew something of
his niece's flight from justice, for his clerk accompanied her
in a postchaise to England, whence she safely reached the

Continent. She is said to have entered a French convent, dying
in the end full of years and grace. Alexander did not long enjoy
his good fortune; presently he was banished for bigamy, but
being allowed some time to settle his affairs, met a violent
death by a fall from a window. Anne Clark, however, survived,
retaining in her experienced bosom the secrets of the house of
Eastmiln.

Not every jury was so eager to convict as that which sent
Patrick Ogilvy to the gallows. On the trial at Glasgow of Jean
Semple in May 1773 for poisoning her husband with arsenic,
no less than fifteen grains of that substance were found in the
deceased's stomach.[1] "The usual experiments," we read, "were
made on it by hot iron, and part of it was given to a chicken,
which died soon after." But this failed to convince the jury,
who returned a verdict of Not Proven. Even more curious was
the scepticism shown by an Aberdeen jury on the trial of Ann
Inglis in 1795.[2] In the homely household of a young farmer,
named Patrick Pirie, this woman combined the offices of
cook and concubine, but her master, desirous of ranging himself, announced his intention to marry another. This was
deeply resented by his lady-help, who was heard to make the
ominous remark that "there would be a burial before a bridal."
Shortly before the wedding, Pirie, a hale man of thirty-two,
who had never had a day's illness, after taking a draught of ale
from the hands of Ann, was seized with violent vomiting and
internal pain; he was attended by a doctor, but died in nine
days, declaring his belief that his servant-mistress had poisoned
him. A post-mortem disclosed "much inflammation in the
stomach, the inner coat of which was corroded and separated
from the adjoining one." No poison was detected in the body,
but the surgeons deponed that the appearances were such as
might have been produced by sulphate of copper or blue
vitriol. A search of Ann's chest brought to light a parcel of that
poison, which she said she had bought as a cure for toothache, though she was never known to suffer from that ailment.

[1] Burnett, p. 584.
[2] *Ibid.*, pp. 9, 393, 547; *Black Kalendar of Aberdeen*, 1854, pp. 139, 140.

The verdict of Not Guilty must have surprised her as much as it did the prosecutor. Strangely enough, another instance of the use of similar means occurred at Aberdeen in 1830,[1] jealousy being also the motive of the crime, where Catherine Humphrey, having quarrelled with her husband about another woman, poured oil of vitriol into his open mouth as he lay asleep. She was convicted and hanged. This, too, was the poison employed by Barbara Malcolm to destroy her own child, for which she was condemned in January 1808.[2]

Such toxicological vagaries are rare; arsenic resumes its rightful place in the case of Matthew Hay, convicted at Ayr in September 1780[3] of poisoning and attempting to poison a whole family. Hay had seduced one of the daughters, and to prevent discovery he did not hesitate to sacrifice, not only the girl herself, but her father, mother and sisters—five lives in all. The parents, however, alone succumbed; the others, after severe sufferings, recovered. Hay, having bought arsenic "for killing rats," called one day on his victim and found her boiling sowens for the domestic meal. He sent her out to get him a drink, and during her absence threw some of the arsenic into the pot and the rest into the seed barrel. All who ate of the food were seized with the usual symptoms of arsenical poisoning, and the father and mother died that night. On a post-mortem examination of the bodies no arsenic was found, but Dr. Black, the eminent chemist, discovered that substance mixed with the sowens and seed; so Hay was, happily, hanged. It is interesting to note that it was upon this trial that Lord Kames made from the bench the judicial joke about "checkmate," which Lockhart in his *Life of Scott* fathered upon Lord Braxfield; also that the counsel for the defence, not the prisoner himself, was his lordship's old opponent at chess.[4]

In the case of Marshall, on the Autumn Circuit at Perth in 1796, the accused's wife died without suspicion of foul play,

[1] *Black Kalendar of Aberdeen*, pp. 207–209; *Edinburgh Medical Journal*, xxxv. 298–316.
[2] Burnett, pp. 9, 549.
[3] *Ibid.*, pp. 9, 11, 546; Hume, i. 284; ii. 69.
[4] Hill Burton's *Narratives from Criminal Trials in Scotland*, ii. 64, 65, n.

which did not arise until two months thereafter, when the body was exhumed and three grains of arsenic were found in the stomach. The prisoner was convicted.[1] At Aberdeen, in 1797, a man named Stewart was found guilty of an attempt to poison by administering arsenic in a ball of oatmeal.[2] In 1800, at Glasgow, one Lockhart and his servant-maid were charged with the murder of Lockhart's wife.[3] No medical man attended the deceased and there was no evidence of the cause of death. It was proved that the husband had bought upon false pretences a large quantity of laudanum, but the body was not opened until a fortnight after death, when the physicians were of opinion that even had laudanum been administered, it could not have been discovered. The accused were acquitted. At Ayr, in April 1810, John M'Millan, from Wigtownshire, was convicted of poisoning with corrosive sublimate Barbara M'Kinnel, a girl who was with child to him.[4]

As we advance into the nineteenth century the field of our investigation, whether by the greater prevalence of poisoning or by the improved methods available for its detection, so largely widens that in the space at my disposal I am able to deal only with the more interesting examples. The crime for which, at Aberdeen, in October 1821, George Thom was brought to book, presents, both as regards manner of perpetration and comprehensiveness of scope, points of resemblance to that of Matthew Hay previously cited.[5] A well-to-do-farmer, who for sixty-one years had enjoyed a high reputation for piety and worth, Thom married his second wife Jean Mitchell, whose brothers and sisters lived at Burnside, a farm in the parish of Keig. By the death of a relation the Mitchells succeeded to a considerable fortune, but the fifth share falling to Mrs. Thom seemed to her spouse a very inadequate provision, and it was obvious that the death of the other legatees would substantially

---

[1] Burnett, pp. 9, 548.
[2] Ibid., pp. 9, 11, 584.
[3] Ibid., pp. 9, 549.
[4] Ibid., p. 10.
[5] Black Kalendar of Aberdeen, pp. 173–180; Edinburgh Medical Journal, xviii. 167.

increase their sister's portion. With a view, therefore, to ac-
celerate her succession he called at Burnside on the eve of the
local "Sacramental Sunday," and announced his intention to
stay the night. After a friendly supper the visitor asked leave
to sleep in the kitchen, but this his host would not permit, and
he was installed in the best bedroom. In the small hours of the
Sunday morning one of the brothers, from his box-bed in the
kitchen, heard somebody moving about the cupboard, but did
not trouble to open the shutter of his insalutary cubicle to see
who was astir so early. When the family met for breakfast,
Thom, hospitably pressed to share the meal, declined on the
plea that he must be off before folks were going to the kirk: it
would never do for one of his godly walk and conversation to
be seen abroad upon the Sabbath day. So, wishing his relatives
a kind farewell, the worthy man set forth. On his way home he
ate at Mains of Cluny a hearty breakfast, though he said he had
been very bad at Burnside after something he had eaten there,
and that but for his promptitude in inducing sickness with a
crow's feather, he would not have lived to tell the tale. Breakfast at Burnside was a simple meal, consisting of porridge,
eaten, in the good Scots fashion, with salt instead of sugar.
That morning one of the brothers thought it had "sweet, sick-
ening taste," the others noticed nothing amiss. Presently all of
them became unwell; the sisters stayed at home, but the brothers struggled to church. James had to go out during the service,
as he "felt himself turning blind"; he found William in the
kirkyard, very sick. All four were for some time seriously ill but
three recovered, William alone dying within the week. They
were attended by a doctor, who seems at first to have had no
suspicions. It appears that from a queer sort of family pride the
survivors wished to hush up the incident; a post-mortem examination, however, was made, and the three surgeons "concurred
in opinion that the deceased had died by means of some deleterious substance taken into the stomach." From the beginning
the Mitchells had suspected their brother-in-law, and when
Thom, uninvited, came with cynical audacity to the funeral,
his presence was forbidden—he "had done ill enough there al-

ready." Told that William had been poisoned, he made the rather inept suggestion that "poison might have been got in the burn from puddocks," to which Helen Mitchell dryly replied that there were no puddocks in the porridge, whereupon Thom took his departure. He was later arrested, tried for murder, found guilty, and sentenced to death. No arsenic was traced to his possession, but an attempt to buy it "to poison rats" was proved by an Aberdeen apothecary. After conviction, Thom earnestly maintained his innocence, but despite edifying behaviour in prison he attempted to get his son to supply him with poison. Finally, the game being up, he confessed that he had mixed arsenic with the salt, not with the meal as had been assumed at the trial.[1] When the execution was over, "the body was subjected to a series of galvanic experiments of which a particular account was afterwards published"—a shocking business in more senses than one.

At Glasgow, in April 1822, Helen Rennie, a domestic servant, was charged with the murder of her illegitimate child.[2] The mother being in service, the little boy was boarded with another woman. One day Rennie called for him and took him away for some hours; he was then in perfect health, but when brought back seemed very ill. She explained that she had given him "some brimstone for the hives." The foster-mother sent for a doctor, who found the child dying. A post-mortem was held, when "two teaspoonfulls" of king's yellow (sulphuret of arsenic) were discovered in the stomach. There was no indication that the child had suffered from hives. Rennie declared that she had bought a half-pennyworth of sulphur, and at her trial a druggist's apprentice (who recalls the assistant of the chemist juryman in Bardell v. Pickwick) deponed that the sulphur and king's yellow were kept respectively in a drawer and in a bottle; he did not recollect having served the prisoner, but was sure he never sold to anyone a half-pennyworth of king's yellow. For the defence, two doctors stated that by an

[1] Such also was the device of the gatekeeper Misard, in La Bête Humaine of Zola.
[2] Edinburgh Evening Courant, 25th April 1822

unskilled eye king's yellow might be mistaken for sulphur. The verdict was, by a majority, Not Guilty, the judge, in discharging the prisoner, remarking that he would have voted with the minority.

The criminal records of 1827 are notable for the occurrence of several important poisoning cases, of which the first is that of Mary Elder or Smith in February of that year.[1] She was the wife of a respectable farmer at West Denside, near Dundee. Among the women employed at the farm was a girl named Margaret Warden, who had engaged the affections of Mrs. Smith's youngest son, a fact which, when discovered by the mother, in view of a previous lapse on the girl's part, that lady bitterly resented. She dismissed Margaret with ignominy; but fearing she was *enceinte*, afterwards induced her to return for the avowed purpose of attempting by illegal means to avert the threatened scandal. Accordingly, with the girl's consent, Mrs. Smith gave her sundry doses, particularly, in presence of Jean Norrie, a fellow-servant, "something in a dram glass" that looked like cream of tartar, with the result that Margaret grew gravely ill, her symptoms being those of arsenical poisoning. A doctor, brought by the girl's mother who had learned of her state, thought she was dying of cholera, which was then rife in the district. Margaret, however, expressed both to her mother and to Norrie suspicion of foul play on the part of her mistress. "Ye ken wha is the occasion o' me lyin' here?" were her last words; "but they'll get their reward. My mistress gave me . . ." but death cut short the sentence. So far as human retribution was concerned Margaret, as we shall see, was not inspired. The girl died and was buried; but somebody talked, so the body was exhumed and examined by three surgeons; on a subsequent analysis the presence of oxide of arsenic was unequivocally detected, and Mrs. Smith was apprehended on the charge of murder. In her declaration before the Sheriff she denied having known of the dead girl's condition, and said she had given her

---

[1] Syme's *Justiciary Reports*, p. 71; *Account of the Medical Evidence in the Case of Mrs. Smith.* By R. Christison, M.D., *Edinburgh Medical Journal*, xxvii. 141; xxviii. 84, 94; *Twelve Scots Trials*, pp. 160–190.

nothing except a dose of castor-oil, and that she (declarant) got no drugs from any person on the Friday preceding the death. All these statements were at the trial proved to be false. In particular, Dr. Dick of Dundee stated that the prisoner, whom he had known for many years, did on the day in question apply to him for "poison for rats"; he gave her an ounce and a half of arsenic in a packet marked "Arsenic—Poison," warning her at the same time to be very careful how she used it. Jeffrey and Cockburn conducted the defence, which rested on two disparate bases—cholera and suicide. The opinion of the Crown experts, including that of Dr. Christison who had made an independent analysis, that the death was due to arsenic, remained unshaken; and Dr. Mackintosh, physician in Edinburgh, called to maintain the theory of death from natural causes, was utterly routed by the Lord Advocate on cross-examination. It would seem that to the evidence of this skilled witness the following amusing extract from Dr. Christison's autobiography refers:

In a trial for poisoning with arsenic—the last occasion on which an attempt was made to dispute the validity of the chemical evidence in arsenical poisoning—Dr. . . . was employed to make a muddle of the professional testimony; and this was how he set about it. The proof, from symptoms during life and morbid appearances after death—apart from irrefragable chemical proof of the presence of arsenic in the stomach—was unusually strong, perhaps singly conclusive. But Dr. . . . had no difficulties. "He had great experience of disease. Vast experience in pathological dissections. There was nothing in the symptoms of the deceased during her life which he had not seen again and again arising from natural disease: nothing in the appearances in the dead body which he had not seen twenty times as arising from natural causes." "But, Dr. . . . ," said the Lord Advocate, "the symptoms you have heard detailed, and which you say may have arisen from natural disease, are also such as arsenic may produce, are they not?" "They may be all produced by natural disease." "So you have already told us. But may they not also be produced by arsenic?" "They may; but natural disease may equally cause

them." "You need not repeat that information, Doctor. Give
me a simple answer to my simple question: May these symptoms be produced by arsenic? Yea or Nay?" "Yes." "Now,
Dr. . . . , you have also told us that the appearances found
after death were such as natural disease may produce. Are they
not also such as may be produced by arsenic?" "Natural causes
may acount for them all," etc. etc., through the same round
of fencing, until he was compelled to admit that arsenic might
produce them. "Now, Doctor," continued the Lord Advocate,
"you have heard the evidence of arsenic having been found in
the stomach of the woman. Are you satisfied that arsenic was
discovered there?" "My Lord, I am no judge of chemical evidence." "Then, Dr. . . . , in that case I must tell you that it
will be my duty to represent to the jury and judges that arsenic
was unequivocally detected; and I ask you this—Suppose arsenic was detected, what in that case do you think was the
cause of these symptoms, and of these signs in the dead body?"
"Natural disease might cause them all." "Yes! Yes! we all
know that. But suppose that arsenic was found in the stomach,
what then would be your opinion as to their cause?" A pause
on the part of the Doctor, now run to earth. "Do you not
think, sir, that in that case arsenic was the cause?" Softly and
reluctantly came the inevitable answer, "Yes." "One more
question, then, and I have done: In your opinion, did this
person die of poisoning with arsenic?" "Yes." "Have you any
doubt of it?" "No." "Then" (*sotto voce*, yet audibly enough),
"what the devil brought you here?" [1]

This instructive passage is in the official report reduced to a
couple of lines.

There was thus no contesting the fact that the girl died of
arsenic, and an attempt to show that she had committed suicide
broke down; nor was Jeffrey more successful in seeking to have
the prisoner's declaration set aside on the ground that at the
time of making it she was unfit to be examined. Yet, after a
trial lasting twenty-two hours, the jury returned a unanimous
verdict of Not Proven, and the prisoner was discharged. Cockburn admits his client's guilt.[2] It seems that she had at first

[1] *Life of Sir Robert Christison*, i. 286–288.
[2] *Circuit Journeys*, p. 12.

meant only to procure abortion, but—*facilis descensus*—was led on to employ the more radical remedy of murder. Sir Walter Scott has recorded his impressions of the trial, which he attended.[1]

A case of peculiar atrocity, exceeding in cold-blooded wickedness even that which we have just considered, was tried at Perth in April of the same year.[2] Two sisters, Margaret and Jean Wishart, kept house together in the High Street of Arbroath, supporting themselves by taking boarders. The younger, Jean, was totally blind and quite dependent on her sister. A young man named Andrew Roy, a wright or carpenter, had lodged with them for five years. He was, as appears, originally the blind girl's lover, and she had borne him a child, which died; afterwards Margaret secured his affections, but later he returned to his first love—which indicates in the words of the Lord Justice-Clerk at the trial, "the most abominable footing on which they were." The discovery by Margaret that Jean was about to become again a mother aroused in her, to quote the same authority, a "fiend-like jealousy," and she determined at all costs to remove her rival. On Tuesday, 3rd October 1826, Margaret gave Jean, who was then in bed expecting shortly to be confined, her supper of porridge, in presence of a neighbour and one of the boarders. No one but Jean ate of it. Twenty minutes after taking it she was seized with sickness and other painful symptoms. Next day she continued very ill, and on Friday gave birth to a child, when Margaret was reluctantly forced to summon a midwife. Jean begged her sister to send for a doctor, a course also repeatedly urged upon her by divers sympathetic matrons, but Margaret replied "that everything had been done that could be done; that a doctor would do no good, and that she was not able to pay one." The gruel which, during the illness, was given both to mother and child, was prepared by her alone, and she showed throughout complete apathy and indifference as to their sufferings. Jean died on Sunday morning,

[1] *Journal*, i. 355, 361.
[2] Syme's Justiciary Reports, Appendix No. I.; *Edinburgh Medical Journal*, xxix. 18.

and as it was obvious that the child too was dying, with similar symptoms, one of the neighbours "brought in a doctor from the street." He said he could do nothing, and being asked by Margaret—an excellent ruse—to look at the dead body of her sister, refused, "as it could do no good." He seems to have had no more confidence in his profession than had the lady of the house. The child died on the following day, and was buried with its ill-fated mother. The authorities, apprised of these doings, ordered an exhumation, and owing to the appearances presented, certain organs were removed for chemical analysis. These were divided into two parts, one being tested by the local doctors and the other sent to Professor Christison for separate examination. Meanwhile Margaret was arrested, and emitted a declaration which the judge afterwards described as "replete with misrepresentation, falsehoods, equivocations and contradictions." On her trial the local doctors stated that arsenic was present in the deceased Jean Wishart's stomach and that her death had been occasioned by that poison. As regards the child, no arsenic was recovered. The tests applied by Dr. Christison in the mother's case yielded incontestable evidence of arsenic, though the quantity procured did not exceed the fortieth part of a grain. The defence relied mainly on the prosecutor's failure to trace to the prisoner the purchase or possession of arsenic, and also upon a peculiar incident connected with one of the Crown witnesses. This woman, Mary Greig, an intimate friend of the Wisharts, had been three times sent for to the prison by Margaret, who finally prevailed upon her to say, in presence of the jailer and two fellow-prisoners, that she (Greig) had gone with the blind woman to three several doctors in the town to buy poison, but without success, and that they had in the end obtained some from a chemist. The truth of this singular statement the witness on oath solemnly denied, explaining that she had been induced to make it solely out of pity for the prisoner, who "grat and urged sore upon her to say these words." The jailer and the other felons were the chief witnesses for the defence, and the judge, in charging the jury, observed that he "had no hesitation in saying he believed Mary Greig in opposition to him and his associates." Andrew Roy had discreetly vanished; but David Edward, another boarder, who bore flagrantly false witness in Margaret's behalf, was committed for perjury. The jury found the pannel guilty of poisoning her sister, but found the poisoning of the child not proven; she was sentenced to death, and was executed at Forfar.

In view of the part played by the prisoners' declarations in the two cases last cited, it may be remarked that although the ostensible object of a judicial declaration is to enable an accused person voluntarily to explain such circumstances as appear to tell against him, in practice it is apt to prove merely a net to entrap him. The uneducated criminal invariably gives himself away, and even intellectual malefactors, however adroit and wary, often are tripped up by its invidious meshes. The wise say nothing, or are content simply to deny the charge; but there is in human nature a curious itch of self-justification which few so situated, be they innocent or guilty, seem able to resist, and to this amiable weakness the judicial declaration ingeniously appeals.

The third poisoning case by which the year 1827 is distinguished is that of Mary Ann Alcorn, a domestic servant, tried in June for administering to her master and mistress, Mr. and Mrs. Roach of Bath Street, Portobello, with intent to murder them, tartar emetic or powder of antimony.[1] Mrs. Roach had told the girl to make a beefsteak pie and to take it to the baker's to be "fired." She did so, and in due course served the pie at table, when it was noticed that the gravy looked white. Mr. Roach ate heartily, his wife but sparingly; after dinner both were taken ill with similar symptoms—sickness, internal pain, swelling, feet and hands cold, perspiration—the husband's being much more violent than those of the wife. In the course of the attack Mr. Roach successively took some strong whisky toddy, two cups of coffee, a glass of brandy, and also "Anderson's Pills," the menstruum being more toddy; but despite the drastic character of this treatment, or perhaps because of it, he "suffered severely afterwards," and for some days his life was

[1] Syme's Justiciary Reports, p. 221.

in danger. Mary Ann, being apprehended, at first denied, but later admitted having put a powder, which she got from a neighbour's servant, into the pie, "merely for a bit of fun." But for the recovery of the subjects the joke would probably have been her last. It appeared that she had been incited to the act by a discharged servant, with a grudge against the Roaches. The doctor who attended the patients held that some preparation of lead, not antimony or tartar emetic, had been employed; and Dr. Christison, while unable to detect any in the remains of the pie, had no doubt whatever that poison of some sort had been swallowed. The prosecutor withdrew the charge of attempt to murder, and upon that of intent to do grievous bodily harm the jury found a verdict of guilty. A sentence of twelve months with hard labour must have gone some way to correct Mary Ann's defective sense of humour, and was certainly, in the circumstances, lenient. The contemporary report describes her as "surprised," but whether agreeably or otherwise does not appear.

We have seen in the case of Mrs. Smith how a timid or stupid jury may, by adopting the Scots form, Not Proven, frustrate the ends of justice. An instance equally scandalous is afforded by the case of John Lovie, tried at Aberdeen in September of the same year for the murder of a servant-girl.[1] This scoundrel, a farmer near Fraserburgh, had seduced one of his maids named Margaret McKessar, who believed and expected that he would marry her. At the date in question she was some five months with child, and their relations were well known to the other inmates of the farm. One of these, Alexander Rannie, a ploughman of seventeen, was asked by his master how much jalap would constitute a fatal dose, and also as to the relative merits of laudanum and arsenic. The lad referred him for information upon these points to one Suttie, "a kind of prophesier in the country," but Lovie does not seem to have consulted that expert. Pursuing his scientific enquiries, Lovie in the beginning of August called at a chemist's shop in Fraserburgh.

[1] Syme's Justiciary Reports, Appendix No. II.; Black Kalendar of Aberdeen, pp. 199, 202; Edinburgh Medical Journal, xxix. 415.

"Would an ounce of jalap be a good dose—not for a beast but for a body?" he asked; being told that it would kill any person, he bought an ounce and said he would divide it. He then asked what was the best poison for rats, and having learned that arsenic was deemed the most efficacious, departed with his purchase. Next day, after dinner, both the ploughman and the girl suffered from a severe attack of dysentery, from which, however, they recovered; so Lovie paid another visit to the chemist, and said he would now take the poison—"they were much infested with rats." He was supplied, according to the guileless fashion of the time, with an ounce of arsenic. On Tuesday, 14th August, Margaret McKessar rose in her usual health, and after breakfast was seized with violent pain and sickness, which continued throughout the morning, till in the afternoon her sufferings were terminated by death. To the master who was "working at his neeps," Rannie the ploughman brought word of her sudden illness, but Lovie continued his labours, merely remarking that if she were so bad as that, "she would not be long to the fore." The girl's mother was at work near him in the same field, but not only did he fail to acquaint her with her daughter's condition, but expressly ordered Rannie not to tell her. When they returned to the farm for dinner the girl was dead. Meanwhile a doctor had been sent for by Lovie's mother; he was from home, but his apprentice came and saw the body; he "tried her mouth with a candle, and said there was no breath there." Margaret was buried on Thursday; there had been some talk of having the body opened, but to this Lovie strenuously objected, craftily representing to the girl's relatives the scandal that would ensue should it be found she was "with bairn." The authorities, however, were less susceptible, and on Saturday the body was exhumed in presence of two surgeons from Fraserburgh, who removed certain organs for chemical analysis, parts of which were sent for separate examination to Dr. Blaikie, Aberdeen, and to Dr. Christison, Edinburgh. These gentlemen duly reported that they found in the stomach and its contents oxide of arsenic, which in their decided opinion was the cause of death. When Lovie heard that the body was to be "lifted" he asked a significant question: "Would it swell if she got poison?"; and later, being advised by a friend inconfident of his innocence "to take the south road," i.e. to fly the country, he denied his guilt, adding that he had never bought, used or seen any poison in his life. As the result of the investigation Lovie was arrested. In his declaration the prisoner took the customary liberties with truth: he never had intimate relations with the girl, and had no suspicion that she was with child; he told the chemist that he wanted stuff "to kill vermin upon black cattle," and was unaware that the substance supplied to him was poison; he used some of it to rub the backs of his cows and laid the remainder in the barn for rats; he knew nothing of the girl's illness until he went home to dinner, and he denied holding with Rannie and others any conversation regarding poison. All these statements were at the trial proved false, the testimony of the Crown witnesses was unscathed by cross-examination, and the defence called no evidence. Cockburn, who was Lovie's counsel, addressed the jury in his behalf, but no report of the speech survives. Mr. Hill Burton, who notices the case, observes: "Mr. Cockburn made at that trial one of his greatest efforts of persuasive oratory, and delivered an oration which, in seductiveness to such a tribunal as he addressed, has probably never been excelled." [1] The effect of this eloquence—a unanimous verdict of Not Proven—was doubtless for Cockburn no less a personal triumph than had been for Jeffrey the acquittal of Mrs. Smith; in the interests of justice it can only be regarded as equally deplorable. Cockburn makes no mention of the case in his *Journal*; one would like to have had his private opinion.

In the minds of most of us the Clyde passenger steamer is associated with summer memories of days passed upon the waters of that noble estuary, and the idea of wrongdoing in such a connection is limited to the occasional excesses of some too-festive voyager. The curious in these matters, however, may recall that in the *Ivanhoe* Lawrie sailed to Arran with his victim Rose, whose body he was to leave hidden amid the lonely

[1] *Narratives from Criminal Trials*, ii. 61.

corries of Goatfell; and that by one or other of the steamers on the "Royal Route" Monson passed to and from Ardlamont upon Cecil Hambrough's affairs, and the mysterious Scott made his exit from the scene of the tragedy. These relations are something of the remotest; yet unlikely as it seems, murder and robbery were once actually done upon a Clyde passenger steamer, for which crimes two persons suffered the last penalty of the law.[1] The *Toward Castle* (like Sir Walter, I love to be particular) was built by William Denny, father of the great shipbuilding firm, at Dumbarton in 1822, ten years after the pioneer *Comet* first threshed with her paddle-wheels the waters of the Firth, and was engined by M'Arthur of Glasgow. A wooden ship of some 79 tons and 45 horse-power, she plied between Glasgow and Loch Fyne, upon the route so long followed by her famous sister, the *Columba*. On 15th December 1828, there embarked at Tarbert upon the *Toward Castle*, then on her return run to Glasgow, a blacksmith and his wife, John and Catherine Stuart, and a mother and daughter named M'Phail. The parties had foregathered at the inn, where Mrs. M'Phail's luggage was lightened by a gauger of two gallons of whisky which she proposed to smuggle. The Stuarts sympathised with her loss, and as the morning was cold upon the water, they suggested a dram in the cabin. There, as she could not read, Mrs. M'Phail consulted them as to the denomination of certain guinea notes. Her hospitable fellow-travellers then pressed her to sample the ship's beer. "It was very bitter," she afterwards told the jury, "I never tasted such infernal strong beer in my life, and I spat out every drop, and wiped my mouth with my apron." As the old woman could by no means be induced to partake further of their bounty, the pair turned their attention to another passenger, a stout merchant from Ulva, Robert Lamont by name, on whose broad bosom the outline of a bulky pocket-book was plainly visible. He was travelling with a cousin, who preferred to remain on deck. Lamont made no difficulty of accepting gratuitous refreshment, but declined to pay for drinks, deeming the price prohibitive—"it cost 9d.

[1] *Trial of John Stuart and Catherine Wright or Stuart.* Edinburgh, 1829.

a bottle"; and so generously did his hosts stand treat that, as appears from the evidence of the steward, they drank the ship dry—"three gills, three bottles of porter, and a dozen of ale; there was no more on board." One tumbler only was in use, and it was noticed that before Lamont drank, Mrs. Stuart "put the tumbler in below her mantle," and once, as her husband was about to drink, she "pulled it from his mouth and spilt it over his breast, and he damned her for it." When the steamer reached Renfrew Ferry, John Lamont went below to look after his relative, whom he found alone in the dark cabin, insensible, with his empty pocket-book lying on the floor at his feet. John at once informed the captain that his cousin had been robbed, whereupon the Stuarts were "laid hold of" and searched, £19, 7s. in notes and silver, and a black purse, all afterwards proved to have been Lamont's property, being found upon them. When at 6 P.M. the *Toward Castle* reached the Broomielaw, Stuart and his wife were taken into custody, and two bottles containing laudanum were discovered in their possession. A doctor, summoned to attend Lamont, applied the stomach-pump, but the patient never regained consciousness, and died that night aboard the boat. On the trial of the Stuarts at Edinburgh in July 1829, the facts already stated were clearly established. Two surgeons, who conducted the post-mortem, deponed that they saw no sign of natural disease; Drs. Ure and Corkindale, who made the chemical analysis, reported that laudanum was present in the contents of the stomach and probably caused the death. No witnesses were called for the defence; the jury found both prisoners guilty, and sentence of death was pronounced accordingly. To their own counsel before the trial the couple fully acknowledged their guilt, and it further appears that they had adopted "doping" as a means of livelihood. The practice seems to have been prevalent at the time and other cases are upon record.

The case of Elizabeth Jeffray, tried at Glasgow in April 1838, is noteworthy not only as one of double murder, but from the fact that there was, in the ordinary sense of the term, no motive for the first crime, it being purely experimental and, as it were, a rehearsal of the second.[1] This woman, whose "well-moulded form and beautiful countenance" favourably impressed her biographer, was in her youth seduced by a "titled villain." After divers less distinguished experiences, she became the wife of a militiaman named Jeffray, and settled at Carluke, where, being unscrupulous and of a passionate temper, she was more feared than beloved by her neighbours. There lodged with her an infirm old pauper, called Mrs. Carl, and a young miner from Skye, named Munro, who had intrusted his savings—some £10 —to his landlady's keeping, and as he was about to leave Carluke, he naturally required restitution. This on various pretexts she delayed to make; there was the expense of her daughter's forthcoming marriage, and it was inconvenient for her then to find the money. Munro continuing to press his claim, early in October Mrs. Jeffray sent to a local druggist by a neighbour's child "a line for 3d. worth of arsenic to poison rats," and obtained half an ounce of that specific. On the night of Wednesday, the 4th, old Mrs. Carl being confined to bed, attended only by a boy, her nephew, Mrs. Jeffray visited the invalid with a drink of warm whisky, meal and cream of tartar, which she said would do her good. The old woman demurred, but Mrs. Jeffray gave a taste to the boy, who, inferring the wholesomeness of the remedy from its repellent flavour, advised his aunt to take it, which she did. Soon after she became violently ill, and the boy, who was himself sick during the night, roused the landlady to tell her that his aunt was dying; but Mrs. Jeffray refused to rise, as it might waken the lodgers. Next morning Mrs. Carl was dead; she was buried and, as Lord Braxfield might have said, "nae mair aboot it." A fortnight later Mrs. Jeffray called upon the druggist and bought another threepennyworth of arsenic, remarking that *"she had killed one rat with the first quantity, and she wanted to try it again."* On Saturday, the 28th, Munro left work early in good health and spirits, and ready for his dinner—porridge—which his landlady had prepared. After eating it he was seized with acute pain,

---

[1] Swinton's Justiciary Reports, ii. 113; *A Sketch of the Life and Trial of Mrs. Jeffray.* Glasgow, 1838.

vomiting, etc., and went to bed, from which he never rose. Terrible thirst was throughout a marked symptom, and from the first, as is expressively recorded, he "took a fear at the porridge." Despite her lodger's sufferings, Mrs. Jeffray would not send for a doctor, alleging to several persons who urged her to do so, that Highland folk were "narrow-minded" and Munro would grudge the expense, also that she had been three times for Dr. Rankine, her own doctor, but he was not to be found. On the Monday night, however, she summoned a surgeon, who "thought it was diarrhœa" and prescribed a rhubarb powder, which he prepared and left with her to be administered. Instead of relieving the patient who was somewhat easier, the powder made him much worse; he died in great agony, and was buried next day. Questioned as to Munro's money, which was known to have been in her hands, Mrs. Jeffray explained that she had given it to him to send to his relatives in Skye. On 3rd November her daughter was married with undue magnificence, the number of the bride's frocks provoking envious comment. A further sensation was provided next day by the exhumation of Munro's body, followed on the 6th by that of Mrs. Carl. As in neither case was there any indication of natural death, Mrs. Jeffray was apprehended, and in due course was indicted for the murders. The chemical analyses, conducted as regards Munro by Drs. Logan and Rankine, and as regards Carl by Professors Traill and Christison, were conclusive of the presence of arsenic, which in the opinion of those experts was undoubtedly the cause of death. It was proved that the prisoner had never called for Dr. Rankine, and that Munro had sent no money home to Skye. For the defence, an attempt to give to the supposititious rodents a local habitation in the garret was unsuccessful. After a trial lasting eighteen hours the jury by a majority found the prisoner guilty, but for some inexplicable reason unanimously recommended her to mercy. The judge in passing sentence observed that he could hardly conceive how a double murder came within the limits of mercy, and as the Home Secretary shared his Lordship's difficulty, Mrs. Jeffray paid the full penalty of her crimes. With characteristic

firmness she refused to confess her guilt, and died inflexible to
the end and unrepentant.

A case of exceptional interest occurring in 1844—the trial of
Christina Gilmour for the murder of her husband—is remarkable both in respect of its unusual features and its surprising
result.[1] The daughter of a substantial farmer in Ayrshire, Christina had been educated somewhat above her condition, and as
she was as fair as accomplished, her parents expected her to
make a good marriage. A suitable *parti* was found in John Gilmour, a Renfrewshire farmer of worth and means, whom Christina was by her family induced to accept, though she had fixed
her heart upon another. The wedding took place in November
1842, and the pair set out for their future home at Inchinnan,
near Renfrew. They had no sooner arrived there than the bride
announced to her husband that she would never live with him
as his wife. How the situation might have developed need not
concern us, for six weeks later John Gilmour was in his grave.
On 26th December Mrs. Gilmour ordered her maidservant,
who was on leave for a couple of days, to buy in Paisley "twopence worth of arsenic to kill rats," which the girl obtained and
on her return delivered to her mistress. On the 29th John Gilmour, a strong man of thirty in perfect health, was seized with
the symptoms characteristic of arsenical poisoning. Notwithstanding the assiduous attentions of his wife he grew gradually
worse. On 6th January Mrs. Gilmour went early to Renfrew for
the alleged purpose of getting "something that would do her
husband good." On her return she inadvertently dropped a
black silk bag, which was picked up by one of the farm hands.
He examined it and showed it to the maid, who gave it to her
mistress. The contents, a little phial of liquid that smelt like
scent and a paper packet marked "Poison," Mrs. Gilmour explained as "turpentine to rub John with." On the 7th a young
lady, describing herself as "Miss Robertson" of Paisley, obtained from a Renfrew chemist twopence worth of arsenic upon
the well-worn pretext. At a later stage three witnesses identified

[1] Broun's Justiciary Reports, ii. 23; *Report of the Trial of Mrs. Gilmour.*
Edinburgh, 1844; *Twelve Scots Trials*, pp. 191–220.

the pseudonymous purchaser with the fair Christina. Though during the illness Mrs. Gilmour represented her husband as refusing medical aid, he had without her knowledge sent for a doctor from Renfrew, but that physician being when he came the worse of drink, was in no condition to make a diagnosis. On the 8th, by request of a relative, Dr. M'Kechnie of Paisley visited the patient. He was not satisfied with the case, and told Mrs. Gilmour to preserve for his examination the vomited matter, etc. Calling next day he asked for these, but she said there was so little that it was not worth keeping. On the 11th the doctor found the patient in a dangerous state. Soon after he left John Gilmour died, expressing a wish "to be opened," and exclaiming with his latest breath, "Oh, that woman!—If you have given me anything, tell me before I die!" The funeral over, Mrs. Gilmour went home to her parents, and resumed correspondence with her first love. Rumour was busy with the farmer's mysterious fate; his wife had told several people that she had married him against her will and "would rather have preferred one Anderson"; in the whole circumstances, especially in view of her repeated purchases of poison, an enquiry was deemed advisable, and on 22nd April the authorities ordered exhumation. Two doctors having reported that the deceased died from the effects of an acrid poison, probably arsenic, the police went down to Ayrshire with a warrant for the widow's arrest. But tidings of what was afoot had been before them, and Mrs. Gilmour had disappeared. She was traced to Liverpool, from which port she had sailed in a packet-ship for America, but her pursuers, taking a Cunard steamer, reached New York before her. After lengthy proceedings, caused by the feigned insanity of the fugitive, she was extradited and brought back to Scotland. In her declaration before the Sheriff the prisoner, abandoning the rat motif, said that being unhappy in her marriage, she bought arsenic for the purpose of suicide, but changing her mind, destroyed it; she gave none to her husband. On 12th January 1844, exactly a year after his death, the widow was brought to trial at Edinburgh. The medical evidence as to the cause of death was incontrovertible; the analytical tests, conducted separately by Drs. M'Kinlay and Christison, established the presence of arsenic in the stomach, liver, and intestines. The defence maintained that John Gilmour had poisoned himself either accidentally or voluntarily, but neither proposition received much support from the evidence. The unanimous opinion of the four Crown doctors that arsenic had been given in repeated doses, disposed of the question of suicide. As to the theory of accident, it appeared that long before his marriage Gilmour once poisoned some rats with arsenic, which he got from a neighbouring farmer; but there was no proof that any of the poison remained in his possession. The defence called no witnesses; and after a damning speech by the Lord Advocate and a sentimental address from the other side, the Lord Justice-Clerk (Hope) charged strongly in favour of an acquittal, and the jury followed the judicial lead. So Christina returned to her native parish, where, though she did not after all get Anderson, she lived to a ripe and venerable age. A certain clergyman told me once that as a boy he often saw her in church—a charming old lady, serene and beautiful, famed throughout the district for her singular piety.

The curious unwillingness of juries to convict a woman upon a charge of poisoning on evidence merely circumstantial however cogent, is, as we have seen and shall continue to find, a marked feature of such cases. A flagrant example is that of Janet Campbell or M'Lellan, tried at Edinburgh in November 1846 for the murder of her husband, James M'Lellan, a weaver at Dunning, Perthshire, nearly thirty years his wife's senior.[1] She had an intrigue with a lodger, resulting in the birth of twins, and the domestic atmosphere was in consequence perturbed. The goodman made a practice at family prayers of referring pointedly to her transgression, which, instead of comforting the fair penitent, so exasperated her that on one occasion she pursued the suppliant with an axe. On 3rd July, M'Lellan, a hale man for his years, was taken ill, with symptoms indicating arsenic, after breakfast prepared by his wife. Next day, feeling "a good deal settleder," he was able to rise, but after

[1] Arkley's Justiciary Reports, p. 137.

breakfast the symptoms recurred in aggravated form. His wife was strangely annoyed when he was sick in a vessel containing "the sow's meat." Advised to invoke medical aid, she refused to do so—"he [her husband] was not so ready sending for skill to her when she needed it"; but M'Lellan insisted on seeing a doctor, as he believed he had been poisoned. Dr. Young, when he came, formed the like opinion, which was confirmed on his detecting arsenic in the vomited matter. The patient died that night, and his widow was arrested. In her declaration the prisoner denied that she ever had in her possession, or attempted to procure, poison. At the trial, it was proved that she applied personally to Dr. Young for arsenic "to poison rats," which, owing to the notoriously strained relations of the spouses, the physician declined to give her; that she then sent a girl, Davidson, to buy arsenic from Dr. Martin, but without success; and that on two occasions within a week of the death she obtained from a chemist by another girl, Aitken, twopence worth of that poison. She explained the second purchase to Aitken by saying that a mason who lodged with her "had tramped upon the saucer in which the former quantity had been placed," which the mason at the trial swore was false. No trace of poison could be found in her house, nor was there any evidence of how she had disposed of it. Dr. Thomson of Perth and Professor Christison found arsenic "to a considerable extent" in the stomach, liver and lungs of the deceased, and were confident that it caused his death. For the defence, Dr. Martin's assistant said that, when the twins were born, M'Lellan asked him for "poison to kill rats," which he refused to supply; and an old flame of M'Lellan's stated that once upon a time she had rejected his suit, whereupon he threatened suicide. But as this incident took place thirty years before, it seemed improbable that the effects would be so far-reaching. The Lord Justice-Clerk told the jury that looking to the whole circumstances of the case, it was impossible to suppose the deceased had poisoned himself; yet that enlightened tribunal returned a verdict of Not Guilty! One wonders what amount of proof *would* have sufficed for those disciples of Didymus.

A case tried at Glasgow in January 1850 is an interesting exception to the general rule I have mentioned. The scene was the village of Strathaven in Lanarkshire; the characters, Margaret Lennox or Hamilton, a young married woman, and her sister-in-law.[1] Jean Hamilton, lately in service with the Rev. Mr. Campbell, an Edinburgh minister, had been seduced by that divine, who paid her £26 as aliment for her expected child. It is gratifying to know that he was in consequence deposed. The girl returned to her mother's house, where in due course she gave birth to a child. She was attended by Margaret, but instead of making a good recovery, she was attacked by frequent sickness. On 7th July Margaret obtained from a doctor for the invalid a calomel powder, upon taking which Jean became violently sick. Margaret undertook to bring the doctor to see her, but failed to do so, and next day the girl died. A post-mortem was held, and on subsequent analyses by Professors Penny and Crawford, twenty grains of arsenic were found in the stomach. Shortly before the death Margaret obtained from an apothecary's wife arsenic "to kill rats," but in her declaration she altered the objective to bugs. The clerical endowment had been placed upon deposit receipt in Jean's name with the local bank. Lord Cockburn, who tried the case, gives the following account of it:

The poisoner had first stolen the bank deposit receipt, and finding that she could not get the money without the owner's signature, she forged it, and then, having committed these two offences, she murdered the victim in order to hide them. She was tried for the whole three crimes. The forgery and the administration of arsenic were very clearly proved. But there was a doubt about the theft, and therefore the jury found it not proved. Yet upon this fact a majority of them grounded by far the most nonsensical recommendation to mercy that any jury known to me ever made themselves ludicrous by. They first recommended without stating any reason, and on being asked what their reason was, they retired, and after consultation returned with these written words, viz.: that they gave the

[1] *Edinburgh Evening Courant*, 12th January 1850.

recommendation "in consequence of the first charge of theft not having been proved, which they believe in a great measure led to the commission of the subsequent crime"! Grammatically, this means that it was their acquittal of the theft that did the mischief, but what they meant was, that the murder was caused by a theft not proved to have existed. It is the most Hibernian recommendation I have ever seen. Though backed by the whole force of the very active party opposed to capital punishment, it failed, and the poor wretch died.[1]

In July of the same year there was tried at Edinburgh a case which, in its hideous blend of hypocrisy and cruelty, anticipates and rivals that of Dr. Pritchard.[2] William Bennison, an Irishman, when a lad of twenty, married Mary Mullen at Armagh in 1838. He deserted her in the following year, and at Paisley bigamously married Jane Hamilton. A few weeks afterwards he returned to Ireland and brought his first wife to Airdrie, where she fell sick and died, probably by poison. He then rejoined his other spouse, to whom he presented the wardrobe of her predecessor as the clothes of "his deceased sister Mary." Later, the second Mrs. Bennison learned that her sister-in-law was alive and well; but her husband explained that the deceased of whom he had spoken was "only his sister in the Lord." Thereafter the couple removed to Edinburgh, where they occupied a flat in Stead's Place, Leith Walk. An enthusiastic Methodist, Bennison received from his pastor at the trial a glowing character. He took the keenest interest in the spiritual welfare of the flock, never missed a meeting, was an eager proselytizer, visited the sick, and possessed a notable gift of fluency in prayer. His character was akin to those "holy Luthers of the preaching North" of whom we read in Synge's *Playboy of the Western World*. The favourite convert of this modern Major Weir was a girl named Robertson, the sharer of his pew in chapel and the consoler of his leisure hours. "Their conversation," says Miss Robertson, "was always of religion." Mrs. Ben-

---

[1] *Circuit Journeys*, pp. 362, 363.
[2] Shaw's Justiciary Reports, p. 453; *A Full Report of the Trial of William Bennison*. Leith, 1850.

nison, though not a strong woman, enjoyed fair health; her sister, Ellen Glass, was surprised to hear from Bennison on Sunday, 14th April, that his wife had been seized with illness and that the doctor despaired of her life. She hastened to the house and found her sister, whom she had seen shortly before in her usual health, violently sick and in great pain. She remained with the sufferer, as, in her own expressive phrase, "she saw that death was on her." As a matter of fact no doctor had seen the patient, and when it was suggested to send for one, Bennison said, "It's of no use; she is going home to glory." Mrs. Bennison told her sister she was taken ill after eating porridge. She died that night. During her last hours her husband, who had asked for the prayers of the congregation, busied himself in preparing "the dead clothes" and writing funeral letters, so that when all was over the final arrangements were well in hand. Advised of his loss—he had never entered the sickroom —he piously remarked, "Thank God! She has gone to glory." The burial took place forthwith, Bennison drawing £11 from divers benefit societies of which he was a member. He informed his tailor, from whom before the death he had bespoken mournings, that he had never seen a "pleasanter" deathbed. Now it happened that, when his wife lay dying, Bennison put out some cooked potatoes, which were devoured by two of the neighbours' dogs; these presently died in agony, the fact aroused suspicion, and a rumour spread that Mrs. Bennison had been poisoned. The widower was much distressed. He called upon a druggist named M'Donald, and referred to a recent purchase by him from M'Donald's wife of half an ounce of arsenic "for rats in the cellar," on which he feared the authorities might put a false construction. He hoped M'Donald would say nothing about it: "As I got it from your wife, you can easily say I did not get it from you." This casuistry not commending itself to the chemist, Bennison said that God had carried him through many difficulties, and would doubtless see him through this one. He was, as will appear, mistaken. Next day the body was exhumed in presence of the bereaved husband, who identified it as that of his "dear Jane." He was subsequently arrested on the charges of bigamy and murder. At his trial Dr. (afterwards Sir Douglas) Maclagan stated that he found arsenic in the stomach and liver of the deceased. He also detected its presence in a vessel into which she had vomited, and in a piece of paper recovered from the grate; but he failed to find any in the bodies of the dogs. From the symptoms, morbid appearances, and results by analysis, he had no hesitation in attributing the death to arsenic. Drs. Spittal and Anderson corroborated. The jury unanimously found the prisoner guilty, and he was sentenced to death. On leaving the dock he made a canting speech, in which he declared his innocence before God and forgave the sins of the Crown witnesses. Bennison in the end confessed his crime—he had put arsenic in the porridge—and was duly executed. Seldom has a fouler scoundrel graced the gallows. His case is the subject of an instructive article in the *Edinburgh Courant*,[1] dealing with the strange affinity between religious enthusiasm and crime.

Apart from those criminals who by the incompetence or pigheadedness of juries escape the grasp of justice, there is a smaller class who owe their immunity from punishment to some loophole in the law itself. Of such technical acquittals three examples may here be noted. At Glasgow in May 1843 Mary M'Farlane or Taylor was charged with a double murder.[2] When the diet was called, objection was taken to the citation of the pannel in respect of an error in date, and the case was certified to the High Court. This certification was fallen from, and no further proceedings were taken. Similar results followed in nineteen other cases at the same circuit. Lord Cockburn, who presided, observes:

> There was also the case of a woman accused of murdering her husband, but it was one of the twenty, and did not come on. It will be a famous case in its day, however. She first committed the capital offence of giving her husband a dose of arsenic, which very nearly killed him, but he survived it. Thinking, truly, that it was her unskillfulness in administering

[1] 29th July 1850.
[2] Broun's Justiciary Reports, i. 550.

that made this dose fail, she resolved to improve herself by a little practice, and then to renew the attempt. She therefore experimented upon a neighbour, whom she killed; and having now ascertained how to proceed, she gave another dose to her spouse, and killed him too. She was indicted for the two murders and the abortive administration, an awkward accumulation of charges. It being in her case that the motion to put off all the trials was made, she was brought to the bar; and, whether it was fancy or not, struck me as having a very singular expression. She was little, apparently middle-aged, modest and gentle looking, with firm-set lips, a pale countenance, and suspicious restless eyes.[1]

This scandalous miscarriage of justice led to an amendment in the practice of citing parties at circuit ayres. The second instance is the case of Janet Hope or Walker at Edinburgh in July 1845.[2] This woman, wife of the landlord of the Blue Bell Inn, Lockerbie, was charged with poisoning by arsenic George Tedcastle, her son by a former husband. While incarcerated in Dumfries jail the prisoner confessed her guilt to the keeper, who had constituted himself her spiritual adviser. At the trial, a question as to what she said to him being disallowed, the prosecutor abandoned the charge, and a verdict of not guilty was returned. The third and most deplorable example occurred at Inverness in April 1852, where Sarah Anderson or Fraser and James Fraser, her son, were convicted of poisoning William Fraser, Inver, Easter Ross, husband of one, and father of the other pannel.[3] Fraser was sixty years of age, his wife forty, and their son seventeen. Purchases of arsenic by Mrs. Fraser at Tain were proved, following upon which the husband became suddenly ill. Before his death she was heard to say that if she were a widow, there would be none happier in Ross-shire. No doctor was sent for, and the man died with all the usual symptoms. Forty-five letters written by mother and son to each other were recovered; and on his judicial examination the son was

[1] *Circuit Journeys*, p. 190.
[2] Broun's Justiciary Reports, ii. 465.
[3] Irvine's Justiciary Reports, i. 1, 66; *Courant; Scotsman;* 17th April 1852.

asked to explain certain passages:—"Hasten the day when you will be a widow"; "I pray to heaven I will soon have it in my power to release you from the tyrant"; "I wish the world were rid of such a monster"; "Many others have wished my father's death as well as I"; "If you have any spunk you will not be long in your present condition," etc. He declared that his father was unkind to his mother—of which, by the way, there was no evidence—and what he meant was, that he hoped soon to be in a position to support her. The mother declared that all the arsenic was consumed by rats. On their trial their guilt was clearly proved, and the jury found accordingly; but sentence was delayed, owing to an objection taken for the defence to the admission of certain evidence. In the list of productions a packet of powder, sent to Dr. Maclagan for analysis, which he found to be arsenic, was described as a "sealed packet," whereas, though the seals were intact, the wrapper had been cut by him in order that he might examine the contents. The point was certified for the consideration of the High Court. On 1st June, before that tribunal, it was further objected that no precise day had been fixed for the diet being called, so the diet was held to have fallen, and the warrant against the prisoners was discharged. On 12th July an attempt by the Crown to proceed against them upon a new indictment failed, the Court holding that, having tholed an assize, they could not again be tried for the same offence. Thus, thanks to these red-tape entanglements, two convicted murderers were restored to society. Lord Cockburn, who presided at their trial, has given his impressions of the case:

> The only interesting case was that of Mrs. and Mr. Fraser, a mother and her son (a lad), who had chosen to poison their father, a shopkeeper in Ross-shire. They thought him a useless creature, and that they would be better without him, especially as the wife had forged his name to bills, in reference to which his removal before they became due would be convenient. I never saw a couple of less amiable devils. The mother, especially, had a cold hard eye, and a pair of thin resolute lips, producing an expression very fit for a remorseless

and steady murderess. She saw her daughter, a little girl, brought in as a witness, and heard her swear that there were no rats in the house and that her father's sufferings were very severe, with a look of calm ferocity which would have done no discredit to the worst woman in hell. They were both convicted, but I fear the gallows won't get its due . . . which will be a pity.[1]

We have seen that his Lordship's fear was justified.

As it too rarely happens that we have the advantage of a judge's private opinion upon cases tried before him, I shall give one other instance from Lord Cockburn's reminiscences: that of Elliott Millar at Jedburgh in September 1847.[2]

The only curious case on this Circuit was that of a worthy husband who wanted to get his spouse killed; but instead of resorting to commonplace violence by himself, he tried to make the law do it. For this purpose he fell upon the device of making it appear that she had poisoned him; for which she was committed for trial and was very near being tried. But suspicion being excited, it was discovered that his whole statements on precognition were false, and all his dexterous imitations of being poisoned, utter fabrications. The result was that he was brought to trial himself for fraud, and was transported for seven years.[3]

It appears that this ingenious rascal complained of illness after breakfast; took an emetic, saying his wife had poisoned him; and preserved for examination the coffee and vomited matter. These on analysis were found to contain sugar of lead, which, as he subsequently confessed, he had himself introduced from a supply obtained by his wife with a view to suicide, in attempting which she was unsuccessful!

Confronted with the task of tackling in a single paragraph the complexities of our greatest cause célèbre, I envy the skill of those caligraphists who within the compass of a threepenny piece can depict our most familiar prayer. But though it is im-

[1] *Circuit Journeys*, p. 377.
[2] Arkley's Justiciary Reports, p. 355.
[3] *Circuit Journeys*, p. 333.

possible in such conditions to appreciate Madeleine Smith's achievement, no paper on Scots poisoning would be complete without her.[1] The daughter of an architect of position in Glasgow, Madeleine at nineteen was a dashing damsel, accomplished and attractive, an ornament of middle-class society in that city. Her charms caught the roving eye of a young Frenchman, L'Angelier, clerk in a commercial house, and he contrived through a common friend an introduction to her in the street. This ill-omened meeting occurred in 1855. Socially, of course, L'Angelier was impossible; but he was a good-looking little "bounder," and the girl fell in love with him. They corresponded constantly, with that amazing mid-Victorian voluminosity which, happily, is a lost art, and met as often as circumstances permitted. No one in Madeleine's set knew of their intimacy; but a romantic spinster friend of L'Angelier, Miss Perry, acted as go-between, and one of the Smith's maids connived at their clandestine meetings. In the spring of 1856 the flirtation developed into an intrigue, the changed relations of the lovers being reflected in the tropical and abandoned tone of the fair correspondent. They addressed one another as "husband" and "wife," and there can be little doubt that in the belief of L'Angelier, as well as by the law of Scotland, they actually were married. An elopement was anticipated, but the gallant's official salary amounted only to ten shillings a week and the lady was quite dependent on her parents, so the prospect was none of the brightest. In November 1856 the Smiths occupied a main-door corner house, No. 7 Blythswood Square. The stanchioned windows of Madeleine's bedroom in the basement opened directly upon, and were partly below the level of, the pavement of the side street; it was the lovers' custom to converse at these, the sunk part formed a convenient letter-box, and when the coast was clear she could take him into the house. In the flat above lived a gentleman named Minnoch, who began to pay his charming neighbour marked attentions. Whether or not the copiousness of her draughts of passion had

[1] Irvine's Justiciary Reports, ii. 641; *Trial of Madeleine Smith*, edited by A. Duncan Smith, 1905.

induced satiety, Madeleine was quick to realise that her position as the wife of a prosperous Glasgow merchant would be very different from her future with the little French clerk, so she gave her responsible wooer every encouragement. On 28th January 1857, with the approbation of her parents, she accepted his hand. Meantime her correspondence with L'Angelier was maintained at the accustomed temperature, till, early in February, she made an effort to break the "engagement," and demanded the return of her letters. Rumours of Mr. Minnoch's attentions had reached L'Angelier; he suspected what was afoot, taxed her with perfidy, and refused to give up the letters to anyone but her father. The mere suggestion drove Madeleine well-nigh crazy: the letters were indeed such as no parent ever read and few daughters could have written; she poured forth frantic appeals for mercy and solemnly denied that she had broken faith; she besought him to come to her and she would explain everything. L'Angelier stood firm; he has been called blackguard and blackmailer; as I read the facts, it was neither revenge nor money that he wanted, but his wife. "I will never give them up," he told his friend Kennedy, "she shall never marry another man so long as I live"; adding with prophetic significance, "Tom, she'll be the death of me." A reconciliation was effected on 12th February, the correspondence was resumed on the old footing, and L'Angelier became again "her love, her pet, her sweet Emile." He told Miss Perry he was to see Madeleine on the 19th. That night he left his lodgings, taking the pass-key as he intended to be late; next morning his landlady found him writhing in agony on his bedroom floor, with all the symptoms of irritant poisoning. Whether the lovers had met or not is disputed, but in his diary, production of which at the trial was disallowed, L'Angelier wrote: "Thurs. 19. Saw Mimi a few moments—was very ill during the night." He recovered, but was never the same man afterwards. At 4 A.M. on Monday, 23rd, L'Angelier rang for his landlady, who found him suffering from another similar attack. The diary records: "Sun. 22. Saw Mimi in drawing-room—Promised me French

Bible—Taken very ill." This meeting is otherwise established under Madeleine's own hand: "You did look bad on Sunday night and Monday morning. I think you get sick with walking home so late and the long want of food, so the next time we meet I shall make you eat a loaf of bread before you go out." L'Angelier said to Miss Perry, "I can't think why I was so unwell after getting coffee and chocolate from her [Madeleine]," referring to two different occasions; "If she were to poison me I would forgive her." He also told his friend Towers that he thought he had been poisoned twice, after taking coffee and cocoa. Now, prior to the first illness, Madeleine made an abortive attempt to procure prussic acid—"for her hands"—but no arsenic could then be traced to her possession. The day before the second attack she bought from Murdoch, a druggist, one ounce of arsenic "to send to the gardener at the country house" —Mr. Smith's summer villa at Row, on the Gareloch. On 5th March L'Angelier, whose jealousy had reawakened, wrote insisting on knowing the truth about Mr. Minnoch; that day Madeleine purchased from Currie, another druggist, a second ounce of arsenic "to kill rats in Blythswood Square," and on the 6th she went with her family for ten days to Bridge of Allan. Mr. Minnoch was of the party, and the wedding was fixed for June. L'Angelier, on sick leave, had gone to Edinburgh, impatiently awaiting Madeleine's return, when everything was to be explained; on the 19th he followed her to Bridge of Allan. But Madeleine had come back on the 17th, and next day she obtained from Currie a third ounce of arsenic —"the first was so effectual." On the evening of Sunday, 22nd, L'Angelier returned to his lodgings: a letter forwarded to him from Glasgow had brought him home in hot haste; he looked well and happy, and after a hasty meal hurried away, saying he might be out late. At 2.30 A.M. his landlady, aroused by the pealing of the door bell, found him doubled up with agony upon the threshold. He was put to bed and a doctor sent for, who formed a hopeful prognosis; "I am far worse than the doctor thinks," cried the patient. He said nothing as to the cause of his illness, but asked to see Miss Perry; when that lady arrived L'Angelier's lips were sealed for ever. In his pocket was found the last letter of a remarkable series:

Why my beloved did you not come to me. Oh beloved are you ill. Come to me sweet one. I waited and waited for you but you came not. I shall wait again to-morrow night same hour and arrangement. Do come sweet love my own dear love of a sweetheart. Come beloved and clasp me to your heart. Come and we shall be happy. A kiss fond love. Adieu with tender embraces ever believe me to be your own ever dear fond MIMI.

The postmark was Glasgow, 21st March. L'Angelier's half of the fatal correspondence was discovered, Madeleine fled to Row and was brought back by her fiancé; an examination of the body pointed to poison, and she was apprehended. In her declaration she said that she had not seen L'Angelier for three weeks; the appointment was for Saturday, 21st, he came neither that night nor the next; her purpose in making it was to tell him of her engagement. As to the arsenic, she used it all as a cosmetic, on the advice of a school-friend. She admitted giving cocoa to L'Angelier once at her window. Of the nine days' wonder of her trial at Edinburgh in July I have small space left to speak. No less than 88 grains of arsenic were found in the body, and the defence made much of the fact that this was the greatest quantity ever detected, arguing that so large a dose indicated suicide rather than murder. The unsoundness of this contention is proved by two subsequent English cases,[1] where 150 and 154 grains respectively were recovered. As regards the first two charges—of administration—the Crown was handicapped by the exclusion of L'Angelier's diary, and in the murder charge, by inability to prove the actual meeting of the parties on the Sunday night. There was proof that L'Angelier had talked once or twice in a vapouring way of suicide, but none that he ever had arsenic in his possession. The prisoner's account of her object in acquiring arsenic was contradicted by her old schoolfellow, and the fact that what she obtained was, in terms of the

[1] R. v. Dodds, 1860, and R. v. Hewitt, 1863.

Statute,[1] mixed with soot and indigo, rendered it strangely un-inviting for toilet purposes. On the other hand, the doctors noticed no colouring matter in the body, but to this point their attention was not then directed. On the question of motive, it was maintained that the prisoner had nothing to gain by L'Angelier's death if her letters remained in his possession. These, however, having neither address nor any signature except "Mimi," afforded little clue to the writer's identity. But surely it was his *silence* that was for her the supreme object: how could that be ensured save by his death? Lord Advocate Moncreiff's masterly address, strong, restrained, convincing, was then, as now, unduly eclipsed by the brilliant emotional speech of John Inglis for the defence, held to be the finest ever delivered in a Scots court. The one appealed to the head, the other to the heart; each pledged his personal belief in the rightness of his cause. Lord Justice-Clerk Hope's charge favoured an acquittal; the jury found the pannel not guilty of the first charge, the other two not proven. In the popular verdict, "If she did not poison him, she ought to have done it," I am unable to concur. The amazing self-command with which the prisoner faced her ordeal, no less than her youth and beauty, inspired the pens of contemporary scribes. During the trial she received many proposals, lay and clerical; her fiancé was not an offerer. A surgeon named Tudor Hora was preferred, with whom she emigrated to Australia. Returning to England after his death, she was married on 4th July 1861 at St. Paul's, Knightsbridge, to Mr. George Wardle, an artist. She is said to have died in Melbourne in 1893.[2]

There is in the trial at Glasgow in December 1857 of John Thomson *alias* Peter Walker, known as the Eaglesham case—the first in Scotland for murder by hydrocyanic or prussic acid—a curious echo of that which we have just considered.[3] Thomson was employed as a journeyman tailor in the village of

[1] 14 Vict. c. 13, s. 3.
[2] *Notes and Queries*, ii. S. iv. 311.
[3] Irvine's Justiciary Reports, ii. 747; *Report of the Trial of John Thomson alias Peter Walker*. Edinburgh, 1858; "Poison and Plagiary," *infra*, pp. 121–142.

Eaglesham, near Glasgow. A girl named Montgomery had rejected his addresses and he vowed revenge. Thomson was much interested in the newspaper reports of Madeleine Smith's trial, discussed the relative drawbacks attending the use of arsenic and of prussic acid, and expressed his strong opinion that she should have been hanged. Having obtained by the carrier's boy from a Glasgow chemist 2 drachms of Scheele's prussic acid, for use as a "hair dye," Thomson on 13th September administered it to Montgomery in beer, leaving the girl locked in her room. She was found in a dying condition, and her death certified as due to apoplexy. On the 23rd, after ordering a second supply, he left his situation for Glasgow, where he attempted gratuitously to poison in whisky Mr. and Mrs. Mason, with whom he lodged. Suspicion was aroused, Montgomery's body was exhumed and examined, and Drs. M'Kinlay and Maclagan detected prussic acid in the stomach and spleen. Convicted on circumstantial evidence, Thomson was executed, confessing his guilt.

Glasgow contributes further to our subject the case of Dr. Pritchard, tried at Edinburgh in July 1865 for the poisoning of his wife by repeated doses of antimony, and of his mother-in-law by antimony and aconite.[1] "When a doctor does go wrong," Mr. Sherlock Holmes once remarked to his egregious colleague, "he is the first of criminals. He has nerve and he has knowledge. Palmer and Pritchard were among the heads of their profession." A hypocritical charlatan with a German diploma, handsome, plausible, and unscrupulous, Pritchard, after a variegated career, came to Glasgow in 1860. Though disliked and distrusted by his medical brethren he acquired a considerable practice; but his reputation suffered by his "treatment" of certain lady patients, and a fire in his house in Berkeley Terrace, involving the mysterious death of a servant girl, followed by a fraudulent claim on an insurance company, hardly enhanced his fame. An adept at self-advertisement, he was an enthusiastic Mason and a popular lecturer on his experiences of for-

[1] Irvine's Justiciary Reports, v. 88; Trial of Dr. Pritchard, edited by William Roughead, 1906.

eign travel, which, as he was unhampered by the laws of truth, were rich in surprising detail. His family worshipped him; his wife, to whom he was flagrantly unfaithful, was ready to accept anything—even poison—at his hands, while of his mother-in-law he is said to have been the idol. In 1864 we find Pritchard established at No. 131 (now 249) Sauchiehall Street, the household consisting of himself, his wife and children, a cook and a nurse-housemaid. The latter, Mary M'Leod, a girl of 16, had been the year before seduced by him and the subject of an illegal operation at his hands. Mrs. Pritchard was aware of the intimacy. Two medical students boarded in the house. Mrs. Pritchard's illness began in October with persistent sickness. In November she went to see her parents, Mr. and Mrs. Taylor, at No. 1 Lauder Road, Edinburgh, where she stayed till Christmas. During the visit she was greatly better, but on her return home the sickness recommenced, occurring after food. Pritchard ascribed her illness to gastric fever, and Dr. Cowan of Edinburgh, her cousin, saw her; he did not consider her seriously ill. On 1st February 1865 she had a violent attack of cramp; Dr. (afterwards Sir William) Gairdner was sent for. The case puzzled him—there were no symptoms of fever, he thought she was intoxicated; so he wrote to the lady's brother, Dr. Michael Taylor, Penrith, recommending her removal to his care; but Pritchard said she was not well enough to travel. Meanwhile Dr. Cowan had told Mrs. Taylor that she ought to go to Glasgow to look after her daughter, and on the 10th the old lady arrived from Edinburgh. She was a hale woman of seventy, but in the habit of taking for neuralgic headaches Battley's Sedative Solution, a preparation of opium. On the 13th some tapioca prepared for the invalid was eaten by Mrs. Taylor, who immediately became sick, remarking that she must have got the same complaint as her daughter, upon whom she was in constant attendance. On the evening of the 24th Mrs. Taylor had tea with the family, wrote some letters in the consulting-room, and walked upstairs to her daughter's room, telling the maid to order sausages for supper. A few minutes later she was seized with illness, and rapidly became unconscious.

Dr. Paterson was summoned, to whom Pritchard falsely stated that the old lady, while writing letters, had fallen off her chair in a fit and was carried upstairs, adding that she was given to liquor. Dr. Paterson examined her; she was dying, said he, under the influence of some strong narcotic, and Pritchard explained that she was in the habit of taking opium. Dr. Paterson was much struck by the ghastly appearance of Mrs. Pritchard, sitting up in bed behind her dying mother. He formed the opinion that she was being poisoned with antimony, but "professional etiquette" prevented him interfering, and he left the house. Mrs. Taylor died that night. In her pocket was found the bottle of Battley, of which Pritchard took possession, saying it would never do for a man in his position to have it talked about. After the death, he met Dr. Paterson in the street and asked him to call on Mrs. Pritchard, which that gentleman did, confirming his impression that she was the victim of foul play. When Pritchard sent to him for Mrs. Taylor's death certificate Dr. Paterson refused to grant it, and wrote to the Registrar that the death was "sudden, unexpected, and to him mysterious"; this he thought should open the eyes of the authorities, but the Registrar destroyed the letter and did nothing further. So Mrs. Taylor was buried by her disconsolate son-in-law in the Grange Cemetery, Edinburgh. Mrs. Pritchard's lingering illness continued, "one day better and two days worse," despite the unremitting care of her loving husband and physician. On 13th March he sent by M'Leod to the patient a piece of cheese, which she asked the girl to taste. Mary did so, and experienced a burning sensation and thirst. The cook, afterwards eating it, became violently sick and had to go to bed. On the 15th Pritchard ordered her to make egg-flip for the invalid. He carried two lumps of sugar from the dining-room into his consulting-room, and from thence to the pantry, where he dropped them into the flip. Mrs. Pritchard took a little and was sick; the cook drank the rest and suffered all night from pain and vomiting. On the 17th Mrs. Pritchard had a severe attack of cramp and became delirious. Dr. Paterson was sent for, and advised a sleeping-draught; as Pritchard said he kept no drugs in the house, Dr. Paterson wrote a prescription and departed. That night Mrs. Pritchard died in her husband's arms, Mary M'Leod lying on a sofa at the foot of the bed. Pritchard took his wife's body to her father's house in Edinburgh, where at his request the coffin was opened in presence of the relatives, that he might kiss his "dearest Mary Jane" for the last time. Not Webster nor Tourneur, those masters of the horrific, ever conceived a scene so cynically atrocious. Meawhile someone had written to the Procurator-Fiscal, calling his attention to these strange deaths; when Pritchard was in Edinburgh his house was searched and the inmates examined, and on his return he was arrested at Queen Street Station for the murder of his wife. On the discovery of antimony in Mrs. Pritchard's body that of Mrs. Taylor was exhumed, and the presence of the same poison being also in her case ascertained, Pritchard was further charged with her murder. The trial took place on 3rd July before the High Court; John Inglis, who had so successfully defended Madeleine Smith, presided as Justice-Clerk; the Solicitor-General (Young) prosecuted, and Mr. Rutherfurd Clark conducted the defence. The medical evidence as to the cause of death was in both cases conclusive. Pritchard had certified that of Mrs. Taylor as "Paralysis, 12 hours; Apoplexy, 1 hour," and that of his wife as "Gastric Fever, 2 months." Mrs. Pritchard's symptoms, as observed by Drs. Cowan, Gairdner and Paterson, directly negatived the truth of this, while other witnesses proved that Mrs. Taylor was quite well until her sudden seizure. There was no sign of apoplexy. The medical and chemical examinations made by Drs. Maclagan, Littlejohn, and Penny established the fact that both bodies contained antimony—that of Mrs. Pritchard being saturated with the poison. Antimony and aconite were found in the bottle of Battley, but no aconite could be detected in Mrs. Taylor's body. The unused tapioca was largely mixed with antimony. As regards possession of poison by the prisoner, despite his statement to Dr. Paterson he was proved to have been from September 1864 to 16th March 1865 a constant purchaser of deadly drugs: strychnia, conium, laudanum, morphia, tartarised antimony, Fleming's tincture of aconite, atropine, etc.; the quantities of antimony and aconite alone being largely in excess of those supplied to other medical men and much greater than could have been required in any ordinary practice. The opportunities for administration were obvious, but the cheese and the egg-flip were the only poisoned articles traced to Pritchard's hand. The Crown case, in other respects impregnable, was weakest upon the question of motive. Pritchard had promised to marry M'Leod if his wife died, and under Mrs. Taylor's settlement he received a life-interest in a few hundred pounds. That he would in any circumstances have married the servant-girl he had long before seduced is incredible; and though his bank account was overdrawn, Mrs. Taylor would have lent him money, as she had previously done. It would be, for him, a sufficient reason for becoming a widower that he was tired of his wife and saw his way to a more attractive match; as for Mrs. Taylor, her presence interfered with his scheme, and we know from his confession that she had "caught M'Leod and him in the consulting-room"; probably she proved less complacent than her daughter on a similar occasion. An attempt by the defence to throw the guilt upon M'Leod failed, and Pritchard afterwards declared her complete innocence. After a five days' trial he was convicted and sentenced to death. Before his execution—the last public one in Glasgow—he confessed his crimes, which he attributed to "the use of ardent spirits"; but there is no evidence of his intemperance: he was too cold-blooded and crafty for that. He retained to the last the cloak of religious hypocrisy which he had worn so long. "I shall meet you in Heaven," said he to the Rev. Dr. Bonar, whom he had asked to pray with him. "Sir," retorted the divine, "we shall meet at the Judgment Seat." On 23rd November 1910, in connection with the demolition of the old South Jail, the courtyard, in which were buried the bodies of executed criminals, was excavated, and among the remains exhumed were those of Dr. Pritchard. Opportunity was taken to examine the skull, a "note" on which, with interesting photographs, was published by Mr. Edington in 1912.[1]

Eugène Marie Chantrelle, teacher of French and amateur physician, was a villain of a ruder type than Pritchard.[2] While employed at Newington Academy, Edinburgh, in 1868 he seduced one of his pupils, a girl of fifteen named Elizabeth Dyer, whom her family, saving her reputation at the cost of her happiness, compelled him to marry. From the first Chantrelle systematically ill-treated his wife, several times she fled from his cruelty to her parents home, but for the sake of her children she as often returned to her tyrant. As his infidelities were frequent and notorious she could readily have obtained divorce; there again, however, she sacrificed herself to her children's welfare. So for ten years the unhappy woman patiently endured her cross. Chantrelle's teaching connection suffered from his profligate and drunken habits, engagements grew scarce, he was in debt and pressed for money, and in October 1877 he insured his wife's life for £1000 with the Accident Assurance Association, having previously ascertained from another office what constituted "accidental" death. This step was against the lady's wish: she told her mother that she was afraid of the consequences, for her husband had more than once threatened to take her life; he was half a doctor, and boasted that he could poison her without detection. The Chantrelles occupied the two upper flats of a common stair, No. 81A George Street, Edinburgh. On New Year's Day 1878 Madame Chantrelle gave the servant a holiday, remaining herself at home with the children. On the maid's return at 10 P.M. Chantrelle told her that his wife, being unwell, had gone to bed. She found her mistress in the back bedroom, "very heavy looking," with the baby beside her. A tumbler of lemonade stood by the bedside, and Madame asked her to peel an orange for her, which was done. Chantrelle slept in the front bedroom with the two older children. Next morn-

---

[1] *Glasgow Medical Journal*, February 1912.
[2] *Trial of E. M. Chantrelle*, edited by A. Duncan Smith, 1906.

ing when the maid rose at seven she heard moaning from her mistress's room, the door of which was partly open and the gas unlit—both contrary to custom. Entering, she saw Madame lying unconscious in the bed, with stains as of vomiting upon the pillow. She called her master, who was in his own bed with the three children. He went with her to the back room and attempted to rouse his wife; the maid advised sending for a doctor. Chantrelle said he heard the baby crying and told her to attend to it; she left the room, but finding the baby still asleep, at once returned, and saw Chantrelle in the act of coming away from the window. "Don't you smell gas?" he asked, and though she did not then do so, immediately afterwards she noticed a slight smell, so she turned off the gas at the meter. Dr. Carmichael was summoned; when he arrived the room was redolent of gas, and Chantrelle explained that there had been an escape. The doctor sent for Dr. (afterwards Sir Henry) Littlejohn, City Medical Officer, "to see a case of coal-gas poisoning," and the patient, in a comatose state, was carried into the front room. Dr. Littlejohn came; he thought she was dying and advised her removal to the Royal Infirmary. Both doctors, in view of the smell and of Chantrelle's false statements, believed her to be suffering from gas. At the Infirmary, Dr. Maclagan, into whose ward she was taken, diagnosed the case as one not of gas, but of narcotic poisoning, probably opium, and it was treated accordingly. At 4 P.M. the patient died without having regained consciousness. Medical and chemical examinations of the body negatived the suggestion that death was due to gas poisoning, but failed to detect the narcotic poison indicated by the symptoms. Fortunately for the ends of justice, in certain stains of vomited matter upon the nightdress and bedclothes Drs. Maclagan and Littlejohn, as well as Professors Crum Brown and Fraser, established by separate analyses the presence of opium, apparently in the form of extract, together with orange pulp. Chantrelle was arrested; although his judicial declaration occupied thirteen hours, the only important point was his statement that he left his wife in her usual health at 1 A.M.; for the rest, the portentous document was devoted to gross and baseless slander of the dead woman. On his trial at Edinburgh in May 1878, for murdering his wife by opium, in orange or lemonade, Lord Moncreiff presided, the Lord Advocate (Watson) appeared for the Crown, and Mr. Trayner for the pannel. The defence maintained that the symptoms and morbid appearances were consistent with gas poisoning, and that the stains were not proved to be the result of vomiting; and indeed, upon the medical evidence alone, the Crown might not have been certain of a conviction. But it was proved that behind the window shutter, from whence, before there was any smell of gas, Chantrelle had been seen by the maid to come, was a disused gas pipe, freshly broken through by wrenching, which, had it been for any time in that condition, must have filled the house with gas; and that while Chantrelle denied that he knew of the pipe being there, he had in 1876 been present when it was repaired, and discussed its position with the workman. It was further proved that on 25th November 1877 Chantrelle bought from a local chemist a drachm of extract of opium, as to the application of which there was no evidence, though a similar purchase by him in 1872 was found in his repositories; also that he had stated to various witnesses that before going to bed he gave his wife a bit of orange and some lemonade, and took the baby away as she was feeling unwell. The jury unanimously found him guilty, and the prisoner, in a rambling statement from the dock, demolished the whole fabric of the defence by arguing that his wife had taken opium voluntarily, and that someone had rubbed the poison on her linen in order to incriminate him. He was condemned to death, and notwithstanding strong efforts made to obtain a reprieve, sentence was duly carried out, the convict refusing to confess his guilt. Had Chantrelle been content simply to turn on the gas that night in his wife's room it is probable that, so far as her case is concerned, he might have "cheated the woodie"; but it was understood at the time that in the event of an acquittal the Crown was prepared to indict him upon another capital charge.

After M. Chantrelle's enforced retirement from practice
the art of poisoning in Scotland sensibly declined. Since his
suspension no other artist of the same school has been, if I
may pursue the metaphor, hung on the line; the present generation furnishes but few performers, whose work, in quantity
inconsiderable, lacks the boldness of design and finish of execution which distinguish that of the older masters.

An unsatisfactory case was that of John Webster, landlord
of Newton Hotel, Kirriemuir, tried at Edinburgh in February
1891, for the murder of his wife by arsenic.[1] In the beginning
of August Mrs. Webster had been suddenly attacked with
vomiting and persistent thirst, and died after three days' illness, attended by her husband. A doctor, called in, thought her
suffering from gastritis, and certified accordingly. Four months
after interment the body was exhumed; it was unusually well
preserved, there were no signs of natural death, and on analysis
arsenic was found in all the organs examined. At the trial expert evidence to that effect was given by Dr. Littlejohn, Mr.
Falconer King, and Professor Crum Brown; death was due to
arsenic, administered in repeated doses. An error in the chemical report as to the amount probably contained in the body
was corrected by the medical witnesses from subsequent experiments. When the diet was first called the Lord Advocate
asked for a postponement, owing to the disappearance of his
principal witness, James Peacock, barman at the hotel. Before the second trial Peacock was discovered drowned in a
reservoir, so his testimony was lost to the Crown. It was
proved that the couple had been on bad terms, and that
Webster had insured his wife's life for £1000. The bed linen
used by the deceased had been partially washed before being
sent to the laundry. No arsenic could be traced to the prisoner's possession, nor any attempt on his part to procure it.
The defence contended that the presence of arsenic in Mrs.
Webster's body was due to her having taken Fowler's Solution; she had consulted in June an unknown medical man,
who gave her medicine which "might have been Fowler"—a

[1] *Scotsman*, 18th, 19th, and 20th February, 1891.

likely prescription for the ailment she admittedly had; but, on the other hand, it was not proved that she ever took any, and none was found in the house. Taylor, by the way, states that there is only one recorded case (1848) in which Fowler's solution has destroyed life.[1] After a three days' trial the jury returned a verdict of not guilty, and the prisoner was discharged.

On 19th November 1906 Mr. William Lennox, Old Cumnock, Ayrshire, received by post an anonymous gift of shortbread, roughly covered with icing, in a parcel containing a card inscribed, "With happy greetings from an old friend." Four persons in the house who tasted the shortbread became seriously ill, with symptoms of strychnine poisoning; one, the housekeeper, Miss M'Kerrow, died next day. Strychnine was ascertained to be the cause of death, and enough of that poison to kill several people was found in the icing. Thomas Mathieson Brown, whose wife was a niece of Mr. Lennox, was arrested in connection with the crime.[2] At the pleading diet, the Procurator-Fiscal produced two medical certificates that the accused was of unsound mind and incapable of pleading to the indictment. It was insisted for the prisoner that he should be allowed to plead not guilty; and the Sheriff reserved the matter for the consideration of the High Court. At the second diet on 18th March 1907, the Solicitor-General left it to the Court to order an investigation as to the prisoner's mental condition. The defence objected, and moved that he should be discharged, as he had not been called upon to plead at the first diet. The Court repelled the motion, and found that it was inexpedient to hold a preliminary enquiry into the pannel's state of mind. He then pleaded not guilty, and the trial proceeded. Evidence was led to prove that the pannel had bought an ounce of strychnine from a Glasgow chemist, and that the card and the address on the parcel were in his handwriting. Expert testimony was given to the effect that he had suffered for years from chronic epileptic insanity. The Lord Justice-General (Dunedin) directed the jury to answer the following

[1] *Medical Jurisprudence*, 1910, ii. 472.
[2] Adam's Justiciary Reports, v. 312.

questions:—(1) Is the prisoner now insane? if not, (2) Did he send the poisoned cake? and if so, (3) Was he insane at the time? The jury, by a majority, found the pannel to be then insane; he was accordingly ordered to be detained during His Majesty's pleasure. Thus the question of his guilt or innocence remained undecided.

A remarkable case which, owing to the self-effacement of the criminal, was never brought to trial occurred at Dalkeith, Mid-Lothian, in 1911.[1] On 3rd February of that year Mr. and Mrs. Hutchison, Bridgend, on the occasion of their silver wedding, entertained a party of friends at a whist drive. After supper coffee was brought in by John Hutchison, the son of the house. Of the eighteen persons present he and three of the guests took none, the other fourteen, including John's fiancée, drank the coffee, were immediately seized with violent sickness, and quickly became prostrate. Medical aid was summoned, and after treatment all but two—Mr. Hutchison and Mr. Clapperton—recovered. Arsenic was ascertained to be the cause of death, and that poison was traced in the remains of the coffee as served. John Hutchison, who had been prompt in administering an emetic to the sufferers, attended the funeral of the victims. He was formerly assistant to his uncle, a chemist in Musselburgh, but though only twenty-four had retired, as appeared, upon his winnings on the Stock Exchange, and his motor car was a feature of the district. On the 14th Hutchison left Dalkeith, ostensibly to visit friends in Newcastle. Meantime the authorities discovered that a bottle containing arsenic was missing from the chemist's shop where he had been recently employed; there were other suspicious circumstances, and a fortnight after the tragedy a warrant was issued for his arrest. Descriptions and photographs of the wanted man were published broadcast; he was tracked to London and from thence to Guernsey, where on the 20th he was discovered in a boarding-house under an assumed name. Questioned by a police-sergeant, he denied his identity and ran upstairs to his bedroom, pursued by the officer. Before the latter

[1] *Dalkeith Advertiser,* 9th, 16th, 23rd February; 2nd March 1911.

could close with him he swallowed the contents of a small phial which he had about him, and fell dead on the spot. An inquest was held, when it was found that death was due to prussic acid. Hutchison, so far from being a man of means, was heavily in debt, and had given way to drink; if there was any financial motive for the commission of the crime it was not disclosed, nor was any evidence as to his mental condition made public.

The next crime to be considered was admittedly the work of a mind deranged. William Watson and his wife were charged at Glasgow in October 1912 with conspiring to murder their children, and with murdering two of them, by cyanide of potassium.[1] The wife pleaded insanity in bar of trial, and upon expert evidence by Drs. Devon and Parker she was ordered to be detained during His Majesty's pleasure. In the husband's case it was proved that he, being a photographer, had obtained four ounces of cyanide, which his wife had persuaded the children to take. After medical evidence that Watson had long suffered from fixed delusions by which his mind was still affected, the judge (Lord Johnston) stopped the case, directing the jury to say whether or not upon the evidence the prisoner was of sound mind; they found that he was insane, and he was ordered to be confined accordingly.

The latest—it were sanguine to suppose the last—poisoning case tried in Scotland is that of John Saunders, gamekeeper, Gosford, Haddingtonshire, at Edinburgh in April 1913, for attempting to poison his wife.[2] It appeared from the evidence that Mrs. Saunders, who had long been in a neurotic condition, began to complain of her food having a strange taste, and displayed after eating symptoms suggestive of poisoning. She was attended by Drs. Gamble and Millar, who treated the case as one of hysteria. To the nurse and others Mrs. Saunders indicated certain articles of food and drink which she said had made her sick, and these were secured for examination. On analyses by Professor Harvey Littlejohn of marmalade, cream,

[1] Official Shorthand Writers' Notes.
[2] *Haddingtonshire Courier*, 25th April 1913.

and biscuit, the presence of strychnine was detected—the total quantity recovered being .323 of a grain. There was no proof of administering or tampering with food by the prisoner, or of his ever having had strychnine in his possession, nor was any motive for the crime alleged. For the defence, Drs. Martine and Gulland testified that Mrs. Saunders suffered from hypochondria, and Sir Thomas Clouston stated that an hysterical woman would do anything to excite sympathy—the theory of the defence being that the symptoms were simulated, and the poison introduced by Mrs. Saunders herself. The prisoner, who bore the highest character, gave evidence in his own behalf; he had patiently endured for many years his wife's peculiar humours, and had never given or sought to give her poison. The jury, by a unanimous verdict of not guilty, acquitted him of the charge.

So much for the past; with regard to the future a recent authority, in an entertaining chapter entitled "Comfortable Words about Poisoning," remarks:—"Everything goes to show that the poisoner of the future will not be a very dreadful person—at any rate, will not be a more dreadful person than the poisoner of the present, unless we credit in the future all the scientific acumen to the villain, and none to those engaged upon the side of justice. For this one dilemma will always remain to the poisoner. If he is ignorant entirely, sheer ignorance will hang him; while, by as much as he knows anything, by so much will he be a marked man, upon whom suspicion will fall." [1]

In concluding this rapid review of four centuries of Scottish poisoning as recorded by various authorities, I am fully conscious of the injustice done to the more important and interesting cases by the compression which my scheme entails; yet I venture to hope that such a survey, bringing together by name, date, and salient features the principal trials of the period covered, may, despite its obvious disadvantages, subserve some useful end.

[1] *Physic and Fiction.* By S. Squire Sprigge, London, 1921, p. 285.

MY FIRST MURDER:

Featuring Jessie King

For I must talk of murders.
—*Titus Andronicus*, Act V. Sc. 1.

(I)

IN THE SECOND YEAR of my apprenticeship as a Writer to Her Majesty's Signet in an Edinburgh law office, there occurred in that venerable city two momentous murder trials. On 18th February, 1889, a woman named Jessie King was charged in the High Court of Justiciary with the strangling in Edinburgh of three infants; and on 8th November of that year, John Watson Laurie was before the same august tribunal indicted for the slaying of Edwin Robert Rose on Goatfell, in the Isle of Arran. Both of these notable sederunts were by me attended, peradventure to the prejudice of my employers' interests, but certainly to my personal advantage: for had I not thus played truant, I had never acquired that taste for trials which has furnished and sustained my interest in them, whether as a collector or a writer, for over forty years. Some of my readers may regret, on other than moral grounds, that I did not stick to my office stool instead of going a-whoring, so to speak, after Themis in her crimson gown, outwith the scope of my employment. But for me those memorable experiences were among the most formative of my literary life. If I had not been present at those trials it is probable that I should never have become a chronicler of crime: and the world would have been (or I flatter myself) the poorer in respect to the eighteen volumes of a criminous cast which I have since, in the appropriate term, perpetrated.

Of the Arran murder I have elsewhere given a full and, I

319

trust, an adequate account.[1] Of Jessie King's case, which is unknown to the present generation, I here propose to essay a brief description. Her trial, apart from its local interest, is less stimulating than Laurie's, for the reason that there was no "fight" in it, and that from the first the verdict was a foregone conclusion. On the other hand, the guilt or innocence of the Arran murderer was stoutly contested in Court, and has been canvassed in the Press both at the time and since. Even to this day, I am given to understand, there are those who still believe him the victim of a judicial miscarriage. If such doubters will purchase and peruse my report of his trial they will not only be doing me a good turn, but will, I pledge my professional reputation, have their minds set at rest. No one, however sceptical, has questioned the guilt of Jessie King or the justice of her sentence.

(II)

It is reckoned among the compensations of advancing years that the mind recalls with vividness occurrences of times past, when, as was the mental experience of Prince Agib's biographer, "a yesterday has faded from its page." Thus, looking back across the gulf which separates the idle apprentice of the 'Eighties from the sedulous historian of to-day, I find I can remember many facts and circumstances of this strange case more clearly than the happening of, say, twelve months ago. The impressionability of youth, the novelty of the adventure, and the arresting quality of the issue: life or death, combined to make the occasion unforgettable.

I sat that day for the first time in the stately courtroom where I have since been privileged to witness such celebrated trials as those made luminous by the names of Laurie, of Mr. Monson, of Oscar Slater, and of Donald Merrett, not to speak of sundry lesser lights in the murky firmament of crime. The

[1] *Trial of John Watson Laurie*, Notable British Trials Series. Edinburg: 1932.

imposing presence on the bench of the Lord Justice-Clerk in his robes of scarlet and white; the attaching charm of the Solicitor-General's voice and manner—surely never was there a more persuasive prosecutor; the miserable little creature in the dock—mean, furtive, shabbily sinister, like a cornered rat; her truculent, robust paramour, with his dirty-grey-bearded face and his bald head, upon which a monstrous wen, big as a hen's egg, rose eminent on the vertex of his naked scalp; the wretched mother weeping in the witness-box over the pitiful relics of the infant she had delivered to its fate; the shameless author of another's shame, callous and unabashed, boldly maintaining that his duty as a father was discharged by payment of £5 to his child's assassin—all these figures I see plain before me as I write. And the final "curtain" of that squalid drama! I can hear to this day, on the return of the fatal verdict, the wave of sound vibrate throughout the crowded benches, when, as the seventeenth-century reporters were wont to record: "the People gave a great Humm"; the moving and impressive words of the judge at the pronouncement of the inevitable sentence; and, above all, the dreadful cries of the doomed woman as she was borne wailing from the bar.

Not an improving spectacle, you may say, for a young gentleman in his teens; yet one calculated to convey a moral lesson by which it is to be hoped he profited. But not, I regret to add, immediately. For the first fruits of the trial took, for me, the form of still further derelictions of duty, being divers unauthorised excursions, during office hours, to view the several *loci* of the crimes. Thus did I successively perlustrate the purlieus of the Dalkeith Road, Stockbridge, and Canonmills, yea, even of grimy Gifford Park, where, although there is no word of it in the indictment, the evil partners were currently believed to have begun their business. The houses proved as uninviting as their sometime occupants, and the Cheyne Street "green" was but a bare backyard. Yet the principle was sound; for I well remember my friend Andrew Lang's advice, given to me a quarter of a century later: "Never write about a case until you have seen the *locus*."

(III)

I had not then read *Weir of Hermiston*, for the excellent reason that that splendid and imperishable fragment was still to be written. Now, I never turn again those pages which tell of Archie Weir's unlucky visit to the Justiciary Court, but they bring back to me the memory of Jessie King. The leading rôles are reversed: Duncan Jopp, "a whey-coloured, misbegotten caitiff," occupies the dock; Janet, his ancient mistress, enters the witness-box "to add the weight of her betrayal."

"Presently, after she was tremblingly embarked on her story, 'And what made ye do this, ye auld runt?' the Court interposed. 'Do you mean to tell me ye was the pannel's mistress?'

" 'If you please, my Loard,' whined the female.

" 'Godsake! ye made a bonny couple,' observed his Lordship; and there was something so formidable and ferocious in his scorn that not even the galleries thought to laugh."

There is, of course, no parallel between the two judges; but the likeness of the sordid protagonists is striking.

So far as literary fame goes, Jessie King was less fortunate than Duncan Jopp. No account of her trial has ever been published; no shorthand notes of the evidence are now available, and I have had to rely, for the ensuing narration, upon the contemporary report of her case in the *Scotsman* newspaper, which, although less full than I could wish it, especially in the matter of the medical evidence and counsels' addresses to the jury, is sufficient for my purpose. I present the facts, generally, as therein set forth; reserving, until we are done with the trial, such comments as occur to me. And so, in the time-honoured order of the Clerk of Justiciary. "Call the diet, Her Majesty's Advocate against Jessie King!"

(IV)

On Monday, 18th February 1889, within the High Court of Justiciary at Edinburgh, took place the trial of Jessie King upon three charges of child-murder. The Lord Justice-Clerk (Lord Kingsburgh) presided; the Solicitor-General (Mr. M. T. Stormonth Darling, Q.C.), assisted by Mr. Graham Murray and Mr. Duncan Robertson, Advocates-Depute, appeared for the Crown; Mr. Fitzroy Bell, advocate, for the defence. The Solicitor-General, by the way, was later to adorn the Bench as Lord Stormonth Darling; Mr. Graham Murray successively became Lord Advocate, Lord President of the Court of Session, and Viscount Dunedin. During the proceedings the Court was crowded to its utmost capacity.

The pannel, "a slightly-made woman of small stature and respectable appearance," was placed in the dock upon the following indictment:—(1) That in April or May 1888, in the house in Ann's Court, Canonmills, then occupied by Thomas Pearson, labourer, she did strangle Alexander Gunn, aged twelve months or thereby, son of Catherine Gunn or Whyte, residing at 6 Huntly Street, Canonmills, and did murder him; (2) in September 1888, in the house in Cheyne Street, Stockbridge, then occupied by the said Thomas Pearson, she did strangle Violet Duncan Tomlinson, aged six weeks or thereby, daughter of Alice Maria Jane Stewart Tomlinson, sometime domestic servant at 3 Coates Place, and now a patient in the Edinburgh Royal Infirmary, or did, by putting her hand upon her mouth, suffocate her, and did murder her; and (3) in October or November 1887, in the house, 24 Dalkeith Road, then occupied by the said Thomas Pearson, she did strangle or in some other manner assault Walter Anderson Campbell, aged five months or thereby, son of Elizabeth Campbell, wireworker, Prestonpans, now deceased, and did murder him. To this indictment the pannel pleaded Not Guilty; a jury was empanelled; and the prosecutor adduced his proof.

(V)

The first witness called for the Crown was Mrs. Catherine Gunn or Whyte, 6 Huntly Street, Canonmills, who said that on 1st May 1887 she was delivered of twin sons. She was then living in Crichton Street and was unmarried. The children were born at 54 Bristo Street, the house of Mrs. Mitchell. Witness was in domestic service and could not herself keep the children. She got Mrs. Henderson, 17 Rose Street, to take charge of them for a weekly payment. She saw them from time to time and they were thriving well. She afterwards got Mrs. Mackay, who had attended her as nurse, to advertise for someone to adopt them. Mrs. Mackay made arrangements for delivering them to the women who were prepared to take them. Witness herself did not see these women. Witness was told that a "Mrs. Macpherson" got Alexander and a Mrs. Henderson—not the Rose Street dame—got Robert. She gave Mrs. Mackay £3 for these women. Since then witness had not seen Alexander. She identified a pair of baby's shoes as those worn by the child when Mrs. Mackay took him away. She also identified other articles of clothing as having belonged to the infant Alexander.

Mrs. Mitchell, 54 Bristo Street, spoke to the birth of the twins at her house on 1st May 1887. About four days afterwards they were taken to Mrs. Henderson's, where they remained till the following April. She knew that Mrs. Mackay advertised for someone to adopt the twins. Witness saw the two women who adopted the children; she recognised the prisoner as the one who, under the name of "Macpherson," got possession of Alexander. He was then in good health. On the last Sunday in September witness went to Ann's Court, Canonmills, to see the child. She found that "Mrs. Macpherson" had left. When the child was given over, witness saw that the prisoner was paid £2. Cross-examined—Alexander was not a strong child, "but strong to be a twin." He was smaller than the other child.

Mrs. Margaret Henderson, 17 Rose Street, stated that in May 1887, Mrs. Mackay, a nurse whom she knew, asked her to take charge of newly born twins. She agreed to do so, and got the children from Mrs. Mitchell. They were then four days old.

Euphemia Mackay, Papcastle, Cockermouth, Cumberland,

stated that she was a monthly nurse (or, as Mrs. Gamp's professional signboard boldly had it, "Midwife"). She was in practice in Edinburgh in 1887, and attended Catherine Gunn, now Mrs. Whyte, when she gave birth to twin boys. The children lived with Mrs. Henderson for about eleven months, till the mother asked witness to advertise for someone to adopt them. She did so, and received twenty-nine replies, one of which was from "Mrs. Macpherson," Ann's Court, Canonmills. "Mrs. Macpherson" took one of the children and Mrs. Henderson the other. The children were brought to her (witness's) house by the mother and handed over there. Witness recognised the prisoner as "Mrs. Macpherson." She saw her get £2 with the child. Witness afterwards called twice to see the child, in April and May. It was then in good health; both "Mr. and Mrs. Macpherson" seemed very fond of it.

Mrs. Elizabeth Mackenzie, 254 Bonnington Road, stated that in March 1888 she was living in Ann's Court, Canonmills. The prisoner, under the name of "Macpherson," rented from her a room for herself and her husband, which they occupied from the beginning of March till the first week of June. They represented themselves to be married persons. On Thursday, 5th April, she was present when the prisoner brought home a male child about a year old. She told witness that it was the child of her husband's sister and her own brother; the mother was ill, and she had been asked to keep it. A neighbour's little girl looked after the child during the day. Witness identified divers articles as worn by the child, whose name, the prisoner said, was Sandie. In May the prisoner announced that she had got another woman to take the child, so witness saw Sandie no more. She also said that the child's mother had died in the Royal Infirmary. The infant was healthy, and the prisoner seemed to treat it with kindness, though the witness had occasion to "check" her for giving it spirits to drink. When witness removed from Ann's Court on 1st June, the "Macphersons" also "flitted." Cross-examined—The child was crying when the prisoner poured the whisky over its throat. She did not know whether the whisky was "neat." "Mr. Macpherson" began to work occasionally four weeks after they came. She identified Thomas Pearson as "Macpherson."

Janet Burnie, the small daughter of William Burnie, 6 Front Baker's Land, Canonmills, said that she knew the prisoner, and remembered her coming with a man "Macpherson" to live in Ann's Court. Witness was employed by the prisoner to nurse a child; she did so from 10 a.m. till 6 p.m. for several months. The child was called Alexander Gunn. She only once saw him ill. She nursed him daily, until going one morning as usual to do so, she found him gone. She asked prisoner where he was, and was told by her that his father had come during the night and taken him away. Witness identified the child's clothing, as worn by him while she nursed him. Cross-examined—She also questioned "Mr. Macpherson," who told her that "the child was away across the water, for the good of its health." Witness only once saw the prisoner the worse of drink. The Lord Justice-Clerk complimented this little girl, when she left the witness-box, on the clearness with which she had given her evidence. The audience's endorsement of his Lordship's commendation was suppressed.

Mrs. Jane Faitchen, Ann's Court, remembered the "Macphersons" coming to Mrs. Mackenzie's house. The prisoner said that the baby belonged to her husband's sister. Cross-examined—She never heard the "Macphersons" quarrelling.

Master Alexander Brown, son of Mrs. Brown, 18 Allan Street, Stockbridge, deponed that in October last, while playing with some other boys in Cheyne Street, he found a parcel, rolled up in a waterproof coat. It lay in a "green" in Cheyne Street, near the door of the prisoner's house. One of the boys kicked it, thinking it was an old pair of boots. Witness and another boy opened the parcel and saw that it contained the dead body of a baby. They informed the police.

Constable Stewart stated that on Friday, 26th October, at half-past one in the afternoon, the last witness and another boy informed him that they had found a bundle containing a dead baby in Cheyne Street. He went to the place, and ascertained the truth of their story. The bundle lay in a "green," twenty yards from the prisoner's house. He conveyed the body, which was much decomposed, to the City mortuary. This concluded the evidence relating to the first charge.

(VI)

Mrs. Tomlinson, wife of Samuel Tomlinson, 6 Wardrop's Court, Lawmarket, and mother of Alice Tomlinson, then in the Royal Infirmary, deponed that on 11th August her daughter gave birth to an illegitimate female child in the Edinburgh Maternity Hospital. She had been in domestic service. The child was brought to witness, who advertised for some person to adopt it. Among a number of applicants, the prisoner's tender was accepted as being the lowest. She said she wanted the child for her sister, "Mrs. Macpherson," who was married to the Duke of Montrose's piper. Her own name she gave as "Mrs. Burns," and her address as Cheyne Street. She said that "Mrs. Macpherson" was then in Edinburgh, and was going to take the child away to the Duke's estate. Witness gave her £2. The child was then a month old. Witness went several times to Cheyne Street to see the child, but she could never get into the house. Eventually she was asked to go to the Police Office, where she identified a dead child as her daughter's baby.

Isabella Banks, daughter of a plasterer in Cheyne Street, said that the prisoner and a man took a room from her father there. They gave their names as "Macpherson." One day the prisoner drove up in a cab with a baby. Witness held the baby while the prisoner paid the cabman. She asked to whom it belonged, and the prisoner said that its mother would soon come for it; that it was a little girl; "and she threw it up in her arms, and said: 'My bonnie wee bairn!'" Witness never saw the child again.

James Banks, her father, deponed that the prisoner and Pearson, under the names of "Mr. and Mrs. Macpherson," occupied a room in his house. Last autumn the prisoner told him "that she had got a child, and £25 to keep it; that she had parted with it to a person, and had given that person £18, leaving £7 for herself." The finding of a dead child in Cheyne Street aroused witness's suspicions, and he communicated these to the police.

Mrs. Banks, his wife, deponed that in June last she let a room to "Mr. and Mrs. Macpherson." They had a coal closet, which they kept locked. Witness was away from home in September, and on her return she learned of the coming and going of the child. She asked what had become of it; to which the prisoner replied (euphemistically) that "she had put it away." She further said that should a servant girl call to see her, witness was to say she was at church. The prisoner was about to be confined, and witness noticed on her bed a child's hat. Asked why she bought a hat before the event, the prisoner said it was her niece's. "Prisoner left to have her baby, and returned." One day witness asked her for the key of the coal closet, which the prisoner refused, "as she had dirty clothes in it." Witness identified a baby's nightdress as one shewn to her by the prisoner, who said it belonged to a child she had when she lived in Canonmills and of whom she was very fond. "Mr. and Mrs. Macpherson" had a private and peculiar "chap" [knock] when they let each other into the house.

James Clark, detective officer in Edinburgh City Police, deponed that he heard of the finding of a dead child in Cheyne Street. From information received from Banks, he saw the accused and asked her what had become of the child Tomlinson. She produced a pair of baby's shoes and a vaccination certificate, and stated that the child was with her sister, the wife of the Duke of Montrose's piper; she referred him to the child's grandmother, as knowing the fact. The Cheyne Street baby being a boy, and the Tomlinson child a girl, witness became suspicious. He searched the house and found the key of the coal closet. Prisoner begged him not to search the closet; and on his telling her that he must do so, she cried: "Get a cab; it's there!" Witness then opened the closet door. Like Mary Blandy when she searched her lover's room, he found more "dirty linen" than he expected. On the bottom shelf lay the body of a female child, wrapped in a canvas cloth; whereupon he locked up the house and took the accused and the body to the Police Office. Returning to the search, he found on the top shelf of the closet a mark corresponding to a child's body, together with several pieces of cloth; also a canister that had contained chloride of lime. The cloth was similar to that wrapped round the body of the Cheyne Street child. At the station, prisoner was formally charged with the murder of the two children; she admitted both charges. Pearson was then apprehended and similarly charged, but denied his guilt. The Cheyne Street body was wrapped first in a newspaper, next in a piece of cloth, and lastly in an oilskin. Witness took from the house a quantity of child's clothing, which he identified as produced.

David Simpson, detective officer, deponed that he accompanied the last witness when he interviewed the prisoner and opened the coal closet. As Clark was about to unlock the door, the accused cried out: "Get a cab; take me to the police office; it is there; I did it!"

Dr. Littlejohn (afterwards Sir Henry, and Professor of Forensic Medicine in Edinburgh University), Medical Office of Health and Surgeon of Police for Edinburgh, stated that, assisted by his son, Dr. Harvey Littlejohn (who later succeeded his father in the Chair), he examined on 27th October in the City mortuary the body of a male child. It was wrapped in an oilskin cloth and presented a mummified appearance. It weighed 11 lb. 4 oz., and was 29 inches in length. A ligature, apparently an apron string, was twice applied round the neck and was embedded in the skin. The rest of the body, with the exception of the limbs, was tightly swathed in cloth. As the result of their examination, they were of opinion that the child was a male, about a year or a year and a half old; that it was healthy; and that the presence of the ligature round the neck could only be satisfactorily accounted for by its having been so placed for the purpose of strangulation. On 4th November, along with Dr. Joseph Bell (the eminent surgeon and the prototype of Sherlock Holmes), witness examined the body of a fully developed female child. It weighed 8 lb. 1 oz. and was 23 inches in length. The lower part of the face was tightly enveloped in a piece of cotton cloth, twisted at the back of the head and knotted at the throat. The cause of death was strangulation by a ligature round the neck.

Dr. Harvey Littlejohn and Dr. Joseph Bell corroborated and concurred. This concluded the proof upon the second charge. It is plain that the medical evidence, as reported, is greatly abridged. The doctors were certainly cross-examined; and as appears from the speech for the defence, they admitted that, owing to the condition of the bodies, the precise cause of death could not be ascertained—it could only be inferred from the ligatures embedded in the necks.

(VII)

Janet Anderson, wife of John Anderson, High Street, Prestonpans, deponed that her sister, Elizabeth Campbell, came to stay with her in March 1887. On 20th May she gave birth to an illegitimate child, a boy, and herself died seven days thereafter. Before she died, she disclosed the name of her seducer, David Finlay. Witness communicated with this man, saying she was willing to adopt the child, provided he would pay aliment. This he refused to do. In August, Finlay wrote that "a party will call for the child to-morrow forenoon," and instructed her to deliver it up accordingly. Next day, 20th August, a man and woman, calling themselves "Stewart," brought a note from Finlay, authorising them to remove the child. Prisoner was the woman and Pearson was the man. The prisoner said she had a baby of the same age which died, and that she had been low-spirited ever since. She explained that "Stewart" was her father. They took away the child, together with its birth certificate and vaccination paper. The latter was duly returned by post, filled up, and was by witness handed to the registrar. The "Stewarts" declined to give her their address. The child was in good health when delivered up to the prisoner. Witness never heard any more about it till the end of November, when a constable came to her with a man whom she identified as "Stewart." Cross-examined—The man conducted the arrangements in taking over the child, and said it would be adopted by his daughter (the prisoner), who was a widow and had lately lost her own child.

David Ferguson Finlay, 16 Lindsay Place, Leith, admitted that he was the father of Elizabeth Campbell's child, born in May 1887. It was at first left in charge of her sister, Mrs. Anderson, for three months. Witness then advertised for someone to adopt it. Among the applications received was one from a person named "Stewart," 24 Dalkeith Road. He identified Pearson and the prisoner as the parties in question, whom he saw when he called at that address. Prisoner said that the man was her father. Witness agreed to let them take the child, and paid them £5 for so doing. From the time he gave prisoner a note to Mrs. Anderson, authorising her to give up the child in August 1887, he had neither seen nor heard of it. He told the "Stewarts" to inform Mrs. Anderson of the whereabouts of the child. Cross-examined—He paid the money to the woman in the man's presence. Witness considered that his duty to the child was done after paying the £5; he never made any further inquiries as to its existence.

Mrs. Elizabeth Penman, 24 Dalkeith Road, said she remembered the prisoner and a man living in the same tenement. The name upon their door was "Pearson." The prisoner said that the man was her uncle. Witness recalled that there was a child about their house for some three months. When it disappeared, she asked what had become of it, and was told by the prisoner that it had been sent away to its aunt. Cross-examined—She had seen the Pearsons the worse of drink.

Mrs. Jane Bookless, 26 Carnegie Street, stated that she had lived for two years before May last at 24 Dalkeith Road. About the end of August the prisoner said she had got a nice healthy boy, the child of her brother at Prestonpans. Witness saw the child there for about three months. Cross-examined—She had seen the prisoner drunk, and had heard her quarrelling with Pearson. She could not say whether he ever thrashed her.

Mrs. Margaret Reid, 82 St. Leonard's Street, stated that while the prisoner lived in Dalkeith Road she asked witness to keep a child, which she did for some time. Witness was a professional nurse, and having to attend a patient in September 1887, she returned the child, a fine healthy boy, to the prisoner.

(VIII)

When the Solicitor-General called his next witness, the paramour of the pannel, there was what the reporters term "sensation in Court." Thomas Pearson, an elderly man of ill-favoured aspect, on entering the witness-box, was warned by his Lordship that as he had been put in the box to give evidence, he could not be again charged with anything connected with the crimes. The only peril he ran was from failure to tell the truth; and he was not entitled to refuse to answer any question, because he could not by so answering incriminate himself. Thus admonished Pearson told his tale. He described himself as a labourer, though the nature of his toil was not specified. He first "took up" with the prisoner, Jessie King, in May 1887. He was then living in Gifford Park, Buccleuch Street. From thence they removed to Dalkeith Road, where they remained for some six months. In November 1887 they went to Canonmills, living first in Baker's Land, and then in Ann's Court, in the house of Mrs. Mackenzie. They next removed to Cheyne Street, Stockbridge. He remembered the child Alexander Gunn being brought by the prisoner to their house in Ann's Court. She had talked before about adopting a child. The child seemed about a year old. He was told nothing of its parentage. He made no objection to her keeping it, which she did for some three weeks. She spoke of getting the child into Miss Stirling's Home for Children. He remembered coming home one night and finding the child gone. The prisoner explained that she had got it into the Home. He proposed to visit the child, but the prisoner informed him that male visitors were not admitted. He did not remember saying anything to Janet Burnie as to what had become of the child. He might have said it was sent across the water, because the prisoner had told him that the children in that Home were sent to Canada. He knew nothing about a baby girl being brought by the prisoner to Cheyne Street. There was a closet in the passage in that house; he did not know whether it was generally kept locked. He certainly was not aware that it contained the dead body of a child. He remembered the disappearance of his oilskin coat, and asking the prisoner for it, when she said she had thrown it out. On their removal from Ann's Court to Cheyne Street the prisoner took with her certain boxes; he did not examine the contents and could not say whether the dead child was among them. While they lived in Dalkeith Road the prisoner got a child from Prestonpans. She answered an advertisement, and he went with her to Prestonpans and got the child from Mrs. Anderson. He wrote the letter returning the vaccination certificate. The child was very young; some weeks after it came he missed it; and the prisoner said she had taken it to Miss Stirling's Home. She told him "he would see the boy running about the Causewayside, with a blue gown on." The reason she gave for parting with the child was that she was tired of it. He wanted to see the child again; but the peculiar regulations of the infant asylum checked his fatherly intention. Cross-examined—The money received from Finlay was expended on the housekeeping. When at Stockbridge, the prisoner informed him that she had got some money from a servant girl in Haddington; that also was applied to meeting the household expenses. The other sums received with the children were devoted to the same object. He and the prisoner never quarrelled, though they might have an occasional "word." "Q.—How many names have you gone under? A.— 'Pearson,' 'Stewart,' and 'Macpherson.' Q.—Why did you use so many? A.—I have gone under the name of 'Macpherson' ever since I was a boy. I used to go to Highland gatherings, and 'Macpherson' was an appropriate name to take on such occasions. You will find my name in the *Scotsman* in 1857, as the winner of a first-class prize. . . ." The reminiscences of the witness were here cut short by emphatic protests from both sides of the bar. Asked why he signed the letter to Prestonpans with the name of "Stewart," witness said it was to make it appear that he was related to the prisoner, who had given the name of "Stewart" to Mrs. Anderson. Re-examined— He passed as "Macpherson" to everybody in Cheyne Street.

John Gunn, sheriff-officer, stated that there was no such place as Miss Stirling's Home in Causewayside; but there was an institution so called in Stockbridge. On inquiry there, he ascertained that no child named Walter Anderson Campbell had ever been in the Home.

Dr. Littlejohn, recalled, stated that along with the police he had twice searched the premises, 24 Dalkeith Road, for the remains of a child. They found nothing. They took up the flooring of two houses and examined the coal cellars of both. They satisfied themselves that there was nothing to their purpose there.

(IX)

The three declarations emitted by the prisoner before trial were read in Court.

In the first she declared she was twenty-seven years of age, unmarried, and did not wish to say anything about the charges made against her.

In the second she stated that on 4th April last she got the child Alexander Gunn from its mother. It was then about eleven months old, and she got £3 to adopt it. Thomas Pearson, with whom she lived, was not willing to take the child, as he said they had enough to do to keep themselves. When she told him that she got £3 for it, he agreed that she should keep it for three or four weeks. She kept it from 4th April to the end of May. Thomas Pearson was very fond of the child; but by the end of May they found they were unable to support it. She tried to get it into a home for children. Among others, she tried Miss Stirling's Home; but all refused to take the child, because it was illegitimate. One Monday, after she had unsuccessfully tried to get the child received into a home, she got very much the worse for drink, and she told Pearson she was going to take the child to Miss Stirling's Home; she had to be there by seven o'clock and would not be back till nine. Pearson went out, and did not come back till ten o'clock. While he was away she strangled the child. She did that because she had no means to support it. After it was dead she put it in a cloth and then into a box. She afterwards put it into a cupboard. It lay there until she removed to Stockbridge, and she put the body in a closet of her house in Stockbridge, where it lay until about a fortnight ago. She wrapped it in Pearson's waterproof coat, in case it should smell. Pearson asked for his coat, and she told him it had been spoiled by green mould and that she threw it out. He said it was a pity. He knew nothing about the death of the child. About a fortnight ago she put the body in a piece of vacant ground in Cheyne Street. One day, passing Miss Stirling's Home, Pearson wanted to go in and see the child, as he wished to buy a toy for it. She put him off by telling him that men were not admitted into the Home.

She got the child Violet Duncan Tomlinson from its grandmother. It was illegitimate, and she got £2 to adopt it. Thomas Pearson knew nothing of that. It was on a Tuesday that she was to get the child, and its mother and grandmother were both present when she got it. That was in the forenoon; and while Pearson was away at his work she brought the child home and gave it some whisky to keep it quiet. The whisky was stronger than she thought, and it took the child's breath away. While the child lay gasping, she put her hand upon its mouth and choked it. After it was dead she put its body in the closet. It lay there until it was found by the police. She had tied a cloth over its mouth for fear it might come alive when she was out, and make a noise.

In her third declaration she declined to say anything about the third child, Walter Anderson Campbell, with whose murder she was also charged.

(X)

The evidence for the Crown being concluded and no witnesses called for the defence, the Solicitor-General intimated that he withdrew the third charge, relating to the Prestonpans child, Walter Anderson Campbell. He then addressed the jury on the other charges, remarking that the case was one distinguished more for its gravity than for its difficulty. Taken along with the prisoner's declarations, the evidence was conclusive of guilt. It was his duty to maintain to the jury that the deaths of these two children were directly and intentionally the work of the prisoner at the bar, and to inform them that he could not find it consistent with his duty to ask them to return a verdict other than that of guilty of murder.

Mr. Fitzroy Bell, in behalf of the prisoner, said that the jury would agree that so far as moral responsibility went, the parents of these children were not without their share. He thought it was for the jury to consider whether it was not in their power to give the prisoner the benefit of such doubts as there were in the case: that, for example, which arose from the fact that the medical evidence shewed that the deaths of the children might have been caused otherwise than by strangulation; and whether, during the whole of the time covered by these matters, the prisoner was not under the influence and control of Pearson, and acting as much for his advantage as for her own. They must carefully consider all the circumstances in regard to Pearson's share in these transactions, and see whether they could not return a verdict of culpable homicide.

(XI)

The Lord Justice-Clerk, in his charge to the jury, referred to the lamentable picture of social life which had been brought before them in this case. It apeared to be quite a common thing for guilty parents practically to get rid of their offspring by paying a few pounds, without having the slightest idea as to what became of the children afterwards, or seeming to care what happened to them. When they (the jury) found, from the evidence, that advertisements for the adoption of such children were answered by some twenty-nine persons, they could not but have the very gravest suspicion that underlying this system of supposed adoption was a state of affairs most dangerous to the moral welfare of society. They must only hope that the disclosures which had been made that day related to an exceptional case. In regard to the discovery of the body of the child in Cheyne Street, twenty yards from the accused's house, and her statement that she had sent the child to Miss Stirling's Home, it would be strange indeed, if the child had been received into that institution, that another child should be found dead, wrapped in things which belonged to the accused. With reference to the second child, his Lordship thought there could be no doubt whatever that the events connected her with the two bodies found in Cheyne Street and in the house where she lived.

It was suggested by the prisoner's counsel that it was possible on the medical evidence to hold that these children might each have died a natural death, in the sense that they did not die by direct violence, but might have been overlain or accidentally suffocated. His Lordship feared that the facts disclosed in evidence absolutely negatived any such idea. The only difficulty which the doctors had in deciding whether strangulation was or was not the immediate cause of death, was the advanced decomposition of the bodies. But if that theory were true, one should have expected that the accused would have taken steps to make it clear that even if strangulation were the cause of death, it had not been brought about by her. One of the children was found with a ligature tied round its neck, and the other with a handkerchief fastened over its mouth; and as men accustomed to deal in a common-sense manner with their own affairs, they would put to themselves this question: Was it credible that a person who now asserted that these children died a natural death would have tied ligatures round their necks in order to produce the impression that some other person had done it? If they could come to that conclusion, they must give effect to it; but he felt bound to say that it did not seem to him a suggestion that could be accepted by anyone.

The most remarkable feature of the case was the concurrence of the two events—so similar in history, in character, and in the way each case was dealt with. While one child was found in Cheyne Street, Stockbridge, it must have lain dead in her house there for a long time, as the mark of its body was discovered on a shelf of a closet in that house. The second child was found in that very closet. These circumstances appeared to his Lordship to be of a very pregnant description; and it was for the jury to consider whether, apart from the prisoner's declaration, they did or did not lead to one certain conclusion.

But that was not all. If they were of opinion that these facts and circumstances were not sufficient to lead them to a conclusion, then it was his duty to tell them that they were bound to take into consideration the prisoner's declarations. By the law as amended within the last two years, a prisoner, in emitting a declaration, was entitled to have the assistance of a law agent, first in private and then while making a declaration.[1] Here a law agent was present; and it could not be said that the prisoner was not in her sober senses at the time, or that she had not been duly cautioned before she made the declaration. What, then, did the declaration disclose? In every respect it confirmed each material particular of the evidence that had been led before them. Her counsel suggested that she had acted, in doing what she did, under the influence of another. His Lordship was afraid that the declaration distinctly negatived that view; it was clear evidence against her that she did these things deliberately and of her own free will.

It had been further suggested that this was a case in which they should return a verdict of culpable homicide; but there

[1] Criminal Procedure (Scotland) Act, 1887 (50 & 51 Vict. cap. 35, s. 17).

was no evidence to shew that these acts were committed in a frenzy or in a state of sudden passion. They were deliberate and intentional; and there was no case known to his Lordship, in which facts such as those in this case were proved, where a verdict of culpable homicide had been returned.

(XII)

At three o'clock in the afternoon the jury retired to consider their verdict. Four minutes later they returned, with a unanimous finding of "Guilty as libelled," on the first two charges.

The verdict being duly recorded by the Clerk of Justiciary and signed by the judge, the Lord Justice-Clerk addressed the prisoner as follows:—"Jessie King—No one who has listened to the evidence at this trial can fail to be satisfied that the jury could come to no other conclusion than that to which they have come in your case. Your days are now numbered. Remember that the sentence of this Court, the penalty of the law, relates to this world only. Do, I entreat you, be persuaded not to harden your heart against the world to come. All that you have done can be blotted out, if you will but repent and turn from it. Listen, I beseech you, to the ministrations you will receive; and as you confessed your crimes in your declaration to man, so also confess them to God, and you may be assured of forgiveness. And now it is my sad duty to pronounce the penalty of the law."

His Lordship then passed sentence of death, ordaining the prisoner to be conveyed to the prison of Edinburgh, and there on the 11th day of March, between the hours of eight and ten o'clock in the forenoon, to be hanged by the neck until she was dead, and her body to be buried within the walls of the prison. "This I pronounce for doom, and may the Lord have mercy upon your soul." The emotion manifested by the judge in his exhortation to repentance was not shared by the prisoner. But no sooner had his Lordship assumed the Black Cap than her face became convulsed, and she uttered continuously heartrending groans till, at the last word of the sentence, she was carried down the stairs from the dock to the cells below. The Court then rose.

(XIII)

At first the condemned woman gave the authorities a deal of trouble. Twice or thrice she tried to commit suicide by strangling herself with strips torn from her skirt, and similar improvised ligatures. But her hand had lost its cunning, for she was less successful than in her previous essays in thuggery. In consequence of these attempts her mental condition was inquired into, but the experts consulted pronounced her entirely sane. Meanwhile, by the intensive culture of the Church—Jessie was a Roman Catholic—she brought forth fruits meet for repentance, and was fortified to endure her earthly punishment.

The execution was conducted by Berry on the appointed day, to the satisfaction of all concerned, in presence of the Bailies, Dr. Henry Hay, surgeon of the prison, and her ghostly counsellor, Canon Donlevy. So died Jessie King the same horrid death whereby she had destroyed those three small lives, and went to her own place. She enjoys distinction as the last woman to be hanged in Edinburgh. When, the other day, the old Calton Jail was demolished, her grave, with that of her neighbour and forerunner, Mons. Chantrelle, was not disturbed; and she still awaits, in that desolate and much-contested site, the imposition of such public buildings as our rulers in their wisdom shall see fit to erect thereon.

Before the end, Jessie King handed to her confessor a written confession of her guilt, which was by him given to Captain Christie, the governor of the prison, who transmitted it to Lord Lothian, the Secretary for Scotland. It was stated in the Press at the time that in this document, while admitting the justice of her sentence, the convict as a dying woman solemnly declared that she committed the crimes at the instigation and with the encouragement and concurrence of "another." The confession was treated as confidential and was not published; but one does not require to possess the acumen of a Dupin or a Holmes to perceive that the unnamed participant is the old-time ornament of Highland games, "Macpherson." None who saw the couple in the flesh can have any doubt as to which of them was the predominant partner. Pearson, as we know, was arrested on the discovery of the murders; but upon his mistress's judicial declaration that he was ignorant of her crimes, he was set at liberty to bear witness for the prosecution. The warning given to him by the Lord Justice-Clerk before he was sworn, shews that he was officially regarded as being art and part in the murders.[1]

Indeed, the Crown here would seem to have been faced with a difficulty similar to that by which, in 1828, the Lord Advocate was confronted in bringing to justice the West Port murderers. There, the four prisoners all denied accession to the crimes. Burke and M'Dougal refused to turn King's evidence, Hare and his helpmate were eager to do so; and although equally guilty, they were reluctantly accepted as witnesses, and thus secured for themselves immunity from the consequences of the crimes. In the present case, Jessie King exonerated her paramour, while he was prepared to testify against her in the witness-box. That his proper place was in the dock beside her must be obvious to anyone who has studied the evidence. But then the Solicitor-General might have failed to obtain a conviction; so he made, like his learned predecessor, the best of a bad job.

The only other point in the case calling for remark is the position of the parents of the little victims. That these heartless wretches were morally, though unfortunately not legally, accessory to the murders admits of no question. Either they well knew what was in store for their infants when they handed them over to a total stranger, without the least inquiry before or after doing so; or their faith in philanthropy was

---

[1] By Scots law a *socius criminis*, examined as a witness in a criminal trial at the instance of the Public Prosecutor, and answering the questions put to him, cannot himself be tried for the offence as to which he has been examined. Cf. the case of *Burke and Hare*, by the present writer. Notable British Trials Series. Edinburgh: 1921, *passim*.

such that they believed another would, for a pound or two, shoulder the burden which they themselves so shamelessly shirked. The fact that a single advertisement for "adoption" produced wellnigh thirty replies from people, as appears, poorer than the parents, is a circumstance, to quote the judge in another connection, "of a very pregnant description."

Lastly, there is one child in this case of whose existence we are informed, but of whose fortunes we hear nothing further. The Cheyne Street landlady deponed: "Prisoner left to have her baby, and returned"—without it. What became of that ill-starred infant? Was it also, in its turn, "adopted"? Like the child that vanished from the dark house in the Dalkeith Road, of whose mortal remains no vestige was ever found, it makes its brief appearance in the grisly drama and then is seen no more.

THE CRIME ON THE
TOWARD CASTLE;

Or, Poison in the Packet

> The poor blunderers can only give him half a pint of
> laudanum . . . and run the risk of detection an hour after
> his death! I think that time is in a circle, and that we re-
> treat as we advance, in spite of our talk of progress.
> Miss BRADDON: *The Trail of the Serpent.*

(I)

THE YEAR 1828 is forever notable in the annals of Scottish
crime by reason of the discovery of the long series of atrocities
known to us as the West Port murders, perpetrated in Edinburgh by Burke and Hare. De Quincey, in a charmingly
macabre essay, has considered murder as a fine art; these
exponents reduced it to a thriving trade. The extent and
effects of their industry are matters of history, Burke enjoying
the further distinction of having added a new word to the
English dictionary: the admirable verb to *Burke:* for an illiterate Irishman no small achievement.

But it is less generally appreciated that the same year witnessed the unmasking of two minor miscreants, who followed
by different methods for profit the same dread business of
murder. The output of these less famous practitioners—seven
similar crimes, for only one of which the partners were indicted
—falls far short of the sixteen transactions recorded in the
books of Messrs. Burke and Hare. The smaller firm, however,
in their modest way also enriched the language by a picturesque phrase: *tipping the Doctor,* which being interpreted,
means, not, giving a physician a gratuity, but the administration to selected subjects, in their drink, of laudanum, with a
view to robbery. If the patient failed to recover and identify

343

the operators, so much the worse for him, so much the better
for them. Some account of the activities of these forgotten and
misguided enthusiasts it is the purpose of the present paper to
supply.

The *Edinburgh Weekly Chronicle*, in commenting on the
quality of the criminal harvest of the year, observes:—

> As has been frequently remarked, there is something pe-
> culiarly horrible, disgusting to the mind, and revolting to the
> heart, in the nature of some of the crimes which have lately
> been brought to light. They seem to be the growth, not of
> famine and misery, but of cunning and hard-heartedness.
> Friends and strangers have alike suffered at the hands of men,
> or rather of monsters, whose trade it has been to practise upon
> their unsuspicious nature, and upon all those easy qualities
> which tend to render life and society happy and united. With
> such facts before our eyes, who can believe that he is safe from
> the snares which it would appear are laid everywhere around
> us? The very bond of a civilised community has been in a
> great measure sundered, and every man is compelled to look
> upon his fellow with distrust and suspicion.

These remarks have reference as well to the case of Burke
and Hare as to that of John Stuart and Catherine Wright, the
protagonists of the present drama.

(II)

Many of my readers must have had the pleasurable experience of sailing down the Clyde and through the Kyles
of Bute to Ardrishaig or Inveraray. Adventurers of yesterday
would plough the waters of that noble estuary in one or other
of the veteran fleet of the venerable MacBrayne. But ancient
and antiquated as were those hardy annuals of the Firth, the
modern Clyde passenger steamer, such as the *King George V.*,
Duchess of Montrose, and *Jeanie Deans*, is not in all respects
more greatly their superior than did they in their turn surpass
in size, speed, and luxury the earlier vessels from which they
have been so splendidly evolved. Thus, for example, in the

year 1828 with which we are here concerned, the four steam-packets of the Castle Company were deemed the last word in comfort and efficiency. A contemporary advertisement, setting forth their claims to the patronage of the coast-bound traveller, is of interest in comparison with an up-to-date steamer time-table of to-day. For the pleasure of reprinting it I am indebted to the research of Captain Williamson, the historian of the Clyde passenger steamer:—

REGULAR CONVEYANCE

To Inveraray every lawful day, and Arran every Tuesday and Saturday.

AT GLASGOW,

The Royal Mail Steam Packets,

Dunoon Castle......................Captain Johnston.
Inveraray Castle.....................Captain Thomson.
Rothesay Castle.....................Captain Adam.
Toward Castle......................Captain Stewart.

The above Packets will Sail as under—calling at Port-Glasgow, Greenock, Gourock, Dunoon, Rothesay, Tarbert, and Lochgilphead.

.   .   .   .

One of the above Packets sails from Glasgow to Inveraray, and one sails from Inveraray to Glasgow, every lawful day; and from Glasgow to Arran every Tuesday and Saturday, leaving Arran for Glasgow every Wednesday and Monday; and to and from Rothesay daily.

One of the Packets sails from Rothesay for Greenock every Sunday morning, at half-past eight o'clock, with the Mail; and leaves Greenock for Rothesay same day at eleven o'clock forenoon.

NOTICE.—Families frequenting the Watering Places to which these Vessels ply will be supplied with Tickets on terms as low as any other Vessel going that way, and they will have the liberty of Sailing in any of the four Castles.

Tickets to be had only of Mr. David M'Donald, Jeweller, No. 134 Trongate.

NOTICE.—Any person putting whisky or other illicit goods on board will be prosecuted.

ESTIMATES WANTED for supplying the above Steam Packets for One Year with the best Hard Coals, commencing on the 1st June next. Those wishing to contract for the same must give in their offers on or before the 25th instant to Alexander Ure, writer, 26 Glassford Street.

A STEWARD WANTED for one of these Vessels. None need apply but those that can be well recommended for sobriety and ability. Certificates to be lodged on or before the 21st instant with

JAMES M'INTOSH,

GLASGOW, 16th May 1829.[1]   99 Main Street, Gorbals.

These vaunted vessels were little better than tug-boats. Built of wood; flush-decked, with no shelter for the passengers except the low bulwarks; with huge paddle-wheels, abaft which soared a slender funnel—in the earlier types used also as a mast! the navigating bridge a plank across the paddle-boxes; and instead of the elaborate engine-room telegraph now in use, a rod with a brass knob, whereby the captain could "knock" down his orders to the engineer. In heavy or wet weather the unhappy passengers were confined to the cabin: a submarine black hole, from which the present-day occupant of an easy-chair on the glazed shelter-deck of the modern pleasure-steamer would recoil with horror and disgust.

The *Toward Castle*, on which we are now about to embark, was built in 1822 by William Denny, founder of the great shipbuilding house at Dumbarton, and was engined by M'Arthur & Co. of Glasgow. Her dimensions were as follows: length, 101 feet; beam, 16 feet; depth, 9 feet; 79 tons register, with engines of the single-beam type and of 45 horse-

[1] *The Clyde Passenger Steamer*, by Captain James Williamson, pp. 54–55 (Glasgow, 1904).

power. She plied upon the route known as "Royal" between Glasgow and Loch Fyne, so long associated with the old *Columba*.

(III)

On 15th December 1828 there boarded the *Toward Castle*, then on her return run to Glasgow from Inveraray, when she called at Tarbert in Loch Fyne, a blacksmith and his wife, John and Catherine Stuart, and a mother and grand-daughter named M'Phail. The parties had forgathered at the inn while awaiting the arrival of the steamer, where Mrs. M'Phail's luggage was lightened by a gauger of two gallons of whisky which, despite the prohibition of the foregoing advertisement, she proposed to smuggle aboard. The Stuarts sympathised with her in her loss; and as the morning was cold upon the water, they suggested a dram in the cabin. There, as she could not read, Mrs. M'Phail consulted them as to the denomination of certain guinea notes in her possession. Her hospitable fellow-travellers then pressed her to sample the ship's beer. "It was very bitter," she afterwards recalled; "I never tasted such infernal strong beer in my life, and I spat out every drop and wiped my mouth with my apron." As the old lady could by no means be persuaded to partake further of their precarious bounty, the pair turned their attention to another passenger, a stout merchant from Ulva, Robert Lamont by name, on whose broad bosom the outline of a bulky pocket-book was plainly visible. He was travelling with a cousin, who preferred to remain on deck. Lamont made no difficulty of accepting gratuitous refreshment, but declined to "stand his hand," deeming the tariff extortionate—"it cost 9d. a bottle": but so generously did his hosts provide drinks that, as we learn from the steward, they drank the ship dry—"three gills, three bottles of porter, and a dozen of ale: there was no more on board." One tumbler only was in use, and it was noticed that before Lamont drank, Mrs. Stuart "put the tumbler in below her mantle," and once, as her husband was about to drink, she "pulled it from his mouth and spilt it over his breast, and he damned her for it."

When the streamer reached Renfrew Ferry, John Lamont went below to summon his relative, whom he found alone in the dark cabin, insensible, with his empty pocket-book lying on the floor at his feet. John at once informed the captain that his cousin had been robbed; whereupon the Stuarts were "laid hold of" and searched, £19, 7s. in notes and silver, and a black purse, afterwards proved to have been Lamont's property, being found on them. At 6 p.m. the *Toward Castle* arrived at the Broomielaw; Stuart and his wife were taken into custody, and two bottles which had contained laudanum were discovered in their possession. A doctor, called to minister to the luckless Lamont, applied the stomach-pump to no effect; the patient never regained consciousness, and died next morning aboard the steamer.

Such is a short statement of the facts, which will enable the reader more easily to appreciate the purport of the evidence led at the trial. I take it from a brief account of the case in an old essay of mine on Scottish poisonings: "Locusta in Scotland."[1] I have been so long accustomed to having my stuff "lifted" without acknowledgment by other writers on crime that I find it refreshing, for a change, thus to pick my own pocket. But I have the uncommon honesty to say so.

(IV)

It was the praiseworthy practice of that day, when newspaper law reports were meagre, to publish on the conclusion of the proceedings separate accounts of famous trials, giving generally the evidence in full, the judge's charge in brief, and sometimes even the addresses of counsel. To such, in the course of my criminous pilgrimage, I have been often and fruitfully indebted. In the present instance there is an excellent

[1] *Glengarry's Way and Other Studies*, p. 83 (Edinburgh, 1922).

report of the proceedings, the title-page whereof reads as follows:

TRIAL of John Stuart, and Catherine Wright, or Stuart, before The High Court of Justiciary, at Edinburgh, on Tuesday, July 14, 1829, for the Murder and Robbery of Robert Lamont, on board the *Toward Castle* steam-boat, while on the passage from Tarbert to Glasgow. [Quotation.] EDINBURGH: Printed for Robert Buchanan, No. 26. George Street. . . . MDCCCXXIX.

The preface is dated July 1829, and the report extends to 47 pages. It ran through two editions; and so successful was the publication that there was issued in the same year a "Third Edition, corrected. To which are added, the Defences of Counsel for the Criminals, and an Account of their Execution, &c." This new edition has been increased to 80 pages, and is that upon which I base my account of the case. It contains a new preface, dated September 1829, which thus explains the occasion of the reprint.

THIRD EDITION.

This Edition has been carefully revised, and it contains the addresses of the Counsel for the pannels, to the Jury.

A variety of unauthenticated and contradictory statements, with regard to the lives and conduct of these criminals, have been published since their execution. On these no reliance can be placed—nor do we consider it conducive to the improvement of public morals, either to trace the steps of profligacy through all the paths and gradations of crime, or to exhibit the foulest victims of the law in their last moments, as invested with the characteristics of saintship and martyrdom. It is indeed, we think, extremely pernicious to represent the language of despair, and perhaps to a certain extent of hypocrisy, in such cases as indications of heartfelt contrition and repentance; and we humbly think a great deal too much publicity is tolerated by public functionaries, to details of the private devotions and last mental agonies of criminals, who have justly forfeited their lives to the laws of their country.

We, therefore, abstain from a repetition of the narratives to which we refer; and think it quite sufficient to quote, from a respectable Edinburgh newspaper (*The Weekly Journal*) a brief account of the public execution of Stuart and his wife.

The publishers shew their good taste and sense of decency thus to break away from the traditional practice of reporting the last hours of the condemned. Criminals well knew what was expected of them in the way of godly conversation and pious sentiments, and their ghostly counsellors played up to them for all they were spiritually worth. From the conversion of Lady Warriston in the Tolbooth, in good King James's glorious days, to the edifying deportment of Mr. William Burke in the Calton Jail, in 1829, we have full descriptions of these moral transformation scenes, which are not less disingenuous than disgusting.

(V)

On Tuesday, 14th July 1829, the High Court of Justiciary met at ten o'clock for the trial of the Stuarts. Lord Gillies presided, the other judges being Lords Pitmilly, Mackenzie, and Moncreiff. Counsel for the Crown were Sir William Rae of St. Catherine's, His Majesty's Advocate, assisted by Robert Dundas and Alexander Wood, Advocates-Depute; James Tytler, W.S., Crown Agent. There appeared for the defence David Milne and William Forbes, advocates, instructed by John Livingston, W.S. The same Crown counsel had conducted the prosecution of Burke and M'Dougal in the preceding December in that Court.

The huge and cumbersome indictment then in use upon which the pannels were arraigned charged them, at vast length and with due forensic verbosity, with the commission of four crimes: (1) upon 15th December 1828, on board the *Toward Castle* steamboat, then on her voyage from Inveraray to Glasgow, "and when the said steamboat was on her way between Tarbert or Tarbet in Argyleshire and Glasgow," wilfully administering to Robert Lamont, then a passenger on the said boat, a quantity of laudanum or other narcotic, noxious, and destructive substance to the Prosecutor unknown, in ale or porter, which they prevailed upon the said Robert to drink, in consequence whereof he died on 16th December, and was thus murdered by them, contrary to the Act 6 Geo. IV. c. 126; (2) administering to Lamont laudanum with intent to murder or disable him or to do him some other grievous bodily harm, and thereafter to steal his property when so murdered or stupefied; (3) stealing a black leather pocketbook, ten bank or bankers' notes for one pound sterling each, a two pound note of the Leith Bank or Banking Company, and seven bank or bankers' notes for one guinea each, as also a black silk purse and some silver money, all as more particularly described in the Inventory of Productions; (4) administering to Mrs. M'Phail and her grand-daughter laudanum, with the like intent. Annexed to the Indictment was a List of Witnesses, thirty-three in number, to be adduced for proving the libel.

The diet being called and both pannels having pleaded Not Guilty, Mr. Milne, as counsel for Stuart, objected to the relevancy of the Indictment on the ground that there was not sufficient specification of the mode in which the poison was administered. For all that appeared, the pannel might have induced the deceased to take the laudanum either as a medicine or as an agreeable stimulant, or even for the purpose of committing suicide. He cited divers decisions whereby libels were held not relevant through similar lack of specification. The Court, without calling on the Crown to reply, repelled the objection. Mr. Forbes then objected to the relevancy on behalf of Wright. The pannels were accused of four different crimes: murder, theft, the common law charge of administering laudanum to any of the lieges to the injury of the person, and the statutory charge of administration with intent to murder or disable. The Prosecutor seemed doubtful whether the medical evidence would bear out the charge of murder; he therefore brought an alternative charge of administration, both under the common law and the statute.

It is not said that Lamont suffered injury in his person at all; yet the injury is an inherent ingredient of the crime. Further, the place of Lamont's death is not mentioned: "It may have been perpetrated in any one of the shires of Argyll, Bute, Dumbarton, Renfrew, or Lanark. . . . Where, then, did Lamont die? Did he die at Tarbert, at Rothesay, at Glasgow, or in England? We obtain no answer to this question from the Indictment." The place of death was not set forth at all. After hearing Dundas in reply, the Court repelled the objections, found the indictment relevant, and remitted it to the knowledge of an assize. A jury was then impannelled and the Prosecutor adduced his proof.

After formal evidence authenticating the prisoners' declarations, John Lamont, farmer, Kilcheoun, in the island of Ulva, was called. Deceased was his cousin; he was a merchant, and was on his way to Glasgow. Witness accompanied him on board the *Toward Castle* at Lochgilphead. After passing the Kyles of Bute, they went below. "We went into a small place beside the steerage, with a table in the middle and a form fixed round it." The cabin was empty. Presently the prisoners came in and witness went on deck. He heard the bell often ring for the steward. Robert came up and invited him to join the party. "I've fallen in with fine company," said he; "you had better come down and take a share." Witness did so. It being suggested that he should "stand his hand," witness declined: "it cost 9d. a bottle."

Mrs. Stuart sat at the door of the little place, and liquor was given to her. She was always next the door and got the liquor. John Stuart sat between her and Robert Lamont. Mrs. Stuart then went away and brought down Mrs. M'Phail. There was only one tumbler used for drink. The first tumbler was poured out to Catherine M'Phail, and when she preed [tasted] the ale she said: "What a bad taste the ale has! I never tasted the like of it." She then put some into her loof [palm] from the bottle. John Stuart wanted to drink it, but his wife would not let him and spilt the tumbler on his breast. Mrs. Stuart coaxed Robert Lamont to drink, saying: "This is your drink; drink some of it."

Witness drank a tumbler; the ale tasted all right to him, but he was "not much acquainted with malt liquor." He felt no ill effects from the draught at that time. He then returned to the deck, leaving the revellers in the cabin. On approaching Glasgow he went below to warn his cousin that he was nearing his journey's end. He found him alone, insensible, his head hanging down between his knees. The familiar bulge made by his pocket-book in his coat was not visible, "and missing this, I was led to think it was away." Witness went on deck and told the captain, who was standing at the gangway awaiting the shore boat, that his relative had been robbed. They returned to the cabin. "Then the captain took the candle that was on the table and looked, and found the book on the floor, with the letters all scattered about." The money was gone. Stuart, his wife, and Mrs. M'Phail were "laid hold of on this." Asked by the captain whether he had any money, Stuart replied that he had nearly £20; and on research £19, 7s., mostly in guinea notes, were found upon him. They were in a black silk purse. Having arrived at the Broomielaw about six o'clock, the captain "sent for surgeons." Robert Lamont died on the steamboat at half-past five next morning. Throughout the night, as he watched by his cousin, witness was very sick and continued ill for some days thereafter. It was not sea-sickness, "being used to the sea." Cross-examined, he heard them singing drinking songs together. They seemed very happy and well pleased with one another.

Catherine M'Phail, wife of Michael M'Phail, hawker in Gorbals, Glasgow, stated that she met the prisoners in a public-house at Tarbert, where she had occasion to change a £1 note before boarding the steamer. She had £16, 10s. 8½d. in notes, silver, and copper. She asked whether it was a pound or a guinea note, as she could not read. The prisoners were in the kitchen; "they were at the fire, sitting taking their gill." On the steamer Mrs. Stuart expressed sorrow for witness's loss of whisky: "the gauger had seized two gallons from me": and invited her to console herself at their expense. There was strong beer on the cabin table. Mrs. Stuart handed her a tumblerful. "I could not drink it, from the bad taste. It was very bitter; I never tasted such infernal strong beer in my life, and I spat out every drop and wiped my mouth with my apron. I put some on my loof [palm] from the bottle and tasted it; the bottle was not so bad as the tumbler." Mrs. Stuart said; "Drink this, Catherine; damn my soul, you'll drink every drop!" Witness drank "down to the rim." Afterwards she became "quite nonsensical" and did not know what happened. She had since been very ill "in her inside."

Margaret M'Phail, Catherine's young grand-daughter, said that she was present in the cabin. She observed that Mrs. Stuart put the tumbler "in below her mantle." She kept it thus for five or ten minutes, then put it on the table, and poured more ale into it. Witness, being allowed a taste, felt sick in two or three minutes and continued ill.

John King, grocer in Greenock, another passenger, having testified to the finding of the unconscious man and of his pocket-book, and the discovery of the money on the prisoner Stuart, Captain William Stewart, master of the *Toward Castle*, deponed that the prisoners joined his vessel at Tarbert, paying 3s. each as their fare. At first they pretended they had no money, and said their property had gone by the *Eclipse*—the Irish boat. He corroborated John Lamont's account, and said that John identified the black purse as Robert's. Catherine M'Corkindale, a passenger, said she overheard the female prisoner say to the other, just before they were taken up, "If anything happen to this man, you'll be blamed for it." Whereupon he gave her a "dunch" and she held her tongue. Alexander Stewart, the steward, said that the party consumed eleven bottles of ale and three of porter, as well as three gills of whisky. There was no more on board.

Una Lamont, Robert's widow, identified her late husband's pocket-book and purse; also a £2 note, which she recognised from a certain red mark upon it. Catherine Lamont, daughter of the deceased, swore to the black purse, which she herself had made for her father. James Maxwell of Aros, who had paid Lamont three pound notes of the Leith Bank four days before his death, identified the notes produced.

Dr. Joseph Fleming, Anderston, said that on 15th December he was called to the *Toward Castle* to see Robert Lamont, whom he found insensible. His extremities were quite cold, his pulse imperceptible, his lips swollen and livid. He was said to be intoxicated; so witness applied the stomach-pump. The results—which smelt strongly of laudanum—were placed in a jar and lodged in the Police Office. James Russell, harbour-master at the Broomielaw, and Angus Cameron, police watchman, corroborated as to the delivery of the jar. Alexander M'Pherson and James Young, police officers, stated that they found upon the male prisoner a large and a small bottle, both of which smelt of laudanum. There was also a smell of whisky in the large bottle.

Dr. James Corkindale, Glasgow, who, along with Dr. Fleming, conducted the post-mortem, proved their joint report.

There were no marks of external violence; neither in the head, chest, or belly could we discover anything different from the ordinary structure or appearance. The stomach contained about a pound of water, somewhat discoloured, and having the smell of spirits, which had been introduced into the stomach after it had been washed out by the use of the pump.

Upon considering this examination in reference to a charge of poisoning by laudanum, we have to state that the total absence of morbid appearances is unfavourable to the supposition that the man died of disease; and it is consistent with our knowledge that poisons of the narcotic or stupefying kind, such as laudanum, are wont to occasion death without producing in any part of the body such changes as are discoverable by dissection.

Cross-examined, death by intoxication might have happened from a person drinking ale, porter, and whisky to excess. The symptoms were equally consistent with death by intoxication. His opinion only amounted to a probability that the man died of laudanum.

Dr. Andrew Ure, Glasgow, proved the chemical report on fluid taken from the stomach, as examined by him and Dr. Corkindale.

We are both satisfied, by frequent trials, that the fluid in the jar had distinctly the peculiar and well-marked smell of laudanum. We subjected the fluid, evidently consisting chiefly of malt liquor, to the operation of various tests, which we know from the science and practice of chemistry are calculated with more or less precision to detect the presence of opium, or its spirituous solution commonly called laudanum. As the ultimate result of these different trials and experiments, carefully and laboriously made, we are led to the opinion that the liquor contained in the jar had a quantity of opium or laudanum mixed with it.

BY THE COURT.—Dr. Ure, you have heard the whole evidence on the trial to-day; what do you conceive to have been the cause of Lamont's death? Do you believe that he was killed by laudanum?

WITNESS.—I think it amounts to a very high probability. My conviction is that he died of narcotism from porter and strong beer, aggravated by opium.

Cross-examined, vegetable poisons are much more difficult to detect than mineral, particularly as to quantity. He inferred that there must have been a considerable quantity of laudanum mixed with Lamont's drink to enable its smell to predominate over that of the beer.

Malcolm Logan, prisoner in the Tolbooth of Edinburgh,[1] deponed that the male accused told every person who came into jail about his case. He told witness that "he kept in with M'Phail that he might try to do her on the passage betwixt Tarbert and Glasgow"; but as we know, the old lady was not to be "done." He saw "something sticking in Lamont's breast pocket," and though he (Lamont) denied having any money on him, deemed him worth the "doing." So Mrs. Stuart put some laudanum into his porter, with the best results. Stuart took his money from the unconscious victim, but "could not

---

[1] Mr. Milne objected to this witness that he had been convicted by a jury of a crime inferring infamy, as instructed by an extract conviction now produced. Mr. Dundas replied that a pardon had been obtained for witness, which he (counsel) now laid upon the table. Dundas won the trick; the Court admitted the evidence.

get the pocket-book into the same place, being large, so he dropped it." They were furnished with a bottle of laudanum, which was half full when they set out. "They kept it for *tipping* anyone *the Doctor* whom they met, meaning that he gave them a dose of laudanum and set them to sleep." Cross-examined, witness admitted that he was then serving a sentence of six months' imprisonment, and was thereafter to be banished for three years. The accused imposed no obligation of secrecy upon witness when he told him his tale.

Archibald Anderson, prisoner in the Tolbooth of Edinburgh, to whom the accused had also confided his story of the crime, corroborated. He told witness that he realised £19 and some odd silver by the transaction. Cross-examined, witness had come from jail that day, where he had been for six months His Majesty's guest. He did not break into a house in Edinburgh two years before, neither was he concerned in the poisoning of a person between Edinburgh and Glasgow about that time.

Gruer M'Gruer, criminal officer, Glasgow, said he took the male accused from Bridewell to the Council Chambers and back again on 10th March. Witness had some conversation with him. "He enquired if I thought whether the evidence of two persons in confinement with him could be taken, for he had been very foolish in telling them, and *if their evidence were good, he was undone.*" He mentioned Anderson. Cross-examined, "We got a gill of whisky, and prisoner got half of it. It was both before and after this that prisoner made acknowledgments." The proof for the Crown was here closed.

Two witnesses only were called for the defence. Dr. Scruton said he kept "an apothecary shop" in Glasgow. He sold a good deal of laudanum, which was used by the working classes as a stimulant. The smallest quantity he sold was a drachm, which contained some sixty drops and cost a penny. Dr. Milner, druggist, High Street, Edinburgh, stated that the practice of taking laudanum as a stimulant was prevalent in that city. He had dozens of customers in a day; in some cases 1½ ounces were taken twice a day for that purpose.

(VI)

The declarations of the prisoners were four in number, each of the accused having been severally twice examined: on 16th and 17th December, and 10th and 11th March respectively. Catherine Wright declared that she was a native of Glasgow, twenty-one years of age, and the wife of John Stuart, blacksmith, then in custody, whom she had married at Gretna six years before.[1] "On Monday was eight days," they sailed from the Broomielaw in the *Eclipse*, bound for Belfast. It became so stormy that the steamer had to put in for shelter to Campbeltown, where declarant and her husband went ashore. They were told that the vessel would sail at six o'clock next morning; "and declarant and her husband went to the quay at five, but were informed that the vessel had set off at twelve the night before." They travelled on foot to Tarbert, where on the following Monday they embarked on the *Toward Castle*, intending to take their passage again at Glasgow for Belfast. Upon going into the cabin, they saw John Lamont and another man sitting together. In their modesty they proposed to withdraw, but the other man insisted that they should come in. "They went in accordingly and had a gill, and after this, some porter, and then strong ale, which the said two men partook of, the company being as it were one party." When it was the declarant's turn to drink she took but half a tumbler, "it not being proper" that she should take more. When they were getting near Glasgow, her husband, who was very drunk, slipped away; "the declarant went in quest of him in case he should fall overboard, and found him lighting his pipe where the engines were working." They returned to the cabin for further refreshment, and the declarant also became the worse of Lamont's hospitality, "for she had taken a good deal" as a precaution against sea-sickness. The other man was asleep, and Lamont became alarmed because he could not rouse him. He found his pocket-book lying at the man's feet.

[1] The legality of her union with Stuart rests upon her *ipsa dixit*. She is generally described as his paramour.

When they embarked at Tarbert she and her husband had between them £20, 4s. Of the two empty bottles found in their possession the one had held whisky, the other laudanum, which her husband kept on account of a liver complaint. Both were empty when they boarded the *Toward Castle*.

John Stuart declared that he was a native of Ireland, thirty-two years of age, and by trade a blacksmith. He concurred generally with his wife. The last time he was in the cabin he saw John Lamont, and the other man, apparently sick, leaning with his head on his breast. John felt about the floor, and picked up a pocket-book which seemed to have fallen from the other's pocket. Declarant did not know the man had a pocket-book until he saw it in Lamont's hand. The money found upon declarant was given to him by his brother in Newcastle three weeks before, "to buy tools and begin to work." He supported his wife's account of the bottles. The last time he had bought laudanum was in Newcastle, when he purchased a pennyworth, which he had used for his complaint. Both bottles were empty when he joined the steamer.

Their second declarations related to the black silk purse, which John said was his property, and which Catherine alleged to have been the work of her own fair hands.

(VII)

The Lord Advocate, in addressing the jury in behalf of the Crown, said that the pannels were charged with murder committed in circumstances of the most atrocious and aggravated nature. It was a crime of so dark a description that in former times by the laws of this country it was held to be a species of treason. In everything they ate, in everything they drank, they ran the risk of death by noxious and deleterious ingredients, provided there were found wretches so unprincipled and sordid as to administer them. It was a crime that called for the severest punishment. If accidental circumstances or stronger constitutions preserved the lives of those to whom poison had been given, it was no merit of the criminals: they had done their part, and were as deeply culpable as if death had followed. His Lordship then went over the evidence, and concluded by stating that the country required protection at their hands. Whatever their verdict might be, they and the public must confess that he had done his duty in bringing that prosecution. He asked for a verdict of guilty against both pannels. It is regrettable that the report gives us nothing of the Lord Advocate's review of the evidence.

Mr. Forbes then addressed the jury for the female accused. The first question they had to determine was, whether the death of Robert Lamont was due to laudanum? He commented on the vagueness of the medical certificates and the defective analysis of the contents of the stomach, and maintained that all the symptoms were identical with those of natural death by intoxication. The prosecutor must either admit that his own witnesses were drunk or that Lamont died of liquor. "Ten bottles of ale, three of porter, and a considerable quantity of whisky are proved by the steward of the vessel to have been consumed in that little cabin! Who drank it?" The women and Lamont said they drank little or nothing; and it was admitted on all hands that the pannels were quite sober. Who, then, but the deceased could have drunk the preponderating share of that heterogeneous mixture? True, a small quantity of laudanum was found in his stomach, but the defence had proved that drug was taken as a stimulant by the lower classes to an appalling extent. Lamont might have been a votary of this disgraceful practice and have taken it himself. In considering the charges against the accused, their cases must be considered separately, for much that was evidence against the male in no degree affected the female. Thus, in considering the culpability of the wife, they must leave out of view the alleged confessions of the husband to Logan and Anderson. "I cannot tell what credit the testimony of these two gentlemen may obtain from you; I cannot tell whether the clanking of the fetters which were struck off before they were brought into your presence may lead you to look upon them with a more favourable eye"; but the production of such witnesses argued in the prosecutor no great opinion of the strength of his case. John Lamont said that Mrs. Stuart drank as much as anyone. With regard to her alleged juggling with the tumbler, counsel observed: "Beware, gentlemen, in your more hilarious moments, of indulging in a fit of absence; beware of leaning back in your chair and placing your glass upon your knee when you are relating some pleasant anecdote. If a man die of intoxication, you will undoubtedly be blamed for it; it will be said that he was poisoned. It will be to no purpose that you protest your innocence by all that is sacred; it will not avail you that you possessed no poison and that none was traced to your possession!" But assuming the guilt of Stuart, how could they take it for granted that his wife was guilty? She may have had her suspicions of the plot, but it would be hard indeed to hold her guilty because she concealed her husband's wickedness and did not denounce him to the captain of the ship. "Never, gentlemen, have I seen a case break down so hopelessly as in the attempt to prove the theft; and if the theft, which was the apparent object of the poisoning, be enveloped in obscurity, the act of poisoning must be doubtful also." It was not contended that Mrs. Stuart took the money, and the notes found on Stuart were not properly identified as having belonged to Lamont. Neither notes nor poison were found in her possession. To enable them to find her guilty it must be proved: (1) that she was seen in the possession of poison; (2) that she had an opportunity of administering it; and (3) that the person died with such symptoms as could only be attributed to poison.

I ask for a verdict of Not Proven. The facts seem to demand no other verdict. This woman ought not to be dragged to the scaffold upon such imperfect evidence. She should not, I confess, be returned upon society free from suspicion. She has not passed through this fiery ordeal with her innocence established beyond the shadow of a doubt; but if you convict upon such evidence, you will give much more weight to it than it deserves.

The address of Mr. Milne for Stuart occupies in the report some seventeen closely printed pages. Life is short, and the art

of forensic eloquence is long; I have not time to follow the
learned counsel throughout his windy paragraphs. Suffice it,
that he maintained that Lamont did not die from the effects
of laudanum, but if he so died, the deed was done by Catherine
Wright, without the knowledge of her husband. He strenuously
attacked the evidence as to Stuart's confession of guilt, and demanded a verdict of acquittal. It is noteworthy that Mr. Milne
devotes much more space to abstract legal theories than to the
proven facts of the case.

We are on firmer ground when we come to the charge of
Lord Gillies. His Lordship observed:—

> It would have afforded satisfaction to my mind in this, as in
> every other case where any doubt exists, to recommend the
> jury to give the accused the benefit of such doubt. But in the
> present instance there is no doubt whatever. It is clear that
> murder has been committed and equally clear that robbery
> has been committed. It was suggested by the learned counsel
> for one of the pannels that the deceased might have taken
> laudanum himself; but is it reasonable to conclude that he
> would at the same time rob himself?

It was proved by an eminent doctor and by the first practical
chemist of the day that this man's body was quite healthy and
that in their belief he died of laudanum. With regard to the
robbery, it was proved that the pannel Stuart had no money
when he went on board, and that soon afterwards he was possessed of a sum, not only about the amount, but in the same
description of notes of which the man had been robbed. A
strong circumstance of corroboration was the little black purse.
That purse was proved to have belonged to the deceased; his
friend saw him with it on the voyage, his daughter recognised
it as her own sewing. It was proved to have been dropped by
the pannel Stuart. "With respect to the murder, the woman
cuts by far the more conspicuous figure. She bought the ale in
which the poison was infused. She neither tasted it herself nor,
aware of its fatal contents, would she allow her husband to do
so." As to the confession, the evidence of Logan and Anderson,
while open to suspicion, gave a clear and distinct narrative of

the whole affair; in the main facts, and even in minute circumstance, they were corroborated by the other evidence.

It is plain that murder and robbery have been committed,
and suspicion rests on none but the prisoners at the bar. They
had the means in their hands, and they had the opportunity
and resolution to use them. I am quite confident that your
verdict will be one according to justice, and one that will give
satisfaction to the country.

Nor was his Lordship's confidence misplaced; after an absence
of five minutes the jury returned a unanimous verdict of Guilty
against both pannels upon all the charges. In pronouncing sentence of death, Lord Gillies observed that the crime of which
they had been convicted was of a most novel, most dangerous,
most subtle, and most daring nature. He ordained the prisoners
to be hanged in Edinburgh on 19th August, and their bodies to
be given to Dr. Monro, Professor of Anatomy in that University, for dissection. The Court then rose.

(VIII)

Less chivalrous than Burke who, on the acquittal of his paramour M'Dougal, congratulated her on her freedom, saying:
"Nelly, you are out of the scrape!" Stuart, after condemnation,
at first ungallantly maintained that his wife had administered
the drug without his knowledge, "for she was in the practice of
mixing the potion." But by the operations of his spiritual advisers he was brought to make a clean breast, as well of his last
as of his former crimes. It is interesting to learn upon his own
authority that Stuart acquired the gentle art of *tipping the
Doctor* in London, where, he states—regrettably for the reputation of that great city—"that a person could there get a lesson
in anything, *however horrid,* for ten shillings," which seems in
the circumstances a reasonable charge.

The *Edinburgh Weekly Chronicle* records such particulars
of his criminous activities as it had been able to collect.

At this moment we could not take upon ourselves to state
with any degree of certainty the exact number who fell victims

to that system of poisoning by which these individuals supported themselves. Stuart, however, confessed that he was aware of no less than seven human beings having died under the application of his deadly drugs. He also mentioned a great many more, of whose fates he had received no precise information. . . . It is supposed that one of their earliest victims was the individual who was poisoned about a year ago under such mysterious circumstances in a public-house at the west end of Princes Street.

I find, on research, this "Mysterious Occurrence" duly noted in the contemporary Press of 28th February 1828. On the afternoon of Tuesday in that week two men and a woman were seen to alight from the Glasgow coach at the east end of Maitland Street, and immediately sought the hospitality of an adjacent tavern. Two gills of rum and a bottle of porter consumed by them were paid for by one of the men with a pound note, of which he received the change. The party was accommodated in a private room. After some time the landlord, whose attention had been otherwise engaged, entered the room. He found the gentleman with the note insensible, and his companions vanished. On his person was found an empty purse: the change had disappeared with his departed friends. Medical aid was promptly summoned; but the unfortunate man died at midnight without regaining consciousness. It was learned that he had left Bathgate that morning with £18 in his pocket. "The guard of the Glasgow coach which brought the party to Edinburgh states that the man and woman who have acted so extraordinary a part in this distressing occurrence, and who have not yet been heard of, were picked up on the road a little beyond Corstorphine." Nor were they heard of again until the affair of the *Toward Castle*.

Their next "subject" was a ferryman at Kirkcudbright, whom they poisoned with laudanum in whisky and robbed of £14. Another was encountered by the pair in Glasgow and induced to go with them into an eating-house in the Bridgegate, where ale and porter were employed as the vehicle of the poison.

Stuart declared that it was his intention to have spared the life of this person, which he could have done by merely giving him a drink of warm milk. This his more sanguine [sic] companion objected to, and urged their immediate departure, to avoid consequences which would have been fatal to them had proper medical evidence been obtained, as in the case of Robert Lamont.

At the time of writing, the *Chronicle* was investigating the circumstances attending the deaths of the remaining three beneficiaries by Mr. Stuart's studies in London, and promised to publish the facts as soon as ascertained. "In all these instances," remarks that journal, "we may state that Wright, whose dispositions proved to be even more blood-thirsty than Stuart's, either from fear or insensibility, acted the more prominent part, and indeed was the great instrument of her paramour's designs." That Catherine Wright played Lady Macbeth to John Stuart's Thane of Cawdor was the belief of those who came in touch with the evil pair after their condemnation. A small incident, occurring in the Lockup-house on the morning of the execution, supports the view that she was, in the vulgar phrase, the better horse. "While he was contented with taking two pinches of snuff, she smoked her pipe four times," and this she did "while listening with apparent earnestness to the pious exhortations of the Rev. Mr. Porter." Stuart's last message was one of gratitude to his legal advisers, with respect to whose services he said "that he was very sorry the lawyers had so little to work on." Whether this has reference to the insufficiency of their fees or to the fragility of the defence, does not appear.

The execution was duly carried out on the appointed day at the head of Libberton's Wynd, whence seven months earlier Burke had departed to his own place. The appeal respectively made by our protagonists to public favour is reflected in the figures of those attending their last appearance. The Burke spectacle drew a crowd of 25,000; the double event, featuring the later performers, only 10,000. After hanging the usual time, their bodies were cut down at nine o'clock and became the property of science, in which form they were at last of some benefit to society.

(IX)

According to the pleasant and salutary custom of the time, there were hawked about the gallows'-foot for a penny, divers villainous ballads, commemorative of the criminals' misdeeds. Three of these, respectively entitled *The Lament of John Stewart* [sic] *and Catherine Wright*, and *Lamentation and Lamentations* of the same, are preserved in the Signet Library at Edinburgh. *The Lament*, which is headed by a quaint woodcut of the *Toward Castle* with a preposterous funnel, gives the following version of the crime.

> The morning was calm as we sail'd through the water,
> Each fond heart was warm, we poor Lamont did flatter;
> For to drink down below we three went together,
> He, poor man, did not know 'twas the last time forever.
>
> .　　.　　.　　.　　.
>
> When lying thus low, we bold did him adventure,
> No one on board did know, we his pockets did enter;
> And we took from the same a pocket-book quite clever,
> The sum we need not name, repent it we shall ever.
>
> .　　.　　.　　.　　.　　.
>
> In steamboats no more will we sail for our pleasure,
> Or on the Irish shore shall we spend stolen treasure;
> For the murders we've done will be told in future ages,
> Compassion we had none, we're a stain to history's pages.

To the *Lamentation* is prefixed a woodcut of the *Toward Castle*, in which that vessel surprisingly figures as a full-rigged ship, under all plain sail! In the text we are furnished with some account of their dealings with *the Doctor*.

A certain man upon a plan he put us both one day,
How we could raise money with ease and no lives take away,
By giving laudanum to them and putting them to sleep,
So by an oath he bound us both the secret for to keep.
In the Bridgegate of Glasgow once this horrid scheme we try'd.

The dose being strong it was not long before the poor man dy'd;
Of the same death, in the Trongate, another dy'd also;
We left the place to shun disgrace, to Ireland we did go.
This practice too in Ireland we followed for some time;
We never thought we would be brought to trial for this crime.

The last line justly defines the attitude of the practitioners:
they were not less sanguinary than sanguine. Familiarity with
murder had, as in the case of Burke and Hare, bred contempt
of consequences, a fact that accounts for the impudent audacity
of the crime for which they suffered.

The *Lamentations* are embellished by a portrait, depicting, it
is claimed, "John Stewart, the Murderer." But unless my memory fails me, I think I have seen the same block do duty for
William Burke, with whom in his day the balladmongers were
also busy.

> But, ah! these days are past and gone,
>   In fetters here we lie,
> Confinèd in a dungeon strong,
>   By men condemned to die.
>
>   .   .   .   .   .
>
> Because God's law we did transgress
>   And would not walk therein,
> But fled the paths of righteousness
>   And trod the paths of sin.
>
>   .   .   .   .   .
>
> Our sentence, therefore, must be just,
>   For God's commandment says:
> "He that doth shed another's blood,
>   His blood must it appease."

The stanzas have about them a rude ring of *The Ballad of
Reading Gaol*, although the fastidious author of that poem
would have shuddered at the vileness of the verse.